Ellis Schreiber

The Life of Augustus Henry Law

Priest of the Society of Jesus

Ellis Schreiber

The Life of Augustus Henry Law
Priest of the Society of Jesus

ISBN/EAN: 9783337233167

Printed in Europe, USA, Canada, Australia, Japan

Cover: Foto ©Raphael Reischuk / pixelio.de

More available books at **www.hansebooks.com**

THE LIFE OF
AUGUSTUS HENRY LAW,

PRIEST OF THE SOCIETY OF JESUS.

BY

ELLIS SCHREIBER.

LONDON:
BURNS AND OATES, LIMITED.

1893.

CONTENTS.

———

uniform and assume the habit of the Society of Jesus.
He tells us himself what was the direct cause of his
resolution.   There was a young lady, the Hon. Augusta
Graves, a daughter of the second Lord Graves, to
whom he had become much attached, and the only
obstacle to his marriage was the limited amount of his
income.   Now he had an uncle, a wealthy Protestant
Bishop, whose wish it had always been, previous to his
choice of the army as a profession, that he should
become a clergyman.   In that case this uncle announced
that he would provide liberally for him, in order to
evince his gratitude to Mr. Law's father, through whose
influence with George IV., when Prince Regent, he
had obtained the bishopric of Bath and Wells.   Hence
by retiring from the army, Mr. Law gratified his uncle's
wish, secured his own worldly prospects, and was
enabled to contract the alliance on which he had set
his heart.   Shortly after the birth of Augustus, in 1833,
he took his M.A. degree, a privilege then granted to
the sons of peers at the end of two and a half
years' residence, and was ordained a minister of the
Established Church.

Although Mr. Law's object in seeking the pastoral
office did not exactly correspond with the aspirations
that candidates for ordination are usually credited with,
namely (as the Protestant service quaintly expresses
it), that of " seeking Christ's sheep in this naughty
world," he was too conscientious to enter upon this
fresh course of life without a full and genuine determination to perform with exactitude all the duties it
involved.   As Rector of a country parish he was very
popular among his parishioners ; he endeared himself
to them by his kindness and his exertions to promote
their temporal and spiritual welfare.   In this he was

greatly assisted by Mrs. Law, who was a singularly charming woman, gifted equally in person and in character. She possessed a cultivated mind, sound judgment, a sweet affectionate disposition, and was besides sincerely religious. Although not more than nineteen years of age at the time of her marriage, she became, as far as this can be said of a non-Catholic, a model wife and mother, and her union with Mr. Law proved an exceptionally happy one. When the ex-officer of the Guards applied himself to the study of divinity at Cambridge, an occupation not a little foreign to his former habits and manner of life, her warmest wish was that he might become a good clergyman. To this end she counselled him: " Read your Bible, but first offer a little prayer to understand it, and think a good deal upon our sinfulness, and what the Saviour has done for us. The earnest and constant wish of my heart is that we may both become not only Christians in name, but in heart and in hope, and that with the same interests, the same feelings, we may journey on with our dearest children on the road to Heaven."

When, after Mr. Law's ordination, he was presented to the living of Yeovilton, Somersetshire, by his uncle the Bishop, and settled down to a country life, Mrs. Law devoted herself to the careful training of her children, the government of her household, and the work of the parish. In these she found her interest and her happiness. " We never see company or go out, except to dinner, and that rarely," she writes. " We lead the same quiet, monotonous lives day by day. I am never so happy as when with my dear children. I walk with Helen (the eldest) every day, and when papa is away, dine with the children at one o'clock. I have got positively to like dining early." The entries in her

diary testify to the simplicity of her tastes, and the
useful nature of her occupations. One morning we
read: "Assisted William (her husband) in writing a
sermon;" the next, "Very busy braiding pinafores for
little boy who crawls about till he makes himself unfit
to be seen." This is almost the first mention of the
subject of this memoir, who made his entry into the
world on October 21, 1833. He was a fine, healthy
child. "Little Boy (or Boykey, as he was called until
his brother Frank appeared upon the scene) is broader
than he is long, and is like no one in particular," is the
account his mother gives of his outer man. Of his
character she says, writing to his father when he was
little more than a year old: " I am afraid many battles
are in store for us with Mr. Augustus. Yesterday
evening he was in an awful passion. It was fearful to
witness. On being taken out of his bath he screamed,
and then held his breath for more than a minute with
the violence of his emotion; at last his mouth and
nails turning quite black, I took him in my arms to
divert him, and found he was in a strong convulsion,
his limbs quite stiff. When he recovered he was
nearly lifeless from the struggle. Poor child, how
I pitied him, and how strongly I felt the imperative
obligation I am under to endeavour to subdue his
violence of temper. He is his naughty papa's *own*
child. Ask your mother if you ever turned black from
rage."

Augustus was about eighteen months old when
a terrible accident occurred to him. Just able to run
alone, he toddled into the dressing-room of a gentleman
who was staying in the house, and seeing on the lower
shelf of the wash-stand a jug or can of boiling water,
peeped into it, curious to discover whence the steam

came. In doing so he probably laid hold of the edge of the jug and tilted it, for the whole contents poured over his chest as he fell backwards, and lodged in the bosom of his frock, which according to the fashion of those days, was very loose in front. Before his cries could summon any one to his assistance, the boiling water had done its work; at first it was feared that the scalds were too large and too deep to heal. Fever set in, and the poor child's strength was reduced to a fearfully low ebb. For weeks he lay day and night on his mother's lap, his sufferings being greatly aggravated by the rough treatment of the country doctor, and the unskilful manner in which he dressed the wounds. But a healthy skin and a good constitution were in his favour, and he was able to pull through, though the nature of the malady rendered recovery a slow and tedious process. The sores gradually closed, but the scars were deep-rooted and remained very red and swollen. In rather more than three months' time the boy was pronounced quite well, and was able to wear a frock again; but he bore the marks of this accident throughout his life, and felt its effects also, for in after-years, when grown up, he attributed to it a weakness of the chest from which he occasionally suffered. One of Mrs. Law's sisters, who happened to be staying in the house when the accident occurred, spent much of her time with the little suffering child, helping to amuse and nurse him. He was ever grateful to her for this, and frequently referred to her kindness when speaking of his childish days.

One might imagine that the indulgence naturally accorded to a sick child would have tended to render Augustus more self-willed and passionate. It seems to have had a contrary effect; at any rate, under the

careful training of his wise and loving mother, though
he retained his high spirit, his character seems to have
developed in the most satisfactory manner. In her
letters to her sisters she often mentions the gentle,
docile disposition of her " soft-eyed darling boy."
" Dustus," as he called himself in his infantile language,
warmly reciprocated his mother's fond affection. " He
was very obedient and devoted to mamma," his sister
Helen says, " always the first to run to her on her
appearance in the nursery, or in the garden where we
were at play, and from her he imbibed the deep faith
and tender piety that distinguished him throughout his
whole life."

Mrs. Law used to set apart two or three hours
every morning to teach her children. But parental
tuition is subject to many interruptions: Mrs. Law's
health was not strong, and the babies came in quick
succession, so that it was necessary to provide for the
elder ones more regular instruction. " I have got a
very nice amiable governess for my ' chicks,' " she tells
her sister. " I think they are improved since her
arrival; they had been running riot sadly before.
Augustus is the little genius. He and Frank are called
pretty. Graves (the fourth child) is as round as a
ball, with a *riante* face, crowned with fiery ringlets."
Augustus had his mother's brown hair, and clear, soft
eyes. A small coloured sketch of him when four and
a half years old, taken by his aunt, Lady Colville,
represents him as a remarkably attractive child, with
a most winning expression of countenance, a delicate
complexion, and bright colour. He was very engaging
in his ways too. One day he surprised and delighted
his mother by giving her a little drawing of his own,
which the children's governess had ingeniously con-

verted into a needle-case, together with a note in his own handwriting, begging her to accept it.

In the winter of 1841, Augustus and Frank were placed with their father's curate, for a few months, to be under his tuition and care during Mr. Law's, and subsequently also Mrs. Law's, absence from home. East Brent was now their home; they had removed thither two years previously, on the living being offered to Mr. Law by the Bishop. The boys got on very well with their tutor; their mother, on her return home, gives the following account of them : " I was enchanted to get home to my dear boys, who were equally pleased to see me. Augustus is grown, and I think improved in looks. Frank is much the same, but both are more boyish than they were. Mr. Simpson speaks very highly of them, but to my sorrow wants to be relieved of them, on account of the noise being too much for his old mother, and we are now on the look-out for a regular school for them. The thought of this breaks my heart, for they are too young to encounter the rough ways and contamination of older boys. Miss them, too, I shall painfully; their merry laugh and cheerful faces form my chief comfort."

It was decided to send Augustus and Frank at midsummer to school at Somerton. Mr. Law was determined in this choice by the advice of an intimate friend, the Rev. W. R. Newbolt, then Vicar of Somerton, who sent his own sons to the school, which was admirably conducted. It was too at an easy distance, Somerton being not more than seventeen miles distant from East Brent. The dreaded moment of separation once over, Mrs. Law did not regret the boys' departure. Time softened the pain of losing them, and such good reports were received of them, that their parents felt they had more reason to be thankful than otherwise. Mrs. Newbolt wrote that Augustus was such a dear boy that there was only a fear of his being spoilt. His mother gave the same account of him when he came home for the holidays. "Augustus' disposition is so sweet that I fear making an idol of him. He is very quick, and is already in fractions. Frank is a regular scamp; both boys are well grown. They have passed a dull Christmas as yet, because I am not strong enough to bear much noise, but we mean to attempt some fun on January 9th, Frank's birthday." On the conclusion of the holidays, the boys left home with smiling faces and apparently with little regret. This was perhaps not exactly flattering to their parents, but at any rate it was a satisfaction to know that the youngsters were happy at school, and that the master to whose care they were entrusted knew how to command their respect and affection. Of this master, Mr. Noon, Augustus often spoke in later years in terms of the highest esteem. There was every reason to be contented with the moral and intellectual progress of the boys, the only exception to be taken was at the companionship into which they were thrown. Some of their schoolfellows were wanting in refinement and good breeding; and the vigilant, anxious mother apprehended the influence that contact with them might have on her sons' manners. "I could wish," she wrote, "that the other pupils were more of their own state in life, as any provincialisms in speech or manner attaching to them in after-life would much preclude their getting on." In commenting on their letters she counsels more attention to spelling, and expresses the hope that they are very good and gentlemanlike at their meals.

The acceptance of the living of East Brent had been contrary to Mrs. Law's wish, and Mr. Law himself afterwards regretted it. The situation was lonely in the extreme. In Dorsetshire they thought they had no society, but at Brent it was not a *façon de parler*. They saw no one, unless a stray curate from a neighbouring parish, who chanced to call. Such perfect seclusion was not desirable, and would have proved intolerable, but for the constant coming and going of visitors, the majority of whom were near relatives, and frequent visits to friends in London and elsewhere. In September, 1843, scarlet-fever broke out in the village, and until the end of the year the Vicarage was a hospital, every one in the house being more or less ill. Mrs. Heneage, Mrs. Law's favourite sister, the same who endeared herself to Augustus by her kindness when he met with his accident, was twice at death's door with low fever, and on the 1st of January was only just well enough to travel, accompanied by Mrs. Law, to London, and thence the next day to her own home in Brighton. Thus the boys' home-coming at Christmas was again not a very merry one. It was, however, bright in comparison with that which awaited them at the close of the year at that time just opening. They joined their mother at Brighton, and spent the greater part of the holidays there, Augustus winning golden opinions from all his relatives on account of his quick intelligence, warm heart, and pleasing manners.

No event of any importance to the family occurred until the 16th of October, when the angel of death visited the quiet Vicarage of East Brent, and a sorrow great and real descended upon that happy household.

The brightness of Mrs. Law's path through life had only been obscured by those passing troubles from which no lot is entirely exempt, and yet she had not allowed herself to be dazzled by worldly joys, or permitted her heart to cling too closely to the earthly objects of her affection. Some time previous to the period at which we have now arrived, writing to her sister, she says: "We must not live as if this world was our lasting home. We must be daily preparing for our eternal habitation, and that cannot be done in the midst of worldly amusements and worldly thoughts. Our spiritual interests are our first consideration, and therefore every other interest should be subservient to them. Let us press forward to the heavenly country, living above this world and its petty cares and deceiving vanities, deceiving because cheating us into forgetting our high calling as Christians, and that we are candidates for a better state. Let us always remember that the world is enmity with God." When the hour of trial came, and the reality of the sentiments she expressed were put to the proof, she stood the test bravely. They were not idle words, but the deep conviction of her soul. On the 5th October, 1844, her eighth child, Augusta, was born, and at first all seemed to go well with both mother and infant. So little cause was there for anxiety, that a few days later, Mr. Law went to Portsmouth to meet his brother, Lord Ellenborough, who was returning to England. The recall of this nobleman from the high office of Governor General of India was a striking exercise of power on the part of the East India Company, but the English Government showed their sense of his services by raising him to an earldom, and conferring on him the Grand Cross of the Bath. Mr. Law was anticipating a pleasant stay in London, when on the morning of the 14th he received a letter by mail train (the electric telegraph was not established in those days) begging him to come home instantly on account of his wife's alarming illness. The next day a further change for the worse in her condition took place, and the doctor said plainly all hope of saving her life was past, it was but a question of hours.

True to the principles she had professed, and acting up to the light that had been vouchsafed to her, this generous woman received with fortitude the announcement of her approaching end. She resigned herself to the will of God, and prepared herself to make the sacrifice of a life that had been most enjoyable to herself, and the prolongation of which appeared most desirable for the sake of her eight young children. Not a murmur escaped her lips, not a word that could increase the agitation of her grief-stricken husband. She gave directions on all matters respecting which her wishes were asked, and repeatedly entreated that her children might never be allowed to forget her. Towards evening, Augustus and Frank, hastily summoned from school by their father, arrived at the Vicarage. As they stood sorrowing by their mother's bedside, she took Augustus' hand, and solemnly bade him throughout his whole life remember, *Thou, God, seest me.* The deep impression these words made on the boy, and the fidelity with which he obeyed the injunction, will be abundantly shown in the course of the present biography.

Shortly before her death, Victor, the two-years-old baby, all the more precious to his mother through his having recently passed through a long and serious illness, was carried into her room by his father. Too young to understand the dread solemnity of the scene, he cried out in his cheeriest tones: "Bye, mamma!

bye, mamma!" She warmly embraced him, calling
him by his pet name, "My Dindin, my Dindin." Then,
at her request, her sister who was present, read to her
a favourite hymn by Mrs. Hemans, the motto of which
is, "God is Love," and the 102nd Psalm, *Benedic anima
mea Dominum.* Thus with the words of praise and
thanksgiving on her lips, she passed into the presence
of the Lord Who had satisfied her desire with good
things, and in the way of Whose commandments,
though not enlightened by the true faith in all its
fulness, it had been her constant endeavour to walk.

We have dwelt somewhat at length on this final
scene of Mrs. Law's life, in order that the loss Augustus
sustained by the early death of his excellent and virtuous
mother may be better appreciated. After the funeral,
at which he and his brother Frank, one on each side
of their bereaved father, followed her as chief mourners
to the grave, the whole family was dispersed, one or
other of the children being taken charge of for a time
by various relatives. Augustus and Frank returned
to school at Somerton, and with them went Graves,
the third boy, then scarcely eight years old. Mr. Law
also left East Brent for several months, as he found
life there too melancholy under such altered circumstances.

At the commencement of Lent in the following
year, he went into residence at Wells, to perform in
person his duties as Chancellor of the diocese, an office
which had been conferred on him by the Bishop shortly
after his ordination, and which he continued to hold
until his conversion in 1851. As Somerton was not
more than fourteen miles from Wells, the three school-
boys had frequent intercourse with their sisters and
younger brothers, and the whole of their midsummer

holidays were spent at their father's house. Some of Augustus' letters from school during this year have been preserved. They are ordinary schoolboy productions, untidily written, consisting of short disjointed sentences about his progress in his studies, and the minor events of school life, ending with affectionate messages to his brothers and sisters. In the first that he wrote after his mother's death, he tells his father that he has counted up all the letters in his possession written by her hand, and finds that he has thirty-seven. Most of these dear letters, he says, have some words of good instruction at the end. The first had been written to him when he was only six years old, a long time back, as it seemed to the boy of eleven, and had been treasured up ever since. Now and again he indulges in moral reflections, as when he states as the result of his experience, that " not many things in this world go as we like, but as God likes."

The following meditation, written by him before he was twelve years old, is hardly what one would expect from a boy of his age, for it was quite original, not a recollection of any sermon or instruction he had heard, nor was it intended for any eye but his own. It shows him to have had a firm grasp of the truths early instilled into his mind by his pious mother, and to have learnt, even at the very outset of his life, to look to the end, and consider the importance of the last things.

"2 Cor. v. 10. 'We must all appear before the judgment-seat of Christ.' That day will be an *awful* one, when our Blessed Lord comes down to judge us. Every one will have to give an account of his deeds, whether they were good or evil ; some will be doomed to eternal destruction and go with the devil and his

wicked angels to Hell, others will go with our Blessed
Saviour to Heaven, where they will live in eternal life
for ever and ever.   Every one will receive his due.
That day the Son of Man will come in His glory and
all His holy angels with Him.   Then shall He sit upon
the throne of His glory, and before Him shall be
gathered all nations.   Some would then have wished
that they had served their Lord when they had time.
So suddenly will that day come to pass, that not even
the angels in Heaven know when it will come to pass,
only the Lord.   Watch therefore, for ye know not what
hour your Lord shall come.   In such an hour as you
think not the Son of Man cometh.   The wicked shall
go away into everlasting punishment, but the righteous
into life eternal.   People cannot think too much of
that awful day.   Some profligate people pass their time
on earth in dissipation and folly, forgetting that in that
day they will have to give an account of all things done
in the body, whether good or evil.   On the other
hand, others always bear in mind that they have to
give an account of themselves on the Judgment Day,
and have set their affections on things above and not
on things of the earth, always calling upon the name of
the Lord, and following His blessed steps.   Then, oh
try, you who wish to live in Heaven with our Blessed
Lord, to follow Christ's example, and then you may be
sure you will live in Heaven in bliss and happiness;
and recollect above all things that we must all appear
before the judgment-seat of Christ, that every one may
receive the things done in his body, according to that
he hath done, whether it be good or bad.   Finis."

Augustus' piety was united with a very cheery and
playful disposition.   There was not a merrier boy in
the school, nor one more ready for innocent fun and

enjoyment.   One of his letters displays not a little malicious triumph in having on one occasion " done " an obnoxious usher.   This individual had officiously interfered when the boys were jumping and dancing in the exuberance of their youthful spirits to the fiddling of one of their comrades, and denounced their harmless merriment as the commencement of rebellion ; but the head master when appealed to, took a more sensible view of the matter.   Augustus was quick-tempered and knew it ; there was something very characteristic in the way he used to warn his brothers or playmates who were trying his temper too much, by saying : " Please don't, or I know I shall get into a rage soon."   With his studies he seem to have got on fairly well.   The half-yearly report of his master at the close of the year announces satisfactory progress.   He was reading Cæsar and Virgil, had begun Greek, and made some acquaintance with Euclid and Algebra ; besides this, he was tolerably proficient in Arithmetic, in English and Roman history, and was learning the elements of French grammar.   He himself says he had been working pretty hard, but he did not get sufficient marks to obtain a prize.

CHAPTER II.

CHOICE OF A PROFESSION. FIRST VOYAGE.

In the autumn of the year 1845, at the close of which we have now arrived, Mr. Law, unable to make up his mind to return to East Brent, and again reside in the desolate Vicarage, peopled as it was with sorrowful associations, had resigned his benefice, and accepted the living of Harborne, near Birmingham, which had been vacated expressly on his behalf by the kindness of a relative. Thus the Christmas holidays were spent by the boys in entirely new surroundings. These holidays were memorable for two other reasons. Before they were ended, an event took place which affected the future of all the children ; their father married again. His choice was no less felicitous this time than it had been on a former occasion. His second wife, a daughter of Sir Henry Montgomery, Bart., of Donegal, proved a kind and tender mother to her step-children, and was sincerely loved by all of them. Many a time in after-years Augustus spoke with affectionate and heartfelt gratitude of all they owed to "dearest May," as he fondly called her. The other cause which rendered these holidays noteworthy was that they marked the conclusion of Augustus' school life. On their way back to Somerton, the three boys remained a short time in London, when they paid a visit to their uncle, Lord Ellenborough, who was then First Lord of the Admiralty. He received them very kindly and tipped them handsomely. With Augustus he appears to have been much taken; almost directly after the boys' departure, he wrote to their father, suggesting that he should make "that fine eldest boy of his" a midshipman. He was old enough, he said, and there were a good many to be appointed at once, so that he could go to sea immediately. This proposal on the part of his brother commended itself to Mr. Law as an excellent opening for his eldest son. He lost no time in informing Augustus of it, leaving him free, however, to fall in with it or not as he pleased. "What do you say," he wrote to him, "to enter Her Majesty's service at once, under the patronage of the First Lord of the Admiralty, instead of remaining six months more at Mr. Noon's, and then going to King Edward's school at Birmingham? No one could enter the navy under better auspices than you would. To secure, however, a continuance of my brother's patronage, it would be necessary for you really to devote yourself to the profession, that you should be a brave, gallant sailor, *very obedient* to the orders of all your superiors, and very diligent in your studies. Of course I should be very sorry to see so much less of you than I should if you remained in England, but I must not let my own feelings stand in the way of your advancement." He ends by bidding him go round after church (the letter was written on Saturday afternoon) to the Vicar, Mr. Newbolt, and talk the matter over with him, and let his father know by return of post what decision he had come to.

Augustus was a little startled at the abruptness of the change proposed in his future. Hitherto he had entertained, and his parents had entertained for him, the idea of becoming a clergyman; but as his uncle's offer was considered to be the best for him, and one not

c

lightly to be declined, he offered no opposition to its acceptance. As a matter of fact, he was scarcely of an age to have made definite choice of a calling in life, and although it was not without some reluctance that he relinquished the prospect of taking Orders, his docile tractable nature readily conformed itself to the wishes and counsels of others. He was a brave, manly lad too, likely to take delight in a seafaring life. His answer to his father's letter ran as follows:

My dearest Papa,—I received your letter this morning, and I think I should like to be a sailor. I hope you will get a ship which is bound for the Mediterranean. I should like to go there better than anywhere. I should *not like* to go quite as soon as you say, for if I could, I should like to see my dear sisters and brothers and all, so very much, before I start. Will you tell me in your next letter when I am to go to London, because I should like to speak to you about it, and will you find out the name of the ship, the name of the captain? I hope it will be bound to the Mediterranean.

Will you thank Lord Ellenborough for me, for having given me such a jolly chance? Give my very best love to all. Will you tell me also how many guns the ship has got? Recollect I can't swim.

Lord Ellenborough was greatly pleased at the boy's readiness to serve afloat. He promised to consult his colleagues as to what would be the best *début* for him; two years' schooling in the *Excellent*, a training-ship for cadets, or actual service either abroad or on the home station. He was inclined to the latter, as the boy was too young for science, but of an age to begin practice.

In less than a week's time Augustus, who notes with delight, as a good augury for his future career, that his birthday is the anniversary of the Battle of Trafalgar, had left Somerton, and received an official announcement of his appointment by the Lords Commissioners of the Admiralty as a naval cadet of H.M.S. *Carysfort*, with directions to repair immediately to Portsmouth to the Commander-in-Chief for examination. This appointment was all the more welcome, because his cousin, the son of the first Mrs. Law's favourite sister, was going out on the same vessel. The *Carysfort* was commanded by Captain Seymour, a very good officer, and was bound for the Cape.

To Portsmouth Augustus accordingly proceeded, accompanied by his father. The examination presented no difficulties; the only requirements in the way of scholarship being a sufficient knowledge of his own language to write from dictation, beside acquaintance with the first four rules of arithmetic, and the rule of three. He remained at Portsmouth while his outfit was being ordered; this included a sword, which replaced the dirk formerly worn by naval cadets. Then Mr. Law returned home, and left his boy to enter upon a sailor's life.

The excitement of preparation had kept up his spirits till then, so that he did not feel the parting as much as one might have expected, and when he went on board the *Carysfort*, at the outset everything wore the charm of novelty. The first day he dined in the gun-room with the lieutenants. Writing home, he says he likes the ship very well, and his hammock too, and tells with not a little importance, how he had eight men to row him—the lad of twelve and a half years old—to the dockyard, where he had to go on duty. Then he begs his father to go to Spithead, where the vessel was to touch before her departure from England, as he wants to ask him about many things.

At length the final leave-taking was over, and the brave little boy was fairly under way, going from all his kind and loving friends, to be tossed about for an indefinite period on the homeless waves. He kept up his heart stoutly, or made a show of doing so, for in writing to his father all he will confess to is: "I must say I was rather sorry at parting from you, but I am happy to say I soon got over it, and now I am as jolly as ever." And he ends: "Hurrah! Please God we shall meet again all happy together. God bless you all."

The vessel was delayed by contrary gales in the bay; this made rather a rough beginning for Augustus, but he soon got over his sickness, and was as merry as need be. The Captain gives a most satisfactory report of him. "He is a very nice and very good boy, and has made himself several friends on board. He is considerably ahead of the rest of his companions as far as books go, and I have no doubt of his doing well in the practical part of his profession, as he appears to take a great liking to it." About two months later the chaplain and acting instructor on board the *Carysfort* says of him: "Mr. Augustus Law promises to be an ornament to his profession. He has evinced even in this short time a great desire to obtain a perfect knowledge of the nautical part of his education, and by his amiable and affectionate disposition has won the esteem and regard of all the officers in the frigate. I can add my testimony to the great progress he has made in his studies while under my charge. The sea seems to agree very well with him."

On account of bad weather, the voyage from Spithead to Madeira lasted nearly four weeks. Augustus writes from the latter place in the most happy and contented spirit : " If you ask me how I like the profession, I can tell you I could like nothing better than a seafaring life. As to there being hardships in life at sea, I don't see that there are any, without you call drinking black water one, which is nothing." With the Portuguese residents on the island he was not very favourably impressed ; he says they are hideous animals and very savage. Whilst off Madeira he spent five days on shore with an aunt who resided there ; she was delighted with the little fellow and thought him the nicest boy she ever knew.

The following letter was written at sea and sent home from the Cape of Good Hope. As it contains a description of his life on board, it shall be given *in extenso :*

H.M.S. *Carysfort,* at sea, lat. 13° 55′, long. 29° 45′.
Friday, May 8th, 1846.

My dearest Papa,—I am going to begin the letter now which I am going to send you from the Cape, and I am thinking that you and all my brothers and sisters would like nothing better than my giving you an account of the sort of way that I pass a day on board ship (at least how a day is spent on board). First of all you must know the watches on board ship are seven. The first night watch begins at eight and ends at twelve ; the second begins at twelve and ends at four (called the middle watch) ; and the third from four to eight, called the morning watch. Then comes the watch from eight in the morning till twelve, the forenoon watch, then from twelve to four in the afternoon, called the afternoon watch, then from four to six,

called the first dog-watch. You must also know we are
in four watches, so that if my watch is from four in the
morning till eight, I have not to watch again until six
in the evening.

Now I will tell you what the employment of each
day is. First of all our hammocks are piped up at
6.30 a.m., and we are all obliged to turn out, without
it is our watch, and then of course we are on deck.
Then we have breakfast at eight, then at nine it is
quarters, *i.e.*, all the officers and men go to their
quarters wherever they are stationed. Some are
stationed, or have quarters, on the quarter-deck, some
on the forecastle, some forward on the main-deck, and
some aft. Each man is stationed to a gun; my
quarters are forward on the main-deck, and every
time when the drum beats to quarters I go there and
muster the men, to see that they are all present
belonging to those quarters. Then about 9.30, after
quarters, we all go in the Captain's cabin to lessons,
and there we stay till half-past eleven, when we go
with our quadrants to take the sun and see what
longitude we are in. At twelve o'clock we have our
dinner; on certain days, twice a week, we have duff
(pudding) and plug (cheese), and we are precious glad
when those days come. Then we can do anything we
like the rest of the day. At six o'clock we have tea,
and then at a quarter-past seven all hammocks are
piped down, and then we turn in if we like, without it
is our watch. About three weeks ago, just a day or
two after we left Madeira, a man fell overboard; we
put the ship about, let go the life-buoy, and did everything we could to save him; we let down both quarter
boats and looked about for him, but the man was
drowned. He fell overboard from the foreyard as we

were exercising in making and shortening sail. It was the first man ever yet drowned in this ship since we left England. It certainly is a very melancholy thing for a man to be lost in that way. Since that, one day just after the drum had beaten a retreat from quarters, I heard the shrill boatswain's whistle, followed by the words, "Hands reef topsails"—just as I heard that, there was "A man overboard!" The truth was, he wanted to go to his station aloft as quick as ever he could, but he missed his footing and fell overboard; but the fellow was a very smart man, and he caught hold of a rope which by accident was hanging over the stern, and by this means he was hauled up on board again, so he was saved.

The next thing I shall tell you is about a man being flogged. This man had insulted one of the officers, so he was put in chains and sentenced to three dozen lashes. So the next morning about half-past seven all hands were piped up. Then the Captain, lieutenants and midshipmen, in full dress, with their swords, came on deck, together with all the other officers and men; and the man was lashed on some gratings, and then the Captain read the article of war by which he was punished, and the order was given : "Boatswain's mate, do your duty," and then he received three dozen lashes on his naked back, and that was the end of it. So all hands were piped down, and all went down below.

The next thing I must tell you is about crossing the line. I dare say you have read about that amusement in many books, all about the shaving, &c. The night before we cross the line I suppose you know there is a sort of ceremony, for old Neptune hails the ship and yells out: "Ship ahoy!" and then the officer of the watch yells out, "Her Majesty's ship *Carysfort*," and

they fling a tar barrel lighted overboard. Then the
next morning we triced up one of the stunsails to
the beams on the main deck and filled it with water,
and then we began. The officers who had not crossed
the line were shaved and ducked first, and then the
men. They let me off very easy. Then we had good
fun all the morning flinging buckets of water at each
other. It was splendid fun. Hip, hip, hurrah!

May 25th.—We are only six hundred miles from
the Cape now, and I hope we shall be at anchor in
St. Simon's Bay before the end of the week. The first
lieutenant has been giving away the boats, and he has
appointed me to the jolly-boat; it is a four-oared boat.
So now I have the charge of that boat, and shall always
go in her when she goes ashore at the Cape of Good
Hope to fetch anything. I have been three months
now in Her Majesty's service, and I must say I like
the navy very much. I don't think there is any one
in the ship happier than me; and I hope some day
(*D.V.*) in about three or four years' time, I may be safe
on old England's shores again. The other day we
practised firing with the great guns at a target (a
grating with a flag stuck on it) and all the guns firing
one after another made such a stunning row; one could
fancy himself in an engagement already.

This letter, at the writer's own request, was sent to
several of his immediate relatives and friends, who
were desirous to hear of his goings on, since he could
not write to each one singly. The same was done with
subsequent letters, provided they contained anything
of special interest. No member of his family could
imagine themselves forgotten, for he rarely, if ever,
writes without mentioning by name every one of his

brothers and sisters, sending messages to each individually, as well as to other relatives and friends at a
distance from his home. Lord Ellenborough, having
read the long letter from the Cape, which was illustrated by a good many pen-and-ink drawings of the
Carysfort at anchor, under double reefed topsails, and
under various amounts of canvas, sincerely congratu-
lated his brother upon it. It was as agreeable a letter,
he said, as a father could wish to receive, the sort of
letter the Duke of Wellington would have written at
thirteen years of age, and as good a one as Nelson
could have written at any time.

Augustus' letters home, still more the pages of his
diary, display a pronounced taste for drawing. The
earlier volumes of the diary more especially, are largely
embellished with sketches, chiefly of a humorous description. Comic figures and grotesque groups of men
and animals, in the style of the title-page of *Punch*,
invariably mark the commencement of a fresh month.
For instance, a band of soldiers is represented as
storming a fort under the banner of the new month,
or a civic procession heralds its arrival. Again, the
departed month is symbolized by a figure in hasty
flight, an officer resigning his command, a ship founder-
ing at sea, or some fanciful device of the kind. Later
on we meet with attempts at landscape-drawing, rocks
and islands descried at sea, and carefully executed
drawings of vessels of various descriptions, from the
stately man-of-war or merchant-ship to the picturesque
junks and humbler craft that ply in foreign harbours.
A large proportion of the illustrations refer to occur-
rences recorded or commented on in the diary; to
these a comic turn is usually given.

Before Augustus' thirteenth birthday he was at

Valparaiso, which did not strike him as "much of a place, not half so good as Sydney or Madeira." He was destined, however, to see a good deal of it, for not until fifteen months had passed did the *Carysfort* prepare to start on the homeward voyage. But in the interim she went cruising about in the Pacific, and Augustus, among new scenes and surroundings, found the time pass very quickly. Whether it is that trifles are of great importance to men at sea, or the law of compensation provides that small events should occur more frequently on the ocean than on land, in order to relieve the tedium of an otherwise monotonous exist-ence, it appears to the reader in turning over the leaves of Augustus' diary, as well of the long letters he was in the habit of writing home, that on most days there has been some incident to record. Almost every page presents something that arrests the attention, and we are tempted to quote from them more largely than our limits will warrant. We must confine ourselves to a few selections.

Whilst at anchor in Valparaiso Bay, Augustus felt for the first time the shock of an earthquake. "It was in the forenoon," he writes, "we were all doing our lessons in the Captain's cabin at the time. It seemed to us as if they were running the heavy guns about on the upper deck, the sensation was most strange. The ship trembled and shook like a leaf. We saw all the people on shore running out of their houses to get clear of them in case they should fall; they knelt down on the ground and sang out: *Misericordia ! Misericordia !* I heard afterwards that some villages were destroyed by the earthquake, but fortunately Valparaiso was not hurt at all, with the exception of some of the houses being almost shaken down."

The first death and burial that occurred on board was naturally an impressive occasion. Augustus had only once been to a funeral before, and that was his mother's. The entry in his diary is as follows:

"August 9th, 1847.—Walter Simpson, the bandmaster, who has been very ill for the last two months, departed this life. Poor man! his disease was consumption, through playing a wind instrument. He was very much lamented by all who knew him. On the following day his body was committed to the deep. At one o'clock the bell was tolled, and every one was sent on deck, the officers in full dress, wearing their swords. The poor man was sewed up in a hammock, put on a grating and covered with a Union Jack. Then he was carried up to the lee gangway, his shipmates and all the principal petty officers standing on each side of the gangway, ready to launch him into the sea. When all was ready, Mr. Onslow (the Chaplain) came on deck in his surplice and read the Burial Service in a very impressive tone. When he said the words: *We therefore commit his body to the deep*, the grating and all was launched overboard; but there was a rope's end made fast to the grating and the Union Jack, so that they were hauled on board again. How solemn a spectacle is a burial at sea! I had never witnessed one before: the splash of the hammock and grating, amidst the silence that prevailed, made one shudder. It was almost a calm too."

We must turn to some entries of a more cheerful character. When occasion offered, the cadets had permission given them to go ashore very frequently, and as Augustus was a favourite with the ship's officers, they often took him with them for an excursion. At Mazatlan about six of them went for a day's shooting in the lagoons, which was quite a novel experience for Augustus. The party rowed ashore at an early hour in the morning, and on arriving, engaged the services of a native boy, whose costume was the simplest imaginable, to wade into the water for them after the game. The principal game was wild duck, snipe, coot, plover, &c. The lakes were said to abound with alligators, but they only came across one, and that a small one. By 9 a.m. the sportsmen had walked seven miles out of Mazatlan, and having reached a hut, they lit a fire and boiled some tea in a portable stove which they had brought, and broiled the coot they had shot. They made a pretty fair breakfast, Augustus says, and during the remainder of the day had very good fun but not much sport. He was allowed to have one shot, and nearly succeeded in hitting a bird. About 6 p.m. they "steered their course" for Mazatlan, and after a jolly good supper, went on board again, and thus closed a very pleasant but rather fatiguing day.

Another time, when the *Carysfort* was at anchor in Conception Bay, the Captain sent for Augustus and asked him if he would like to go with him for a cruise to the town of Penco. Of course there could be but one answer to such a question. The party started about ten o'clock, and after rather a difficult sail, owing to the extreme shallowness of the water, landed at Penco. The boat's crew were told to get their dinners, whilst the officers went up to inspect the old fortress. Wandering about the town, they met with a priest who told them where the smelting-houses were. "As they were a good way off," Augustus writes, "we thought it best to go in the pinnace, so we had to disturb the men at their dinners, and get the boat under weigh again. When we got opposite to the houses, we anchored, and leaving the crew to finish their dinner, we walked up to the houses. We found the overseer there, he was a Chilian. He showed us all over the place, and explained the process of purifying the copper. It has to be melted three times before it is quite pure. I was much interested in seeing the men taking off the scum with a long iron hoe. After they have got off all the scum, they make a small opening and out runs the beautiful vermillion-coloured copper; it is a grand sight and well worth seeing. When the stream of melted copper comes in contact with damp ground, it begins to fizz like fun. It did so once while we were looking on, and we had to run out of its way. The heat was tremendous. In different places there were large heaps of copper ore. I took some pieces which I intend to bring home with me. The overseer told us that no less than 8,000 tons were exported from that place every year. The houses have only been built two years. When he had shown us everything that there was to be seen, he took us into his house, and gave us some very fine strawberries. They were delicious, and formed a most acceptable refreshment after the heat of the furnaces. Then we walked through the fields till we came to where the pinnace men were, and we had our dinner under the shade of a high hedge. We had a capital dinner, with plenty of wine, ale, brandy, and rum. We gave a bottle of rum to the boat's crew, and then went down to the boat and shoved off. On the way back we ran upon a rock, but managed to get off without much trouble. The coast is a very unsafe one for ships, if they stand at all close in."

While returning to Valparaiso, an accident occurred which afforded Augustus considerable amusement; at least he gives a humorous account of it. The crew happened to descry a turtle, and the Captain ordered the jolly-boat to be lowered in view of capturing the prize. "Perceval (one of the cadets) got into the boat with the crew, but directly she touched the water she capsized. The crew escaped with a wetting, but Perceval fell into the water, floundering about, and turning over and over. At last he came up, puffing and blowing like a porpoise, and yelled out at the top of his voice for help, when he was as safe as could be, for he was holding on like grim death to about three or four oars, masts, &c. Finally he managed to scramble into the boat, and was hauled on board by a rope's end under his shoulders, looking like a drowned rat. In the meanwhile they had lowered the cutter to pick up the coxswain, who was far astern, and the gear of the boat, which had drifted some hundred yards astern. The only things lost were the sails, so there was not much harm done, but we saw nothing more of the turtle."

Another time the whole ship's company had a very narrow escape. For a whole night, unknown to any one on board, the *Carysfort* was in danger of catching fire. Augustus gives a brief account of what might have been a terrible catastrophe. "The first thing in the morning, one of the men going into the boatswain's store-room, found half the foreign ensigns completely burnt. The evening before, two or three farces had been acted on board, and a pantomime. It appears that the managers of the play, being in a great hurry to get the things put away after they had finished, had been so careless as to wrap a match, which they did not see was ignited, in the ensigns. The consequence was they smouldered away; it is a lucky thing that they were made of linen instead of bunting."

On the 25th of November, 1847, he hears the
" jolly news" that they are to take in freight at once,
and on December 1st to sail for England. The next
day he writes to his father in the highest spirits. " I
cannot express my joy, you will hardly believe what
I say. The *Carysfort* is homeward bound ! ! ! Hurrah,
hurrah! I am not going to write a long letter, for
about three or four weeks after you get this I hope I
shall see you. It makes me very happy to think of
going home. May God preserve me in health and
safety till I get home to see you, dearest papa."

His account of the Christmas Day which followed,
when they had been three weeks at sea, shows that in
heart he was already in England.

" I dined in the cabin with Captain Seymour,
Mr. Onslow, and six of the officers. We had a very
good dinner, notwithstanding I think that a Christmas
dinner on board a ship at sea is rather dull than
otherwise. After the Captain's dinner was finished,
some of the men dressed up like clowns, and were
singing songs, dancing, &c., until three bells in the
last dog-watch. It was tolerably good fun. There was
also a magic-lantern on the lower deck which was
conducted pretty well. A good many men were very
drunk. I often thought during the day of the contrast
between a Christmas at home and on board ship."
The festivities on New Year's Day seem to have
awakened a similar longing for home. " A whole lot
of the men dressed up as before on Christmas Day.
They acted ' King Charles defeating the Moorish
knight,' which I remember having been acted at
Mr. Newbolt's at Somerton in the year 1845. *I wish
I was there now.* What jolly times those were !"

In another place he enumerates the presents he has

collected for his "dearest brothers and sisters," consisting of beautiful and rare shells, baskets made of
hair by the Mexicans, a stick made out of a whale's jaw,
some ponchos, one of the caps worn in Madeira, and
various other curiosities which he has picked up in the
places he has visited ; anticipating with childish delight
the pleasure they will give to the destined recipients.
Before he reached England he was made a midshipman, when but fourteen years old, having passed the
examinations and received his certificates on the
homeward voyage.

While the *Carysfort* lay in Bahia Bay, Augustus
had a pleasant excursion on shore. He went with
Mr. Onslow to call on an English merchant residing
there, whose brother Mr. Onslow had known at College,
and who kindly invited them to his house. "We went,"
he says, "for a long and very beautiful walk, and had
a splendid view. The neighbourhood of Bahia is most
beautiful, it cuts Valparaiso out and out, excepting as
to the climate, which is exceedingly hot from about
11 a.m. to 5 p.m., although it is pleasant in the
morning and evening. We saw lots of fruit-trees,
cocoanut-trees, jack-fruit, a kind of date, bananas,
palm-trees, &c. A large proportion of the population
are blacks. There is an extensive trade carried on
here in slaves. I am glad to say they are treated here
on the whole a good deal better than in the West
Indies. A number of them get their living by carrying
sedan chairs. When they are carrying any heavy
weight they make a horrid row. The next day we
hired a boat and pulled round to a point near Bomfim
Church, about six miles from the town, and walked
up to the church. The first thing we saw when we
got near it was a tremendous show of a kind of painted

scenery, more befitting a theatre than a church. The choir is beautifully fitted up, and the altar is a most splendid piece of workmanship, with a great deal of gilding about it. After we had seen the choir, we went up into the tower, and saw the machinery of the clock, which is very curious and elaborate : it was made by a Brazilian. After that we went into a side chapel, where were a quantity of pictures offered by persons who had been saved (as they pretended) by the inter-position of the Saint *Bomfim*. Bomfim[1] means *good end;* he is the patron of sailors, and whenever they are in danger they call upon the Saint. If they are saved from destruction, they offer a picture representing the dangerous situation they were in. Thus there was a painting of an English ship running down a Brazilian whale-boat (here he gives a good sketch of a British man-of-war at full sail, with a rowing boat under her bows, while the figure of the Saint appears above in an aureole of light). The men called on 'Bomfim,' and were saved. The picture was painted to com-memorate their deliverance. After we had seen all there was to be seen, we went away." This was perhaps the little Protestant's first visit to a Catholic church, and his first introduction to devotion to the saints; those saints of whom he was to become not very long after, a close and fervent follower.

The principal charm in the details Augustus Law gives of his life on board ship, or when ashore in distant climes; of his duties, his studies, his pleasures; of his impressions of places and people during his first two years at sea, consists in the insight they afford into his

---

[1] It is clear that Augustus is wrong in thinking that this was the name of a Saint. The devotion, perhaps at a shrine of our Lady, is for a happy death.

D

character. What a cheerful, contented disposition the
pages exhibit! What wise determination to make the
best of hardships, for hardships there must necessarily
have been many in a sea-faring life for a young boy,
accustomed to the comforts of a well-appointed household; one who had, moreover, never evinced any predilection or received any previous preparation for the career
on which he was suddenly launched. Never does one
meet with a single complaint, either of his companions,
his work, or the treatment he receives from his superiors.
It is only by the pleasure and relief he expresses at
some change that has been effected, or some fresh
arrangement that has been made, that one gathers that
any disagreeables existed. Nor is it only a cheerful
spirit that he manifests, but an affectionate heart, a
decided character, and high religious principle. When
it is remembered at what an early age he was taken
from home and country, and launched on the wide seas
in the company of strangers, exposed to see and hear
much that it was, to say the least, most undesirable for
so young a boy to see and hear, it seems wonderful
that he should preserve his innocence unsullied, and
have the courage to adhere conscientiously to the
Christian principles and pious practices taught him in
his childhood. The testimony of the chaplain on this
point, as well as to his progress in seamanship and
nautical astronomy, must have been very gratifying to
his father. "Augustus is going on in the same steady
way," he writes from Valparaiso, "as ever, not only in
his studies and duties as an officer, but especially in
those things which are of more value than all, and
which will in the end tend to carry him through the
world as an honourable, just, and good officer. He very
often comes into my cabin in the evening and reads

the Psalms and Lessons appointed for the day by our Church. He did this of his own accord, which indeed says much for him."

And at the end of the voyage, he speaks in still more emphatic terms: " I hasten with real pleasure to give you a few lines touching your dear little son, in whose welfare I shall ever be warmly interested. You will receive him as he left you, pure in principle, and uncontaminated by the vices that he may have seen during the last two years. I cannot say too much for his Christian character, which has been witnessed by all. Evidently by nature and disposition he was intended for a holier and a higher calling, and he has sometimes expressed a wish to me on that head. Still he can shine forth well in his present profession, and guided by his early training will be an honour and an ornament to it. His mathematical abilities are very good, and he is gifted with the power of finding out many things which those much older than himself cannot manage; I mean especially geometry, algebraic and trigonometrical problems."

As the good chaplain surmised, Augustus was indeed destined by God for a higher and holier calling, although a very different one to that which he would have marked out for him.

During the detention of the *Carysfort* at Portsmouth, Augustus had the honour of being invited by the Admiral to dinner, in acknowledgment of the excellent place he had taken in the examinations on board, and of the high character for general good conduct he bore among the officers of the ship. Under such circumstances, how joyous was the newly-made midshipman's first home-coming.

CHAPTER III.

At the close of his first voyage, Augustus Law went home for a holiday of six or eight weeks. It was spent in free and happy intercourse with the members of his family, his affection for whom had suffered no diminution during his two years' absence. Of course he found that some changes had taken place; his eldest sister Helen was no longer a little girl, his brother Frank was preparing for the military academy at Woolwich; "old" Graves, as he was familiarly called, had been removed from Somerton school, and the future calling of his younger brothers was already matter of discussion. Besides this, a baby-boy and girl whom he had not yet seen were installed in the nursery of Harborne Vicarage; with these he quickly made friends, and became a great favourite, as he was at all times with little children. But however pleasant it was to have his son at home again, Mr. Law wisely lost no time in obtaining another appointment for him. The result of his application at the Admiralty was that Augustus and his cousin Algernon (now Admiral Sir A. C. F. Heneage) were appointed to H.M.S. *Hastings*, which was to sail for the East Indies on July 1st.

This fresh parting, when the time came, proved more painful for Augustus than the first. He had not acquired that love of the blue water which makes the true salt restless on shore even amid the happiest surroundings. He confesses to having been rather down in the mouth after bidding his father good-bye at Portsmouth, but he turns it off with a laugh, telling him as a good joke that some of the fellows had mistaken their relationship to one another, and had asked him whether that young fellow with the red whiskers was not his brother.

Unfortunately when the *Hastings* had only left Portsmouth a few days, small-pox broke out on board. Consequently the yellow flag had to be hoisted, and when she reached Madeira, no one could go ashore, much to Augustus' annoyance. It was so tantalizing, he writes, to look at that beautiful Madeira, and not be able to leave the ship. He, with a number of others, was vaccinated, and so escaped the disease; but about twenty-five men had it, and rather badly too.

Thrown as he now was among a fresh set of associates, Augustus naturally made new friends. One of the ship's officers, Lieutenant Hancock, took a great liking to the bright, intelligent boy, and made a companion of him. He encouraged and helped him in his religious practices, and allowed him to make use of his cabin. " He is a very nice man," Augustus says, " quite like a father to me, and I like him all the more because he is such a good Christian. He has given me leave to go into his cabin; I go there of an evening to read the Lessons for the day, and to say my prayers. He is the best friend I have, or ever shall have, in the navy." Mr. Hancock had a good many volumes of sermons, which he used to lend to his little friend, or read with him. Amongst these were some of Manning's;

Augustus mentions one, on Holiness in Childhood,
which they both thought very beautiful. They often
had long talks (we ought rather to say *yarns*) together.
"One day," Augustus writes in his diary, "whilst I
was reading in Mr. Hancock's cabin, he happened to
ask me how long my mother had been dead, and I
could not refrain from tears. But directly he saw his
question had brought back to my mind painful recollections, he was so sorry for it, and consoled me as
much as he could. The most singular thing was that
he selected to read to me the 103rd Psalm [in our
version 102nd] the very one that my dearest mother
desired to be read to her when she was on her death-
bed. This shows what a good kind man he is. I cannot
thank him too much for his kindness to me." This
incident also shows how tender was the love wherewith
Augustus cherished his mother's memory. He seldom
failed to chronicle October 16th in his diary as "the
anniversary of my dear mother's death," and to inscribe
on the same page the words which on her death-bed
she bade him ever remember: "Thou, God, seest me."
The Commander, too, noticed Augustus, and expressed
his approval of his attention to religion. One day he
spoke to him on the main-deck, and told him he would
give him all the assistance in his power with regard
to explaining anything he might read in the Bible.
"This was very kind of him," Augustus adds gratefully.
"I do not think there are many Commanders in the
service who would trouble their heads about a midshipman." Perhaps the officer would have said there were
not many midshipmen who would care that he should
trouble his head about them, or at any rate who would
repay a few kind words, as Augustus Law did, with
gratitude and affectionate respect.

Nothing particular occurred on the voyage out to Hong Kong, which was reached on the 14th December. During the months spent there life seems to have been easy and agreeable; in the forenoon there was school, mathematics, nautical astronomy, and navigation being the subjects of study; in the afternoon there were entertainments on board, and plenty of leave to go ashore, where the club, cricket, bathing, shooting expeditions, &c., offered attractions to suit all tastes. But although Augustus took part in all these amusements, when Christmas Day comes, he thinks a good deal about how his dearest father, May (Mrs. Law), and all his dear brothers and sisters are enjoying themselves at the happy home from which he is an exile; at Easter he says: " How different was my last Easter Day, spent at Harborne with you, my dearest father."

On her way to Singapore, the *Hastings* touched at Manilla. Manilla Bay is a very beautiful bay, thirty to forty miles long. Augustus says there was nothing to see in the town; he does not appear to have visited the rope and cigar manufactories, the latter of which is said to give employment to eight thousand women and girls between the ages of eleven and sixty.

Like many religious Protestants, Augustus had strict ideas with regard to the obligation of abstaining from servile work on Sundays, and he did not at all approve of the manner in which that day was observed on board the *Hastings*. Soon after she left England, an order came down from the Captain to send the day's work in on Sundays just the same as on other days; at this Augustus expresses himself as much surprised, since he thought that avoidable work should not be imposed on any one on Sundays, as it is, or ought to be, a day of rest. Sometimes, to his great disgust, they actually

washed decks about ten o'olock on Sunday morning.
On the first Sunday after their arrival at Trincomalee,
Augustus was employed in taking some one to another
vessel in the bay, and in conveying some of the Admiral's
luggage ashore. When he got back, the church pendant
was hoisted, and he found to his chagrin, that the
service was half over. In the afternoon he went twice
more to the Admiral's house with his "traps," and
once with the officers ashore. "Altogether," he writes
in his diary, "I spent a most unsatisfactory Sunday.
It was certainly *worthy* of the *Hastings.*" Another time
he says how he dislikes the way naval officers have of
asking a number of people to dine on *Sundays.*

The Admiral (Sir Francis Collier) had a very large
house at Trincomalee, and frequently invited Augustus,
whose fine qualities he appreciated, to dine and sleep.
During the voyage, he had taken a good deal of notice of
him, singling him out for many little attentions. Once he
spoke of him as being the flower of his flock. However
Augustus, although by no means insensible to the kindness shown him, did not hold the Admiral in particularly
high esteem. His sense of right and wrong was shocked
by the language he made use of when addressing the
officers ; moreover, the Admiral had a dislike to sermons,
and frequently sent to request the chaplain to omit his
customary discourse at the Sunday morning service.
Sometimes for as many as four consecutive Sundays
he allowed no sermon. This seems a strange thing
for a lad of fifteen to take exception at, but Augustus
really enjoyed sermons, and was sorry to be deprived
of them. He listened most attentively, and made an
invariable practice of entering in his diary the text
from which the chaplain preached, adding a short
summary of the instruction, with his impression of it.

The following extract will serve as an example. "Onslow never preached, in my humble opinion, a better sermon than he did to-day, as it was so very plain and easy for the men, and in fact, I was very glad to see several men listening very attentively to it. May the good seed not be sown in vain. It was from St. Matt. xxi. 28—30. Onslow showed how very well the case of the second son (who said, ' I go, sir, but went not ') might be applied to ourselves, inasmuch as we too often vainly imagine that we can do good deeds, &c., which, when the time comes, we shrink from. He then went on to show how you may have faith, but if it is without the fruits of faith, the works whereby faith is manifested, what would it profit?" Very often, when the ship was anchored off any large town, he would go ashore after dinner on Sundays, with one of his friends, to attend the afternoon service, and hear another sermon; failing this, he applied himself to a volume of printed sermons. The entries in his journal during the year 1850, while he was in Chinese waters, show how truly religious was his mind, and what good use he made of the graces within his reach. "Read the fourth, fifth, and sixth of Moberly's sermons at Winchester. I am quite delighted with them. Let people who laugh at religion say what they will; but if they knew what happiness I have whilst I am reading these sermons, I am sure they would try to get it too by reading them. May I by God's grace be enabled to perform what is enjoined and avoid what is condemned by His commandments." And again: "On reading a sermon on the words, ' Agree with thine adversary quickly,' I asked myself what was my own conduct in this respect. My heart condemned me when I thought of the second master leaving the ship. He

certainly was my enemy, and although I said good-
bye to him, I did not perfectly part with him in
peace."

The entry on his seventeenth birthday, which
occurred in this year, shall be given in full.

"October 21st.—Begun taking charge of the main-
deck. May God give me grace to begin this eighteenth
year of my existence, go through it, and end it, in His
fear. May I constantly remember that God's all-seeing
eye is on me at all times. May I keep my heart with
all diligence, for out of it are the issues of life. May
I in all things acknowledge Him, for He shall direct
my paths, and may the Holy Spirit's sacred fire burn
everything contrary to itself out of my impure heart;
and may God, of His infinite goodness and mercy,
forgive me all my sins, and give me true repentance
for all my wicked and sinful deeds, through my blessed
and merciful Saviour, Jesus Christ. Amen."

Keeping constantly in mind, as it will be observed
that he did, his mother's dying admonition, no wonder
that his conduct exemplified the saying of St. Thomas
of Aquin : "He that shall walk faithfully in God's
sight, always ready to render to Him an account of
His actions, shall not be separated from Him by con-
senting to sin." Throughout his life at sea we do not
hear of Augustus being guilty of any serious offence,
although, as may be imagined, he occasionally merited
punishment for some slight neglect of duty or breach
of discipline. He was rather careless in leaving his
things about, and often got a "rowing" for not having
put them in their proper places. On one occasion he
records that he received a severe reproof from the Commander for "sky-larking" during his watch. Another
time he had his leave to go ashore stopped for a week

on account of some misdemeanour. Once he was left standing in "the bitts,"[1] even when the Admiral came on board to inspect the ship, for having, in a fit of temper, flung a book at a brother midshipman. Again, for neglecting to take his log to the cabin according to rule, he was sentenced to be kept on deck for six hours ; but he tells us, after he had been on the poop about an hour, the Captain called him up, and after lecturing him on the necessity of obedience, the soul of discipline, he told him he might go below.

Another day the Captain had gone on shore, and Augustus, who was on watch at the time he was expected to return, not anticipating that he would come off in the rain that was falling heavily, was not keeping as sharp a look-out as he ought to have kept. The first he knew of his being alongside was that the coxswain came up the ladder and said the Captain was waiting alongside for man-ropes. When he came up on deck, there was naturally "a row in the house." Augustus was punished (most naturally, as he acknowledges) for his remissness in attention to duty with "watch and watch till further orders." But from this he was released on the next day but one, at which he says, "I was not at all displeased." Instances of this sort might be multiplied ; every one is aware how perfect is the order and how strict the discipline maintained on board a man-of-war. For this reason the naval service was for Augustus, as it has been in the case of several other Jesuits, an excellent preparation for the religious novitiate. From the outset of his career the finger of God is discernible, leading him through many shifts and channels to the

---

[1] An ordinary punishment on board ship. The bitts are strong posts of wood or iron to which cables are made fast.

peaceful haven where at a later period he cast anchor with a willing and joyful heart.

As it was for the most part on account of forgetfulness that Augustus got "rowings," he determined to correct this fault. "I wish I had a better memory," he writes, "I am now trying to improve it, by learning by heart." And what, it may be asked, does he select to be learnt by heart? "I think," he continues, "that to commit to memory some of the psalms might be of infinite value to me. I learnt one of those appointed for to-day, 'Whoso dwelleth under the defence of the Most High'" (Psalm 90. *Qui habitat*). Thus, while pacing the lonely deck during the silent watches of the night, this young sailor occupied his thoughts, not with the frivolities on which we too often allow our minds to dwell during the hours of solitude, but with the recollection of the protection of his God extended over him, of the guardianship of the angels to whose charge he was committed. And shortly after, he experienced the truth of the gracious promise that no evil should happen unto him, in his preservation from what might have been a terrible accident, or more likely, sudden death. He chronicles the occurrence in the following brief manner: "I had quite a providential escape during the exercising, viz., a block very nearly struck me on the head, it in fact just fell at my feet. It fell out of the mizzen-top. If I had been only two inches further forward, the chances are that it would have killed me on the spot. How thankful ought I to be to God for all His mercies to me!"

While the *Hastings* was in Trincomalee Bay, Augustus had a pleasant little holiday. The Admiral asked him if he would like to go to Madras, to pay a visit to Sir Henry Montgomery (brother to Mrs. Law). Of course he said yes ; so it was arranged that he should take his passage in the *Fury*, and stay a few days at his house. This visit he thoroughly enjoyed, and when writing home, spoke in the warmest terms of the kindness shown him. " I was never so sorry to leave a place," he says. His host and hostess on their part expressed the pleasure it had given them to have the boy with them : " Such a fine fellow, so well disposed, and possessed of such good feeling and high principle."

On his return to Hong Kong, the appearance of some pirates caused considerable excitement. The account of their capture may be given in Augustus' own words.

" A new steamer has arrived with the news that the *Columbine* yesterday gave chase to a lot of pirate junks, and that as they were taking one of them, the Chinese blew their junk up rather than be taken. In the explosion poor Goddard (a midshipman) and three or four men were killed, besides six or seven badly wounded and burnt. The first thing that was done was to signal to the *Fury* to get her steam up with all possible speed, and start in pursuit of the pirates. So she hoisted her Blue Peter at the fore, and fired guns continually to bring her men who were on leave on board. Our barge was manned, and besides her own crew were the launch's crew and also her marines. About dusk the *Fury* got under weigh with the barge in tow. I was employed most of the afternoon and evening in taking the wounded men on board the *Alligator*. Some of the poor fellows looked very dreadful. Two were in cots. After information of the arrange-ments for the burial of poor Goddard, I went on board the *Canton*, and he was put into the coffin and taken ashore, and some of my boat's crew went up to Happy

Valley with the hearse, to take the coffin out when they got there. I did not get on board till eleven; I was very tired. When the steamer left the *Columbine*, she had hemmed in nine junks in three different bays. I hope our fellows will be all right."

The next day but one intelligence arrived that all the piratical junks had been taken, and some three or four hundred Chinese had been killed. On the following day the *Fury* steamed into harbour with the *Columbine*, and the men and officers belonging to the *Hastings* came on board. Their description of the action was this: "They arrived at the place about midnight, and when daylight dawned commenced firing with the great guns. Some of the larger junks (there was one 150 feet long) returned the fire with great vigour, but after five or six discharges of grape and canister from the *Fury's* 84-pounders, they fired little or not at all, and then the *Fury* went on firing without stopping for four or five hours. The rest of the time they were up there, they were employed in setting fire to and destroying the junks, and also their guns. The pirates had a regular dockyard full of stores, and a most beautiful junk building on the stocks, which was of course also destroyed. The pirates were not at all afraid of the *Columbine*, for they gave out they were coming in to clean their bottoms before going out again, and were in fact doing so when the *Fury* arrived. There was only one man slightly wounded on the *Fury* in his leg. Very few shots struck her."

But they had not done with the pirates yet. Two or three weeks later a fresh expedition was made against them by the *Fury*, in which fifty of the *Hastings* marines joined, with some of the officers. Amongst the latter was Lieutenant Hancock, who distinguished himself greatly by his gallant conduct. Augustus Law would much have liked to have been one of the party and accompanied his friend. During their absence a little adventure came in his way. He was sent out with two of the ship's boats to the succour of five Chinese sailors, who were supposed to have been capsized. The men were picked up, but the truth of the matter turned out to be that they had been up to no good; and having had a scuffle with the master of the junk on which they were employed, he had, with Chinese disregard of life, intentionally pitched them overboard. Their rescuers, therefore, had little thanks for saving them from a watery grave.

The termination of the encounter with the pirates is related in the following words by one of the officers engaged in it. " We had been cruising about in the Gulf of Tonquin for some days, when groups of piratical junks came in sight, which seemed to be as great strangers in the labyrinth of creeks as ourselves. Before night twenty-four of these were totally destroyed and their people killed, drowned, or in the hands of the Cochin-Chinese, who were hunting them down with bamboo-spears, or they perished in the swamps which for miles round bound the waters we were in. A gallant affair took place the next day. Lieutenant Hancock, of the *Hastings*, in the paddle-box boat of the *Fury*, attacked nine large junks, who tried their best to beat him off, and although they maintained a well-directed fire for two hours, were at last, by the beautiful practice from his 24-pound howitzers, forced, after terrific slaughter, to give in, and their junks met the common fate. Nothing but the exceedingly good management of his boat saved his people. Not a soul' was wounded or hurt, although grape in showers fell around, and his ammunition was reduced to seven rounds." Augustus adds: "I was very glad to find they were all right, especially *dear* Hancock."

The Admiral was so well pleased with the result of the expedition against the pirates, that he wrote a letter to the Captain of the *Hastings*, which was read after church on the upper-deck on Sunday, to the whole ship's company, complimenting him on the behaviour of his men. This must have been one of the last letters the Admiral (Sir Francis Collier) wrote, for in three weeks from that day tidings came off from shore of his death. This Sunday Augustus was not defrauded of a sermon. On the contrary, he had the opportunity of hearing two, as we learn from his diary. "Mr. Onslow preached from the twentieth chapter of the First Book of Samuel (1st Kings), part of the twentieth verse. 'Truly as the Lord liveth, and thy soul liveth, there is but a step between me and death.' It was a very nice sermon on the uncertainty of life. At one o'clock I took Onslow on board the *Alligator* to preach." It is needless to add that the pious middy formed part of the chaplain's audience. On the morrow the funeral took place in the Hong Kong burial-ground. "At a quarter to three all the boats were manned. The marines went in the launch, the petty officers in the pinnace, the gun-room officers in the barge, and some of the ward-room officers in the first cutter. The Commander in the second gig was superintending. While we were going ashore the *Hastings* was firing minute-guns, and when we were on shore the fort fired minute-guns. The procession was formed at the bottom of the hill. The 95th band went first, Onslow and two officers second, then the two surgeons. The Admiral's coxswain carried the flag half-mast high on a staff before the coffin, and the galleys and bargemen pulled the coffin on a field-piece. The whole way was lined by the 95th, 96th, and Rifles on each side of the road. Altogether the ceremony was performed very well. There were a good many civilians there. When the service was over we all went down to the boats, and at sunset the Admiral's flag was hauled down."

Amongst the changes ensuing upon the death of Sir Francis Collier was the promotion of Lieutenant Hancock to the rank of Commander, in consequence of which he left the *Hastings* and returned to England. Augustus expresses himself as very, very sorry to lose this friend, from whom he had received great kindness, "so much more than I deserve," as he modestly adds. He regretted also being no longer able to go to his cabin whenever he wanted a quiet hour to himself, but he did not on that account give up his daily habit of reading and prayer, for in that he found real happiness. He availed himself of the opportunity offered by the return of Lieutenant Hancock to England, to send home a set of carved chessmen and a few Chinese curiosities for his father and sisters. When forwarding these little gifts to Harborne Vicarage, Lieutenant Hancock wrote to Mr. Law, speaking of his son in terms of real affection, saying what a fine character he was, and how universally beloved on board ship.

The departure of his friend made Augustus more anxious than ever to get away from Hong Kong. The *Hastings* had been a long time in the harbour, and he was getting very tired of the place, although the surrounding scenery is extremely beautiful, and he enjoyed many delightful walks and excursions on shore. "The country is hilly," he says, "abounding in deep ravines, with streams rushing among the rocks. Looking

E

across the green plains, or walking in the woods, one
might fancy oneself in one of old England's parks."
But a sailor loves to be out at sea, and Augustus was
heartily glad when the *Amazon* came from Singapore to
relieve them, and orders were given to prepare for
a cruise. On the way to Penang they touched at
Malacca, where new scenes presented themselves, in
which he found fresh sources of interest. ,

"Malacca is a very inconvenient place to land at,
for at low water our cutter cannot approach within
seven hundred yards or so of the shore. We had to
get into a canoe, and were dragged through the mud to
the land. As we were walking about the town we came
to a mosque. We were standing at the steps looking
at the Mahommedans praying, when a Malay came
to worship, and seeing us waiting there, he patted
Mr. Ewan (my companion) familiarly on the back, and
said: 'My good fellow, take off your shoes and wash
your feet and come in.' We told him we would rather
not, we could see enough where we were. We then
saw him go to a large round basin of water, and he
took off everything except his trousers, and then washed
his hands, face, and feet, and rinsed his mouth out.
There were several others besides him doing the same
thing; when he had finished his ablutions he put on his
outer garments and went in to pray. The altar was at
the west end of the mosque, and all the worshippers
were facing it; they seemed to be very devout, and the
mosque looked clean and orderly. Just as we were
leaving, the man who had already spoken to us came
back, he made us go into his house, which was close by,
and sit down. He had a very long yarn with us. He
told us that the Malays here disliked the English very
much, as they drew their conclusions as to their general

character from the behaviour of the drunken sailors they saw. He also told us that he kept a school at Singapore, and had come to his native place for a month. This was his fasting month; he said he had to attend prayers at the mosque five times a day. What an example to us Christians! Passing a Roman Catholic church on our way, we stopped and went in. It is certainly a very good church for this place, a better one than I ever expected to see. There were three recesses in the north side of the building. The one nearest the west end contained images of St. Peter (with the keys) and St. Paul (with a sword in one hand and a book in the other). In the next recess was a figure lying down, stretched at full length, of our Most Blessed Saviour Jesus Christ. The holes in the hands and feet were plainly visible, the blood was flowing from them. It made me quite shudder when I first saw it. The recess at the east end was the vestry; there we saw the Latin prayer-books. I looked for the Collect, Gospel, and Epistle for this week, and found it was the same as in our prayer-book."

Not many lads of his age would have cared to turn over the pages of a Catholic missal, and fewer still perhaps would have known or cared to know, whether the Gospel and Epistle were identical with those that had been read in the Anglican service on the previous Sunday. The compassion excited in his mind by the representation of the dead Christ is also characteristic. Later on in his life, as we shall see, a profound devotion to the mysteries of our Lord's Passion was one of the distinctive features of his piety.

CHAPTER IV.

CONVERSION.

THE *Amazon*, whose arrival at Hong Kong the *Hastings* had awaited before putting out to sea, was a fine corvette of twenty-six guns. As soon as she hove in sight Augustus took a fancy to her, and whilst absent on the cruise conceived a strong desire to join her. He was getting very tired of being in a flag-ship, as there was always a family on board, which makes a ship very un-man-of-war-like, and at the best he disliked a line of battle ship. There had been changes too on board the *Hastings* since the Admiral's death, and it is always disagreeable to persons who have grown accustomed to a certain system to be required to fall into a new one, as is generally the case when the senior officers of a ship are changed. The disagreeables under these circumstances mostly fall to the lot of the subordinate officers. But the principal reason that made Augustus desirous of joining the *Amazon* was that in October of the next year her time would be up, and she would probably be back in England about the following February. In that month Augustus would have been six years in the service, and be ready to pass as mate, although he would have to postpone passing until October, when he would attain the required age, nineteen years. Accordingly, on the return of the *Hastings* to Hong Kong some six months later, he asked the Captain for permission to change ships. He said he would think about it; but a few days later, when Augustus repeated his request, he refused to let him go. This was a sore disappointment for Augustus. He had been over the *Amazon*, and everything he saw confirmed his wish to make the exchange. The surgeon promised him the run of his cabin, which would be a great boon, as it would ensure privacy for the performance of his devotions. But though he had to see the *Amazon* leave the harbour without him, Augustus could not give up all hope of obtaining his object. He writes in his diary: "I do not know what I shall do, if I do not join the *Amazon*. I have set my heart upon it." Writing to his father he says: "If you approve of the exchange, you had better get me appointed from the Admiralty, which will ensure my joining her, in case Captain Austen should refuse me again at Singapore. I intend asking him again. How jolly it would be if I could manage it. I should then be home in a year from the time you receive this letter."

Augustus did ask again, when, in the early part of 1851, he was again at Singapore. There, as he anticipated, he found the *Amazon*. This time he was allowed to go, and he did so the next day, to his great satisfaction. The following letter to his father is written in the best of good spirits.

H.M.S. *Amazon*,
Penang, February 23rd, 1851.

Dearest Father,—Here I am, you see, in the *Amazon* at last. I am appointed "supernumerary to await a vacancy," so the first vacancy that occurs I shall pop in. I hope you will be satisfied with what

I have done. I shall be home, God willing, in a year from the present time. I like the ship very much indeed. All my mess-mates are very good fellows, especially the first lieutenant, who is a very smart officer and first-rate seaman. He has been twenty-two years in the service and always afloat. Our berth is a much larger and better one than the one on the *Carysfort.* We sailed from Singapore on the 9th and arrived here on the 14th. To-morrow we sail for Acheen, where you know I have been before in the old *Hastings*, thence we shall go back to Singapore, touching perhaps at some places on our way. The night we arrived here a ship caught fire, and was burnt down nearly to the water's edge. Had she rung her fire-bell in time we might have saved her. The Captain, who unluckily for him was the owner, was on shore at the time, and the mate (selfish man) did not seem to care about any one's things but his own. If you remember, when we were here on the *Hastings* a ship was burnt; since that and before this last, another met with a like fate, so Penang seems to be a regular place for fires, at least nautical ones.

How jolly it will be to meet again after nearly four years' absence! as I expect we shall arrive in England about February. I intend to buy you two thousand Manilla cheroots; I hope you will like them. I shall try and get them as old as I can. I smoke a little now.

The following letter was written to his father on his return to Singapore after a short cruise.

H.M.S. *Amazon*,
Singapore, May 31st, 1851.

Here we are again at Singapore. I hope by the English mail, which is expected soon, that I shall get my letters regularly again and directed to the *Amazon*. I hope my uncle Ellenborough will not be annoyed at my having exchanged, as I see he would rather I had shared the fortunes of the *Hastings*. One good thing in this ship is that the Captain never stays in harbour long together, but about once a month takes a few days' cruise. Out of the one hundred and twelve days I have been in her we have been forty at sea. Now I will tell you what we have been doing since I last wrote. On the 4th the English mail arrived with the intelligence that she had passed a ship on shore on the Pyramid shoal. Directly we heard that we bent sails, hoisted the boats in, and away we went. The Pyramid shoal is about one hundred and fifty miles from here on the way to Penang. The name of the vessel was the *Charles Forbes*, she was a fine ship of nine hundred tons. She ran on it on the morning of the 2nd in a thick fog and then a heavy squall. The next day we met her two boats. The Captain with his mates and crew had given up the ship for a bad job, and were making for Singapore. They had as much opium stowed away in the boats as they could hold. We took the Captain on board of us, and proceeded on our way. The *Charles Forbes* was laden with four thousand bales of cotton and about thirty cases of opium. The next day at daybreak we sighted the wreck, and about 1 p.m. anchored close to her, and sent our two cutters to get the opium. They brought it off, and about eight the same evening we sent a party of men to break the cotton out—it is stowed very thick together—and put it on the upper deck ready for removal in the morning. But just at midnight it began to blow very hard from the S.W., so we sent the boats for our men and brought them off the wreck. In the morning we saw the unfortunate vessel breaking up very fast; by 9 a.m. it was completely broken up, and as far as we could see, there was one uninterrupted line to leeward of bales of cotton, planks, spars, &c. So there was an end of the *Charles Forbes.* The poor Captain was on the poop watching her break up; he looked very much down in the mouth. We were rather sorry, as we expected to have got her off the shoal, and to get lots of salvage money by her. The Captain of her said he was a poorer man now than when he arrived out here some fourteen years ago, without a sixpence; now he is in the same condition *plus* a wife and children. We weighed anchor and sailed for Singapore. The salvage money is in court now, because the agent offered us a fifth of the value of the opium, but the Captain would not take that, and put in our claim for half. If we get the half, it will be about four dollars a share, and as midshipmen have seven shares, I shall get twenty-eight dollars. But on the whole, I do not think men-of-war ought to get salvage, for what is their duty if not to look after their own merchantmen? While we were at anchor off the shoal, we saved a merchant-ship from being wrecked, by signalling to her: "You are running into danger," and by firing three guns to attract her attention to the signal. So at any rate, if one ship was lost, we saved another.

Of Augustus' attachment to his father and home circle, and his ever present thought of them, these simple unaffected letters afford abundant proof. The affectionate messages invariably sent to his brothers and sisters, mentioning each one by name, evince the deep interest he constantly took in all that concerned them, notwithstanding his having been separated from them at so early an age, and his long absences at sea. During the short intervals he spent at home, too, it generally happened that some of his elder brothers and sisters were away at school, so that in reality he saw very little of them. Their birthdays he never forgot, as his journal bears witness, for each anniversary as it recurs is duly noted, and seldom without the addition of some pious remark or good wish. In one place he writes: "How thankful I ought to be to God for all His blessings, in having given me such a dear father, step-mother, brothers, and sisters. May my constant prayer be that I may be more thankful for His mercies, and also show it by following His blessed will in all things that I do." To one so fond of home, the prospect of returning to England in a few months' time afforded intense delight. "I am very anxious," he writes, "to see you all again. God grant us a happy meeting soon. Oh, how I wish we were off now! Tell them all how *happy*, *happy* I shall be to see all their dear faces again."

Before the time for the earnestly desired meeting arrived, an event took place, of which a passing mention has already been made, and which not only materially affected Augustus' future, but, as will be seen, was the means of directing the whole current of his life into a totally different channel. We refer to Mr. Law's reception into the Church. In order briefly to trace the path whereby he was led thither, it will be necessary to recur to the period when he assumed the charge of a parish and first began to direct his attention to religious questions. The country clergy were then divided into two classes, those who claimed the title of "orthodox," and those who called themselves "evangelicals." With the latter party Mr. Law's inclinations led him at the outset to ally himself, and when the Oxford tracts subsequently found their way into the hands of every country parson, although impressed by the arguments they contained, he did not accept the doctrinal views set forth in them. As time went on, however, his opinions underwent an entire change; by degrees he came to regard the Anglican Church as the purest branch of the Catholic Church, and to look upon those who forsook her communion much as he would, when in the army, have looked upon deserters from his regiment. The occasional misgivings that arose in his mind were easily silenced, until the judgment in the Gorham case, when the highest tribunal in the Church of England decreed that belief in the regenerating power of baptism might be asserted or denied at the option of her members, opened his eyes to the true character of the Establishment. He was not long in arriving at the conviction that in the Catholic Church alone were to be found the abiding signs of the Holy Spirit's unchangeable presence. Feeling that under the circumstances he was no longer justified in officiating as a clergyman, he communicated his difficulties to the Bishop, and obtained from him six months' leave of absence for the purpose of studying at leisure some books recommended by Dr. Pusey as likely to bring him back to his former allegiance.

At this juncture Mr. Law thought it right to acquaint his eldest son with his doubts and mental anxieties. Hitherto topics of this nature had never been alluded to between them, hence Augustus was not a little surprised at the contents of his father's letter. The subject of the Gorham controversy had indeed already attracted his attention, for in a letter to a friend, he had asked to be told the truth of the matter, remarking that he was very sorry to hear of the disagreement, and wondered such a case should be brought before the Council, not before the Bishops. But he was far from suspecting the influence which the decision would have upon his father. All, however, he could say in reply to the unexpected intelligence was that he hoped with all his heart that God would direct his father to the truth, adding that he would try to be what he wished him in his letter to be, instant in prayer to God to guide them all into the truth, and striving to serve God better than he had done of late. And when Mr. Law, referring to temporal considerations, speaks of the pain that it will cause him to entail upon his wife and children the sacrifices which the resignation of his living and Chancellorship, and the consequent serious reduction of his income will involve, Augustus begs that his father will have no regret on this score in as far as he is concerned. To give practical proof of his willingness to bear his part in the sacrifices his father predicts, he adds that since every unnecessary expense, however small, ought to be avoided, he does not care to have the *Illustrated London News* sent out to him any longer, as the Captain was always kind enough to lend him the papers. " I shall look forward anxiously to your next letter," he says, " in which you say you will write more fully, as I wish to know all your reasons. May God bless and preserve you, and guide us all to the truth through Jesus Christ."

The perusal of the books recommended by Dr. Pusey produced no change in Mr. Law's sentiments, except that of strengthening his conviction of the truth of Catholicism. The fact of Archdeacon, after-

wards Cardinal, Manning having joined the Catholic
Church had a great effect on him, and thus before the
expiration of the allotted term, he resigned his benefices,
and made his abjuration at Oscott, on September 19th,
1851. At the same time he resigned all the prospects
of high position and rich emolument which his family
connections would not have failed to secure for him
amongst the Anglicans.

Having become a Catholic himself, he was naturally
desirous that his children should embrace the same
saving faith. Shortly before writing to Augustus to
announce that the final step had been taken, he sent
out a parcel of books and pamphlets on controversial
subjects which he wished him to read with prayerful
attention. After despatching this parcel to Singapore,
he heard that an order had been sent out some six
weeks previously for the immediate return of the
Amazon. He therefore feared that neither letter nor
books would reach his son before his departure, and
that he would arrive in England in ignorance of the
changes that had taken place. However, through what
Mr. Law regarded as a merciful interposition of Providence, not only did considerable delay occur in the
transmission of the Admiralty despatches, but when
the Captain of the *Amazon* at length received the order
to set sail for England, he was unable to comply with
it at once, on account of some repairs being required
before the ship entered upon so long a voyage. Thus
Augustus, whose own good sense suggested to him that
if such a step was right and necessary on his father's
part, it must be equally so on his own, had ample time
to investigate the claims of the Catholic Church on his
allegiance, and acquaint himself with her teaching.

On the day following the receipt of the tidings of

his father's reception into the Church, he wrote: " I
have read some of that Catechism already that you
sent me. I am very glad, dearest father, that you are
so happy. May God bless you for ever and ever."
Then his dutiful, affectionate heart prompts him to
add: " If ever a son ought to feel grateful to a dear
father for his kindness and trouble about him, it is I."
The books he appears to have read with great eagerness, devoting a considerable portion of each day to
the study of them. They were chiefly Cardinal
Wiseman's *Lectures of the Catholic Religion*, Keenan's
Controversial Catechism, Orsini's *Life of the Blessed Virgin*,
and *The See of Peter*, by Allies. Soon after receiving
these volumes he asked a shipmate, Quartermaster
Grant, who was a Catholic, whether he was allowed
to read the Bible. He said certainly, whereupon
Augustus began to think the Roman Catholic Church
was not so black as it is painted. He expresses his
amazement too at the arguments put forward in the
books; they appeared to him quite irresistible.

Naturally enough Augustus, who was but eighteen
years old, felt the need of oral instruction, and looked
anxiously for some one to aid him in his course of
inquiry, and answer the difficulties that arose in his
mind. He owns that he feels quite in a state of doubt
about the two Churches, and wishes he could obtain
enlightenment on the points that perplexed him. He
took Mr. Waldron, the chaplain and naval instructor
of the *Amazon*, into his confidence, and told him about
the books he had received and was studying. On his
mentioning the *Life of the Blessed Virgin*, Mr. Waldron
burst into a fit of derisive laughter. After that no
assistance could be expected from him in the search
for truth, but still Augustus discussed theological

questions with him now and again. He was not long
left without the guide he needed. One Sunday afternoon he went ashore with Mr. Waldron. Before church
they both went to call on Father Barbe, a French
missioner, with whom they had a "yarn." He invited
them to return after the service and have tea with
him; this Augustus did, while Mr. Waldron spent the
evening elsewhere. We give the account of his visit in
his own simple words:

"After leaving the English church, I went towards
M. Barbe's house, but spent about half an hour cruising
about the Roman Catholic church before I found it.
M. Barbe is a very good kind of old fellow. On my
asking about St. Francis Xavier, he told me the church
in ruins at the top of the hill at Malacca was dedicated
to him, and that it was the church he used to preach
in. He told me also that St. Francis Xavier had
performed several miracles there; among others, that
he raised from the dead a girl who had been dead three
days. He also told me about the Roman Catholic
missions in China. The Catholic church here cost
£18,000. The subscriptions were raised by the residents.
I left his house about ten o'clock, and he would walk
part of the way down to the landing-place. He has
asked me to witness the baptism of twenty-one Chinese
on Wednesday at 6 a.m. I am getting a better opinion
of the Catholic Church every day. M. Barbe lent me
a small book, written by Manning, proving the truth
of the Catholic Church, and I asked him to lend me
an English missal, which he very kindly did."

On reading the foregoing extract from his diary, one
cannot fail to be struck by the singular coincidence
that the first Saint in whom Augustus Law took an
interest, should have been not only a Jesuit and a

missioner, as he himself subsequently became, but also the very one of all others whom he was most closely to resemble in the circumstances of his death.

A few days later, he went to return the books, and had another conversation with M. Barbe, about the benefits of confession, among other things. This good priest was instrumental in removing many of his prejudices; he liked him much, and felt the reality of the religion he professed. On leaving Singapore, he says: " Upon my word, what I have seen of the Catholic clergy here at least has given me a high opinion of these men. I shall find out if there are any at Trincomalee, and if so, shall go and see them."

How quickly a conversion is made where there is a man of good-will! Augustus' prejudices and mis-apprehensions vanished as smoke before the wind, or the shades of night before the rising sun. His receptive and docile mind drank in eagerly all the teaching of the Church; the posture of his soul seems to have resembled that of the man in the Gospel who had been born blind, who said: " Who is He, Lord, that I may believe on Him?" And when the great Teacher of mankind revealed Himself to him, he said: " I believe, Lord. And falling down, he adored Him." Augustus had no sooner received the gift of faith than he was desirous of acting up to it. His interviews with the French priest at Singapore nearly resulted in his being received before he quitted the East, despite the reiterated assurances of the chaplain that nothing a Roman Catholic says about his creed is to be believed. On reflection, however, he thought it better for the sake of avoiding all appearance of precipitation, to take more time for the consideration of so important a matter, and wait until he could talk it over with his father.

The *Amazon* set sail from Singapore on January 5, 1852. The homeward voyage, a remarkably favourable one, was accomplished in three months; it offers no features of special interest as far as external events are concerned. It is on Augustus' inner life that our interest centres at present. The record of the books he was reading: Ecclesiastical biographies, Cardinal Wiseman's lectures, Manning's sermons, Law's *Serious Call*, and others of a similar nature, the extracts copied into his journal, and passing notes of the impressions he received, give an insight into his thoughts and feelings at this period, the period of transition from the bondage of error into the liberty of the children of God. He was now more than ever in earnest about religion. To him it had ever been a matter of primary importance, and his example had been a fruitful source of edification to others. When first he went on board the *Hastings* as a midshipman, he found his companions of the gun-room given to ridicule religion. Augustus was accustomed never to omit saying his prayers on going to bed, accordingly the first night he knelt down as usual to repeat his prayers. This was the occasion of a good deal of rough joking and banter on the part of his fellow-midshipmen, but no amount of scoffing had any effect on him. He continued to kneel down every night without heeding his companions, and very soon one and another of the lads began to follow his example, until at last the custom of saying night prayers became quite general among them. Admiral Beamish, who was one of Augustus' comrades on board the *Hastings*, has often said that Augustus was quite the most conscientious and pure-minded midshipman he ever met with. He was as full of fun as any one, but a joke lost its point with him if it savoured in the

least of impurity, and all his mates were so fond of
him that they would not by word or action wound his
sensibility in this respect. If this was true of him as
a Protestant, how much more when his mind had
opened to receive Catholic truth. As he draws nearer
to the Church, one may observe a growing desire to
be watchful over himself, to resist temptation, to be
exact in the performance of duty, to direct his whole
life according to the will of God. His constant prayer
is that he may be kept at peace, that God would grant
him a quiet mind, and resolve his remaining doubts.
On February 18th, the day when he had served his
time for mate, he writes: "One of my most besetting
sins is pride. What a mischievous sin is that! it
destroys every Christian grace. How truly St. James
writes when he says that he who commits one sin is
guilty of all. I have had one or two rows with the
First Lieutenant through the instrumentality of that
sin. May God grant me His saving grace through
Jesus Christ to get rid of this unchristian spirit." Again
on Ash Wednesday he says: "May I observe the day
in proper manner, by repenting deeply of my sins
and in keeping it as Holy Church directs. Let me
remember St. Benedict's rules, and try to act up to
them, and also think particularly of Christ's Death on
the Cross for us miserable sinners."

On April 29th, the *Amazon* cast anchor in Spithead
harbour, and Augustus gave thanks to God for having
brought him safely home, and protected him from
dangers and sickness during the voyage. His father
met him the same day, and he was allowed to go on
shore until 8 a.m. on the morrow. He records his
delight at being once more with his father. They dined

F

at an hotel and sat together till past midnight, " as happy as two kings."

Augustus' wish was to obtain leave to spend six weeks at least with his family, no unreasonable request, one would think, after four years' absence at sea. His principal object was, not to amuse himself and enjoy life, but to make up his mind about religion, since, as he said, he did not like being in doubt on that matter. When pay-day came, he received £67. It was seldom, the clerk observed, that a midshipman received as much at the pay-table. This testified to his careful habits. Unfortunately his pleasure was damped by getting, only a few hours' before, an appointment to the *Encounter*, with orders to join her immediately. This he feared would interfere with the desired leave, but it was not so, and he was able to proceed to London, where his father was then residing. On May 16th, scarcely more than a fortnight after his return, he was received into the Church by the Bishop of Southwark (Dr. Grant). Two or three hours' conversation with that Prelate on the preceding day had thoroughly convinced him of the supremacy of the See of Peter, the only subject on which any remnant of doubt lingered in his mind. Mr. Law was naturally much delighted at this speedy answer to his prayers on behalf of his eldest son. He never anticipated that Augustus would make so little difficulty about embracing the true faith, and had arranged that shortly after his return to England, novenas for his conversion should be offered by various religious communities at home and abroad. But in this instance God's gracious promise to the Prophet, " Before they call, I will hear,"[1] was signally fulfilled. On the day preceding that fixed for the com-

---

[1] Isaias lxv. 24.

mencement of the novenas, he was received into the Church. Thus the voice of supplication was changed into the voice of thanksgiving.

A week later, Augustus made his First Communion, and chose St. Aloysius Gonzaga for his patron saint. The reason he gave for this choice was that the virtues that specially distinguished St. Aloysius were those whereof he himself stood most in need. The persons who knew him best would hardly have been of the same opinion. On the contrary, they would have said that he already in some measure resembled the Saint. His innocence and purity of heart were of no common order; he had a most lowly opinion of himself; he spoke in terms which might have appeared exaggerated of the sins of his past life; and worldly pleasures, even in their most harmless form, had little more attraction for the pious midshipman than they had for the saintly youth whom he proposed to himself as his model. Almost all his time and thoughts were devoted to the study of holy things and attendance at religious services. Visits to his relatives, a large number of whom were then living in or near town, and to the various Catholic churches of the metropolis, seemed to have been his principal diversion during the period of his leave.

When this time had expired, and he had rejoined his ship, Augustus Law was for three weeks so unwell as to be hardly able to leave his hammock. As long as a member of the ship's company is on the sick-list, he is not required to attend Divine worship; thus it was not until his third Sunday on board the *Encounter*, that the moment came for Augustus to declare himself a Catholic, and ask exemption from attendance at the Protestant service. The refusal to join in any religious exercises with those who are outside the pale of the

Church is an ordeal from which every recent convert shrinks, and for many it proves a painful duty. In this case, however, no difficulty was experienced. While the preparations for the service were being made, Augustus sent to inquire whether he could speak to the Captain. The answer was in the affirmative. As soon as he entered the cabin, the Captain asked in a very kind manner, " Well, Mr. Law, what is it? " " Can you excuse me from attending service? I am a Catholic," was Augustus' rejoinder. " Oh, certainly, certainly," the Captain replied; " you can do just as you like about that." For this permission, given so pleasantly, Augustus was not a little thankful; while the others were at their service, he got down the *Golden Manual* from his shelf, and read the prayers for Mass in undisturbed solitude.

On the following day the vessel cast anchor in the Tagus, and Augustus, who had quite recovered from his indisposition, rejoiced in the prospect of being able to approach the sacraments, and go to Mass and Vespers on the next Sunday at the English College in Lisbon. At the earliest opportunity he went on shore with one of his messmates, and leaving him to make purchases in the town, made his way to the College. " That alone," he said, " had any attraction for me." He made acquaintance with some of the students, who were very civil and friendly, and with the Superior, who showed him over the College, and treated him with great kindness. Another day he got leave to go ashore at 5 a.m. After going to Confession and Communion, he breakfasted at the College and stayed until eleven, talking with the Superior. The latter, writing to Mr. Law, told him that the childlike docility and guileless confidence of the young middy won for him the favour and affection of all the inmates of the College.

His stay in the Tagus was a very short one. The *Encounter* joined the Admiral's squadron, then cruising in the Mediterranean. Augustus was stationed in the signals, which means that he had to keep a sharp look-out on the flagship's movements and signals, and repeat them. This duty kept him on deck all day, so that he really had no time to himself, and complained that he could scarcely find leisure to say his morning prayers. But the manœuvres the squadron went through were often a beautiful sight, and he acknowledges that they were a compensation for having come out there. On September 1st he was again at Spithead, with the prospect of being soon paid off. When pay-day came, he was reappointed to the *Encounter*, but permission was subsequently given for him to join the *Excellent* at Portsmouth until further orders, for the purpose of studying for the examination he would have to pass in October. We are now approaching a turning-point in Augustus Law's career. A question more important than that of the rank he was to hold in Her Majesty's navy presented itself for decision.

CHAPTER V.

As the result of the examination Augustus Law passed
in the autumn of 1852, he obtained a first-class certificate in seamanship, but in the other subjects his
papers were unfortunately not quite up to the mark.
Consequently he failed to get his commission as Lieutenant, as would have been the case had he passed
with full numbers for navigation and gunnery and a
first-class certificate for seamanship. He now held
the rank of mate, or, as it is at present called, of
Second Lieutenant. Mr. Law, solicitous for his son's
promotion, endeavoured to get him recommended for
a lieutenancy, through the influence of one of the
Admiralty Lords. But Lord Ellenborough was no
longer the First Lord, and the Duke who had succeeded
him in that office did not see fit to promote his pre-
decessor's nephew. This caused more disappointment
to Mr. Law than to Augustus. To him the failure
seemed a matter of small moment. God destined him
for a higher service; already he heard the voice bidding
him leave all and follow Christ, and the ardour that
filled his soul quelled all desire for fame and promotion.

It will be remembered that in his school-boy days,
previous to his receiving from his uncle the offer of a
cadetship, Augustus had cherished the idea of becoming a minister. This project he relinquished, chiefly

in deference to his father's wishes, certainly not without
a considerable measure of regret on his own part.
Although he got on well in the navy, and by his warm-
heartedness and strict attention to duty won golden
opinions from both his comrades and superior officers,
oftentimes while serving afloat, as he acknowledged
later, the conviction forced itself upon him that a seafaring life was not the one that really suited his inclinations, nor for which he was best fitted. More than once
he seriously thought of asking his father to take him out
of the navy and educate him for the clerical profession.
Fear lest his father, who had a large family to provide
for, should find difficulty in meeting the expenses he
would incur at the University, alone deterred him from
urging this request. Thus we see that even while a
Protestant, the idea of embracing a calling which would
give a religious colouring to his outward life and occupations, continued to attract him. How much the
more, when he had been some months a Catholic, did
his thoughts turn with earnest longing towards the
highest calling of man upon earth, and the desire to
consecrate himself to God in the sacerdotal state, take
possession of his heart. When he visited the College
at Lisbon, where English students were preparing for
the priesthood, and he contrasted the life they led with
his own on board a man-of-war, he felt how infinitely
preferable theirs was, how far more in accordance with
his truest inclinations, his inmost convictions and
aspirations. This thought was constantly before his
mind, and he earnestly entreated the Holy Spirit to
enlighten him, that he might perceive and follow the
will of God in his regard.

On his return from the Mediterranean, he informed
his father of his wish to become a priest. Mr. Law

did not discourage the project, or place any obstacle in the way of its accomplishment. He merely insisted that Augustus should wait a year, in order to test the reality of his vocation before applying to the Board of Admiralty for his discharge. Meanwhile, he desired him to prosecute his studies on board the gunnery-ship at Portsmouth, to which he had been appointed.

According to the regular order of things, after passing his examination, Augustus ought to have re-joined the *Encounter*, which was to sail from England in November. But Mr. Law, who was extremely adverse to his son's going to sea again, had, by apply-ing at head-quarters, obtained his permanent appoint-ment to the *Excellent*. At this, the Captain of the *Encounter* was somewhat aggrieved. He had been asked as a favour to lend Augustus to the *Excellent* in order that he might prepare for the examination, and when that was over, he expected him to return to his own ship. Instead of this, without a word of explanation, Augustus joined the *Excellent*, and an order to discharge him was sent to the Captain of the *Encounter*, who thus found himself, on the eve of going to sea, compelled to seek another officer to fill the place left vacant by his departure. He naturally con-sidered that the course of procedure on the part of those interested in the young man had not been either fair or courteous, and expressed this opinion in a letter to Mr. Law. The latter hastened to offer apologies and explanations, which the Captain accepted as satis-factory. Augustus himself would have much preferred to go to sea. He thought besides that it would be better for his health, as the *Excellent* was by no means a comfortable ship, and while on board of her he was scarcely ever without a cold. He was, however, obliged to make up his mind to remain there, for when he wrote to tell his father he would much rather go to sea, the answer he received was a long extract from St. Jerome on the necessity of mortifying our own will.

In the following March, Augustus obtained leave of absence, a portion of which he employed in making a retreat with the Redemptorists at Clapham. A rule of life to be observed on board the *Excellent* that he drew up for himself whilst there, will serve as a model to persons in the world who wish to live for the greater glory of God, and who cherish the hope of embracing at a future period the religious life.

A Short Rule of Life for the "Excellent."

6.30. Rise and dress, not forgetting to make the sign of the Cross directly I awake, and to let the first words uttered be Jesus, Mary. Offer myself and all that belongs to me to God, and make acts of faith, hope, charity, contrition, and thanksgiving. Whilst washing and dressing, repeat the *De profundis, Miserere, Gloria in Excelsis*, or any other psalms or prayers I know. After being dressed, let me go up into the study, or into as retired a place as I can, and say my prayers; let them be from the heart. Let the Litany of the Holy Name, or some other litany, be said amongst them. A little before 7.30, let me make a spiritual Communion, and then make my meditation, as Father Coffin used to make it with me.

At 8, breakfast. On fasting and abstinence-days, no butter. Let me be as temperate as I can, and always offer up something to Jesus.

After breakfast, meditate again on the same subject,

or some other devotions. After Divisions[1] at 8.30, repeat a *Pater noster* and *Ave Maria*, and offer up my duty to God. Make an act of contrition and love of God, and say a Hail Mary every time the bell strikes, as I find I can, without detriment to the duty I am engaged in.

At noon, examination of conscience, acts of faith, prayers for the dead, offerings of the Precious Blood, with hymn. When that is finished, spiritual reading, or Lives of the Saints. At 1 p.m., as after Divisions (see above). From 3.45 to 4.30, meditate for ten minutes on the same subject as the morning, then spiritual reading or Lives of the Saints.

After dinner till 6, free time; 6 to 7, Latin; 7 to 8, free time, letters, &c.; 8 to 8.30, tea; 8.30 to 9.30, Euclid, gunnery, logarithms, &c.; 9.30 to 10, Rosary; 10 to 10.30, spiritual reading, night prayers, and bed.

On Tuesdays, instead of the offerings to the Precious Blood, the Rosary of the Sacred Heart. On Thursdays, Devotions to the Blessed Sacrament. On Fridays, the Seven Words on the Cross. On Saturdays, the Seven Dolours of Mary.

On resuming his duties at Portsmouth, he wrote to his father that his desire to become a priest was just the same as ever, and he wished the time was come when he could leave the navy. Earnestly desirous as he was for the conversion of his brother Frank (then Second Lieutenant R.A.), the only member of the family who had not become a Catholic, he suggests that during the approaching month of May a special

---

[1] Divisions, *i.e.*, setting apart a portion of the ship's company for a certain service. The master's division steer the ship and work the sails, the engineer's division manage the engines, the powder division provide the guns with ammunition, &c., and so forth.

effort might be made to obtain this grace for him. " Every one of us might write to the Catholics we know, and get them to say the *Memorare*, and some other little prayer or hymn, such as the *Salve Regina*, or to repeat a certain number of times, ' Our Lady of Victories, pray for him,' daily throughout the month of May. If each of us were to ask even ten to join, there would be a good many praying to our Blessed Lady. And what may we not hope for in the month of May!" We are not told whether this suggestion was acted upon, but we know that it was in May two years later, that the brother for whom so many prayers were offered was received into the Church, on the eve of his embarkation with a detachment of his regiment for the Crimea.

About this time Augustus thought it his duty to acquaint Lord Ellenborough with the resolution he had formed to enter the priesthood. He was aware that this announcement would be most displeasing to his uncle, who from the outset had taken the kindest interest in him, and who looked forward to his distinguishing himself greatly in the service. With the utmost candour and simplicity he laid before him the state of his mind, and his conviction that to become a priest would be more conducive to his spiritual interests, to which all earthly interests must be sacrificed. His only regret therefore, he said, in leaving the navy was that he would incur the disapproval of his uncle, and other dear relations, to whom he was indebted for so much kindness. Lord Ellenborough's answer was as follows :

My dear Augustus,—I certainly am very sorry to hear that you think of leaving the navy to become a priest.

A man may be good and do good to others by his advice and example in whatever situation he may be placed, and the more he is brought into communication with large numbers of persons exposed to great temptations, the more good he may do, by showing that they can be effectually resisted. I doubt whether any priest was ever a better man than Lord Collingwood, and you will not easily find one better than Captain Chads. Solitude and celibacy, though they may diminish in some cases the number of bad actions, may not impose restraint upon bad thoughts, and God knows men's thoughts and will judge them by those, as well as by their actions. You are making a great mistake as to happiness here, without at all improving your chance of happiness hereafter.

The remark Augustus makes upon this letter is that it is kind enough, and free from bigotry. It is, in fact, just what one might expect from a sensible Protestant and prudent man of the world. The writer of it did not perceive, as we do, that the zeal of the Lord was consuming the young man's heart; and when that flame is kindled no one may quench it, or prevent it from burning up like chaff worldly calculations and interests, turning into glowing ardour past languor and delaying doubts, elevating the powers and affections of the soul until they rise like incense on the altar of God. About this time we find a long meditation written by Augustus, on the certainty of being saved or lost; of this we give the concluding portion.

St. Philip Neri used to say, Heaven is not made for the slothful, let me take care that I do not come under that head. If I have been slothful and idle,

seldom exerting myself to do anything for the glory of
God, let me arouse myself. Stir thyself up, O my soul!
Lament thy defects. Beseech God to pardon them, and
endeavour for the future to lead a better life. And as,
O Lord, following the vocation that Thou hast marked
out for me is necessary for my salvation, show me Thy
will; I will do it. If I have made a mistake in believing
I am called to the priesthood, let it not be too late.
Call me back before it is too late, O Lord. But if it is
Thy blessed will that I should be a priest, let me devote
myself to Thee more and more, and try to make Thee
loved by every one. Give me the graces necessary for
such an awful office; and then, O Lord, Thy will be done
with regard to whether I shall be a regular or a secular.
And if I am to be a regular, Thy will be done again with
regard to what Order, whether Jesuits, Redemptorists,
or Passionists. Let Thy will be always beloved and
sought after by me. Lord, hear my prayer. St. Teresa
said to her religious: " One soul, my daughters, one
eternity." If one only considered in his heart these
words, *One soul, one eternity.* What volumes they express!
Yes, I have only one soul, and if that is lost, all is lost,
and for ever too. How precious then ought this soul to
be to me. How careful I am for my body, that nothing
hurts it, that it never wants for anything; but how
differently I behave in regard to my soul. I do not
mind my poor soul going through all sorts of dangers,
and if it wants food (prayer or meditation), it must wait
until it is convenient to the body. How long is it to be
this way? One soul, one eternity. Think on these
words, and you will say it shall be so no longer. O my
Blessed Saviour, forgive my many treasons and infi-
delities. Come Thyself and feed my soul spiritually
with the Bread of Life. Grant that I may never be

separated from Thee. Mary, my dear Mother, intercede for me, and obtain for me final perseverance. St.Joseph, St. Aloysius, St. Francis Xavier, obtain for me the love of God.

From this outpouring of Augustus' inmost heart it will be seen that the question of his vocation to the priesthood was not the only one to be decided. Another had presented itself: Was he called to enter a Religious Order? During his retreat at Clapham he had read St. Alphonsus Liguori on the Religious State, and ever since had felt a strong attraction to the religious life. In how many Christian souls has not the perusal of that little work awakened a desire to follow the counsels of perfection? The reason he gave to his father for his preference of the religious life was that he did not consider himself to possess sufficient decision of character and self-reliance for a secular priest, and that he should work much better under obedience than as his own master, or placed in a position of authority over others. In reality, though he was perhaps hardly conscious of it himself, the charity of Christ was urging him to make a complete holocaust of himself. *Omnia pro Christo* was the motto he adopted, and to which he endeavoured to conform himself. He knew well that, in the words of the *Imitation*,[1] to obtain all it was necessary to forsake all, to resign himself always and at all times, as in great things, so also in little. With this object he wished to leave off smoking, which had become a fixed habit with him, almost a necessity. The difficulty he found in making this daily sacrifice was almost insurmountable. Again and again he resolved to break through the habit, and took

---

[1] Bk. iii. ch. 37.

himself to task for not putting his resolution into practice. "How long," he asks himself, "am I to be held in bondage by the devil in regard to smoking?" Again and again he enumerates the reasons for and against the use of tobacco, and tells himself how vastly the latter preponderáte over the former. By giving up his pipe, he argued, he would gain time, at least an hour a day, and money, a trifling sum certainly, but one that might be better spent. By denying himself in a spirit of penance and for the love of God, he would also gain merit; and since he must give it up eventually, better sooner than later. Smoking was a pleasure of the senses, and he had read in St. Alphonsus, that indulgence of the pleasures of the senses was incompatible with a holy life. On the other hand, his natural man urged that it was a great luxury at very small cost; that it was useful in preserving him from infection; that there was no harm in smoking while he was in the navy, and that it in no wise interfered with his devotions. Finally, to put an end to his hesitation, he consulted Father Coffin, who had given him his retreat at Clapham, on the matter, and was advised by him not to attempt too much at first, but to restrict himself for the present to a limited number of pipes, three or four only, perhaps, in the course of the day. Whether or no Augustus followed this advice, at any rate he did not entirely give up smoking until he became a religious. The habit proved easier to overcome than he had anticipated. On being asked by a friend, some six months after he entered the Novitiate, whether he did not feel the want of his pipe, he replied that he must own that just at the outset he used to miss it very much, especially after dinner, but that after the first week or two he scarcely ever thought of it.

The autumn of 1853, when the fixed time of proba-
tion was ended, found Augustus unwavering in his
determination to offer himself for the priesthood.
Cardinal Wiseman kindly volunteered to send him to
the English College in Rome, and the only reason
apparently why this offer was not accepted was that
Augustus feared lest he should not be free to enter a
Religious Order if, after two or three years of study, he
should feel called to do so. He wished to apply for his
discharge from the service at once, but to this Mr. Law
would not consent. The plan he proposed was that
Augustus should obtain leave to remain twelve months
on shore, his name being still retained on the Navy
List, and he meanwhile pursuing his studies either at
home, or in some school or college. This plan did not
commend itself at all to Augustus. He felt he could
never again take any real interest in the service; that
to prosecute his studies with undivided attention and
application would be impossible amid the distractions
and interruptions which would beset him whilst living
under his father's roof, and he could not hope to obtain
admission into any seminary or college free of charge
under the proposed conditions. Moreover, as no reason
of a satisfactory nature could be given to the naval
authorities for the desired permission for a twelve
months' absence from his ship, without altogether
leaving the service, the petition was not favourably
received by the Admiralty. While the matter was
pending, Augustus caught scarlet-fever, and was sent
to Haslar, the naval hospital near Portsmouth. The
attack appears to have been a very slight one, for in
three or four weeks' time he had completely recovered.

Immediately upon leaving the hospital he went to
make a retreat. This time it was to Hodder House,

near Stonyhurst, that he went, where the Jesuit
Noviceship then was. Whilst there he came to a
final decision in regard to his state of life, electing
the religious in preference to any other, as that in
which he considered he would be best able to serve
God. The next thing to be done was to make
choice of an Order. The Society of Jesus and the
Order of the Most Holy Redeemer were the only
two he knew much about, except the Cistercian, and
of that he feared that he could not bear the severity of
the Rule. Before he went to Hodder, his inclinations
led him in the direction of the Redemptorists. All that
he saw while in their house at Clapham, pleased and
attracted him. The constant cheerfulness of its inmates
in particular impressed him most favourably. Father
Coffin, C.SS.R., too, who was his director, had told him
that from what he knew of him, he considered him well
suited for the life of a Redemptorist. With the writings
of the Founder of the Order, St. Alphonsus Liguori,
he had already made himself acquainted, and was
much delighted with them. Besides the treatise on the
Religious State, of which mention has been made, the
little book of meditations entitled *The Way of Salvation*,
was an especial favourite. He had used it daily for
several months past; speaking of it, he says: " I
spent many a happy half-hour with it on board the
Excellent, the half-hour before breakfast; and I found it
a pleasant companion when left to myself for twenty-
one days in Haslar Hospital." But it was not for
nought that he had placed himself under the special
patronage of St. Aloysius, that he daily commended
himself to the Saints of the Society, and invoked their
intercession on his behalf. The principal reason why
he did not at first think much of becoming a Jesuit was

G

because he imagined he should have to pass some very difficult examination before admission into the Society, and for that his scanty knowledge of Latin disqualified him. When once this apprehension was removed, and he found no preparation was required, but that he could be admitted at once, and pursue his study of Latin during the two years' novitiate, the scale quickly turned in favour of the Society.

The admirable organization of the Society, the perfect discipline maintained among its members, naturally commended themselves to one trained as he had been in the naval service. And when he acquainted himself more fully with the history of the Society, its work, its triumphs, its reverses, its persecutions, its suppression, its resurrection not to another and a new life but to the self-same life it had ever led, all hesitation vanished; and now he determined to enrol himself under the banner of St. Ignatius, thenceforward to follow him as he had followed Christ.

Meanwhile Mr. Law was still carrying on negotiations at the Admiralty in the hope of obtaining his object, and getting his son's name retained on the Navy List, in case he should not adhere to his purpose of taking Orders, and wish to resume the sword and epaulettes of a lieutenant R.N. The protracted discussions and letters to and fro worried and agitated Augustus. He longed once for all to put an end to the harassing suspense, to cast aside the considerations of worldly prudence, and without further delay and hesitation retire from the navy. He had counted the cost, and was prepared to make whatever sacrifice might be required of him. At length his father withdrew his opposition, and Augustus, delighted to find himself free to obey the impulses of grace, applied at once for his discharge. This he did with the full approval of the Captain of the *Excellent*, who behaved with the utmost kindness, and made no objection to Augustus leaving the ship, although he did not pretend to understand the motives that actuated him. The order for his discharge arrived on the 8th of December, and on the 15th of the following January he entered the Novitiate of the Society of Jesus.

Of the intervening six weeks scarcely any record exists. His diary, which, ever since he first went to sea, had been the faithful chronicle of all his thoughts and actions, is a blank. Letters to his father there are none, for the time was spent under his roof. Only from letters addressed to Augustus, speaking of the step he had taken, do we gather in what light his friends regarded it. Most of these were written in a kindly spirit, but few exhibit the complete absence of prejudice, or attempt at remonstrance, which characterizes the subjoined note, penned by one of his uncles, the Hon. Henry Law.

I only heard on Saturday last of your determination to leave the navy and become a priest. I do not write in the hope of dissuading you from that course, but simply lest my total silence should imply indifference as to what became of you. This I can never feel. I lay no blame upon you for following the course you conscientiously believe to be the right one, and only hope that should you hereafter feel any misgiving, you will not be deterred by false shame from acknowledging your change of mind, before you have bound yourself by an irrevocable vow. You will have my sincerest prayers for your happiness here and hereafter.

Of the vexation and disappointment experienced by his uncle and kind patron, Lord Ellenborough, mention has already been made. One can hardly wonder that similar sentiments were entertained by many other Protestant relatives and friends of the family. All who were connected with the navy, more especially Augustus' former shipmates and fellow-officers, greatly regretted his retirement, on account of the loss he would be to the service as an officer. They all had but one opinion of him, that as a sailor his main idea had been attention to duty and forgetfulness of self. The moral influence exercised on those around him by a man of such character is an element of strength in a mess or on board ship. There appeared besides every prospect that he would distinguish himself, and rise to the head of his profession, when a wider sphere would be open to him, and his power to influence for good the men under his command would be incalculable.

Of his final parting from the immediate members of his family nothing is told us. It may be imagined that the severance of the endearing ties that bound so affectionate a son and brother to his home must have been most painful to nature. The following story appears to have afforded consolation both to Augustus and to his relatives under these circumstances. It is, moreover, interesting in itself, so that we have a double plea for inserting it here. The Jesuit concerned in the narrative was living when it was related to Augustus.

A young man entered the Society of Jesus in France. About the same time his father and brother, both of whom had given up their religion, sailed for some distant port. The vessel was wrecked, and all on board were supposed to have been lost. When the

news reached the Jesuit in question, he naturally feared
much for the souls of his father and brother. Many
years later, after he had become a priest, he was one
day visiting a hospital, when he was called to the
bedside of a soldier who was dangerously ill. He found
the poor fellow to be as sick in soul as in body. After
doing his utmost to awaken him to contrition, and
induce him to make his peace with God, he put a few
questions to him, by means of which he discovered that
the man was his brother. Fearing to overtax the
strength of the sick man, he did not make himself known
to him, but went straight home, and told his Superior
what had occurred. After a moment's reflection, the
Superior bade him not to return to the hospital, but
leave his brother to the mercy of God, and trouble
himself no more about him. The Jesuit Father was
astonished at this answer ; a strong temptation assailed
him, which, after a severe struggle, he generously
repelled. Two or three days after he was removed to
another place.

Four years passed away, and the Jesuit Father
happened to be giving a mission in the town where he
had met with his brother. One day a woman came
into the sacristy, and said to him : " I have not come
to ask you to hear my confession, Father, but to give
you a message from the *Curé*. He has ordered me to
tell you from our Blessed Lady, that your father, who
was shipwrecked fifteen years ago, before he sank
below the waters made a good act of contrition, and
saved his soul." The Jesuit, who had never seen the
woman before, and whom she too now saw for the first
time, was amazed at what she said. She seemed a
poor, simple woman, but was far advanced in the
knowledge of God. After a moment's pause, she

continued : " Your brother, whom you recognized here four years ago, saved himself by clinging to a plank, but he narrowly escaped death. He enlisted in the army, and lived in neglect of God. His salvation was the reward of the act of obedience you performed on his account ; two days after you saw him, he died in excellent dispositions. I am also charged to tell you that our Blessed Lady desires you should know that scarcely any souls who have relatives in religion are lost ; for Almighty God is so pleased with the sacrifices made by a good religious, that in virtue of them, He gives great graces to their relations to enable them to save their souls. Thus very few of them are lost eternally."

Before Augustus Law takes leave of his friends in the world, we must add a few words respecting his personal appearance. He was at that time twenty years of age, of about an average height, rather broad-shouldered, but not otherwise of a robust build. He had lost the good looks of his boyhood, but his brown eyes still had the soft, gentle expression his mother loved so well, and a somewhat wide mouth gave a good-humoured look to his frank, open countenance. As a boy he was slight in figure, and looked well in his midshipman's uniform ; and when he exchanged the gold-laced cap for a cocked hat and epaulettes, every one pronounced him to be a smart-looking young officer. When we next see him he will have assumed the habit of the sons of St. Ignatius, and this he will still be wearing when he is laid in his lonely grave on the African plains.

CHAPTER VI.

FIRST YEARS IN THE SOCIETY.

A TRULY simple and hidden life, such as was really led in the Holy House of Nazareth, cannot be written about, and hence it is not described in the Gospels. The life of a novice in a religious house is likewise a hidden life; a life of prayer, of obedience, of self-denial. Consequently we shall have little to relate concerning Augustus during his two years' novitiate, except such information as can be gleaned from his letters, and from the recollections of his fellow-novices. The latter all formed a high opinion of him; let us listen to one of them while he recalls his impression of the whilom sailor.

"What I chiefly remarked about Augustus Law, when I knew him in the Novitiate, was the charming simplicity of his character. I never knew him do anything that I should have thought of recording, nor did I ever hear him say anything that was striking. He was an unpretending, unconscious, happy youth, who took the world as he found it, and never thought that the weather, or the food, or his professors, were not up to the mark. He had the great gift of living the 'common life,' and probably with St. John Berchmans, he found his 'greatest mortification' in it. He had the spirit of sanctity about him, and differed, as far as I can judge, from so many others merely in this, that he never lost it." The speaker of these words was already a priest when he began his novitiate. He remembers that Augustus, ever anxious to learn something connected with his future calling, used when walking out with him, to "pick his companion's brains," asking him questions of theology, and endeavouring to gain from him some knowledge of the duties and privileges of the priesthood.

But we must hear what Augustus has to say for himself concerning the new life upon which he has entered. About a month after he had left home, he wrote to his father: "I am very, very happy here, and by the assistance of God's grace, I hope to live and die in the Society of Jesus. It seemed rather strange to me at first when people whom I had never seen before called me *Brother* Law. There are, I think, altogether twenty novices. I have learnt how to serve Mass, to serve at table, &c., and am learning to bind books, so that I shall be quite accomplished soon. It is such a capital thing here that we never have an idle moment; besides, Latin takes up most of my *ad libitum* time. I am going through Cæsar. Give my very best love to all." And concluding the same letter a week later, he adds: "I am getting happier every day. Best love to all again. You cannot think what beautiful exhortations Father Clarke (the novice-master) gives us."

During the first month of his residence at Hodder, Augustus employed his spare time in filling a little book with long and minute counsels addressed to his younger brother Frederick (now retired Commander R.N.), who was just about to enter upon the career he himself had abandoned, and in whom he took a peculiar interest. These counsels are very edifying. We give a few extracts from the closely-written pages.

On attending to the Duties of Religion.

Heretofore you have always gone to Mass, prayers, confession, and other religious duties almost as a matter of course. For even if you had not felt disposed to perform these essential duties, you would have done so either from force of example, or from being obliged by the rules of the school. But when you enter the navy you cannot lean upon these safeguards. It will be all optional with you. You will have to look after yourself and no one will say, Come to Mass, or, You should be going to confession, or, Are you going to receive the Blessed Sacrament to-morrow? None of this; on the contrary, you will be told that going to confession so often is all nonsense, as I remember being told, when one of my messmates asked me how often I went to confession, and I told him: Once a week when I could, and if that could not be done, as often as I had opportunity. And surely in the navy you will want strength, light, and grace from our Lord to carry you through so many dangers, difficulties, and temptations which you will experience. Then for the love of Jesus and Mary, go to confession as often as you can, and let it be the first thing you do when you go on shore. Even if you could only get one day's leave, because the ship was only going to stop a day or two, I do not think there is any question what you should do. For the thing is, Shall I go to confession and thus make myself at peace with God, and be at ease the rest of the voyage? Or shall I go and amuse myself and then not feel exactly comfortable when I get to sea again, for I had my opportunity of going to confession, and never went? You know a little of Latin and a little of French. I should certainly advise you to perfect yourself in one of them at least. Perhaps French would be best, although, if you can manage to understand Latin sufficiently to make your confession in it, it would be of more universal use.

And now a few words on meditation. All Catholics are earnestly recommended to practise meditation once a day, and that for at the very least a quarter of an hour. You will find lots of time for this holy exercise, I am certain of that. The best time I should think would be before breakfast, which is nearly always at 8, and you are turned out of your hammock at about 6.30. So if you take half an hour for dressing, you can have a full hour for anything you like. What better time than this for going into your berth, or mess-room, and saying your prayers—offering up all your actions, thoughts, and words of the day to God, and making half an hour's meditation. Supposing with all your endeavours to get half an hour's quiet during the day for meditation you cannot get it, well, there are the night-watches to fall back upon, in which you will generally find plenty of time for reflection and thought. Of course you must never neglect your *duty* in order to meditate. That obviously would be wrong, but there are so many portions of the watch in which you have nothing to do but to walk up and down the deck. Then is the time for you to meditate, say the Rosary, &c. When you have got into the ways of a ship, you will find you will have plenty of time for prayer without inter-fering with your duty. St. Alphonsus Liguori says of mental prayer: Without this it will be difficult for the soul to continue long in the grace of God.

Although when at sea, you of course cannot attend Mass personally, yet you can unite your intention with the priests who are offering up the Holy Sacrifice

throughout the world. It is a pleasant thing to think
of, that whatever time of the day it is, the Holy Sacrifice
is being offered up somewhere. . . . So at any time in
the day or night, you can be in spirit at Mass. In that
beautiful book of meditations by St. Alphonsus which
I have given you, you will find everything that you
could want for guiding you through difficulties and
temptations. I hope you will make use of it often.
When in danger of the body at sea in any way, or
anywhere else, make a fervent act of contrition and
love of God, and then trust in God whatever happens.

I suppose it is almost superfluous to tell you that you
should respect and obey your superior officers. You
must see that where there is no discipline there will not
be much peace and comfort, whether it be a monastery,
a regiment of soldiers, or a ship. I just mention this to
warn you never to speak badly of your superior or
senior officers, down in your berth or elsewhere. You
will hear a good many do this though, and call them
all the names they can think of, because they do something or say something they do not like. There are
many reasons why you should refrain from doing this.
First your duty as a Christian and a Catholic tells you
to speak evil of no man. Moreover, it is expressly
against the rules of the service, and may get you into
scrapes from being overheard. Then after all, what
good do you get by it? It makes no one happier
to abuse another. So do not join with others in
speaking evil of superior officers. If you can say
something good of the man talked about, say it. With
regard to addressing superior officers, always speak
respectfully, whoever and whatever they may be, for .
bear in mind, it is not the man as he is you pay respect
to, but the office as captain, commander, lieutenant, &c.

After several other pages filled with wise and judicious counsels on various other points, he concludes with these words:

Make yourself as good an officer and sailor as you can, all for the glory of God. Give a good example to all your shipmates. You must not be surprised at being bothered about your religion. I advise you never to let them put you out of temper on account of it, for if you do, they will only go on the more. First endeavour when any one speaks to you about our holy religion in public, to turn off the conversation. I am almost glad they tease you about it, for I hope it will make you prize your faith (the greatest blessing God bestows) all the more, and also make you keep closer than ever to Jesus and Mary. Jesus never forgets those who are persecuted for the holy faith.

Later on, writing to his father about this same sailor-brother, he says: " We must pray hard for him, for sailors do not get many advantages in the religious way. However, God no doubt will give him great graces. Captain Jerningham told me he was a much better Catholic on board a ship, amongst all the cursing, swearing, &c., than when living quietly on shore with all the advantages of hearing Mass, &c. The fact is, that on board a ship in the Royal Navy, one is often the only Catholic officer, so all eyes are turned on him to see how 'the Catholic' behaves, and I fancy this is a great incentive to leading a good life."

We may conclude that Mrs. Law was somewhat alarmed in regard to the ascetic practices of Hodder, for Augustus continues: " I hope Father Clarke gave May a full description of the 'frightful' austerities we poor novices undergo. Fred will soon be amongst the *real* austerities—walking for four hours in the middle of the night, wet through sometimes, and with a very cold piercing wind, not to forget living upon 'salt-junk and maggoty biscuit' for about sixty days, at the same time being on short allowance of water. Tell May that directly that I find our austerities get up to that I will write in all haste to her. I am very jolly and happy."

Another time he writes: "I little thought two years ago what blessings God had in store for me. How good He has been to us all! Tell Helen and all, I would write to them individually, but since every one sees my letter, it would be no good, besides every minute at Hodder is precious. No time is thrown away, and really the time I have been here seems to have passed away so very quickly."

The following notes, jotted down for his own instruction and encouragement at the commencement of the first retreat he made as a religious, may be of some interest to the reader.

The Advantages of a Retreat.

1. I merit. There is some difficulty about it. We praise the three Kings for the long journey they took to see the Infant Jesus; to many persons an eight days' retreat is a thing of greater difficulty than a long journey. Let us endeavour to be looking for Him as they did. *Ubi est qui natus est?*

We bless Cleophas and his friend because our Lord found them talking about Himself. We shall be like them for these eight days. Daniel was told: " From the beginning of thy prayers the word went forth and

I am come to show it thee, because thou art a man of desires."[1] Later on, the Angel gives him the same name, adding: "Peace be to thee, take courage and be strong." What an encouragement! Let the same be said to us. God seemed pleased at seeing Job serving Him so faithfully. *Numquid considerasti servum meum Job?* He appears glad to find some one who will serve Him sincerely. He says now: Have you seen that Brother, how he is meditating, how he is visiting Me? He was grateful to the woman who anointed His feet, so that He said no one should ever preach Him without that being preached that she did.

2. The memory, imagination, intellect, and will being concentrated on one thing, they are used with more effect. *Pluribus intentus minor est ad singula sensus.* Hence guard of the eyes, silence are recommended. The thoughts are to be confined to congruous subjects. This helps a good deal, and makes the work much easier and lighter.

3. The more we are removed from men and external work the nearer we come to God and His angels, and the more readily do we hear God. Hence God often spoke to men in their sleep, as to Jacob and to St. Joseph. In retirement we see heavenly things with a keener sight: hence, *vacate et videte quum ego sum Deus.* And *accedite ad eum et illuminamini.* We are perhaps blind, and want to see. We see the difficulties and do not see what there is to help us. In retirement we learn how to make God sweeter to us than creatures: *delectare in Domino.* Here we have plenty of time. To run a few steps may not make you warm; if you walk for an hour, you will get heat.

[1] Daniel ix. 23.

In September, 1854, the happy monotony of the life
in the Jesuit Novitiate was broken by an unusual and
exciting event.   This was none other than the transfer
of the Novitiate from the north to the south of England.
" Wonderful to relate," Augustus writes to his father,
" I actually have news, news from Hodder ! Hodder is
no longer the Jesuit Novitiate. ' Business is removed'
to Beaumont Lodge, Old Windsor. Fancy the Jesuits
in sight of Windsor Castle, for I believe we are only two
miles away from it." This removal of the Novitiate from
Hodder, where it had been for more than fifty years,
took almost every one by surprise. No one except the
solicitors who transacted the business knew for whom
the property was purchased. One fine day the work-
men who had been engaged in making alterations and
doing repairs disappeared, and were replaced by a
number of active young students, some of whom set to
work plastering and painting the interior of the house,
whilst others lent a helping hand at fixing and arranging
things. On this occasion Augustus Law could turn his
former experience as a sailor to good account. A priest
who had charge of the novices at that time remembers
that he was remarkably helpful in making everything
ship-shape, and displayed wonderful ingenuity in stow-
ing the baggage away in the smallest possible space.
It was some time before it was generally known who
the new-comers were. The Novice Master, Father
Thomas Clarke, was supposed to be the Principal of
an Academy for gentlemen's sons. When the truth
leaked out, a considerable outcry was made. Even the
friends of the Society deemed it somewhat imprudent
to place the Novitiate under the walls, so to speak, of
Windsor Castle. The Jesuits had however no cause
to regret the move ; the advantages derived from being

within easy reach of London, at least every one will understand.

Augustus for one was well pleased with the change. He thought Beaumont a very healthy place, and rejoiced in the facilities now afforded him for seeing his father occasionally. His fervour as a novice did not diminish the warmth of natural affection, but that affection was supernaturalized, and his first thought was of the eternal good of those he loved.

" If I have been negligent in writing lately," he says at the commencement of 1855, "I have not forgotten you and my dear brothers and sisters at Mass every day. I have now been a year and more out of the navy. You must imagine my name has been on the Navy List all this time, viz., for the year you wished it to be, for if it had, it would now be all the same. On the 15th I have been the year in the Noviceship. Thanks to God, I am still of the same mind, only much more strengthened in it than when I first joined, and I hope by the grace of Jesus Who mercifully brought me here, to live and die in this same dear Society of His."

In January of the next year, Augustus pronounced his first vows. Even those who know him only from these pages will be able to conjecture the fervour wherewith he made this entire dedication of himself to the service of God. Let us listen to his own words at the time.

"One object, one mark to be looked at and aimed at, one straight path which leads to God's praise and glory to be walked along. And all things around me to be used for that one object, that one mark. Otherwise I have missed my road, I have failed in life, I am ruined. Nothing to be aimed at for its own sake, only God."

At the close of his novitiate, his Superiors, desirous that he should improve his knowledge of French, sent him to St. Acheul, near Amiens, for his rhetoric. On the way thither he was allowed, at Mr. Law's request, to spend a couple of days with his family, who were then residing at Boulogne. He gave much edification by his religious obedience on that occasion, gently but firmly adhering to what he believed to be his Superior's intentions even in the most trivial matters, notwithstanding the efforts made to persuade him to the contrary. A few months later, he wrote the following letter to his brother Graves, who after a short time spent at Addiscombe, had renounced his intention of entering the army for the sake of joining the Oratory of St. Philip. In familiar letters such as this, and others that have been quoted, the writer unconsciously paints himself, and gives an insight into his amiable, affectionate character, his simple, earnest piety.

A.M.D.G.

Pentecost, May 11, 1856.
College of St. Acheul, Amiens.

I must commence my letter by wishing you all the gifts of the Holy Ghost and of Mary, since to-day it is Pentecost, and the month of Mary is not ended. You will have heard that papa, May, and Maud came over here to see me. We went over the Cathedral and over a hospital kept by the Sisters of Charity. I think they were very well pleased with their day. You know also that they are about to live at Hampton Court, close to Beaumont Lodge.[1] I hope papa will be able to do

---

[1] The apartments in Hampton Court Palace occupied by Mr. Law's family were originally given to Lady Montgomery and her two then unmarried daughters. The elder of these married, as we have seen, Mr. Law. Some years after Lady Montgomery's death, the other daughter,

something for the mission at Sunbury, which is about
three miles from Hampton Court. Our novices catechize
there. You will be glad to hear, if you do not know
it already, that *All for Jesus* has been translated into
French. Walking from the railway-station to our
College, I saw it in a shop window. Do you remember
the Jesuit Captain Wood, R.N.? He is dead. He
died of consumption at Malta; we are extremely sorry
to lose him. He was so good. I saw him at Ryde,
and he was two or three months with me at Beaumont.
The state of his health prevented him from finishing
his course of theology. I beg your prayers for his
soul. I have taken him for my patron, since I think
he is bound to hear a brother sailor-Jesuit.

May 17th.—You would like, I dare say, to hear what
I am studying. Well, now I can understand my French
Brothers, provided they do not talk very fast, and I
can speak a little; as to reading a French book, that
is easy compared with speaking. I hope by September
to know French very tolerably. As to Latin, I read
Cicero, Virgil, &c., and write themes and verses occasionally. Greek I am just beginning to look up again.
I follow the class I am in *quoad fieri potest*, but I bestow
my principal pains on French and Latin. I was
thinking of threatening you with the bother of reading
a badly-written Latin letter, but I will spare you the
penance this time. I get up at 4 a.m.; meditation
from 4.30 to 5.30; then Mass; 6, study; 7, breakfast,
study, &c.; 8 to 10, class; 10 to 10.15, manual work;
10.15 to 11.15, study; examen; 12, dinner and recrea-

---

on her marriage with Sir Thomas Whichcote, made over to Mrs. Law her
right to the apartments in the Palace. The family, who had been living
first in London, then at Boulogne, since Mr. Law's resignation of his
living of Harborne, removed thither, and they have resided there ever since.

tion till 1.15; study; 2.30 to 4.30, class; 7, supper and recreation; 8.15, litanies; 8.30, preparation for meditation; 8.45, examen; 9, bed. The after-dinner recreation is in French; after supper, Latin. On Tuesdays and Thursdays we have a walk in the garden and no class. Every alternate Tuesday we spend at our country house and have games, &c., no study. Such is my day, dearest Graves, and I suppose yours is much the same. How much happier we are, working away for God's glory, than we were while working for our own amusement in the world. One of your old schoolmates is here, he begs to be remembered most kindly to you. We are in the same class in rhetoric. He was delighted to hear that you were at the Oratory. I shall be most happy to get a line from you, when you can spare the time. And I beg your prayers, dearest brother, most heartily. We three, Helen, you, and I, ought to pray well for one another. I shall never forget that happy meeting at the Convent in Blandford Square. There we were all three, after being knocked about in the world for a long time, enlisted at length in Jesus Christ's service; one an Oratorian, one a Sister of Mercy, one a Jesuit. Jesus and Mary be praised!

To this little group of religious, a fourth was shortly after added, when Mr. Law's second daughter, Matilda, became a nun in the Convent of the Visitation at Westbury-on-Trym. She was Augustus' favourite sister; on hearing of her vocation and entrance upon the religious life, he gave thanks to God, and said, in his humility, that he wished he could imitate her fervour and her love.

In the course of the year 1857 it was found that the climate at Amiens did not agree with Augustus. The

state of his health became very unsatisfactory, so
much so that the Provincial was informed of it. He
was consequently recalled to England, and sent to
pursue his studies at the Seminary at Stonyhurst.
There he remained for two years. During this period
we are told that he was noted for three characteristics :
the first of these being a deep interest in and close
application to the study of philosophy, in which his
health obliged him to be rather a careful thinker than
an extensive reader. During walks, or strolls in the
garden at the time of recreation, he was always anxious
to discuss some philosophical question with his companion. The second point in his character, which
manifested itself so strongly afterwards, was an intense
zeal for missionary work. He was ever studying how
he might best put plain truths in a simple and practical
way before the young and before the poor and ill-
instructed, and was glad of every opportunity of practising himself in the catechisms given by the scholastics
in the villages at a short distance from the Seminary.
To the third point remarked in him he was also faithful
through life, and this was his devoted admiration of
the writings of St. John Chrysostom. While his fellow-
students were humorously called by the names of the
authors for whom they had a special predilection,
Brother Law was in his turn denominated " St. Chrysostom." He devoted a quarter of an hour every day
to reading his favourite Father in the original text.
And though he was not familiar with the language, at
any rate not at all proficient in it, the Greek seemed to
explain itself to him by some spiritual process in a
wonderful manner. " If one reads St. Chrysostom's
writings with a pen in one's hand," he writes in his
note-book, " it is hard work, for you might write nearly

every word down ; everything is so lucid, so eloquent,
so pious." Some years later, writing to his father from
Berbice, he says he would give anything for a volume
of St. Chrysostom in Greek, and asks him whether he
could pick up an odd volume in some second-hand
book-shop. And in his sermons and written meditations, we find him continually quoting this favourite
writer.

At Stonyhurst, as in the Novitiate, Brother Law
was much liked by his Superiors on account of his
diligent and intelligent observance of the Rule, and
by his companions, a large proportion of whom were
old friends, having been his fellow-novices, on account
of his entire unselfishness, and the almost unvarying
brightness of his disposition. The former trait was
one which had distinguished him from his boyhood,
and he practised it with so much freedom and ease that
it wore the semblance of a natural gift rather than of
an acquired virtue. Even in the nursery he was
always ready to leave his games to render a service to
any one, and he was just the same now, ingenious in
finding occasions for exercising his charity. Towards
the sick he was kindness itself. At every free moment
he would visit their rooms on some pretext or another,
to tell them any scrap of news, or amusing intelligence
that he had heard ; sometimes only to stir the fire, and
see if anything was wanted.

One may judge of the spirit in which he lived
from the following remarks on prayer and hints for
the practice of self-denial which he wrote during his
first year at Stonyhurst, and which were intended
to guide him in his intercourse with God and with his
neighbour.

On Prayer.

1. It is good to persevere calmly when in desolation, and it is also well:

2. To be simple in prayer.

3. To persuade oneself that the prayer of St. Ignatius consists in applying the memory, understanding, and will to some truth, aided by the light of the Holy Ghost, and that one can make an excellent meditation without the least bit of sensible consolation, for this is wholly in God's gift. We must pray as well as think.

4. It requires an effort sometimes even to start it. Nothing in this world can be done without some labour.

5. I should not go to prayer expecting consolation, but I ought to prepare myself to plod along as well as I can, and leave the rest to God. For consolation, unction, clear lights, &c., are a pure gift. (*Vide* remark 3.)

6. It appears to me that to well prepare two points suffices; for, *de facto*, I seldom use more than one.

7. Take the truth or fact to be meditated upon, and exercise your memory, understanding, and will upon it, not hampering yourself with too many divisions of the subject. It is well, however, to know them so as to have them at hand, but going through each division hampers the mind.

8. There is a mean to be observed. I must not pass all the time in reflection. I must use the colloquies to God and the saints. I must expose my doubts, wants, necessities, troubles, anxieties; I must ask, beg, implore, &c. Reflection will help prayer, and prayer reflection.

9. Results of some examinations after meditation. (1) Humility is very necessary; perhaps for want of it

I do not have good meditations. (2) I ought to say to myself, What fruit do you wish to get from this meditation ?

A.M.D.G.

Acts of self-denial for the love of God, which can easily be practised, no one seeing them.

In honour of B.V.M.	1.	To serve tea at breakfast.
St. Ignatius.	2.	Not to look at the newspaper.
St. F. Xavier.	3.	To give way to every one in the house in passages, &c.
St. Aloysius.	4.	To resist a desire to say such and such a thing of self.
V. Berchmans.	5.	To leave the choice of the walk to another.
St. F. Borgia.	6.	Not to excuse myself if accused or scolded.
St. Aloysius.	7.	To keep custody of the eyes during meals.
St. Aloysius.	8.	To do the same a short distance in walking.
St. Ignatius.	9.	Not to sit during meditation, nor to walk up and down.
St. Ignatius.	10.	Not to talk disparagingly of, or comment upon, the arrangements of Superiors. It is against obedience and does no good to any one.
	11.	The same as to the Professors.
V. P. Claver.	12.	To resist the inclination to speak disparagingly of the sayings and doings of another—an equal—and

	to seek reasons as far as possible for defending them.
V. P. Claver.	13. If an unkind thing should be said to me, to return a kind word; if I should have a repugnance to the person, a still kinder.
V. P. Claver.	14. If an uncivil thing is done to me, to return a civil.

On the conclusion of the two years, Augustus Law went to the preparatory school at Hodder, to teach a class of little boys. He writes thence: "I am very happy, have lots to do always, and like my occupation very much. I thank God for the happiness I find here." This arrangement was but a temporary one. After a few weeks his first regular term of external work was to begin at Glasgow, whither, in the next chapter, we shall follow him.

CHAPTER VII.

PREPARATION FOR THE PRIESTHOOD.

In the summer of 1859, the time when Augustus Law went to Glasgow, the College of St. Aloysius had not long been opened. The number of pupils was between fifty and sixty; the staff of teachers, on which Augustus was placed, consisted of two Jesuit Fathers and two members of the Society who were not yet ordained. There were besides three other Fathers in the town, in charge of the flourishing mission church of St. Joseph, where one of the younger masters of the school used to go every Sunday to help in the catechizing. Augustus threw himself into this new work with the utmost zeal and energy. As a teacher he was careful and painstaking, but it was not to this that the great popularity he speedily acquired amongst the boys was owing. He knew that it is out of the class-room that children's hearts must be won; the master who holds himself aloof from his pupils in the hour of recreation may be respected and feared, but will not be loved. Therefore he entered into all their sports with a hearty good-will, to all appearance enjoying himself in the playground as much as the lads for whose sake he was there. His great object was to make every one happy, and all who went to him with the little troubles of school-life, found him as ready to help them in their difficulties and to conjure away their griefs, as to join

in a game of football, or make up the number wanted
in the cricket-field. There was a fund of humour about
him, too, which delighted the boys. Many a time he
would keep a whole roomful amused and merry by
drawing good-natured caricatures, and sketching droll
figures—a talent we have seen him to possess while
turning over the pages of his diary. When the boys
went out for a country walk, his company was eagerly
sought after, for he would entertain the little group
which pressed around him—the discipline observed in
the town being relaxed—by relating incidents that had
occurred during his voyages. One story that he was
fond of telling was how one day while walking in
Singapore, he met a crowd of natives running down a
street and round a corner at full speed, as if they were
escaping for their lives. On looking about to discover
the cause of their terror and precipitate flight, he
descried a rollicking British tar, more than " half seas
over," who held a stone jar containing liquor in each
hand, pursuing the swarthy crowd as well as his
unsteady steps would allow, uttering noisy but harmless imprecations. " I must confess that I felt a certain
pride in my fellow-countryman," he used to conclude,
with a laugh that lighted up his countenance and gave
a merry twinkle to his eye. He willingly recalled his
seafaring life, for his love for the navy was second only
to his love for the Society, and he was accustomed to
say it was the finest service in the world. His conversation often savoured of the salt water, and the expressions
he had learnt to make use of when he wore the blue
jacket, sometimes rose to his lips after the habit and
biretta had become his garb. When asked one day by
the Superior whether the boys were assembled in the
chapel, his reply, given with perfect gravity, called a

smile to the countenance of his interrogator: "All hands on their knees, sir." This habit of employing nautical terms he never completely lost. Years after the time of which we are speaking, when a missioner in Demerara, he went a long ride to baptize a child "up country." The horse returned to its stable rider-less, and considerable anxiety was felt as to its rider's fate. He presently made his appearance on foot, saying in explanation: "I moored my mare to the garden gate, but while I was gone, she drifted away. However, as she steered straight for the harbour, there was no harm done."

Augustus did not content himself with providing amusement for the boys under his charge, his thoughts were ever bent on promoting their edification. In his free time he planned many a scheme for their moral or spiritual improvement. Religious dramas for acting in school were then not common; he undertook to write a short play for performance at St. Aloysius'. The subject he chose was the martyrdom of St. Hermene-gild, at the period of the Arian persecution. A library for the use of the boys was much wanted, but the school at its commencement was poor, and the required sum, inconsiderable though it was, was not forthcoming. Augustus exerted himself to obtain the funds; with a donation from his father, and the help of a few friends, the library was soon started, and placed on a firm footing.

But the strain of teaching proved too much for his health; on the commencement of the summer holidays in July, 1862, he quitted Glasgow, and returned to Roehampton to recruit his strength. We cannot do better than close the period of his connection with the College of St. Aloysius by transcribing a portion of a letter written by one of his former pupils, after the news of his death had reached England. It was addressed to Augustus' father, to whom the writer was a complete stranger.

" It is now twenty-three years since I had the good fortune of becoming acquainted with your saintly son. I was then a mere child in his class in the Jesuit College at Glasgow, during his first years of teaching, but the impression he then made upon me by his pure, self-denying life, has never been effaced. There was no one who did not love Mr. Law, as we called him ; but on account of his special kindness to me, I am sure no one loved him more dearly than I did. He it was who prepared me for my First Communion, and I still preserve in my breviary the little picture he gave me on that occasion. This picture, and some of his letters, written to me in after-years, are my most precious treasures. To the deep impression he made upon me by his genuine piety, and to the great interest he took in me, I owe under God my call to the Society of which he was so exemplary a member. The highest ambition of my religious life has ever been to be like him. I never knew any man so devoted and self-sacrificing as he."

After a few days spent in retreat at Roehampton, Augustus went to Beaumont Lodge, where he remained more than two months. His health improved very slowly ; the least extra exertion threw him back, and desirous as he was to begin work again, he was forced to admit that he did not feel equal to it. For some time it was a question whether it would not be advisable to send him out of England to some warmer climate, but in October, 1862, he had recovered his strength sufficiently to commence his course of theology at

St. Beuno's, although he had to keep on the sick-list for several months longer.

The College of St. Beuno stands upon a terraced height in the vale of the Clwydd, amid the most romantic scenery of North Wales, and commands an extensive view of the surrounding country. The situation is beautiful indeed in summer, although in winter it is somewhat bleak, being exposed to the storms that sweep across the ocean, and to the rough winds that howl around the mountain tops. In this remote and lonely spot Augustus spent what he was wont to call the four happiest years of his life. The absolute quietude and seclusion was grateful to him in his impaired state of health ; his silent communings with Nature were soothing after the bustle and activity of school-life in a large and noisy town. The study of theology, moreover, was one in which he took intense delight, while among his fellow-students and the Professors of the College he found agreeable and congenial companionship.

Augustus applied himself to his studies with the same energy and oneness of purpose that he had displayed when he filled the post of teacher instead of learner. He was considered one of the best and most solid theological students of his time ; certainly there was not one more anxious to profit by the instructions of his Professors, more desirous of drawing the spiritual honey from the rocks where it was stored. The Holy Scriptures, for which from his childhood he had a profound veneration, and which when a sailor, he was accustomed to read and reflect upon, were to him a source of infinite pleasure and profit. Among the notes written at this time for no eye but his own, the following passage occurs :

There is the saying: *Timeo hominem unius libri.* Now for a priest, for instance, if he takes the Holy Scriptures. In addition to the wonderful things that are always said about them, as being God's written Word: (1) It is the best book to know well for ordinary controversies, for few Protestants care a rush for the Fathers. (2) Nowhere can you find better illustrations for sermons than in Bible history. Apart from Chrysostom being a Saint, how well he uses for illustrations the persons and events of Holy Scripture. (3) However tired you are, you can always read the Holy Scriptures, and take delight in them, for they speak more to the heart than to the head. (4) Here we must not pass by how much they help to our individual instruction and exhortation; it is on this account that our Rev. Father General commends the constant reading of the Scriptures so much to our Fathers, saying that is what we Jesuits should read and study, rather than periodicals and newspapers. The holy Curé d'Ars gave the fondness for reading newspapers as one of the causes why priests did not become saints. St. Augustine says of the Scriptures: *Sint castæ deliciæ meæ scripturæ tuæ, Domine.*

The frequency and remarkable appositeness with which Augustus quoted the Scriptures is sufficient proof how thorough a knowledge and how clear an understanding he had acquired of the truths contained in them. He might almost be said to have been himself "a man of one book" had there not been another, second only to Holy Scripture, of which indeed it forms the supplement, viz., the Catechism of the Council of Trent. The esteem he entertained for it is expressed on another page of his note-book.

What can be said too much of the great Catechism?
We might say to it, as the Church says to the Blessed
Virgin: *Gaude, Catechisme Conc. Trid., tu solus cunctas
hæreses interemisti in toto mundo.* One might well venture
to say that all that great controversy which has agitated
France and Germany these late years, about the rela-
tion between faith and reason, might have been avoided,
if what the Catechism says upon faith and reason had
been studied or even read. It is a wonderful book.
And each time you read it you see something new.
Perhaps some think that having studied theology
they have no more need of it. But it is *after* having
studied theology that it is most useful. (1) It recalls
all your theology to mind as you read it. (2) From
knowing theology you can see and appreciate its
beauties more fully. (3) There is such an unction in
it that it puts you in love with the Catholic Church
and her doctrines; I mean rather, it increases your
love and renders it more tender and enraptured.

The invigorating air of the Welsh mountains did
not have the beneficial effect that was anticipated in
restoring Augustus' strength. The condition of his
health continued to be far from satisfactory, though he
made the best of it in his letters, in which some allusion
to it is occasionally made. " Thanks to St. Joseph, my
health improves gradually." Or again: " My health
seems improving little by little; I can walk fairly now;
one day I accomplished ten miles without very great
difficulty." But although he wrote hopefully about
himself, there is no doubt that he felt weak and ill, and
sometimes even feared lest his strength should not hold
out until the conclusion of the ordinary term of preparation for the priesthood. It was this fear that prompted

him at the end of his second year at St. Beuno's, to beg Father Seed, who was then Provincial, that he might be put into the short course of theology, in order that he might be ordained as soon as possible, and fulfil his ardent desire to work for the good of souls. His request was complied with. But when Father Bottalla, who was the Professor of Theology, heard of it, he very much disapproved of the change, and endeavoured by every means in his power to persuade Father Seed to revoke the permission he had given, and put Augustus back into the long course. The principal reasons he urged were that in the first place Augustus was naturally so clever that he could pass all the examinations without any severe application on his part being required, and in the second place, he considered him possessed of such excellent qualities, prudence, mildness, and firm-ness, that later on, no better man could be found to rule the Province. Father Seed saw the justice of these arguments, and at once reversed his decision. Augustus' name was accordingly struck out from the list of the short course. This he at first very much regretted, but in the end he saw that it was for the best, and expressed his gratitude to Father Bottalla for what he had done.

Father Bottalla was not singular in the opinion he had formed as to Augustus Law's suitability for a ruler. Another Jesuit Father, speaking of him after his death, said the same: "What an excellent Provincial he would have made! He had so thoroughly the spirit of St. Ignatius. What confidence we should have had in him. *Vere Jesuita es tu*, must be the conviction of every one who had been associated with him in the Colleges or in community life, or who studies the meditations and notes of retreats in which the secrets of his soul

are revealed." The estimate Augustus formed of himself was a very different one. "I am but half a Jesuit,"
he says. "I have been ten years in the Society, and
am miles off being a true Jesuit." And again: "What
ought a priest and a Jesuit to be in thoughts, words,
and actions, and what am I as God sees me? A
whited sepulchre, fair without, foul within." This
lowly opinion of himself was no morbid feeling engen-
dered by bad health, but the firm conviction of his
heart, a prevailing sentiment which distinguished him,
as will be seen, throughout his life.

His physical weakness rarely affected his spirits at
this time. The joyousness of his disposition mastered
the depression that often arises from bodily infirmity.
There was not a trace of gloom or melancholy about
him, and he was ever ready to sympathize with the
difficulties and troubles of his companions. Amongst
the latter the foreigners especially appreciated the
power he displayed of entering into their feelings in
regard to trifling matters which were trying to them
as strangers, and "the Captain," as he was familiarly
called, was long held in affectionate remembrance by
many a foreign Father who had been his fellow-student
at St. Beuno's, as one who was far more warm-hearted
and sympathetic than the English are usually considered to be by men of other nationalities.

Amongst the scholastics at that time studying
theology at St. Beuno's were four French students,
who were learning English in view of going out to
the Indian missions. Whether it was association with
them that fired Augustus' enthusiastic temperament,
or whether his old love of activity and movement
awoke within him, we cannot tell; at any rate he
conceived an ardent desire to devote himself to the

I

work of foreign missions. Perhaps the fact had something to do with it that the first Catholics with whom
he had become acquainted, who had instructed him in
the faith, and edified him by their manner of life, were
the good Fathers who were labouring on the distant
shores of China, and in the seaports of India and
Ceylon. However this may be, the desire within him
grew more intense, until it was brought to a climax by
the arrival in England of Father St. Cyr, one of the
Fathers of the Madura Mission.

This zealous and experienced missioner came over
on a begging expedition, as funds were greatly needed
for his large and flourishing mission. There were in
his district about 142,500 Catholics; in the year preceding his departure, no less than 1,000 adults had been
converted to the faith. His proposal was not only to
appeal to the charity of the faithful to help this important work, but to endeavour to obtain assistance from
the English Government. During the time of the
Mutiny, one of the Jesuit Fathers had offered the
services of some thousand Indians, whose fidelity could
thoroughly be relied upon, to the Government, to
suppress the insurrection should it break out in
Southern India. Father St. Cyr thought that facts
such as this, proving so undeniably that the influence
of the missioners tended to strengthen and uphold
British rule in India, would have weight with the
Government, and procure a hearing for him at the
India Office. He was not entirely unknown there,
as he had made the acquaintance of Sir Henry Montgomery during the residence of the latter in India, and
he hoped that he would support his petition. Sir Henry
Montgomery was Augustus' uncle, a fact of which he,
anxious to introduce himself to the notice of one whom

he already regarded in the light of his future Superior,
hastened to inform the good missioner when he came
to St. Beuno's. It soon transpired that Augustus' sister
and brother-in-law, Mr. and Mrs. Cary-Elwes, had
returned from India in the same steamer that had
brought Father St. Cyr to England; that he had made
friends with them, and that the impression on both
sides had been of the most agreeable description. This
was a fresh bond, on the strength of which Augustus
opened his heart to his new friend, and confided to him
his hopes and aspirations. Father St. Cyr, who had
come to Europe in quest of subjects as well as of
money, did not discourage the project; he recommended him to seek in prayer to learn the will of God
in regard to his destination. Soon after, Augustus,
hearing that an English Jesuit was much wanted at
Negapatam, offered himself to his Superiors for the
college there. We are not told what was the nature
of the answer he received: but thenceforth no more
mention is made of the Madura Mission. Father
Bottalla was strongly opposed to the idea of Augustus,
one of his dearest pupils, in whom he took a warm
interest, going on the foreign missions. He was very
sorry when, about a year after his ordination, Augustus
was sent to Demerara, and later on to Africa, for he
considered that thus a man of great promise, whose
career might have been one of eminent usefulness to
the Society, was lost to the English Province.

But Augustus is as yet only a scholastic; we will
now listen to what another Father tells us about him
during the period of his preparation for the priesthood.

"I made his acquaintance," Father Wynne writes, ·
"when he came to St. Beuno's as a scholastic. He
had *learned the ropes* of religious life in our Novitiate,

and was studying the *navigation* of the bark of Peter.
We were at that time building a church and forming a
congregation at Rhyl, and Rhyl became a centre of
furious attacks from the 'Protestant Alliance' and all
the fanatics of the neighbourhood. Scurrilous pamphlets
and articles in the local newspapers appeared, in which
the old bugbear of the 'blind obedience of the Jesuits'
was much insisted on. Father Law, although he was
only a student, not yet a priest, came down to Rhyl,
and gave three lectures in my school which were well
attended by both Catholics and Protestants, on 'The
blind obedience of the Jesuits compared with the
discipline in Her Majesty's navy.' The lectures were
very amusing, full of sailors' yarns and jokes, inter-
spersed with a little sound theology and a great deal of
common sense. The lecturer showed very satisfactorily
that the obedience required by Her Most Gracious
Majesty of her officers in the naval service was much
'blinder' in its character than that demanded of Jesuits
by their Superiors."

Augustus was always desirous to turn to account
his nautical experience and knowledge of sailors' ways.
On the occasion of being sent, during one Holy Week,
to assist the Father in charge of the mission at Rhyl,
he used to go down of a morning as early as he could
to the beach, in the hope of meeting with a sailor or
fisherman whom he could draw into conversation about
God and his spiritual state. For this his acquaintance
with a seafaring life, and the good companionship he
was always ready to claim with all who followed it,
afforded him many facilities.

It was on this account that he wrote to his brother
Frederick, who was rapidly rising in the profession he
had himself abandoned, more frequently than to any

other of his brothers or sisters. He felt that counsels
and admonitions from the lips of one who had passed
through the same training and knew all his circumstances, would have with his sailor-brother a weight
which no others could possess. We will give an
extract or two from the letters he wrote to him from
St. Beuno's.

"I got your letter about three or four weeks ago,
and thank you very much for it, and for the news you
gave about yourself. I was amused at your row about
the insertion of *Roman* Catholics in the log, and perhaps
you did right in remaining firm after once rubbing it
out on the slate. But I do not think in general it would
be prudent to kick up a shindy about those kinds of
things. It is true Protestants give us the name of
Roman Catholics in their sense wrongly. But on the
other hand, it is one of our greatest glories to call
ourselves *Roman* Catholics in *our* sense, *i.e.*, meaning
thereby that there can be no true Catholics who are not
united with the Head of the Church, the Bishop of
Rome. They call us 'Papists,' too, meaning it for a
reproach. But what does it mean? 'Papista' means
a follower or adherent of 'Papa,' the Pope. And we
Catholics are glad to be Papists in this sense. Of
course when they call us Papists they do not mean to
compliment us, and hence the sting. So, old fellow,
though I admire your zeal for your religion, still, if I
were you, I would not have a row if not called for
especially, as you will lose friends by it. Of course
I do not mean that you should hide your religion, or be
ashamed of it, or not defend it, or even not have a row
if necessary. No, I only mean in such a case as the
last, I would look before I leapt. I hope you will write
soon again, and tell me how you are getting on, and

whether there are any new rows. Go to confession, dear old boy, if you have an opportunity. Pray for me. If ever your ship comes round to Liverpool, you must give me a hail here."

"You cannot think how interesting your letters are to me. Graves tells me you were very much disgusted at the state of religion in Madeira, and from all accounts very justly. Well, all we can do is to remember what our Lord said: *Necesse est ut sint scandala*, and to pity the miserable state of the scandal-givers. However, it is to be hoped that you will see some brighter examples where you are now. I hope you will be able to go to Madagascar or Mauritius or Bourbon. I think the priests there are all French Jesuits, and zealous, holy men. I dare say some of them can speak English, and I am sure they will receive you kindly. If you happen to go to any of those places, tell me how you get on, &c., and whenever you learn anything interesting about the Catholic foreign missions, or anything laughable or absurd about the Protestant ones, tell me, as it is both interesting and useful to know them. There are four different stations of Jesuits in Bourbon and about twenty-three priests, three in Mauritius, nine in Madagascar. I was delighted to hear you had been to your duties before leaving England. God will bless you, old fellow, if you stick to your spirituals, and when you say your prayers, remember me in them."

The year before his ordination he wrote thus:

"In September next year, please God, I shall be ordained priest. What a happiness it will be for me you can well imagine, and for you too; you will have another priest amongst your brothers, however unworthy, to say Holy Mass every day at God's altar; where of course it is not likely you will be forgotten.

Now you must pray away during the interval to prepare me for saying Mass well for you. I suppose you will scarcely be at home as soon as September next year; but if you are, you shall be dragged up here if possible, to be present at the ordination. The news I heard of you gave me great joy from what it indirectly hinted, which was that my dear old Fred does not forget God and does not neglect holy confession. God loves you very much, dear old fellow, and takes great care of you. My health is improving, thank God, little by little, and I can now take pretty long walks, if I may call five miles and back a long walk. You must ask St. Joseph to give me perfect health, that I may be able to work hard for God's glory."

It was not only to his sailor-brother that Augustus could give good advice. The following letter to his sister, a nun in the Monastery of the Visitation, contains admirable counsels for the spiritual life, and shows that he was fast becoming a master in the science of the saints. It is dated from St. Beuno's, on the eve of Corpus Christi, 1865 :

I take advantage of my writing to wish dear papa many happy returns of his birthday, to send you a few lines in answer to your last welcome letter. You must excuse a rather short letter, as I have my hands pretty full. Now I shall begin to " blow you up " if you make too much of difficulties. Difficulties we must have, and especially from vainglory, because we all think we are such great people. But you remember how St. Gertrude was taught to manage these things. She was taught by our Lord to look on the *bright side* of everything. At least as far as I remember, all our Blessed Lord's instructions to her tended that way.

You know there is such a thing as wishing to be too perfect. You understand in what sense I mean. So do not fret. I am sure people who lead a religious life and who are anxious to please God in all things often think *too much about themselves.* They fret and tease themselves. I remember hearing read in the refectory of a Father Cortez, S.J., who was much troubled with scruples. Well, the Blessed Virgin appeared to him and told him to pray for the souls in Purgatory. I thought to myself, Now what is the philosophy of that? There must have been some reason why the Blessed Virgin gave that particular remedy for that particular disease. And I came to the conclusion that the reason was that thinking of others takes our thoughts off ourselves. Do not you think that must have been the reason? You understand, dearest sister, what I mean, and that I do not accuse you of being scrupulous. Besides, if you were, scrupulousness may come from no fault of ours, and may be also very useful. But what I mean is that we must keep moderation in all things. *Ne quid nimis.*

As to confession. If you were only allowed to hear Mass once a week, still obedience is better than sacrifice, and therefore also better than confession twice a week. Now I hope again, dearest sister, nothing too harsh has been said. But I have had all these bothers myself and shall have them to the end of my life. But we will both make a good act of hope, and go on our way rejoicing.

In this hopeful spirit he looked forward to his approaching ordination. A little anecdote copied into his note-book gives an indication of the feelings with which he regarded this great epoch of his life.

" St. Francis of Assisi, when a deacon and thinking of becoming a priest, had a vision, wherein an angel showed him a vase of water as clear as crystal, to represent the purity which becomes a priest. The Saint was so struck with this, that he would never be a priest." Deeply as Augustus felt his own unworthiness to stand at the altar of God, he yet anticipated joyfully the time when he should receive the Divine commission to go and work in the Lord's vineyard, strong in the assurance: *omnia possum in eo qui me confortat.* His meditations at this period were frequently, as may be supposed, on the dignity and responsibilities of the priesthood. With one of these we may fittingly conclude the present chapter.

Of what use is a priest if he does not live for God alone, Whose priest he is? His life is useless, frivolous, if not spent for God. *Ut quid occupat terram?* Think over what is expected of you by the Church, the Society, your flock, even by Protestants. If not for God and for the salvation of souls, of what use are you?

What is it that will make me what I ought to be? For I am weak, and careless in the use of means. It is the love of God. Can I then ever cease praying for it?

How strong is the force of example! It is far stronger than words. And what an example is expected from priests, who are the *Forma gregis.* St. Paul said, " Be ye imitators of me, as I am of Christ." A priest ought to be able to say that. St. Paul told Timothy, and in telling him, he spoke to all priests, " Be thou an example of the faithful, in conversation, in charity, in faith, in chastity;" and then he tells him not to neglect the grace that is in him, and that his profiting should be manifest to all.[1]   As profiting comes from self-denial (*tantum proficies, quantum tibi ipsi vim intuleris*), I see what I must pray for. Let me delight the Church of God by becoming a holy priest, like Simon the High Priest, who "shone in his days as a morning star in the midst of a cloud, and as the moon at the full.   And as the sun when it shineth, so did he shine in the Temple of God.   And as the rainbow giving light in the bright clouds, and as the flower of roses in the days of the spring, and as the lilies that are on the brink of the water, and as the sweet-smelling frankincense in the time of summer.   As a bright fire and frankincense burning in the fire.   As a massy vessel of gold adorned with every precious stone.   As an olive-tree budding forth and a cypress-tree rearing itself on high.   When he put on the robe of glory and was clothed with the perfection of power."[2]   See how many similes the Holy Ghost employs to describe a holy priest. He compares him to all that is most brilliant and beautiful and fragrant in the heavens and the earth that God made. Let me study these things, that I may be what the Holy Ghost would have me to be.

---

[1] 1 Timothy iv. 12.   [2] Ecclus. l. 6—11.

CHAPTER VIII.

On the day after his ordination, which took place on September 24, 1865, Father Law said his first Mass at St. Asaph, and immediately afterwards left for Hampton Court, in company with his father, who had of course been present at his ordination, and had also been privileged to serve his Mass. At the Palace he met many of the friends of his earlier days, and was most cordially welcomed by them—by none more so than by Sir George and Lady Seymour, and their son, Admiral Seymour. Sir George had been the Admiral commanding on the Pacific station, when Augustus, a boy of twelve, joined the squadron as naval cadet on board the *Carysfort*, of which his son was then Captain. It will be remembered that Augustus met with much kindness from the Captain, and that the report the latter gave of him to his parents was most laudatory. On the following Sunday Father Law preached his first sermon at Kingston-on-Thames. As it was Rosary Sunday, he chose for the subject of his discourse the Rosary; the most efficacious, as has been well said, of all modes of prayer after the Holy Sacrifice and the Divine Office, and not restricted to the use of the few, but within the reach of every Christian, from the highest to the lowest. After giving a short history of the institution of the Rosary, Father Law proceeded

to explain, in earnest and simple language, the nature
and value of this beautiful devotion—one very dear to
his own heart. The following notes form a kind of
synopsis of the latter part of his sermon :

There is no devotion in the Church sweeter than
the Rosary, and none more powerful. Why this is we
will now consider. First, it breathes nothing but Jesus
and Mary, than which nothing can be sweeter. Its
fifteen mysteries place them before us and put us in their
blessed presence. Saying the Rosary is holding sweet
converse with Mary, and speaking to her about her
Divine Son, and about herself. And what can be more
powerful to keep us from sin, and to plant virtue in us,
than to live with Jesus and Mary, to talk with them, to
accustom ourselves to their ways of thinking, speaking,
and acting, which we do by being much in their company—at one moment being present at the manger, at
another at the foot of the Cross, at another contemplating our Lord and His Blessed Mother in Heaven.
But then we are reminded in the Rosary that this
meditation and contemplation of our Lord's life is not
to be a mere speculation, but is to bear its own proper
fruit. That fruit is expressed in the petitions of the
Our Father and the Hail Mary. We look at our Lord
and our Blessed Lady, and our hearts get warmed and
seek an outlet in words. At once there are the ardent
petitions of the Our Father and Hail Mary, which will
express the most fervent desires that any saint ever
had. In a word, there is nothing like the mysteries of
the Rosary to excite us to pray ; nothing like the two
prayers, the *Pater* and *Ave*, to express what we would
pray for. For whether you are in joy or in sorrow, in
hope or in fear, near God or far away from God, still

those two prayers will always fall in with your desires, and exactly suit your particular circumstances. But all this and much more is better understood by using the Rosary than by talking about its use.

St. Bernard says: *Totum nos habere voluit per Mariam* —"God desires that we should receive all through Mary." This is just what is admirably done in the Rosary; all the fruit of our Blessed Lord's Infancy, Passion, Resurrection, Ascension, is given to us through Mary's hands. And who can walk with us hand in hand through our Lord's life and Passion and glorified life better than Mary? Who can teach us to meditate upon these mysteries better than she who "kept all these things, pondering them in her heart"?

An anecdote, of which the preacher made use to illustrate the importance of the daily recitation of the Rosary, finds no place in these notes. It is, however, too interesting to be altogether omitted.

A young French officer, whose life was far from being a model one, and who was careless as to the practice of his religion, had bound himself by a promise to say the Rosary every day. To whom, or under what circumstances, the promise was made, we are not told. One thing, however, is certain, that it was faithfully kept for a considerable number of years.

But for every one who pledges himself to any rule, the occasion must come when the rule grows irksome, and so it was with the officer in question. One day, during the Crimean War, he returned at nightfall to his tent so utterly worn out with fatigue that he threw himself at once on his bed, and instantly dropped into a sound sleep. Before midnight he awoke, or rather his Guardian Angel woke him, and he remembered that he had not said his Rosary. As may be imagined, he felt not a little disinclined to get up and recite it. For a while he lay still, debating what he should do. At last he said to himself: "I never broke my word to any man, and I will not do so to our Blessed Lady." He sprang up, and as one after another he told his beads, feelings of contrition for his past sins began to steal into his heart. By the time the Rosary was finished he was conscious of an intense desire to go to confession. Kneeling down, he made a solemn promise to do so, saying aloud, "I will go to confession to-morrow morning." "And why not now?" asked a familiar voice out of the darkness. It was that of the army chaplain, Father Damas, S.J., who through the providence of God happened to be passing at that moment, and overheard the officer's words. Impressed by the coincidence, he readily consented, and made his confession. Early on the following day he heard Father Damas' Mass, and received Holy Communion.

A few hours later the troops were called out to attack the Russians. Almost the first shot fired by the enemy struck the young officer and killed him on the spot. The Rosary had done its work.

What would have been Mr. Law's feelings, on that Rosary Sunday, as he looked with fatherly pride and pleasure at his eldest son, had he known under what circumstances that son would spend his last Rosary Sunday upon earth. It is said that the foreknowledge of the cruel sufferings and ignominious death awaiting her Divine Son was the sharpest sword that pierced our Lady's heart. And had it been told to the fond father that, exactly fifteen years later, Augustus would be dying of hunger and privation in a remote and savage country, surely the joy of his heart would have been largely mingled with sorrow. But the future is mercifully hidden from us; nothing occurred to cast a shade of gloom over the happy days the newly-ordained priest spent under his father's roof. And when his week's leave was at an end, it was in good health and cheerful spirits that he left Hampton Court to return to St. Beuno's, in order to complete the prescribed course of his theological studies.

Four years may perhaps seem a long time to be devoted to the study of theology alone, but it is none too much, as Father Law himself was fain to acknow-ledge, despite his impatient desire to engage in active work. This desire grew stronger within him as the time approached for him to commence his apostolic labours. The devotion of his days to meditation, to study, to occasional preaching, did not satisfy the craving of his ardent nature. It was his ambition to offer himself as a holocaust on the altar of sacrifice. Every day in the Mass, as he elevated the chalice, he prayed that the grace of martyrdom might be granted him. One may almost say that it was painful to his generous soul to receive so much, and give nothing in return.

The notes of his meditations at this time express these sentiments; they are in strong contrast to the self-seeking egotism of the present day, which too often makes itself felt even in regard to the things of God.

When asking God for things, we should be ready to give too. This way is of common use in the Holy Scriptures; we have instances of it in the example of Jacob after the vision of angels. "He made a vow,

saying : If God shall be with me, and shall keep me in
the way by which I walk, &c., the Lord shall be my
God."[1]   Jephte, too, makes a promise to God, that if
he should gain the victory over the Ammonites against
whom he was going to fight, he would offer as a holocaust whoever should first meet him on his return.[2]
And in Anna's prayer for a son : " She made a vow,
saying, O Lord of hosts, if Thou wilt look down on
the affliction of Thy servant, and wilt be mindful of
me, and wilt give Thy servant a man-child, I will give
him to the Lord all the days of his life."[3] This practice
is common also in Catholic countries, as we see from
the custom of the Portuguese, who, when they wish
much for anything, invariably make their *promessas.*
Making such promises shows that a man is in earnest,
and ready to give something for what he desires and
expects.   How God appreciates, if we may so speak,
the little things we do for Him, the services we render
Him, the little efforts we make to show our love to
Him, in return for what He has done for us.

Jesus Christ went freely to His Passion.   *Oblatus est
quia ipse voluit.* If I compassionate Him, plunged into all
these waves of suffering and sorrow for my sins, should
not I on my part say, *Voluntarie sacrificabo tibi ?* When
He has so freely and willingly sacrificed Himself for
me, when He has done such great things as He has
done for me, am I to haggle about what and how much
I will do for Him ?   Am I to measure out to Him with
a niggardly hand, and go only so far as is necessary to
avoid mortal or venial sin ? *Lex non est posita justis.*
The really just measure by the law of love written in
their hearts by the Holy Ghost.   To give everything is
little to them when they think Whom they are giving

---

[1] Genesis xxviii. 20, 21.   [2] Judges xi. 30, 31.   [3] 1 Kings i. 11.

to. " I am giving to God," they say; "to God Who
has suffered for me and died for me, so do not speak to
me of measures, and how much." " If a man should
give all the substance of his house for love, he shall
despise it as nothing."[1] " My God, when shall I love
Thee?" says St. Bonaventure. It is impossible, if I
have a heart at all, not to feel myself obliged to refuse
nothing to Jesus Christ. He spares nothing for me,
and He is God. Can I, who have been and am the
" Achan " of the Church, refuse anything to Him ? If
Jesus Christ has shown in so many ways His tender
love for me, such as I am; if He has been so prodigal
in His generosity, what can I say but *charitas Christi
urget nos ?* What can I say but that I am driven and
forced to love Him, and do all that He asks of me? to
devote my life and my whole self to His service ?

It will be remembered that Augustus Law, about
a year before his ordination, had asked that he might
be chosen for the foreign missions. He had refrained
from again urging this request, although his heart was
as much set on it as ever, for he considered it more in
accordance with the spirit of obedience to leave the
decision entirely to the judgment of his Superiors. Not
until the time came for him to leave St. Beuno's was he
informed that they saw fit to accede to his wishes. He
was not however destined to follow, as he had hoped,
on the footsteps of St. Francis Xavier. India was not
to be the sphere of his missionary labours. Each
Province of the Society of Jesus has some foreign
mission especially confided to its charge. England has
the West Indies. To the West Indies consequently

---

[1] Cant. viii. 7.

J

Father Law was to be sent. "I am bound for Jamaica," he writes, "and I like the idea very well. It is a happiness to me to think that obedience sends me there."

In the interim he went to Edinburgh for about three months, to "supply" in the absence of one of the resident Fathers. Demerara was ultimately chosen for his destination. In the last week of October, Mr. Law, who was then at Boulogne, received a telegram from Augustus announcing his immediate departure. He crossed over to Folkestone by the next boat, in order to meet him at Southampton, whence the steamer was to start. Whilst the father and son were walking up and down on deck an hour or two before the final farewell, an incident occurred which at the time afforded them much amusement. Augustus, who had left his father for a few minutes to see about the bestowal of his luggage, on returning to him, exclaimed with the greatest glee, "Fancy my good fortune! Among my fellow-passengers to Demerara there is a brother-priest!" When interrogated as to how he had become aware of the fact, he answered emphatically that he had *seen* him.

Presently the supposed priest came in sight, and was pointed out to Mr. Law, who, being better acquainted than his son with the "get-up" of Anglican clergymen, expressed his doubts as to whether the individual in question really was a Catholic priest. But Augustus' hopes so far predominated over everything his father said, that nothing would satisfy him but to address the gentleman, and express the pleasure it gave him to think that he would have the company during the voyage of one who was like himself, a priest. The person he addressed drew himself up, and replied stiffly: "I certainly consider myself to be a priest, sir, but I almost doubt whether you would be willing to accord me that title; I am the Archdeacon of ——." Augustus' countenance fell, and he was at a loss what to answer; but Mr. Law, who had been standing by, stepped up, and saying, "I told you, Augustus, that you were mistaken," endeavoured to enter into conversation with the Anglican dignitary on the subject of a religious question then engaging the attention of the High Church party. The Archdeacon, however, refused to be drawn into any discussion, and politely explained that he had not taken his passage in the steamer, but had only come on board to see a friend off.

The tidings that Augustus was to go out to the West Indies was most unwelcome to Mr. Law. He had much desired that his son should remain in England, and he feared besides lest, as his health was still far from robust, the yellow fever, which proves fatal to so many Europeans, should carry him off. He acquiesced, however, in the separation with a cheerfulness that delighted Augustus, who had feared to encounter considerable opposition from him. In his first letter from sea he alludes to his father's dread of the fever. "Even should I fall a victim to 'Yellow Jack,' as the sailors call it, I could not die a better death, after martyrdom; and I hope that in such a case God in His mercy might overlook all my short-comings. However, by the help of your prayers, I trust God may spare me many years to labour for His glory, and if it be His will, to see you again, my dear, dear father." He continues: "I shall be so delighted when Friday morning comes, for I shall, I hope, be able then to say Mass at St. Thomas'. It will almost

appear to me like a first Mass. Before this voyage, I
had only missed saying Mass one day since my ordination."

Father Law was not disappointed in his hope of
being able to say Mass at St. Thomas'. He also had
an opportunity of which he gladly availed himself when
the ship touched at Santa Lucia and at Barbadoes.
The voyage passed pleasantly. The Sunday after they
left St. Thomas' a man on board got the yellow fever.
He was a Protestant, and there was a parson on board;
but either because he did not know of the man being
ill, or because of apprehension for his own safety, he
did not visit him. So Father Law went to him, and
did what he could for him, although, as he confessed,
he felt "a little funky."[1] The patient was the ship's
baker, the fifth baker, as the doctor informed Father
Law, who had been attacked by the fever. The
coincidence is curious, and would lead one to imagine
that there was something in the work of bread-making
that predisposes a man to take the infection. The four
others had all died, and this poor fellow was landed at
Barbadoes, with little chance of recovery.

The tropical climate, which he compares to that of
Singapore, suited Father Law admirably. A few
months after his arrival he reported himself to be in
capital health. He had one attack of fever, but only
a very slight one, and he never experienced a touch
of it afterwards. This he attributed to the care of
St. Peter Claver, for he always carried on his person a
relic of that Saint. His time on the way out had been
devoted to learning Portuguese, which to any one

[1] The yellow fever is now believed not to be contagious, but Father
Law, like the majority of persons at that time, was under the impression
that it was so in a high degree.

possessing a knowledge of Latin and French offers no
great difficulty. By the end of the voyage he could
read the New Testament with facility, and could speak
a little; in a year's time he had mastered the language
sufficiently to carry on a conversation, and even to
preach in it.

It was at Berbice, seventy or eighty miles from
Demerara, that Father Law was stationed. He liked
the place extremely, and said that he felt more energy
for everything he undertook than he had felt for years
past. This was doubtless owing to the improvement
in his health, which continued to be much better than
it was in England. It was well that he did feel up to
the mark, for a wide field for exertion was open before
him. He found a heterogeneous medley of nationalities
congregated at Berbice; Portuguese, English, Chinese,
Dutch, French, with the creole modifications of each.
His letters indicate that he was very happy in their
midst. Gradually he won the confidence and affection
of these various characters, and laboured successfully
amongst them, converting many to the faith. As long
distances had often to be traversed in answering sick-
calls to the outlying hamlets and scattered homesteads,
and in visiting the hospital, which, formerly within a
stone's throw of the church, had been moved to a
fresh site outside the town, the Catholics subscribed
to purchase a horse for him. By this means he was
spared a great deal of fatigue. The first time he
mounted his horse, an accident happened that might
have been a sad catastrophe. As the country is perfectly flat, the land is drained by ditches in every
direction, so that one cannot get up to any house
without crossing a wooden bridge, generally unprotected by a railing. Father Law had just returned

from his first ride when he stopped on the bridge leading into the garden of his house to speak to some one
who had come to say that his services were required
in another direction. Forgetting how narrow was the
bridge on which he was standing, Father Law at once
turned the horse's head round, and down went the
animal's hind legs into the ditch. Fortunately it did
not go head over heels immediately, so Father Law
had time to jump off before it rolled over. The ditch
was rather deep, so that the horse could not regain its
footing, but floundered about until it was pulled out with
ropes. It sustained no injury, but from that time forth
Father Law was very cautious about executing any
manœuvres while crossing the bridges.

He had not been long in Berbice before he went out
to the Chinese settlement, about a mile and a half from
New Amsterdam, to see the Catholics there. On his
first visit he experienced great difficulty in getting the
aid of the interpreter for the plantation. The man
was somewhat unwell, had been roused out of sleep,
and gave his services very grudgingly. On going there
a second time Father Law found him in a better
humour, and by dint of dexterous handling, got all he
wanted out of him. At last the man delighted him by
saying that he was thinking of becoming a Catholic.
"God grant it!" exclaims the zealous missionary.
"What a blessing it would be. He speaks English
well and fluently, and might be the instrument in God's
hands of converting the whole Chinese village." Father
Law began to take a special interest in the Chinese
settlers. One result of his visits was that he succeeded
in getting four boys to his school. He describes one
of them as a jolly little fellow, and says that if the boy
continues to promise well, he means to take special

care of him, so that in time, if God should so will, he might become a priest and labour out there amongst his countrymen. This seems looking rather far into the future, but we know Father Law's sanguine temperament, and after all, a beginning must be made betimes if anything satisfactory is to be accomplished.

He soon found it would be necessary for him to learn a little of the Chinese language. His account of his first attempts is amusing. He found a number of poor coolies, or Chinamen, in the hospital where he attended the sick Portuguese. Seeing the consolation that his ministrations afforded to their Catholic neighbours, the dying Chinese made signs for him to come to their bed-sides. Father Law was in despair at being utterly unable to make himself intelligible to them. So he got hold of a Protestant Bible-reader, and gave him half-a-crown to put into Chinese some simple sentences and teach him how to pronounce them. With the help of the Chinese themselves he soon got to know a few of the most necessary words and phrases, and made a sort of dictionary for himself. He baptized a number of these coolies before he had seen a single printed book to help him with the language. As soon as he had attained tolerable proficiency in Portuguese, he applied himself vigorously to the study of Chinese. " I have not much time to give to it," he says, "not more than half an hour every day, but little as that is I shall get on. A knowledge of the language would be of immense use to me, and besides, learning these languages keeps one occupied in every spare five minutes."

Whilst attending the hospital, Father Law tried to make friends with all the sick, as far as he could. Amongst them he met with a Swedish sailor, a

Protestant, and a nice old fellow. His calling gave him a special claim on the attention of the ex-lieutenant R.N., who gave him a call every day when he went to the hospital, and lent him a Catholic story-book. The man was delighted with the book, and told Father Law that it made him think of times long gone by, when, a little boy at school, he used to contradict his master at catechism, and tell him the Roman Catholic Church must be the true one because it was the old one. Some arguments employed in the books made a great impression on the man, whose mind appeared already prepared for the reception of the truth. After his discharge from the hospital he called on Father Law, and asked to be put into the way of becoming a Catholic.

There was a good deal to be done in the colony in the way of converting Protestants. Father Law used to preach every Sunday on some Catholic dogma or some doctrine that was disputed or misapprehended by heretics. Many Protestants used to go to hear these sermons. But far more efficacious than lectures or controversial topics in bringing souls to the Church was the edification afforded by the untiring zeal and devotion of such men as Father Law and the other Jesuits of the mission. The Protestants could not understand the affection manifested everywhere by the Catholics for their priest whenever he visited a town. Father Ragazzini, Father Law's colleague at New Amsterdam, gave an account of his reception at Albion, a place about seventeen miles distant, where he met with a perfect ovation. The parson was so much surprised at witnessing this that he asked Father Ragazzini how often he came up there. " I was once up here for a day," was the reply. " Strange," said the parson. Then Father Ragazzini got about forty

Portuguese to clean out a large unused warehouse ready for Mass. As many hands make light work, and all worked with a good-will, it was soon done. "How much did you pay those men?" the parson inquired. "Nothing at all," said Father Ragazzini. "Strange," said the parson. "You speak English fairly," he further remarked, "how long have you been learning it?" "I have been working at it about five months." "Strange," once more ejaculated the parson, eyeing, as he took his departure, the wonder-working Jesuit with no little curiosity, and perhaps some degree of envy.

Augustus much preferred the free life of a missioner to the civilization of towns. During his residence in Demerara, he had once to give a mission to a number of people who were camping out in the fields (for what reason it is not stated). He discarded the tent pitched for his accommodation, climbed up a tree with the agility of a cat, and fixed up a hammock aloft, so that he could keep his congregation well under his eye. There was no need of a bell to announce Mass in the morning. The people saw their *padre* at his toilet in the tree, and assembled in readiness accordingly.

Plenty of exercise on horseback and on foot he thoroughly enjoyed, and it suited him excellently. The heat was never too much for him. Although the thermometer was 80° to 84° in the shade, it did not cause him the slightest inconvenience. "I am quite in love with this colony," he wrote. "If it was better known at home, many people would come out for the sake of their health, especially persons suffering from weakness in the chest. I never in my life had such health as in this much-abused country. I keep so well that I need no change, and am ready to live and die out here. I have now pretty well attained to the proper voice of a ' Law.' You remember what poor Father Faber used to say, ' Now *do* speak with a voice as much resembling a zephyr as any son of William Law can.' "

Even in Demerara, of which he speaks so enthusiastically, if any extra exertion had been required of him, Father Law's chest grew weak, and he was compelled to rest his voice for a time. He soon recovered from these " tires, not sickness," as he used to call them, and was ready for hard work again. The reader will understand that he had scant leisure for letter-writing. Still, he contrived to write home frequently, if not lengthily. His letters contained interesting details of his life in the colony. Several of these have been preserved by his father's care, but the greater number were mislaid or lost in transmission from hand to hand, for it was Mr. Law's habit to pass them on to other near relatives. We will transcribe one which was written during the third year of his residence in British Guiana.

I have quite lately returned from the Essequibo coast, where I made my retreat. I had never been there before. It is a finer coast than this, and far more active and lively. Father Swift, who met me at the steamer, and drove me to his house, about seven miles, began apologizing for the roads being so bad, as there had been such heavy rain, at which I was quite surprised, for their worst roads are almost equal to the streets in our town. His house was only about twenty yards from the sea at high water, where there is a nice sandy beach and a breeze, a strong trade wind, coming straight from the Atlantic. As I had one day free each

side of the eight days of retreat, I was taken along the
coast by Father Swift. We went on about seventeen
miles further from his house, and that, with the seven
on the steamer, gave me a sight of twenty-four miles of
that coast. Father Swift has under his care the western
extremity of British Guiana, and I have the eastern, so
we guard the outposts. The furthest village I reached
was called—what do you think?—Hampton Court!
There Father Swift found a dying Portuguese woman.
He gave her Extreme Unction, whilst I catechized the
Portuguese children. I returned here last Wednesday,
all the better for my trip. I was a little in want of a
change of air, as I was tired, and am now, thanks
to God, set up again. But it is quite strange that
I never get fever, so few escape having occasional
touches of it. Father Meyer, the consumptive Father
who was with me, died on May 28th. I wrote to his
father on his death, and also to the Provincial a still
further account, begging him to send it on to his father.
He died in a way that was all that could be wished,
resigned and pious. I was present and gave him the
last absolutions, which he asked for by signs, as he
could not speak. I was a novice with him at Beaumont
Lodge. It was a very touching thing to see him finish
his last few lines to his father, a week before he died.[1]
When he had finished and given the paper to me, as
if they were the last parting words to his father, as
indeed they turned out to be, he burst into tears. I
did not like to mention this little fact to his father,
because I thought his death would be sufficiently affecting, but he will come to know it.

---

[1] Father Law might have seen in this act a forecast of what he himself
would do, twelve years later, in another clime, under still sadder circumstances.

Chinese gets on slowly, but surely, I hope. I have so many other things to attend to. Pray that I may sanctify my own soul and gain many others. Get prayers too, for the same object, and do not forget, dear father, that prayers are for missioners and for missions, what money and ammunition and the commissariat are for armies. You cannot do without them. Thank dear old Fred for his letter. He asks for one all for himself. How greedy of him! But I will try on another occasion. In the meantime he must look upon my letters as circulars, or general "orders," I was going to say, to keep to the naval expression. By the way, some great astronomical swell has been frightening people in this colony by saying we are to be treated to a tidal wave of thirty feet in height out here on the 5th October. Now as ordinary spring-tides sometimes trickle across our roads here, and we are quite flat, without a hill for forty miles into the interior, you see where we should be with his wave. Our Bishop goes to the Council in a week or two, and if the wave comes, he will find himself minus his diocese. However, I believe the wave is not specially for British Guiana, but for somewhere in the West Indies. Whether scientific men can foresee tidal waves I do not know, and so I do not really know whether to treat the thing seriously or not.

Leaving the wave to God's providence, I must now shorten sail and bring ship to anchor. Let us remember each other before Jesus in the Blessed Sacrament. I like that way the Portuguese and Italians have of saying "Jesus sacramented"—*Jesu sacramentado.* If I had my way I would make it English. Best love to all at home.

In connection with the Vatican Council, he writes: "What a glorious event the Council will be! Even here it is in the mouths of Protestants as well as Catholics. Last Sunday evening the Methodist ministers, &c., begged their people to pray for the Council, to enlighten the Pope and the Bishops, and *make them read their Bibles !* It was, I dare say, very well meant."

About a year later he wrote the following letter to his brother, Captain Victor Law, Madras Cavalry, whose wife had died.

I have just received a letter from father in which he tells me of your sad loss, and I cannot do otherwise than write a few lines to you, dear old fellow, to condole with you in it. And the first consolation you must have is what is found in the words you wrote in your letter to father, not long before her death. " God's holy will be done." Yes, dear Vic, that is *the* consolation. God measures out things for our souls and for eternity, and when we think a little on this, and then on His infinite power, and then on His infinite wisdom, and then on His infinite goodness, and all three seeking out the good of our souls for all eternity, we can at least come with resignation to say: "God's holy will be done." But for all that we feel such heavy blows : we must feel them, and so I beg our dear Lord and our Lady to help you well in your affliction. I have no doubt dear papa and your own devout heart will do much to help you through. I thank God for my part, for lending you such a holy soul, as your wife seems to have been, even for a short time. I will not forget her in my poor prayers, and in my mementoes at Mass, where she shall always be in every Mass I say. Also

I will pray that God may support you through your affliction. I am very well, thank God, and have plenty of work, and little time to do it in. Pray for me that, while I preach to others, I myself do not become a castaway. There is some talk of my going home about autumn to make what is called my tertianship, which is a kind of second noviceship and lasts a year. Time will show whether I shall go or not. In the meantime I must prepare myself to profit by that precious year. There are all sorts of nations here to work amongst. As for my Chinese, I get on little by little. It is leisure I want for studying it, not inclination, for it is interesting enough, especially when you know a few words. I must now finish, again condoling with you, and promising prayers both for you and your wife. I remain your most affectionate brother.

Another letter of good advice to his brother Frederick (Commander Law) is dated from Berbice.

I must write you a line in answer to your last. I heartily condole with you on being put into a Guardo— about the most stupid existence for a true naval officer that can well be imagined, I should think. However, out of evil may come good. You may find time for study, either in your own profession, or in matters that would come in useful by-and-by, such as languages. And of course, dear old boy, all the more time to think of your soul. This last is my way of consoling those who are kept long in hospital or in prison. You will probably put yourself among the last. You might *perfect* your French, for I suppose you know something of it already. Or you might make yourself learned in controversy. At any rate do not lose your time, but do something useful *ad majorem Dei gloriam.* If you want to know something about myself, I am very well, except that for the last three weeks I have had severe attacks of lumbago and rheumatism, which I am glad to say are just about saying good-bye. It is the first taste of anything like sickness I have ever had out here—now for more than four and a half years. Good-bye, dear old boy; don't forget prayers and the sacraments, nor me in them.

CHAPTER IX.

TERTIANSHIP. MISSION WORK IN SCOTLAND.

Notwithstanding his eloquent defence of what he called the healthiest of Britannia's colonies, Father Law was not destined to spend the remainder of his life in the West Indies, as he had expressed himself willing to do. In the autumn of 1871 he was recalled to England for the year of tertianship or second novice-ship, which the Rule requires of every Jesuit ordained in the Society. Although the call of authority found him ready to obey with cheerfulness and promptitude, it was impossible for him not to feel sorrow at leaving Berbice. The climate seemed, as he said, made for him and he for it, and his work, in spite of difficulties, was exactly what, had the option been given him, he would have chosen for himself. Yet it is doubtful whether he would have been left much longer in the West Indies if his presence had not been required in Europe on account of making his tertianship. Five years in such a mission as Berbice is a fair term of service, and many a stronger man than he would have been unable to remain there half as long, or accomplish half as much as he had done. In fact, the immense amount of work he joyfully undertook, and of which he made so light, had begun to tell on him to some extent, although he would not allow this, nor could he be persuaded to relax his exertions. The change, he said, was clearly for the good of his soul, not of his body, and he did not disguise the fact that he should only be too delighted to return to the scene of his labours if his Superiors should see fit for him to do so.

If it was not without heartfelt regret that Father Law bade farewell to Berbice, how much greater was the grief of the inhabitants of the district under his charge when they heard of the approaching separation. They thankfully acknowledged the benefit his ministrations had been to them, and the profit they had derived from his instructions. The kindness and fatherly solicitude he had shown in each individual member of his flock, the interest he took in their concerns, had not been unappreciated. His tender charity also to those outside the fold, his devotion to their welfare, his unwearied zeal for their salvation, had not failed to evoke feelings of affection and confidence. He had besides enlarged and beautified the church, established confraternities and sodalities, increased the congregation by the conversion of many unbelievers and the reclaim of many careless and indifferent Catholics. The deep gratitude of all the inhabitants for the good he had effected amongst them, and their sorrow at parting from one from whom they had received so much sympathy and kindness, was expressed in an address, signed by about three hundred persons of different nationalities, the presentation of which was no mere formality, but prompted by the sincere and genuine feeling of their hearts.

Father Law himself was fain to acknowledge with thankfulness that an abundant blessing had attended his first experience of missionary work. Not only had his efforts for the good of souls been wonderfully successful, but strength and energy in an unusual

K

measure had been granted to him. He had been
enabled to carry on his apostolic labours for a longer
period than any of his predecessors in the mission had
done. And now he was not returning to his native land
like so many of them, utterly broken down in health
and incapacitated, at least temporarily, for active work.
True, he had been of late somewhat indisposed, suffering from ague and rheumatism, but he was still full of
vigour and in good spirits, anticipating with gladness
the time when, after an interval of rest and refreshment
to his soul, he should again go forth to teach and to
preach. On his arrival in England, Father Law spent
a week with his relatives at Hampton Court, permission
for this having been obtained by Mr. Law from the
Father Provincial. At the end of the week he went to
Roehampton to begin his tertianship.

The English climate towards the close of the year
is not calculated to dispel ague, nor is the pale sunshine
of the brief November day likely to prove exhilarating
to one who can bear without inconvenience the heat
of the tropics. The grounds of Manresa House, too,
shady and pleasant in summer, do not appear to
advantage when a chill mist clings to the face of the
earth, and the sere and yellow leaves float "each to
its rest beneath the parent shade." In spite of these
surroundings, Father Law's buoyant spirits kept him
up for a time. Writing to his father early in January,
he gives a good report of his health. After expressing
the pious hope that all at home may receive from the
Infant Jesus and His Holy Mother good New Year's
gifts, such as the world cannot give, he begs for prayers
that they may be merciful to him, and enable him to
make a devout tertianship. He had been out a little,
he said, to Westminster for a few days at Christmas,

to Sydenham for a day or two; and when he wrote, he was giving a retreat to a gentleman in the house. So he had not given up all active work. In February, he went to Commercial Road, Woolwich, to assist the Fathers who were giving a mission there. "I began unwell," he said, "but returned much better. Hard work agrees with me." The mission was very successful, and Father Law was so much liked that he went again to Woolwich for Holy Week and Low Week, during both of which he gave two instructions daily.

Hard work may have suited his inclinations, but it did not suit his strength. Two or three weeks later, he gives a very different account of himself. He writes from Blackpool, for it was found impossible for him to remain any longer at Roehampton. "I am here now for change of air, as what with ague in winter in this barbarous country, then jaundice, then some six weeks of hard work giving missions, I was ready for a rest. So I was ordered to come here, and do nothing for a month." The month prescribed for his sojourn at Blackpool was prolonged to nearly three. Although he called himself very lazy, he was content to rest a while, nay, glad of the enforced idleness for his own soul's sake. He spent his time in prayer, in study of the Holy Scripture, and in learning the Chinese language.

The fact that he pursued his study of Chinese, and devoted a good deal of his leisure to it, is in itself sufficient proof that he quite expected to return to Demerara, for of course it would be useless to him in England. At any rate he was most desirous to return, and was not very well pleased when he heard that Father Swift, who was out with him in Demerara, had, while discussing the subject with the Provincial, put a spoke in his wheel. The Provincial talked of sending Father Law back in a month or two, whereupon Father Swift had said that he thought it would be un-advisable that either he, or the other Father who would accompany him, should go out at that time of year, and thus come in for the greatest heat at Demerara. With regard to the other Father, whoever he might be, Augustus agreed that it might not be good for him, but as for himself he did not think that the heat would do him any harm, since he had so recently come from the West Indies, and had been so well whilst there. However, as the weather was now getting warm in England, he was not sorry to stay at home during the summer months, in order to get up his health and strength.

His next move was to Bournemouth for a few weeks, to supply the place of a Father who was absent. Then he went to Roehampton, to make the usual retreat prior to taking the last vows. The notes made by Father Law during this retreat have been preserved. They were put down on paper without the slightest thought of their ever falling into the hands of others, and are an unconscious revelation of his own beautiful character. We have from time to time inserted one or other of his private meditations in the pages of this memoir, not only because the writer is himself reflected in them as in a mirror, but in order that others reading them, may profit by the lights granted by God to a spiritual man.

It is indeed a privilege and a pleasure to be afforded a glimpse into the secrets of a soul so humble and so detached. The list he makes of the *dona particularia*, the special mercies which stand out prominently in the past, and for which special thanks are to be rendered to the God Who has led him thus far on his journey, is most edifying. The persons and incidents referred to will almost all be familiar to the reader.

Dona Particularia.

(1) Having had a good and pious mother. Her recommending me at her death-bed to remember, "Thou, God, seest me" (I once behaved rudely and disobediently to her). (2) Having a pious and generous father. (3) Being brought up in Puseyite principles, learning to "believe what the Church teaches." (4) Having a good schoolmaster in Noon (the head of the school at Somerton), who was God-fearing and just. A good example in Digby Newbolt (a fellow-pupil at the same school). Remember my unkindness to the poor Russian boy L. (5) A kind and good stepmother. (6) Onslow, the chaplain, a good and pious man, gave me excellent advice. (7) Digan (an officer on board the *Hastings*) encouraged me to read the Scriptures. (8) The sermon Blomfield preached at my Confirmation impressed me. (9) All the good I received from dear Hancock's acquaintance (I often did not heed him). (10) Dr. Scot's saying, "If God is not very merciful, it will go hard with some of us." (11) Beamish and Haverfield's example, and that of Pike the gunner. (12) That sudden light "about Heaven." (13) Being saved from the marling-spike falling on me.[1] (14) The example of Lieutenant Mould, on board the *Amazon*. (15) Waldron taking me to the Abbé Barbe at Singapore. (16) The grace given me not to give up reading pious books. (17) My father's conversion. (18) All Dr. Grant

---

[1] A marling-spike is a ponderous iron implement shaped like a pin, used on shipboard to separate the strands of a rope in splicing. Father Law probably refers to the narrow escape from death mentioned on p. 44.

did for me. My own conversion. (19) The retreat
at Clapham; Father Coffin's instructions. (20) The
attack of scarlatina, and removal to Haslar Hospital,
which gave me time for meditation. (21) Retreat at
Hodder. My vocation. (22) Father Clarke's kindness
to me during my novitiate.

Who is there who estimates at its full value the
importance and force of example? Many souls might
be stimulated to nobler actions did they think of the
effect their conduct had on others. And where can
the man be found who, looking back over nearly forty
years of life, can say as Augustus Law could, that he
had always followed the good example and avoided
the evil?

Few indeed are the sins that even his sensitive
conscience recalls to mind whilst he thus enumerates,
ad obtinendum amorem Dei, the mercies he has received.
Happy he who has nothing more serious whereof to
accuse himself! From this retrospect of the past,
Father Law proceeds to review the present, to consider
what it is he urges in preaching to others, and ask
himself whether his practice is in accordance with his
precept.

1. I recommend much the living with God's eye
upon us, and looking for His praise, as God's judgment
is the only one worth caring for.

2. I enlarge much upon the advantage of prayer,
and speak of how we ought to have great confidence,
looking upon it as an immense power.

3. I remind people how they should look upon
themselves as *ulcus et apostema*, as brands rescued
from Hell, if they have committed even one mortal

sin; and how they ought to live in a penitential spirit.

4. I speak much about the immense graces promised to a forgiving and merciful spirit, and say that people should be delighted to get an opportunity of forgiving, since the reward is so unspeakable.

5. I exhort much to often recalling to mind the memory of Jesus Christ, and say this is a beginning of devotion to the Sacred Heart; and I repeat often those words, " Do this in memory of Me."

6. I exhort people always to look upon God as their Father, and I urge them to say the petitions of the Our Father with all fervour. I recommend them strongly to prepare their minds before beginning prayer, according to the admonition of St. Ignatius.

7. I am accustomed, in fact, to say that everything depends upon how we pray. The above are some of the things I most frequently preach upon. Do I practise them? " Thou therefore that teachest another teachest not thyself."

How many seculars shame me to very confusion by their faith, fervour, piety, devotion, and love. Yet I say the Breviary, offer up the Holy Mass, and receive our Lord every day! When I think of my light and knowledge and then of my actions, of my office as a priest and how I perform it, I am terrified. *Da te ad compunctionem et invenies devotionem.*

The compunction he felt was without any element of discouragement. " I feel great confidence," he writes, " in asking for the gift of contrition, because I am sure God will be ready to grant a thing He loves so much and that He can ' never despise.' I like to go over in thought the definition of penance given by the

Catechism of Trent. Interior penance is to turn with all one's soul to God, to hate and forsake one's sins, and to resolve to amend one's corrupt ways and habits; all this with hope of pardon from God's mercy."

Up to the time of taking his final vows (August 15, 1872), and indeed for two or three weeks after, Father Law was left in ignorance as to what his future movements were to be. That he was tolerably confident of being sent back to Demerara there is little doubt; that he was extremely anxious to return thither is quite certain. It could not be denied that he was better qualified for work there than in England. He had written from Blackpool to the Father Provincial, to say how well he was feeling, in the hope that this might influence his decision, and turn the scale in favour of the West Indies. In every letter to his relatives he mentions the subject. "I do not know my destination as yet," he writes from Mount St. Mary's, where in the commencement of September he went to give the community retreat. "I hear I am to return to Demerara, but up till now the Provincial has not written. I shall not be sure about the matter until I am on board the steamer at Southampton." When he was informed that not Demerara but Dalkeith was to be the sphere of his ministerial labours, not a word of disappointment or annoyance escaped him. On the contrary, he accepted the decision of his Superiors gladly and willingly. He did not altogether abandon the hope that his wishes might yet be fulfilled, and comforted himself with the thought that with "plenty of fresh air" he might get his strength back fully, and so be ready to go back to Demerara the next autumn "quite refitted."

He entered upon his work at Dalkeith, which is

near Edinburgh, with the greatest zest and vigour. The little outlying village of Pathhead was committed to his charge and he took immense interest in it. Lady Lothian, who had built the chapel of the little mission, half-amused and much edified at the zeal he manifested, called the place *New Berbice*. Wherever Father Law found souls to be benefited, sinners to be reclaimed, he cared not what trouble he put himself to. The Protestant inhabitants of Pathhead were not ill-disposed towards Catholics, and he found great favour with them. His cheerful, friendly manner and ready sympathy made its way to the hearts even of the reserved and cautious Scotch. Before he had been there many months he had received several persons into the Church. He made himself one with the people, with their interests and their wants. From his own lips we learn the secret of the influence he exercised and the success he achieved. Personal kindness to individuals, and extreme charity to his public opponents, were the weapons wherewith he broke down prejudices and won hearts. "To-day," he says, "I married my former schoolmistress of Pathhead to a Catholic of Peebles. The old father was present. A few months ago, he had turned his daughter out of doors for becoming a Catholic. To-day he was present when the bride and bridegroom went to Communion, and at the marriage ceremony. We, that is the father and I, made great friends at the marriage-breakfast, to which I was invited, and at which I said grace, &c. When I was going to take my leave, one of the friends of the family, a Protestant, got up and made me a very complimentary speech, saying that he had never been in a Catholic church before, but that he had been much pleased with all he had seen, &c. So all went off beautifully. Last Sunday night I preached on the Notes of the Church. Half the audience were Protestants. I hope you will pray for the conversion of these poor Scotch. They are awfully ignorant of the Catholic Church. A certain Dr. Wylie spoke at a Protestant institution meeting in Edinburgh lately. He said he " considered Catholicism and heathenism as one and the same thing." This was received with applause. Did not I give it him and his applauders on Sunday! Only I spoke kindly of them. I said that if Dr. Wylie had read the Life of St. Stanislaus, and would not believe the miracles, nor even half the rest, if he would only believe one quarter of what was related of him, he would, like St. Peter, weep for the remainder of his life tears of contrition for having vilified a Saint of God, and considered him to be the offspring of a body which was one and the same thing with heathenism."

During the winter spent at Dalkeith, Father Law wrote occasionally for the *Messenger of the Sacred Heart*. His contributions are for the most part signed *Lex fidelis*, a fanciful pseudonym devised by the late Father William Maher, who was then editor of the *Messenger*, because of the writer's name being Law, and because he proved faithful to a promise given some time previously that if he had time he would try and send a few articles for publication. Sometimes, however, they are signed *A. L.* This again, Father Law explains to his father, was Father Maher's doing, not his own, " although," he adds, " it is true I am in the habit of leaving out the H——, not I hope at the beginning of words, but in the middle of my initials." In the *Messenger* for March, 1873, Father Law contributes some very beautiful principles and practices concerning prayer, gathered from the Life of B. Peter Fabre, one of the first companions of St. Ignatius. In the following numbers there runs a dialogue, in which Augustus' old love of the sea comes again to the fore, in union with his admiration of St. Chrysostom's writings. The scene is on board a vessel at sea, and the speakers, contemporaries of St. Chrysostom, converse about his sermons. The Captain of the ship relates to a merchant, one of the passengers, his recollections of what he has heard from the lips of the holy Patriarch at Constantinople. Speaking of the uses of sorrow, the pious Captain quotes the following words of the Saint, which, in the absence of books, he has stored in his retentive memory.

"God has given us the power of sorrowing; why, and to what end? For no other end but that you may use it to wash away your sins. Let an example show how true this is. Medicines were made for those diseases only which they can cure, and are useful for those alone. For instance, if a medicine has been tried for many diseases and has failed in curing any of them, but when applied in the case of one disease has removed it at once, we conclude directly that that medicine was made for that disease and that alone. Now sorrow is a medicine; apply it then in the case of all the miseries of this life, and see which it heals, and learn from that for what it was made, and why the power of sorrowing was implanted in our hearts by God. You have lost all your property and are reduced to beggary; add sorrow, does it give you back your riches? No; then it was not made for loss of riches. You are annoyed and insulted and injured by your neighbour; add sorrow, and what do you gain by the addition? Does it lessen the annoyance, remove the insult, or compensate for the injury? No; it was not then made for annoyances or insults or injuries. You have lost a dear wife or child; you grieve, lament, sorrow. Does this recall your wife or child to life? No; such grief is natural, but it heals nothing here. It was not then made for loss of wife or children. You are on a sick-bed, you lose patience, you sorrow. Does this help you? No; it only increases your sickness. It was not then made for sickness. But you have sinned, and you sorrow for your sin, and at once the sin is forgiven. Sorrow was then made for sin, and for sin alone. For it was used as a medicine for other miseries, and failed to cure them. Applied to sin it cures it at once. 'Blessed are they that mourn, for they shall be comforted.'"

Father Law's style was not particularly striking or fluent or graceful, but it was clear and easy, and brought out his meaning well. He did not continue long to write for the *Messenger*, as the calls upon his time became too numerous and engrossing to allow of literary work, which, it must be owned, was not much to his taste. Later on, when he was in Edinburgh, he was asked by Father Christie to write something for *Catholic Progress*, a little periodical he was then managing. Father Law declined on the plea that what with parish work, and occasional retreats or missions given elsewhere, his hands were too full to undertake anything more. Besides he was at that time engaged in revising the old translation (1688) of the Catechism of the Council of Trent. But in order that Father Christie might not lose a hoped-for contribution, Augustus wrote to his father, suggesting that he should send a paper or two to *Catholic Progress* in his stead.

When he had been about a year at Dalkeith, the Provincial sent him to a consulting physician to be examined, to see if he were fit to return to the West Indies. The report was that he was still suffering from nervous depression—the effect of his five years' work in Demerara—so that his immediate return thither could not be recommended, he had better remain another winter in Europe. This was a fresh disappointment for Father Law, especially as the medical verdict, like that of the practitioner he was in the habit of consulting, pronounced his chest to be quite sound. "So you see," he writes to his father, " I must remain content for another year at least. I dare say you will be quite satisfied with the doctor's decision. Whether I shall stay here I do not know. The fine air of the hills about here, and the amount of walking I have, have done me a great deal of good.

CHAPTER X

THE autumn of 1873 brought a change of place for
Father Law, although not the one he wished for. He
was moved to Galashiels, close to the Tweed, where
again he found plenty to be done. There was a good
deal of drunkenness in the place, and he entered with
great ardour into a crusade against it. He had just
returned from a mission in a parish where the
" Crusade " had been established, and much good done
thereby. Whilst there he learnt how it worked, and
came back stored with new ideas and projects. A little
band of teetotallers was formed in Galashiels, and
named " Crusaders." When the members had fought
bravely for six months, they were entitled to wear a
cross. Thus the crusade obtained a firm footing, and
acquired an *esprit de corps* which always accompanies
societies when properly established and rightly conducted. Father Law found the good it effected in
reclaiming men and making them attend to their duties
was wonderful.

There were also a good many Protestants at
Galashiels whom he desired and hoped to bring into
the Church. He wrote to his sister at Westbury to
ask her prayers and those of the community for these
persons. " Human respect is very strong here, as it is
everywhere, and it keeps many from entering God's

Church. Some Protestants have even let that out
themselves. So do ask our Blessed Lady to give
us some good conversions, real, fervent conversions.
Especially pray for those who are like Mary Magdalene
at the tomb, seeking Jesus Christ, and who see Him in
the Catholic Church and ' know not that it is Jesus.'
It only wants a little word from our Lord to show them
that He is to be found in the Catholic Church, as it
only wanted one word from our Lord to show Mary
Magdalene Who it was she was taking for the gardener.
And indeed it is often the same word that our Lord
said then that is wanted now—Mary—especially in this
month. I must end by begging you to recommend me
much to Mary, I will do the same for you."

O si scires donum Dei! was a frequent expression
on Father Law's lips in regard to non-Catholics.
His efforts for the conversion of the Protestants in
Galashiels were very successful, as much so perhaps
on the whole as his exertions for the suppression of
drunkenness. In no place where he was for so short
a time did he leave a more lasting proof of his labours.
His whole soul was in his work. His plain-spoken,
yet thoughtful and stirring sermons pleased the blunt,
straightforward Scotch, and went with force and
efficacy to their hearts. There was the same honest
unpretentiousness about his sermons that there was
about himself. His brother Graves tells us that a
friend of his one day informed him that a stranger,
a Jesuit, had preached at the chapel of the town
where he lived, and from the likeness he thought it
must have been his brother. The sermon had two
or three sea-stories in it, and what particularly struck ·
the hearer, was that after expounding two reasons for a
General Judgment, the preacher went on : " The third

reason is—well, I forget the third reason now, but I dare say I shall remember it before my sermon is done." And sure enough, after a few minutes he suddenly exclaimed, " Ah, I remember it now. The third reason is so and so." On hearing this, Mr. Graves Law said to his friend with a smile, " That was undoubtedly my brother ; " and so it turned out to be.

Father Law never cared much about his personal appearance. When a boy, it was with difficulty that he could be persuaded to take pains with his dress. After he became a religious, he took no thought about his outer man as far as his clothes were concerned. He did not mind how shabby he was ; the battered old head-gear in which he sometimes, when a priest, presented himself on his visits to his relatives, was a standing joke against him. One of his brothers remembers one particular hat in the last stage of decrepitude which he persuaded Augustus to leave with him as a curiosity. It was a nondescript sort of wide-awake, which had served him apparently for years at Demerara. It had had a new crown and a new brim, and at last there was scarcely a thread of the original hat left. It could not be tolerated in London, so Augustus had, not without considerable regret, to consent that it should be discarded. Although he was most scrupulous as to cleanliness and neatness, he could not be made to see that his clothes were too shabby to wear, it was only in deference to the opinion of others that he provided himself with new ones.

Later on, when at the Cape, he thought himself at liberty to indulge his love of holy poverty to the full. One who knew him out there, says the first thought on seeing him was : " At any rate as regards the vow of poverty he is a good religious!" His coat was rusty and threadbare, and as for his hat, it had weathered storm and sunshine for so long a period that no one could possibly conjecture what had been its original form. But this peculiarity (if we may thus term it) was far from making an unpleasant impression, there was, on the contrary, something attractive about it. His voice and bearing and manner were so out of keeping with his poverty-stricken appearance, that it gave him more weight, especially with the poorer members of his flock. They felt that for their sakes, like his Divine Master, he had made himself poor, and they respected him for it. The poor had indeed every reason to rejoice in their pastor's mortifications in this as well as in other matters, since they benefited largely by them.

In Scotland, Father Law's indifference in regard to apparel, together with his kindness to the poor, was a sore trial to his housekeeper. She complained that her master, in whom she took the greatest pride, never had anything fit to wear, and that if he had he never kept it. One day she was bewailing herself that he had scarcely a pocket-handkerchief left, when a lady offered to provide him with these and other articles. "You must give him the commonest-looking, coarsest hand-kerchiefs you can find, or he will give them away the next day," the housekeeper replied. He was accordingly presented with a quantity of rough blue cotton hand-kerchiefs with large round spots, and of these he was particularly proud. Shirts and socks were surreptitiously placed in his drawers, but unless the old tattered things were taken away, he would pick out all the best of his new stock as soon as he saw them, and give them away, keeping the worn-out ones for his own use as before.

I.

It is needless to say that a man of this stamp was much beloved by the poorer members of his flock. From his youth up he always had a great love of the poor. This was due in a great measure to the training of his excellent mother, who was ever thoughtful of the needs and troubles of the poor in her husband's parish. She used also to interest her children in their welfare, taking them with her when she visited the sick or aged, and allowing them to accompany the servants whom she sent to the cottagers with gifts of nourishment or clothing, and even themselves to carry some portion of her bounties. When he was at home from sea, Augustus was never asked in vain for an alms, in fact, with a sailor's liberality, he used to give away all he had in his pocket. The last time he was on leave, before he quitted the navy, he went with his eldest sister to the Little Sisters of the Poor, and saw all the old people under their charge. They could not say enough in his praise; one old woman was so touched by his kindness to her that the tears ran down her wrinkled cheeks. He took her by the hand, and told her she must not cry, for he would surely come to see her again. So he did, but the poor old woman was then beyond the need of his consolation; in the interval the hand of death had removed her from this valley of tears.

As we have already said, Father Law delighted in children. They were very fond of him too, and used to run to meet him when they saw him coming. Almost every day he went to the schools, if only just to see what was going on. He made much of their hymn-singing, and was very impatient with the Scotch habit of drawling out the tunes in a solemn fashion. "Come, give us some more jolly tunes," he would say, "and faster, faster. I like a good noise."

Two of his favourite hymns were the hymn to the Blessed Sacrament, " Jesus, my Lord, my God, my all," and " Faith of our Fathers." When the children were singing them, he could not refrain from joining in himself, right heartily. He often said that he considered singing hymns in the vernacular a great means of engrafting the faith deeply in the hearts of the children, since they seldom forgot them in after-life. Many a time a Catholic who had for years never entered a church, or who had become neglectful of religion through living out of reach of the means of grace, has been touched, and awakened to a sense of his duty by hearing once more the familiar strains of some simple hymn, learnt at school and sung in church in the days of his childhood. Father Law made the singing of hymns a feature in the public retreats he gave. The instructions and meditations were invariably closed by some appropriate hymn. One which he himself wrote when he was in charge of the mission at Berbice, and which has been set to music, may be suitably introduced here.

THE CHURCH IS ONE.

The Church is One ; her Faith is One,
  For Truth is One alone ;
She has one Head in Peter's Chair,
  Placed there by God the Son.

I know the marks, I see the signs
  Of Christ's own Church so fair ;
Oh, may her beauty and her truth
  Spread widely everywhere.

She brings forth saints of wondrous life,
  'Tis done by her alone ;
And Christ works wonders through their hands
  Thus stamping them His own.

    I know the marks, &c.

From pole to pole, from east to west
  The Holy Church is spread ;
The rich, the poor, all nations, tribes
  Into her fold are led.

> I know the marks, &c.

In one long line, from Peter down
  Her ministers descend ;
They teach till now what Peter taught
And will unto the end.

> I know the marks, &c.

While at Galashiels, Father Law wrote the following letter to his sister in the Convent of the Visitation at Westbury. We insert it here, because it gives an insight into his own spiritual life.

Really it is too bad of me not writing for so long a time, but I think I can say I have had very little time. But that was not a good excuse. I could, if I had tried, have found time to write to a dear sister who prays so much for me.

I am very glad that you take to the Spiritual Exercises pure. Father Gallwey recommended me to write my own meditations from the Gospels, and I have done this now for nearly two years.[1] And I find it of great service. It is very hard to get meditations that will suit every one. It is almost impossible. The Gospels are like the manna, "having in them the sweetness of *every* taste." "Serving *every* man's will, it was turned to what *every* man liked."[2] There is another thing that writing one's own meditations does. It makes one take such an interest in the Gospels. I

---

[1] A few of Father Law's meditations will be given as an Appendix to this memoir. The reflections they contain are simple, practical, and suggestive.

[2] Wisdom xvi. 20, 21.

never felt the same interest in them till I began to
write my own meditations. There is besides another
advantage, one that St. Ignatius mentions in the second
or third annotation : " we take more interest in what we
have found out ourselves with our own labour." This
is another instance of how our holy Founder always
used nature to build grace upon. I read something in
St. John of the Cross the other day which delighted me
very much. He was speaking to people who seek after
revelations, visions, &c. " You have everything in the
Gospels. Jesus Christ the Eternal Word is your revelation. Him you may gaze upon as depicted in the
Gospels. If you would have 'locutions,' &c., there
you have His words. What do you want more?" It
was something like this and it consoled me, because it
shows the dignity of meditating upon the Gospel. Now
I must finish for the present, for I have my hands very
full with the charge of this mission. Do pray for your
poor brother. I enclose what I promised. They are
simply notes for my own use, and I only send them at
your request.

OFFICE.

1. Before beginning, a *Pater*. Then *Quo vado? Ad
quid? Coram quo?*

2. Leave the earth. Ascend to Heaven. *Cum
Angelis et archangelis, dominationibus et omni militia cælestis
exercitus, hymnum gloriæ canimus, &c.*

3.
> *Sed illa sedes cælitum
> Semper exultat laudibus,
> Illi canentes jungimur
> Almæ Sionis æmuli.*

(Laud. Ded. Eccles.)

But that sweet heavenly choir
Ever exults in praise.
We too, with Sion join
A rival song to raise.

4. You are praying in the name of the whole Church. You are an ambassador. It is your " office " as a priest.

5. It is the best way of benefiting your flock. Prayer does more than talking.

6. " The sacrifice of praise shall glorify me; and there is the way by which I will show him the salvation of God."[1]

7. God Himself has drawn up the petition, so you may be sure of being heard. " My words that I have put in thy mouth."[2]

8. Do not hurry. You can be doing nothing better for yourself or mankind.

9. Say it as your last Office, as though everything depended upon *this* Office.

10. St. Mary Magdalen de' Pazzi was filled with joy when she heard the bells for Office.

11. Say the *Pater*, *Ave*, and *Credo*, slowly, as St. Francis of Assisi used to do. Turn your prayers into Mary's by the *Ave;* make an act of adoration and of love out of the *Gloria*.

12. " *Si psalmus orat, orate; si gemit, gemite; si sperat, sperate.*" (St. Aug. in Psalm xxx.)

13. More reverence when speaking to God or the saints. (St. Ignatius.)

14. The Office is our consolation in this place of exile.

15. Make the Office a real prayer. (Father Weld.)

---

[1] Psalm xlix. 23.   [2] Isaias lix. 21.

16. *Psallite sapienter.* What a man repeats with his mouth, let him feel in his soul. (St. Edmund Cant.)

17. *Non vox, sed votum ; non chordula musica, sed cor ; non cantans sed amans cantat in aure Dei.* (St. Aug. ex Corn. a Lap.)

18. For the praises and blessings we offer to God, He bestows His blessings on us. What we present to Him returns to ourselves with an increase which becomes His liberality and greatness. (St. Stephen of Grandmont.)

About Father Law's piety there was nothing at all rigid or severe. On the contrary, it was characterized by a cheerfulness, hopefulness, and general charity which served to inspire in those who knew him a greater love for the holy faith which was the mighty and constant power directing his daily life. He speaks of himself in the lowliest terms, calling himself only a half-formed Jesuit; but this only shows how high a standard he placed before his eyes. In the same spirit of humility he prayed God to send him trials, because he was so cowardly in inflicting penances on himself. Whatever were the austerities he practised (of these no mention is of course made), he never imposed them on others. Whatever tended to depression he invariably reprehended. For instance, he expostulated with his father, who was an inveterate smoker, because on going to make a retreat he proposed to try and do without his pipe. "I always thought you too strict in your ideas about a retreat," he wrote. "In your case I think no director would counsel you to give up smoking, as the privation would only cause distraction and prevent the good of the retreat."

Although Father Law seemed to be doing so much good in Galashiels, after a year's residence at the mission he was again moved. In the autumn of 1874 he acquainted his father with the fresh change. " Here I am now, stationed in Edinburgh, as I was eight years ago when beginning mission life. I have got very little to tell you, but I have plenty to do here, and shall have more and more, as I get better acquainted with the place. I was very sorry to leave Galashiels, but then we are soldiers and must go where we are sent." Somewhat later he says he likes Edinburgh very much. The wider sphere of activity pleased him, he spent whole days looking up the worst cases in the Westport and Grassmarket, on his return home relating with the greatest glee the adventures he had met with. He loved to seek out wanderers and with persuasions and entreaties to bring them to the feet of Christ. Patiently and eagerly he went again and again, waiting for the opportune moment when the soul seemed disposed to receive the words of exhortation. First he would do his utmost to relieve the most pressing temporal wants of the indigent poor, before seeking to awaken them to a sense of their spiritual destitution. One day he found a poor woman in an apparently dying state, laying on the floor in a miserable little room, with no one to look after her, and nothing to eat. She had strayed from the Church for more than fifteen years. Father Law took her his own dinner that same day, got a charitable lady to provide for her immediate necessities, and saw her comfortably sheltered in the hospital. She recovered, and became a fervent Christian. During the remainder of her life she daily offered an act of thanksgiving for her rescue from apostacy, and a prayer for the zealous priest who had been instrumental in effecting it. He had a special love for great sinners. Perhaps it was the innocency of his own past life which made him feel a peculiar pity and tenderness for transgressors. He could not rest until he got the sinner to confession, and then he could not console and notice and encourage them enough. Some one once said to him, " I really think you like great sinners better than good people," and he said promptly, " Well, I do. I have found that they are almost always peculiarly nice characters." Then he proceeded to explain how often people were led into sin by yielding to warm feelings and even generous impulses, which more correct people were not capable of experiencing; moreover, great sin often prepares the soul for great contrition, and even for great sanctity. Sometimes it must be confessed, Father Law's warm-hearted and confiding nature led him into what looked like imprudence, but it was not easy to restrain him in his zeal for souls.

As had been the case before, Father Law now again found that hard work in a crowded city, although it satisfied the craving of his heart, did not agree with his health. It did not compensate for the loss of the fresh air of Galashiels. He broke down, and was compelled to go for a week to Oban to recruit his strength. It was impossible to deny that he could not stand the work of a missionary priest in a large town. At the close of Holy Week he was generally more or less invalided. This was not solely on account of the physical fatigue occasioned by the greater number of services and the long hours in the confessional, but also because of the emotion produced by the contemplation of the events commemorated at that holy season. His power of realization was so great that he seemed to witness the cruel scenes of our Lord's Passion enacted anew before his eyes. He has been seen to shudder and turn pale when meditating upon the Crucifixion, and has been heard to say that he could hear the blows of the hammer almost as distinctly as if the nails were then really being driven into the sacred hands of the Redeemer. This he said quite simply, as if he thought everybody did the same. He had a great devotion to our Lord's Passion, and the remembrance of it seemed ever present to his mind. Those who have been privileged to hear him speak on this subject, will doubtless recollect how he loved to repeat the words of St. Bernard: "Nothing touches me more deeply, affects me more forcibly, kindles me more warmly, makes Thee appear more lovely in my eyes, O good Jesu, than the chalice Thou didst drink, the work of our redemption Thou didst accomplish." "How intense," he would continue, "is the pain our Lord endures! There is no comfort, no ease for Him either of body or of soul. And He suffers all so willingly, so devotedly; suffers it, too, for my sake. *Omnia hæc pro me.* And I am so cold, so insensible! What shall I do, what shall I say? Go, wretch, and hide yourself; or rather go to the Mother of Sorrows, and ask her to enable you to share in those sufferings; by her transfixed heart entreat her, *Sancta Mater, istud agas, Crucifixi fige plagas cordi meo valide.*"

When speaking of the infinite virtue of our Lord's Passion for the conversion of sinners, even of those who crucified Him afresh by mortal sin, Father Law sometimes related the following anecdote. His fondness for it, as well as its own interest, will be sufficient excuse for its insertion here.

There was a Christian living in Beyrout, who when he removed to another town, happened to leave behind him an image of Jesus Christ in the rooms he had occupied. A Jew took the lodging the man left, but did not notice the image. A few days later he asked another Jew to dine with him, and this man, seeing the image, was very angry and informed against his friend. Next morning the priests of the synagogue came in a body to the house, and finding the image there as they had been told, turned the Jew in whose room they found it out of the synagogue. Then they took down the image, and said: "As our fathers mocked the Nazarene, so let us now mock Him." Then they spat upon the figure of our Lord, struck it, pierced and cut it, and uttered all manner of insults against Him Whom it represented. Finally they said: "We have heard that nails were driven into His hands and feet, let us do the same." Thus they imitated as far as possible all that was done to our Lord in His Passion; and when they had gone through it all, at last they got a sharp stiletto, and pierced the side of the defaced and disfigured image, as the side of the Redeemer was pierced by the lance. But when they did this, immediately blood and water flowed from it. When they saw this, they exclaimed: "The Christians say the Nazarene healed the sick. Let us take this blood and water to the synagogue, and call the sick, and anoint them with it, and see if what they say is true. Thereupon they collected the blood and water in a vessel, took it to the synagogue, and in mockery invited all who were sick to come and be cured. A paralytic came, and a man blind from his birth; both were cured. Other sick persons came. All were healed of whatever diseases and infirmities they had. The synagogue could not contain the multitudes that flocked thither. Then the priests of the synagogue and all the congregation of the Jews believed on Jesus Christ, saying: "Glory to Thee, O Christ." They went in a body to the Bishop Adeodatus to be baptized. And their synagogue was converted into a church.

Perhaps it was a presentiment that the time was approaching when he would be called upon to follow in the footsteps of our Lord which caused Father Law to dwell more frequently upon the sufferings and labours of the Redeemer. He was acting upon the counsels St. Bernard gives in a passage from his sermons, which was no less a favourite with him than that we have just quoted. "Do you, dearest brethren, collect for yourself a precious bundle made up of the anxieties and bitternesses of our Lord and put it into the centre of your hearts, so that it may abide between your breasts. For if you only keep before your eyes Him Whom you carry, be sure that seeing the sufferings of your Lord, you will bear your own more lightly." "In that bundle then" (thus Father Law concludes one of his meditations), "I will put the prayer of Agony in the Garden, the bloody sweat, the weariness and sadness of His Sacred Humanity, the kiss of Judas, the flight of the disciples, the scourges, the crown of thorns, the Cross, the desolation of His blessed Soul. And when I sign myself with the Cross, I should imagine myself by that action, as it were, placing that *fasciculus myrrhæ* between my breasts."

In the beginning of September, 1875, he was told that he was shortly to sail for Grahamstown, Cape of Good Hope. Bishop Ricards (of the Eastern District of the

Cape Colony) was going out with several priests and a numerous body of Catholics, and Father Law was to join this party. It was not as one of the staff of missionaries that he was going out, of this the state of his health would not permit; he was sent to teach philosophy and theology to the more advanced pupils in the College recently founded at Grahamstown by Bishop Ricards. As this College had not been opened long, the number of students in the higher classes would be small and the work light.

Having received orders to go to Grahamstown, Father Law turned his face towards Africa, where he was destined if not actually to shed his blood, yet to lay down his life for the cause of the Gospel, and thus to earn the crown of martyrdom which he had so often prayed to obtain. In the interval before leaving England he had to make his retreat of eight days; the remainder of the time was devoted to taking leave of his relatives. He went over to Boulogne, to say good-bye to his sister, Mrs. Cary-Elwes, who was then residing there with her family, and paid hurried visits to other relatives and friends. On the 21st September the last farewells were spoken. His father was much grieved at parting from his son; his grief would have been still greater had he known that the farewell was a final one, and he should see his face no more.

CHAPTER XI

LIFE AT GRAHAMSTOWN.

WE must resume our history of Father Law some eight months after his departure from England, since, unfortunately for his biographer, the letters he wrote in the interval, giving an account of the voyage out to the Cape, of his fellow-passengers, of the hearty reception the Bishop met with, have been lost. Almost all, too, of those which the members of his family received from him during the four years of his residence at St. Aidan's College have shared the same fate. Thus we are almost exclusively dependent upon the reminiscences of those who knew him at Grahamstown[1] for details of his life whilst there.

His first impressions of the new country seem to have been favourable, at any rate as far as externals are concerned. With the climate he was much pleased; he said it was the finest he had ever known. After he had been there a few weeks he felt that he was getting stronger. But with regard to his work disappointment awaited him. The labours of an apostle and evangelist were those wherein his soul delighted. Life in the College was of too uniform a nature, and the scope afforded for his activity too limited to suit either his inclinations or his health. Besides, he felt himself to be comparatively useless. On arriving he

---

[1] Grahamstown is one of the principal towns of the Cape Colony. It has a population of over twenty thousand, and is about three hundred and eighty miles west of Capetown.

found that there were no pupils actually ready to learn
philosophy and theology, to teach which he had been
sent out, and only two in prospect. So he had to help
in the ordinary school work, and this soon proved too
much for him. He tried first one class, then another,
hoping to find one which was not beyond his powers.
But the exertion was much the same in all, he was
obliged to give it up and confine himself to teaching
three little boys, who required individual instruction
for a time. Later on the two theological students who
were preparing for the priesthood were placed under
his charge, and he also filled the post of Spiritual
Father to the boys. In this capacity he was a tender
and loving guide, and most judicious also, for he understood boys well, and could enter into their difficulties
and temptations. He spared no pains to ground them
well in Christian doctrine, and make religious instruction interesting to them. His lectures on the Catechism
were most carefully prepared beforehand, and enriched
with illustrations and anecdotes which he had collected
from the Bible, the lives of saints, and other sources,
for the purpose of elucidating the various points and
impressing them on the memory. He used to say it
was a great mistake to think that little or no previous
preparation was necessary for catechetical instruction.
He considered just as much to be needed as for a
sermon to adults, since the work of the catechist did
not yield in importance to that of the preacher. Of
the two it was even more important, for the doctrines
and commands of the Church once deeply impressed
on the receptive mind of the young would never be
forgotten, and in after-life be a guide to the obedient
or a monitor to the erring. Thus it was that his
instructions were eagerly listened to, and what has

often been regarded as a tedious half-hour by boys, was looked forward to with interest and pleasure.

Out of school hours, too, his watchful eye was always over the boys, and he embraced every opportunity of teaching them to overcome themselves, and practise acts of virtue. At one time he suggested that whenever one of them felt himself tempted to yield to passion, or to carry out his own will at all costs, he should make a sacrifice of his own inclinations to our Blessed Lady and offer it up as a fragrant rose on her altar. Thus it became no uncommon thing when some dispute arose amongst the boys, and an open quarrel seemed imminent, to hear the cry: "A rose for Father Law! a rose for our Lady!" and in a few moments the disturbance was quelled and all strife was at an end.

In dealing with some of the pupils no small measure of patience and forbearance was needed, for many of them were imperfectly instructed, or had been subjected to bad influences. Three of the boys especially gave Father Law a great deal of trouble. They were brothers, and in the absence of any Catholic boarding-school, before St. Aidan's was opened, they had been placed by their parents in an Anglican school, with the proviso that no attempt should be made to turn them from their faith. But far from this condition being observed by the authorities, the boys were compelled to attend sermons and instructions in which the Catholic Church was defamed and vilified, and the usual Protestant arguments urged against her teaching. The boys who were very young, and owing to the negligence of their parents, Catholics in little more than name, drank in all these untruths, and abandoned every endeavour to practise the religion in which they had been brought up. When their father removed them

from the Protestant College and placed them at
St. Aidan's, they at first proved very rebellious, refusing
to make the sign of the Cross, or to attend Mass with
their fellow-pupils. Moreover, they persisted in repeating the slanders and accusations they had heard against
priests, and even ventured to speak with contempt of
the Vicar of Jesus Christ. The Rector of the College,
fearful lest these unruly subjects might spread insub-
ordination amongst his flock, or even lessen the loyal
devotion of their companions to the Church, and
diminish their respect for their teachers, at last wrote
to request their father to remove them from St. Aidan's.
Meanwhile Father Law determined to take them in
hand, and try what he could do to reform them.
He began his mission by contriving, whenever he went
for a walk, to choose the eldest of the brothers as his
companion, and laying himself out to make an impression on him. With many an amusing tale of life on
board ship, of adventure in distant climes did he beguile
the way, until the boy forgot his prejudices, and asked
nothing better than the society of so entertaining a
talker. Flattered by the attention shown him by one
who was in the position of a master, and finding
himself on that account an object of envy to his schoolfellows, he readily yielded to Father Law's influence,
and gave him his entire confidence. It was then no
difficult task to win him back to the faith. Judicious
kindness, coupled with the example of their elder
brother, accomplished as much with the two younger
boys, who from the outset had shown themselves far
less stubborn and aggressive than the eldest, and thus
Father Law's triumph was complete. No more was
said about expelling the boys ; of their own accord they
expressed the wish to go to confession and receive

M

Holy Communion. This they did in the happiest dispositions, the younger ones in their fervour asking permission to remain in chapel for a second Mass in thanksgiving. Many a hearty *Deo gratias* arose from Father Law's heart on the day that witnessed the return of these poor children to the fold whence they had been seduced by the craft of the tempter.

The following letter, addressed to a little nephew of eleven years of age who had just begun his school life, was written by Father Law shortly before he started for the Zambesi Mission. It is very characteristic of him, and may fitly be introduced here in connection with the subject of which we have been speaking, his tact in the management of boys.

Thank you for your long letter which I received some time ago. I suppose I was very busy at the time, and afterwards forgot to answer it.

I am so glad that you want to be a priest and a Jesuit. And you must begin at once to train yourself for it. Your best way will be to be very fond of your prayers. For if you grow up to be a lover of prayer, you are sure to make a good priest and Jesuit. Look forward to your morning and evening prayers, and to Mass and to Communion as to a feast. And before you begin your prayers always think for the space of an Our Father what you are going to do, and in Whose presence you are going to be whilst you are praying.

I hope you will pray for me, as the Mission we are going on will have difficulties and the devil will not be pleased at his kingdom being interfered with.

Give my love to all your brothers and sisters.

Your most affectionate uncle,

A. LAW, S.J.

In consequence of his being incapacitated by the weakness of his chest from undertaking regular teaching in the College, Father Law had leisure for work of a more strictly ministerial nature. His assistance was not required in the parish, for it was in the charge of two able priests, but his services were greatly in request for retreats and missions in towns more or less distant from Grahamstown. It was while he was giving a retreat at Capetown, about a year after he landed in Africa, that an unexpected pleasure presented itself, in the arrival at the Cape of his brother, Colonel Frank Law, who had been appointed to the command of the Royal Artillery at the commencement of the Kafir War. The two brothers had seen each other but rarely and for a short time since the days when they were at school together, but their mutual affection had remained unchanged. This brief period of intercourse was very welcome to both; many happy memories of bygone days were revived, many a half-forgotten incident was called to mind, many a confidence exchanged between them while they sat and smoked together, or walked out during the intervals when Augustus' duties left him free. Colonel Law was hospitably entertained by the Bishop and clergy, and Augustus had the opportunity of making friends with the officers of his brother's regiment, with some of whom he was not altogether unacquainted. Before they parted, the soldier proceeding to the seat of war, the priest returning to the scene of his labours, Augustus did not fail to do his utmost to strengthen his brother's faith, and to urge him to more assiduity in the performance of his religious duties. This was their last meeting on earth.

At the time of which we are speaking, the roads

about Grahamstown were very rough and unfinished;
the only means of transit from one town to another
was the mail-cart, which was drawn by four horses.
Father Law often travelled in it when going backwards
and forwards to Port Elizabeth[1] and other towns to
give missions and retreats. These carts were driven
by colonial-born men; one of the drivers, a fine, sturdy
fellow, caught cold; and the cold being neglected, rapid
consumption set in. He was taken to the hospital, and
feeling his end drawing near, he requested one of the
Sisters to send for Father Law, as he desired to die a
Catholic. On being asked his reason, he replied that
he had often driven Father Law to and from Port
Elizabeth, and he had been so much impressed by his
holiness and by several conversations which he had
with him on the subject of religion, that he wanted to
see him again, and be received into the Church before
he died. Father Law baptized the man, administered
the sacraments to him, and had the satisfaction of
knowing that he made a pious and edifying end.
Shortly after his wife with her two children became
Catholics. Nor was this the only instance in which
the seed Father Law cast upon the wayside was known
to spring up and bear fruit. Another case, somewhat
similar to the one just related, occurred after he had
left Grahamstown. A half-caste man, also a mail-cart
driver, who had led a very irregular life, fell ill; on the
approach of death he asked to see a priest, saying that
through the conversations he had had with Father Law
he was thoroughly convinced of the truth of the Catholic
religion, and was desirous of confessing his sins and
making his peace with God in the appointed way before
his departure from this world.

[1] Port Elizabeth is seventy-five miles distant from Grahamstown.

As in Scotland and in Demerara, so in Africa Father Law was ever in quest of sinners to be reclaimed, heretics to be converted. In one of his rambles he accidentally met with an old man, infirm and ill, in a state of great destitution, sitting helplessly by an empty hearth. The hovel in which he was living was too far distant from Grahamstown to admit of frequent visits on foot, so Father Law borrowed a horse, and every day, even sometimes twice a day, he might be seen on his way thither, carrying with him a little nourishing soup that he had procured, or some food that he had saved from his own meals to tempt the sick man's appetite. Whilst ministering thus attentively to his corporal wants, he inquired into the old man's spiritual state. Alas! he had no religion, and did not feel the need of any; his past life presented a sad record of sin and crime. Perceiving that he had not much longer to live, Father Law exerted himself to the utmost to rouse him from his apathy, and awaken him to a sense of his danger. His persevering efforts were not in vain; the old man consented to be baptized; he listened attentively to the instructions Father Law gave him, he was prepared for death, and departed this life in contrite and peaceful dispositions.

Although in general Father Law's labours for the salvation of souls were eminently successful, it must not be supposed that failure and disappointment never fell to his lot. Had it been so, his experience would have differed from that of every other priest who works in the vineyard of the Lord. During one of his walks he had occasion to address a few questions to a man whom he discovered to be a German Catholic living with a Hottentot woman in the outskirts of the town. He visited the house, and found there a coloured woman

who could not speak a word of English, surrounded by a
crowd of half-caste, unbaptized children, growing up like
heathens.   He baptized the children, and persuaded
the man to be married to the woman, but he could do
no more.   The father could not be prevailed upon to
return to the practice of his religion ; nor, so degraded
had he become through constant contact with the
coloured races, could he be induced to take steps for
the proper education of his numerous and neglected
offspring.

It was not alone among the poorer classes that
Father Law's influence for good made itself felt.   Many
of the residents in Grahamstown were much attached
to him, and found his ever-ready sympathy and counsel
their greatest help in times of trial.   He was so cheerful
and encouraging that his very presence seemed to dispel
gloom and despondency, and lead one to take a brighter
and more hopeful view of things.   One lady in particular, who was married to a Protestant, and had
encountered many difficulties and troubles, speaks of
him with the warmest gratitude.   " He never came to
see me," she writes, " without saying a word or two to
help me on, and make my burden lighter.   Although
his attempts to reclaim from his evil ways one who
caused me much trouble and anxiety were unavailing,
his patient efforts were the means of saving the soul of
my father, an old military man who had spent the
greater part of his life in India, and for thirty years
had utterly neglected religion.   He was an object of
great solicitude to Father Law ; many an hour he
spent chatting with him, watching for the opportune
moment when he might turn his thoughts to spiritual
things, and draw his soul to God.   Shortly before he
started on the Zambesi Mission, he said to me : ' The

old Major is breaking up fast; these old men who have roughed it in India often die very suddenly. I must not go away before I get him to his duties.' His earnest persuasions and entreaties had not, however, the desired effect; my father grew irritable when pressed, saying he would approach the sacraments, but must have time. When Father Law was obliged to leave, his last thought and prayer was for the old Major, that his heart might be touched by grace. Nor was this prayer fruitless. Soon after his departure my father of his own accord made a full confession of his whole life, and received the sacraments with contrition and fervour, to the great joy of myself and my children. A few days later he had a stroke of apoplexy; after a few weeks, during a considerable portion of which he was insensible, he died, fortified with the last rites of the Church, and blessing Father Law for having induced him to make his peace with God ere it was too late."

Father Law's unbounded joy at rescuing a sinner was sometimes almost amusing to witness. His countenance literally beamed with happiness and delight. On one occasion he was sitting on the hill-side near St. Aidan's, amid a group of students, with whom he was having a debate on some question of theology, when a man came up and asked whether they could tell him where to find Father Law. "I am Father Law," he answered, springing to his feet with alacrity. The man appeared somewhat taken by surprise, but recovering himself, he led Father Law aside, and told him that he was a Catholic, and for many years had not approached the sacraments. Now his conscience left him no rest, and he was resolved to lay down his burden of guilt and misery. Father Law's face was radiant with delight; he grasped the penitent by the hand and led

him to the confessional.   In the space of about half an
hour he returned, overcome with emotion, yet full of joy.

The ways of God towards sinners in the Sacrament
of Penance was a subject on which he delighted to
dwell. He frequently made it the topic of his discourses
when addressing the young students at the College.
"When we see," he would say, "how sweetly and
kindly God deals with the sinner, it should teach us
never to condemn any one even in our thoughts. We
may condemn others for faults which our Lord has
long ago forgiven and forgotten. Even those who have
wearied themselves in the way of iniquity He is ready
to forgive at the first acknowledgment of their guilt.
No one hated sin like Jesus Christ, and no one dealt
more lovingly with the sinner. I always feel this when
meditating on the story of the woman taken in adultery.
' Bowing Himself down, He wrote with His finger on
the ground.' Mark His Divine consideration for the
sinner. He bows down that He may appear not to see
her, and thus spare her shame. And what does He
write upon the ground? Her sins, that they may be
obliterated, and no trace of them may remain. ' Go,
and sin no more.' "

It might be imagined that so zealous a seeker of
souls would be regarded with no good-will by the
Protestant ministers of the town. This, however, was
far from being the case. He was on most friendly
terms with them. One, the Rev. Mr. Packman, spoke
of him after his death with affectionate gratitude, saying
he should never forget the kindness he received from
him when laid up with fever. Father Law used to
visit him, sit up with him at night, and show him
every attention.

During the last two years of his residence at

Grahamstown, Father Law acted as confessor to the Convent of Our Lady of Good Hope. He was much beloved there, not only as a valued spiritual guide, but on account of his many acts of thoughtful kindness towards the Sisters and the children under their charge, and the practical help he was always ready to afford them. Almost every day he would run in to see how they were getting on in the school. On one occasion, seeing a young Sister poring over some maps with a very puzzled expression of countenance, he asked her if she were in any difficulty? She replied, yes; that in teaching Scripture history to the children she found it impossible to point out the places mentioned, as on no map that they had were they marked. Father Law only smiled, but in a few days he brought her a large map of Palestine which he had drawn and coloured himself, with all the principal towns and districts marked in large letters, suitable for a class of children. This emboldened the Sister to ask for a map of Greece on the same scale; her request was most willingly granted, and the two maps still decorate the walls of one of the class-rooms of the school. The Sisters also possess many memorials of Father Law in the form of verses composed for various festivals and special occasions. His readiness to write these verses procured for him the playful title of "our Poet Laureate." Other carefully preserved treasures are notes of Father Law's retreats. Whenever he gave a retreat to a religious community, he made it his aim to produce some permanent fruit. For this end he would write out instructions for the guidance of each individual Sister. These he called "schemes." There was a "scheme" for the reciting of the Divine Office; a "scheme" for the particular examen, a "scheme" for the meditation, and

so on. It will readily be conceived that he was long
and lovingly remembered at the convent after he had
left Grahamstown.

An extract from a letter written by a lady who
was brought into close contact with Father Law
during his residence at Grahamstown, and with whom
he kept up a correspondence for some months after
he started on his last fatal journey, will afford us
a clear and interesting view of his energetic and
unselfish character. It was addressed to Mr. Law, to
whom the writer was a complete stranger, soon after
his son's death, and contains many warm expressions
of affection and veneration for him, as well as of
profound grief at his loss. Father Law had been
instrumental in the conversion of this lady, who had
been born in Basutoland, being the daughter of a
French Protestant missionary. He also received her
children into the Church. Her husband, a Government
employé, was, owing to his professional duties calling
him to a distance, soon removed from Father Law's
influence ; yet he too eventually became a Catholic,
under circumstances which left little room for doubt
that it was to the prayers of the zealous missioner that
his obedience to the promptings of grace was due.

I had three Kafir girls in my service whom Father
Law, always on the outlook for souls to be won for
God, instructed and received into the Church. He
had already endeared himself to them by the cheerful,
kindly notice he took of them ; hardly ever did he come
to my house—and he was a frequent visitor there—
without going into the kitchen to say a word to his
children, as he called them. The circumstances connected with the baptism of one of these servants,

Betsey by name, have impressed themselves deeply on my memory, and they may perhaps interest you, as being highly characteristic of your dear son.

The day fixed for Betsey to be baptized was one which was a little family festival with us, and it had been arranged that the school-children should come to my house that afternoon to give a simple kind of musical entertainment, which they dignified by the name of a "concert." At this concert Father Law had promised to be present, but he did not put in an appearance until it was almost over. Then he only came to the door seemingly much agitated, and asked for the Superior of the school, who had come with the children. When she returned from speaking to him, she whispered to me, "Father Law begs you will excuse him, he is not able to come." Although she said no more at the time, I perceived from her altered countenance that something disastrous had happened. Afterwards she told me that one of the boys belonging to St. Aidan's had been drowned, whilst bathing in a pond situated in a thickly-wooded valley near the College. Father Law had desired her not to say a word of this before the entertainment was over, for fear of spoiling the children's pleasure. On hearing of the accident he had hastened to the spot, and had been a long time in the water endeavouring to recover the body. Finding himself unable to do so, he had returned in order to obtain assistance. Notwithstanding his anxiety and grief, he had not forgotten our little entertainment, and had been so thoughtful as to come round to explain his non-appearance.

I had made an appointment with him that afternoon to go to the College with Betsey, who was to make her confession and be baptized, but on hearing the sad

intelligence, I hesitated whether to go, as I thought
Father Law would probably be otherwise engaged.
Finally, however, I decided to take the girl to the
chapel, in case he might be there. Just as we reached
the College, one of the other Fathers came up on
horseback, and told me that Father Law had at last
succeeded in recovering the body, and was bringing it
home. We went into the chapel to pray for the poor
boy who had thus suddenly been taken from our midst,
and presently Father Law came to us, pale and cold
and wet. He had not even waited to change his clothes,
and the water was still dripping from his hair. He
would not hear of our going away, but asked us to wait
a little while, as the boys were coming into the chapel
to say the Rosary. I listened to his voice as in clear,
calm tones he recited the prayers, and wondered that
he could so far control his emotion, the more so as the
responses were broken by the sobs of the boys, who
were overcome with grief at the death of their comrade.
When the Rosary was ended, he said a few words to
them, and dismissed them. Then he called me to
make my confession, as it was my usual day. I wished
to postpone it to another occasion, but he would not
allow me to do so. Afterwards he summoned Betsey,
and when he had heard her confession, he baptized
her. He was perfectly collected, but he looked very
ill, and his hands were so cold that he let fall the glass
basin that contained the water. In his joy at witnessing the new birth of a soul to the life of grace, he
seemed to forget all else ; laying his hand on the girl's
shoulder, he said smilingly, "Now you are a true
Christian, a real Catholic, just as real a one as the
Pope himself!" Turning to me, he added, "Now
mind, she is your sister in Jesus Christ."

This poor girl had before she entered my service, been led astray by an unprincipled man. Of this fact I was not aware when I engaged her. Father Law, with her consent, told me her secret; he did so most tenderly, begging me to make no change in my treatment of her in consequence of her fault, but to be very kind and loving towards her. He also sought out the man, and persuaded him to marry her, he himself performing the ceremony in the Cathedral. Very probably the man would have been converted had Father Law not left Grahamstown; as it was he took to bad ways and deserted his wife, and presently disappeared altogether. The girl was compelled to go to service again; she has remained true to her religion, and cherishes the memory of Father Law with much affectionate remembrance. I wish I could tell you how much he was loved and respected here, and what a void his departure caused amongst us. The poor especially miss him. Many who were beyond the reach of ordinary parish care he constantly visited, cheered, and helped, and many who might never have repented in their lives were brought back to God through him, and now live to bless his memory. Whenever we found a bad Catholic our first thought was to get Father Law to visit him; he always went at once, and never failed to leave some blessing behind from his holy words and influence. He sought out good souls amongst the poor coloured people, and made them fervent and devout Catholics. I have no doubt that had he stayed longer in Grahamstown, he would have made many converts amongst the Kafirs; they were attracted by his pleasant genial manner, and the simple, plain way in which he placed before them the great truths of Christianity. One day when talking to me about his intention of learning Zulu, and the difficulty of finding any intelligent person who could teach it to him properly, he said, " Well, I shall not require as many words as most men, very few will do for me, and those short and simple ones. I shall never want to call a house a residence or a habitation." Then he laughed heartily. His teacher was an old man of no education, most incapable, but possessed of an excellent opinion of himself. Father Law liked to call him by his unwieldy native name, *Umtakababa* (son of my father), whereas he was commonly known amongst our people under the familiar appellation " Jim." The patronizing manner that this old man assumed towards his pupil amused the latter immensely. One day he asked him what was the word for priest. "*Umfundisi*" (teacher), he replied, adding with an absurd affectation of dignity, " You are *Umfundisi*, I also am *Umfundisi*." When Father Law was appointed to the Zambesi Mission, he wanted Jim to go with him; but the old man, elated by his promotion to the post of Professor of Zulu, refused to go unless a salary of £8 a month was promised to him. This demand was exorbitant, and could not be acceded to, so Jim was left behind. He informed his friends that he was extremely sorry Father Law should be deprived of his assistance, yet he could not be spared to accompany him, as the Bishop wished him to remain in Grahamstown to take care of the Sisters at the convent.

I cannot close this letter without mentioning our beloved Father Law's wonderful humility. This was, I think, the most prominent trait in his character. He used frequently to say to me, " My child, do not be satisfied until you love to be humbled ! " This precept was certainly carried out most fully in his own practice.

He did not simply bear insults with patience, he courted them and rejoiced in them. In all his letters to me there breathes this same spirit of genuine, heartfelt humility. He spoke of himself in the lowliest terms ; I have even heard him call himself, in accents of sorrow and shame, "a disgrace to the priesthood."

The incidents related above testify better than any mere words could do, how just is the character for earnest, unaffected piety, self-sacrificing zeal and tender consideration for others which we have described as distinguishing him throughout his career as a Jesuit. As he applied himself in Demerara to the study of the Chinese language, that he might be able to instruct the coolies, so largely employed in that colony, so in his post at Grahamstown, the same true missionary spirit incited him to begin to learn the Zulu tongue, in order that he might teach the Kafirs, even before he heard that he was chosen to form part of the little band who were to start for the Zambesi about Easter, 1879.

We now stand on the threshold of the final stage in Father Law's career. It is the shortest, if we reckon by time ; the longest, if it is regarded in the light of eternity. The interest of his whole life centres in the history of a few eventful months, and they cast a halo of glory and grandeur over the years of which we have already traced the course.

CHAPTER XII.

THE COMMENCEMENT OF THE ZAMBESI MISSION.

BEFORE entering upon the last and most important stage of Father Law's career, it will be well briefly to relate the circumstances under which the enterprise whereof he was one of the earliest pioneers and the first martyr, was planned and prepared.

In 1875, Bishop Ricards, the Vicar-Apostolic of the Eastern District of the Cape Colony, went to Rome, in order to lay before the Holy See the spiritual needs of South Central Africa. During his sojourn there, he proposed that a Jesuit College should be erected at Grahamstown for the purpose of training young men for the work of evangelization. This offer was accepted with gladness by the General of the Society; for it was seen that such a foundation might lead to very great results at no distant date. It would serve as a basis for missionary operations in the interior of Southern Africa beyond the English colonies. The hour long prepared in the secret counsels of God for the conquest of the Gospel in the southern portion of the vast continent seemed at length to have dawned.

The College of St. Aidan was opened in 1876, and in the following year the arrangements for the mission to the Zambesi began to take definite shape. Not until the very end of the year did it receive the formal sanction of Cardinal Franchi, the Prefect of the

Propaganda, at the time when Mr. Stanley was engaged in his adventurous passage of the Congo. The territory assigned to the Society of Jesus extends from the Limpopo, or Crocodile River, the northern boundary of the Transvaal, to the tenth degree of south latitude, and from the Portuguese possessions on the east coast to the twenty-second meridian of east longitude. It embraces the enormous area of nine hundred thousand English square miles, and includes the powerful kingdom of the Zambesi, as well as four hundred miles of unexplored country to the north of that river, the lands of the fierce Zulu tribes, the Matabele and the Abagasi, Lake Nyassa, the great Kalahari desert, the semi-civilized kingdom of the Khame, and the lands of other scattered tribes.[1]

The General of the Jesuits confided the charge of this Mission to Father Weld, of the English Province : he chose for the organizer and Superior of the expedition Father Depelchin, a Belgian, who had passed eighteen years in the Indian Mission. It was proposed to establish the head-quarters of the Mission in the neighbourhood of the Victoria Falls on the Zambesi River. This spot could be reached by three different routes. The most obvious of these was to follow the course of the great river itself from its mouth upwards through Portuguese territory to the interior. Another, starting from Zanzibar, led in a south-easterly direction by Lake Nyassa, through a country desolated by the slave-trade, and a third and longer one, from Grahamstown through Kimberley and the Transvaal. Of the

---

[1] Since the treaty with Lo Bengula, in 1891, the whole of the vast territory assigned by the Propaganda to the missioners of the Society of Jesus has passed under the British flag, and is subject to the rule of the British South African Company.

N

latter route, which lay through British territory, choice was made, since its greater length is compensated for by preponderating advantages. In the first place, the road passes through a healthy country, exempt from the swamp-fevers of the coast. Secondly, its freedom from the terrible tsetse-fly admits of the use of ox-wagons, thus rendering comparatively easy the chief difficulty of African travel, that of transport. Thirdly, it offers facilities for keeping up communication with the towns, by establishing intermediate stations among friendly tribes, which the state of the country in other directions renders impossible. Commercial enterprise has since opened up the regions of South Central Africa, and the country beyond the Zambesi is no longer a trackless desert. At the time that our missionaries started on their expedition, the votaries of trade had unconsciously prepared a highway for the Gospel, for the route they were about to follow was the one already marked out by the footsteps of the trader.

It will be understood that for the expenses of an expedition on so large a scale a considerable sum was requisite. The question of raising funds was the next to be considered. The Society for the Propagation of the Faith in Lyons contributed liberally towards providing the means of conveyance for the missionaries; for the remainder they were dependent on the charity of the faithful. Father Depelchin devoted a whole year to collecting money; he and two of the Fathers he had chosen to accompany him on the Mission visited all the principal towns of Germany, Holland, and Belgium in quest of alms. The appeal was generously responded to, and much interest was awakened in the projected enterprise.

On January 3, 1879, Father Depelchin and nine companions (Fathers Terörde, Blanca, Croonenberghs, and Fuchs, Brothers Nigg, Paravicini, Hedley, de Vylder, and de Sadeleer) sailed from England. Their voyage was signalized by an interesting occurrence. The vessel met with an accident to her machinery, which compelled her to make for Ascension. There were on the island fourteen Catholics, who had not seen a priest for nine years, and there Father Fuchs was able to receive into the Church an English Protestant, formerly a Freemason, who, having been converted by his Catholic wife, had been waiting for three years to make his abjuration. During the ten days of the Fathers' compulsory sojourn there, a man-of-war came into the harbour for coaling; and on Sunday Father Fuchs, hearing that there were Catholics among the soldiers on board, obtained permission from the Commander for them to go ashore to hear Mass in the little chapel of the hospital.

On the 13th of March the missioners reached Grahamstown. The outbreak of hostilities in Zululand, and the recent disaster the British forces had met with in the war with Cetewayo, seemed to menace the safety of the routes into the interior. It was therefore deemed advisable to postpone the journey for a short time, until the English flag should have recovered its prestige. The delay was but a brief one, and it proved of service to the missioners, since it gave time to complete their preparations, and afforded them an opportunity to acquire some knowledge of the languages of the tribes with whom they would have intercourse. Their departure was fixed for the 16th of April.

It has already been mentioned that Father Law

was appointed to the Mission of the Zambesi. Missionary work had ever been the chief object of his desires, and he counted it as the greatest privilege to have been chosen for it. One of the Fathers at St. Aidan's said, " New life seemed to have been given him when he received the tidings of his appointment." In view of this he had, for the last two years, as has been said, been studying the Zulu language, and was now able to constitute himself the teacher of his colleagues. They all began to learn Zulu, with the exception of Father Terörde, who applied himself to the study of the Betchuana dialect, as he was destined to labour amongst that tribe. With the assistance of an intelligent young native he succeeded in translating Deharbe's short catechism into that language. Father Law had already compiled a vocabulary of the Zulu tongue, and had commenced writing a short manual containing the rudiments of Christian doctrine. Zulu has no affinity with any European language. Like the other Kafir tongues, it is only spoken, not written, and like them, is governed by clear and precise rules which greatly facilitate its acquisition. He had besides been diligently practising the flageolet and concertina, in the hope that music, which we are told "hath charms to soothe the savage breast," might attract the natives, and lead them to assemble for religious instruction. A zealous convert of Grahamstown, who was much attached to Father Law, had also painted a large picture of the Crucifixion, introducing a group of Zulus kneeling in reverent devotion at the foot of the Cross. This painting, in which by a pardonable historical inaccuracy a spiritual truth was conveyed, was to be rolled up and taken with the missioners, to be displayed on suitable occasions. Thus art was made to play her part as the handmaid of religion; and the sign of our redemption was to prove, as it has done in all countries and at all times, the book of the unlearned, the book which was to teach them the lesson necessary for their eternal salvation.

By Easter every preparation for the journey was completed. Easter Tuesday, April 16th, the eve of the departure of the expedition, was kept as a solemn festival by all the inhabitants of Grahamstown. Father Depelchin sang High Mass in the Cathedral, *coram episcopo*, to ask the blessing of God on the Mission, the six Fathers, with the five lay-brothers, being all gathered round the altar and taking part in the ceremony. The church was decorated as if for a great feast, and was crowded in every part. All eyes were fixed on the little band of Christian heroes, who at the voice of the Vicar of Jesus Christ, had left home and friends and country in the hope of evangelizing, at the hazard of their own lives, the savage tribes of the Zambesi. After the Gospel the Bishop, crozier in hand, preached an eloquent sermon, in which he dwelt especially on the spirit of charity that has ever prompted the missioners of the Catholic Church to sacrifice themselves for the salvation of souls. It was this same patient charity, this spirit of self-sacrifice, that nerved the band of missioners now about to start for the region of the Upper Zambesi, to make a settlement, if possible, perhaps in the midst of enemies, at any rate among beings suspicious, crafty, treacherous, incapable of appreciating the motives of unselfish devotion, ready in obedience to the first irrational impulse to persecute or massacre their benefactors.

After the Mass, Father Depelchin, kneeling at the foot of the altar, recited the prayers of the *Itinerarium*, the same that were to be said daily by the missioners before proceeding on their journey. The Bishop and all in the sanctuary responded, and the ceremony ended with the *Laudate Dominum omnes gentes*, which was sung with great fervour and enthusiasm. On the clergy leaving the sanctuary a banner of the Sacred Heart, the gift of some ladies of Bruges, blessed and indulgenced by the Holy Father, was borne aloft at the head of the procession. Many of the people remained in the church, insisting upon receiving a last blessing from the Fathers. Pressing round them, they threw themselves on the ground, and wept as they kissed their hands, and also their feet, remembering the words: "How beautiful are the feet of them that preach the Gospel of peace, of them that bring glad tidings of good things."[1] The scene was a touching one, recalling the farewell of St. Paul to the elders of Ephesus, as Father Depelchin addressed a few words to those gathered around him, thanking them for the kind sympathy they had shown in the undertaking, and exhorting them to pray for its success.

On the evening of the day fixed for starting, a large crowd assembled in the plain stretching in front of the College of St. Aidan, to witness the preparations for the departure. The four wagons were already packed, and just as night cast her shadow on the scene, the fifty-eight magnificent oxen which made up the four teams were inspanned. To these wagons, for some of them their only home for nearly twelve months to come. the Superior led the Fathers and Brothers; the Bishop was awaiting them to give his blessing to the caravan. according to the form prescribed by the Roman ritual. The prayers were read by the fitful light of a lantern

[1] Romans x. 15.

held by one of the Fathers, and then the last heartfelt
God-speed was given to this band of apostolic men,
who were to be the pioneers of the Gospel in the
remote interior.

The good Catholics of Grahamstown had rendered
much assistance to the missioners in their preparations
for the journey. In fact the reverence and sympathy
manifested by all the inhabitants for the Fathers
during their short sojourn amongst them, was almost
incredible. A wagon was needed to carry away all
the things that had been prepared at the convent by
the Sisters and their pupils for the Zambesi Mission;
and the Sisters had taken much pains to instruct the
Brothers and initiate them in many little arts and
accomplishments likely to prove useful to them when
they found themselves in the interior of Africa. At
the hour of parting many a tear was shed, especially
in taking leave of Father Law, whose departure was a
real grief to his friends. The lady of whom mention
has already been made, who painted for him the picture
of the Crucifixion, writing shortly after the expedition
had started, says: "The day of his going was one of
great mourning, and will long be remembered here.
Father Law himself felt leaving very much; how
indeed could he do otherwise? Yet he never changed
in his bright cheerfulness to the last, thinking of each
one he had known, and addressing some words of
consolation to each. Our only comfort was to know
that he was called to a larger and higher sphere of
usefulness, and we could not help even catching some
of his pleasure and delight at the thought of all the
hardships and sacrifices before him, which he was so
willing, so anxious to meet for God's sake."

For the first stage of the journey, to Kimberley, the

capital of the Diamond Fields, which would be reached in about five weeks, Father Depelchin was not going to accompany the expedition. He purposed leaving Grahamstown a few days later, and proceeding by mail-cart to Kimberley, where he hoped to meet Sir Bartle Frere, the Governor. He had known him in India, and counted on obtaining from him valuable information and assistance, especially recommendations to the chiefs of the country, which would be of great service to the Mission. During his absence, Father Law was to act as Superior. He had already been appointed Minister, and in this capacity had exhibited great skill and thoughtfulness in foreseeing the wants of those for whom he was to provide. His early training was of use to him here; in fact, the post of head of the caravan was no unsuitable one for the whilom naval lieutenant. If the camel is the ship of the desert, says the German explorer Mohr, so assuredly the wagon is the ship of South Africa. A cumbrous and roomy vehicle, it serves, like a vessel at sea, all the purposes of dwelling-place, conveyance, and store-house. Father Law's knowledge of nautical astronomy also stood him in good stead on this expedition, as it enabled him to take observations of latitude and longitude, and to make useful charts of the country passed through. But before following our travellers on their long journey, we will say a few words about their equipment.

The caravan was organized on the model of trading expeditions to the interior. Four huge, firmly-built wagons, on wheels six feet in height, had been purchased at the cost of £110 each. They were painted in brilliant colours, and placed severally under the patronage of a Saint of the Society. They were to be the domicile of the missioners during the succeeding months. Each one was to accommodate three passengers, and to carry two and a half tons of weight in addition, the body of the vehicle being packed with stores to the height of four and a half feet, and the whole covered with a canvas roof. Fifty-eight oxen were also purchased at the price of £12 per head; a high price, cattle being very dear at that time. A conductor was engaged for the journey, who was to receive £10 a month; and for every conveyance a driver and a leader were hired, to be paid at the rate of 30s. a month. A stock of provisions for six months was laid in, besides a supply of goods available for barter with the natives on the way. In all, the expenses of the expedition amounted to £4,000. Father Depelchin thus describes the start of the missioners:

" At length they depart; the four wagons drawn each by a team of fourteen or sixteen oxen, moved down in a trot into the valley, soon to ascend the slope of the little hill opposite, overlooking the town, and begin their journey. The wagon *Claver*, loaded with provisions, is at the head of the caravan; on the top of the baggage are lodged Father Law, the guide, and Brother Hedley (chosen probably to accompany Father Law because he was the only other Englishman in the company, and had also formerly been a sailor). Next follows the wagon of *de Britto*,[1] with the two German Fathers and Brother Nigg, who was to act as cook. The third wagon is dedicated to St. Francis Xavier, and under the *ægis* of this great apostle are sheltered Father Croonenberghs and Brother de Sadeleer. Lastly, the wagon of St. Ignatius, drawn by fourteen splendid ·

---

[1] Blessed John de Britto was a Jesuit missioner, martyred in Japan.

bullocks as black as ebony, brings up the rear of the caravan, and wheels off in a cloud of dust Father Blanca and the two remaining Brothers.

"*In nomine Domini*, the Mission of Zambesi is started. Who is to stop it? In five weeks' time our little band of fearless missionaries is to meet me at Kimberley, to enter together the territory where the great fight is to begin. *Gloria in excelsis Deo*."

CHAPTER XIII.

THE FIRST STAGE OF THE JOURNEY.

In the course of this biography we have seen Augustus Law under very different aspects and amid very different surroundings. From the time when a schoolboy he stood sobbing by his dying mother's side, and was told by her to remember continually the ever-watchful eye of God upon him, we have followed him in his voyages to every quarter of the world : India, China, Australia, New Zealand, South America, the islands of the Pacific. We have seen him handling the ropes of a ship of war, sweeping the corridors at Manresa, studying theology at St. Beuno's, preaching at Edinburgh, teaching coolies in Demerara. Everywhere and always he is the same : simple, pure, courageous, unselfish. We now ask the reader to accompany him on his last journey, one from which there will be no return, for it will lead to his eternal home.

The journal which Father Depelchin requested Father Law to keep during this first portion of the journey, while he acted as Superior, has unfortunately been lost ; we are consequently dependent on the letters of the travellers for details of their perilous and adventurous life. These letters, while they mention the trials and privations which belong to missionary life in general, contain a great deal that is peculiar to Africa : they reveal the hopes and fears of the apostolic

labourers themselves, who might be too sanguine or too
desponding, but were always full of devotedness to the
great cause for which they had offered themselves.

A description of the first day's journey, from the
journal of Father Terörde, will give an idea of the
country at the outset. "At half-past seven, the wagons
were brought together and the oxen outspanned, to
feed in the best of pastures. On our left was a large
farm, serving at the same time for hotel and post-office.
On our right was the bed of a stream with a slender
thread of water, on the opposite bank of which rose a
hill a thousand feet in height. Within half an hour
three altars were erected at the foot of this hill, and in
this solitude of Nature three priests offered the Holy
Sacrifice. Turtle-doves and other birds composed the
choir. At four o'clock we started again, some on foot.
After leaving the neighbourhood of the farm we found
ourselves alone with the beauties of Nature. The way
led by the side of a winding river. The solitude was
extreme; there was not a house, not a hut, not a
human being, nothing but birds, countless birds, gave
life to the scene. Cactus and mimosa clothed the
slopes, and under their shade thousands of the most
varied and beautiful flowers and grasses were blooming.
The wild geranium was conspicuous for its beauty;
but, what seems to be a characteristic of South Africa,
not a tree, not a twig was without thorns. In comparison with other parts, the earth here does indeed bring
forth thorns and thistles." During the following night
the wagons passed the ridge of hills leading up to the
first plateau under circumstances which the travellers
would not easily forget. The significant name Helleport,
given to the pass by the old Dutch settlers, suggests an
idea of the difficulty of the passage for heavily-laden

vehicles. Through the darkness they have to force their way over what we should call impassable roads, inflicting on the unaccustomed traveller a jolting which, to say the least, renders sleep impossible. It is not surprising that one wagon became so embedded in the mire as to require all resources at hand to extricate it ; and to add to the difficulty, a violent storm of thunder and lightning, which had long been gathering, broke out just when this untoward accident occurred. The reader may conceive the situation, the fury of the storm, the shouts of the Kafirs, the darkness of the night broken only by the lightning, the torrents of rain. All this with a wagon embedded on the brink of a yawning abyss, showed these inexperienced travellers something of the dangers they had undertaken to encounter. "It was too dangerous," writes one of them, "to remain in the wagons, but scarcely less so to venture on foot; we rejoiced when the lightning came, as it showed where we could place our feet in safety."[1]

On the following day the party crossed the Great Fish River. The track led up its course for a period of five days, during which they journeyed through an almost uninhabited country to a little place called Goba, consisting of five houses, the largest settlement in the first fifty miles of their journey. They then passed through the deep gorge which the river has cut for itself in the central range of mountains. The scenery here is described as magnificent. Enormous masses of rock, piled one above another, rise up to the height of several thousand feet above the road, whilst

[1] The chief cause for alarm during a thunder-storm in South African travelling is lest the lightning should ignite the store of powder always carried in one of the wagons, and the whole caravan be blown up.

the slender stream flows in a deep chasm more than a hundred feet below it.

The work of inspanning or yoking the oxen was difficult at the outset. It usually is so with these uncouth beasts when first they are brought together. But when they have become accustomed to their work, and to each other, all goes on smoothly and they range themselves in rows each in its proper place, and are yoked in without much trouble. They feed only during the day; for this reason when a night halt is made they are not outspanned, but are allowed to lie down to rest at their posts, like soldiers ready for battle.

On Father Law, as the Superior, the duty of reporting the progress of the expedition devolved. About a week after the departure from Grahamstown he wrote to Father Weld as follows:

We go about fifteen miles a day in the wagon, which is the ordinary day's work for bullocks on a long journey. Our order of life is on the whole pretty regular. This is it more or less: 4 p.m. inspan and go on until about 9 p.m., when we outspan and have supper. Then the Litanies of the Blessed Virgin are sung; examen; then inspan again about 2 or 3 a.m., and go on until sunrise; outspan, and all say Mass, those of us at least who are able; then breakfast, various occupations, &c., until 1.30, when we say Litanies of the Saints and the *Itinerarium* all together, and make our examen. Dinner at 2. At 4 p.m. we start again, some of the Fathers walk on ahead of the wagons and get in about an hour later. Then you might hear in the twilight sounds of music from the wagon of Brother Nigg—his concertina; and from the back wagon sounds, but alas! only broken sounds,

from the flageolet of Father Law.   After supper we go
to bed.

You will be anxious to hear how we get on with
our guide.   Well, we are delighted with him.   He is
a perfect gentleman ; he points out nice quiet places to
say Mass in all of his own accord.   He knows his
business perfectly, and gets on well with the drivers.
Even they are very nice and civil.   We are all getting
fearful appetites with this gipsy life, and the health of
all is very good.   Wagon life is a continual picnic ;
but not only are the meals picnic, but also the washing
and sleeping and everything else.   As for myself, I like
it immensely; my appetite is shockingly great, and I
am getting stronger every day.

"For the spiritual exercises," another of the
travellers tells us, " signals are given with whistles, and
the whole party forms a perfect travelling community.
Father Fuchs, our musical director, is practising
hymns for May.   The devotions of the Month of Mary
are to be kept up as in every well-ordered house of
our Society, in order to obtain the protection of our
Immaculate Mother on this expedition."

It was well for the travellers that their health and
spirits were good, for even at the early stages of their
progress they had many hardships to endure.   The
cold upon the high plateaus was often intense, so much
so that the Fathers could not sleep, and were not
unfrequently forced to leave the wagons.   Father
Terörde writes that he never suffered so much from
cold while saying Mass, as on this journey.   Sometimes
the icy wind was accompanied by still more icy rain,
which penetrated the tent-like covering of the wagons, .
and rendered it impossible to light fires for comfort or

for the purposes of cooking at the end of a weary
march. They had frequently to content themselves
with the most meagre fare. What their bread was
may be supposed when we are told that it was hastily
kneaded and baked in an oven extemporized by one
not too well acquainted with the art. For meat they
were principally dependent upon the guns of some of
the party, and it often happened that the hunters
returned from a foraging expedition with an empty
bag. On such occasions the meals were not of a very
substantial character. Sometimes, however, a watchful
Providence sent them assistance when it could be least
expected. One miserable day, when a pitiless rain
was beating down, and the chase had been singularly
unproductive, a Protestant farmer appeared upon the
scene, bringing with him a supply of bread, fresh meat,
and milk. He had made acquaintance with one of the
party at Grahamstown, where his daughter was at
school, and had come five miles to meet the travellers,
and wish them God-speed. Indeed the many acts of
kindness they met with from all classes were most
cheering for the missioners.

At the little town of Cradock they found much
to console them. Amongst a population of about two
thousand, there were thirty Catholics, without either
priest or church. Having been told by the Bishop that
the missioners would pass through the town, this little
flock awaited their coming in glad expectation. On
their arrival a Protestant presented himself, offering a
room in his house for a chapel. The offer was thankfully accepted. The Fathers had got faculties for the
two vicariates through which their route lay, in order
that they might be able to do some good to the
Catholics they might meet with on their way. The

remainder of the day was spent in finding out the Catholics and inviting them to approach the sacraments. Father Law visited all the English; he found to his sorrow that many had fallen away for want of instruction. Father Terörde sought out the German families; in the evening he employed himself in converting the room which had been placed at their disposal into a temporary chapel. The banner of the Sacred Heart served for an altar-piece, and the decorations were such as the simple character of their portable wardrobe could afford. The poor people had never seen an altar so beautifully adorned. On the following morning almost every one of the Catholics attended Mass; two-thirds of the congregation went to the sacraments, three of them, between the ages of fifteen and twenty-five, made their First Communion. Father Law gave a short instruction in English. On the missioners, before taking their departure, going to thank their host for his kindness, they received from him a fresh mark of good-will, a gift of about five pounds in English money and a sack of potatoes for the journey. And yet Cradock is a most Protestant place, where to declare oneself a Catholic is to expose oneself to obloquy and derision in the streets. The finger of scorn was in fact pointed at the Fathers. May God reward liberally those who did not fear to show kindness to His servants! On the evening of the same day, one of the Fathers had occasion to purchase some medicaments for his medicine-chest, an antidote for the bite of serpents, &c. On his laying the money on the counter, the druggist returned it to him, saying that although he was himself a Protestant, he would not think of taking payment from a missionary.

At Colesberg, another small town of about a thousand

inhabitants, there were three churches for the Protestant
sects, Calvinist Boers, Anglicans, and Methodists. Our
missioners found eight or nine Catholics, who had not
seen a priest for six years. Father Law baptized a
child, and while the other Fathers set forward on the
march, he remained behind with Father Croonenberghs,
in order that these forsaken Catholics might have the
happiness of assisting at the Holy Sacrifice. Two
children received their First Communion from his
hands. Father Croonenberghs said Mass in the prison,
the jailor and two of the prisoners being Catholics. At
another settlement on the route there was one Catholic,
who was overjoyed at seeing so many priests. After
this there was not much scope for the exercise of their
zeal, as they soon entered within the sphere of the
Kimberley mission.

Whilst speaking of the assistance rendered to the
missioners by the thoughtful kindness of their fellow-
men, we must not omit to mention their heavenly
protectors. The favour and help extended to them
by St. Anthony was strikingly apparent on several
occasions. "What have we not to thank this great
Saint for!" writes Father Terörde; "there is not one
amongst us who has not experienced his friendly aid.
It was indeed not in vain that for two months before
we left Brussels, we kept a taper burning continually
upon his altar." Before the expedition started, Father
Law was in consternation at finding he had mislaid his
pocket-book, the loss of which, especially at such a
moment, would have been irreparable. After looking
for it in every place where it appeared possible that
he might have left it, he appealed to St. Anthony, and
almost immediately it was found in one of the wagons,
where so small and inconspicuous an object stood

every chance of slipping out of sight. One of the many instances in which the Saint befriended the missioners on their journey is related by Father Terörde. At the halt one day Brother Nigg's keys could nowhere be discovered. This was a matter that affected the whole party, for several of the keys belonged to the kitchen department. The Brother was urged to pray to St. Anthony, but at first he could not be prevailed upon to do so. He could not, he said, venture to ask the Saint to do so much for him, and he knew that he would have to go back a great distance to recover the keys. Presently, however, as search proved unavailing, and the hungry travellers were waiting for their supper, he yielded to their persuasions. No sooner was his prayer ended than a native came running up, asking whether they had not lost a bunch of keys? He had found them five miles off, and had hastened after the caravan to restore them.

"After passing Cradock," writes Father Weld in his interesting pamphlet on the Zambesi Mission, "the country becomes dreary and barren in the extreme. For a fortnight our travellers journeyed over dusty plains, showing no vegetation whatever, except a scanty covering of parched grass, affording poor fodder for the cattle: no trees and no water except in the deeply-cut bed of a few streams, or where a natural ravine had made a reservoir. In such spots the industry of the Dutch settlers had made a centre of richness and beauty. Every fruit of temperate and semi-tropical climes is found there in abundance. Great herds of cattle and sheep are attached to these farms, and find pasture on the plains. On most occasions the new-comer is interested by the sight of a large flock of ostriches. At Fish River the Fathers were disturbed while offering the Holy Sacrifice in the open air by a flock of these creatures poking their long curious necks about the altar. In every halt, as will be understood, the first things sought for were wood and water, but in crossing these plains firewood was nowhere to be had, the only fuel available being the dung of the animals, carefully collected at the outspans. Throughout this district, which becomes more stony and barren when the Orange Free State is entered, the presence of water alone determines the possibility of human life and cultivation. This is sufficiently indicated by the names of Adam's-fontein, Macassa-fontein, &c., which we find recorded as halting-places on the road.

"On the 3rd of May the travellers reached the Orange River, which is described as being just there about as wide as the Rhine at Cologne, and some three feet deep. As this is one of the principal fords of the river over which the traffic between the Colony and the interior is carried, there are few spots whereat the characteristic features of African travel can be seen to more advantage. It frequently happens that a hundred of these huge wagons pass the river here in a single day, laden with wool, hides, and ivory for the coast, or with European goods for the interior. At the time the missioners reached the ford there were twenty-five other wagons awaiting their turn to pass. It is difficult to form a true conception of the scene; the assembly of so many of these unwieldy vehicles, each with its team of fourteen to eighteen oxen, the wild-looking Kafirs, representing all the types of South Africa, with their repulsive features, their broad hats, their strangely, or rather slightly-clad forms, the bellowing of five hundred or more oxen, the cries of the drivers, the cracking of whips, all this amid the placid beauty of a

fine river gently flowing between banks clothed with
the richest foliage, must have left an impression upon
the mind not easily to be effaced. But all this will
soon pass, for civilization has invaded the land. A
large iron bridge is by this time constructed, and
passengers are whirled over the river with as little
emotion as over the Thames at Richmond."

In the early part of May, Father Terörde tells us,
the caravan journeyed for several days over a dreary
wilderness of sand and stones. Happily the lay-brothers
had, in the last town passed through, laid in a store of
wood, otherwise they would not have had so much as a
cup of coffee. The jolting of the wagons was at times
so violent that the Fathers could not rest at night, and
were fain to rise and proceed a while on foot in the
darkness, rather than any longer be tossed about on
the hard boards. At such times they would beguile
the way by reciting litanies, or awaken the echoes with
the sweet strains of the *O Sanctissima*. On the evening
of the 9th they reached the Modder, a river which has
cut a way for itself through a deep bed of clay, and
on this account is most difficult of passage. It is
approached by a steep and dangerous descent. On
reaching the ford, our travellers found that a wagon
belonging to another caravan which had preceded them
was stuck fast in the mud in the middle of the stream.
Though the Kafirs shrieked and yelled, and used their
long whips unmercifully, and the oxen leapt and
struggled, it was impossible to move the vehicle, which
was embedded up to the axle-trees in the slimy bed of
the river. It was ten o'clock at night, the missioners
had alighted, and it was proposed to take supper on
the spot where they were. To this the guide would not
consent. The prospect of further waiting must have

been unpleasant enough. The following amusing extract from a letter informs us how the difficulty was overcome. "It was necessary to search for a more practicable ford, and this Brother Nigg, borne on the back of a tall and powerful native, proceeded to do, carrying aloft a huge coffee-pot and some sticks of wood. He was speedily followed by another Brother, mounted on another Basuto, bearing a load of bread and bacon. Then our four equipages, like a flying battery, entered the stream at a gallop, crossed without obstacle, and ascended the further bank in full view of our unfortunate friends fast mired in the stream. Brother Nigg had meanwhile filled his coffee-pot and lighted a fire, and prepared supper on the summit of a little slope, so, like the disciples on the shores of Genezareth, we found a warm meal awaiting us." Meanwhile a second team of oxen had been yoked to the wagon in distress, and it was at length extricated, though not without first breaking the chains.

Notwithstanding all these hardships, Father Law, when writing to Father Depelchin to announce their near approach to Kimberley, was able to report : "We are all in capital spirits, and we have met with no mishap whatever on the road. On the contrary, we have been gifted with great appetites, and I think you will find us all looking quite robust."

It will be remembered that in our account of Augustus Law's youthful days, it was remarked that one of the most prominent features in his character was his contented and cheerful disposition. As a naval cadet he bore without a word of complaint the many disagreeables and hardships inseparable from what was then, even more than it is now, an undeniably hard life. The happy gift of looking at the bright side, and always making the best of things, did not forsake him as years went on. On the contrary, his sanguine temperament was strengthened, and his natural cheerfulness enhanced by the joy of the Holy Ghost and the anticipation of eternal glory. As Superior of the missionary expedition he was invariably ready to help and encourage his fellow-travellers under adverse circumstances, and communicate to them his own buoyant spirits and genial good-humour. "I have not yet suffered as much on this journey," he often said, "as I did when serving Her Majesty in the navy." Thus the hearts of the missioners were light, and they could look forward with hopefulness to the great work before them, as they sat in the wagons studying the native languages, and regarding all things as light, provided only they were enabled to plant the Cross in the vast region before them. It was this that led them on, and to support them, they daily partook of that Heavenly Manna which gives courage to martyrs, solace to the afflicted, and makes suffering desirable and attractive.

On Sunday, 11th of May, a day on which the Society of Jesus commemorates one of its most remarkable Saints, Francis di Geronimo, the caravan reached Kimberley, the capital of Griqualand. In 1879, the town was still chiefly known under the name of "the Rush," on account of the haste wherewith the people flocked thither in 1870, on the discovery of diamonds in the immediate vicinity. Father Depelchin, who had been there since April 30th, came out to an outlying hamlet to meet his brethren, in order that the little band, half-smothered as they were with the dust of the arid plains they were traversing, bronzed by the sun of Africa, weather-beaten through exposure to wind and storm, might under his auspices make their entry into the town.

CHAPTER XIV.

IT was during the journey from Grahamstown to
Kimberley, of which some details were given in the
preceding chapter, that Father Law received intelligence from home of an event which could not be
regarded by the members of his family otherwise than
as a great calamity, and was a source of the greatest
grief to himself. One of his brothers unhappily threw
off his allegiance to the Church. The letter that
Augustus wrote to his father shows how he felt for him
under this sad affliction.

I received a letter from you a few days ago in which
you tell me you had received mine about Frank's safety
after the Tsanhlana massacre. I do not think I answered
that letter, so I must give you a line or two now. I
am afraid poor Graves' apostasy has beaten you down
much, judging from your letter, dearest father, and no
wonder indeed. Still, keep up your spirits for our sake.
All of us want you still, dearest father, and to see you
alive yet for many years, to encourage us and help us
on. For you are not only an earthly father to us.
Under God we all owe the faith to you. And we do
not want to lose our father in the faith. When God's
will calls you, we shall bow to it. But do not hasten
your death by sorrow, for our sakes we beg this.

Comfort yourself by the thought that not only all of our family who are Catholics are praying for him, but also many good and holy souls in many parts of the world.

Please pray for our Mission. It is prayer that converts souls. And will you get prayers from any Catholics you meet as well? God bless you, dearest father. Every little suffering I get in our Mission shall be offered up for my dear brother's conversion. I am glad that *nolens volens* I shall have to suffer some little trials in our Mission, as I am such a miserable fellow at doing anything of that kind voluntarily. And let us pray that beautiful consoling prayer of David: *Mirifica misericordias tuas, Domine, qui salvos facis sperantes in te—* " Make wonderful Thy mercies, O Lord, Thou Who savest those who hope in Thee." Think over these words, dearest father, and they will help you much. I shall always pray that before you leave this world you may see poor Graves again a good Catholic.

Your most affectionate son,

A. H. LAW, S.J.

Again somewhat later, referring to the same brother in a letter to his sister, he says, " I read with sad interest your account of the poor dear fellow. Oh, dear Maude, cannot we force the Sacred Heart to lead him back? Let us persevere in prayer and never despair. I think one way is for us all to love God more intensely than ever, and be very generous to Him. And when one is generous to God, is God ever niggardly in return?" From this time forth the spiritual interests of this brother were continually present to his mind. Scarcely did he write a letter to friends in Grahamstown or elsewhere, without earnestly soliciting prayers on his brother's behalf. Sorrow and anxiety on his account seem to have cast a shadow over the remaining portion of Augustus' life: in most of the letters he subsequently wrote a strain of melancholy is perceptible which formerly was absent from them. For him he offered up all the sufferings— and they were greater than his generous heart antici- pated—that fell to his lot during the last eighteen months he spent on earth; for him he made the sacri- fice of his life; to him he turned, as will be seen, when standing on the threshold of another world, to utter one last entreaty that he would come back to the faith he had forsaken.

We must now revert to the band of missioners, whom we left at the gates of Kimberley. The reception they met with from the Catholics of the town was of the warmest description. The two priests, Oblates of Mary Immaculate, went to meet them, and insisted that Father Depelchin should take up his quarters in their house. Father Law also accepted the hospitality offered him by one of the inhabitants for the sake of convenience, as he was a sort of adjutant to Father Depelchin, as well as procurator to the community. For the rest, on account of the scantiness of the fodder in the immediate vicinity of the town, it was necessary to make the encampment about six miles further in a northerly direction, where pasture was good and water abundant. But before we speak of Kimberley, and of the good people who in this remote part of Africa opened their arms in welcome to the servants of Jesus Christ, a few words must be said about the diamond- mines, which give importance to this locality.

Father Depelchin calls Kimberley a town of iron and diamonds; for the houses, churches, schools, public buildings are all of iron or zinc, the walls being lined with bricks or felt, as a protection against heat in summer and cold in winter, while mats or carpets are spread on the clay soil. These houses are quickly erected, and were therefore best adapted to shelter the thousands who swarmed to Kimberley when it was first known that diamonds in plenty were to be found there. The discovery of these gems, Father Weld tells us, on the banks of the Vaal is not new. A missionary map published in 1750 has the words, " Here be diamonds," in large letters on the very spot where are now the diamond-fields ; and certain stone instruments left behind by the ancient bushmen are considered as proofs that those ingenious savages knew the use of the diamond for boring purposes. But like so many other things, diamonds had to be rediscovered in our own day. It was only in 1868 that the eyes of practical men were opened to the fact that untold treasures of wealth were being trodden under foot in the near neighbourhood of the confluence of the Vaal and the Orange River. Diamonds were picked out of the mud with which a Boer's cottage was plastered. A Dutch housewife having shown a passing traveller some stones she had picked up, it was found there were fifteen diamonds among them. The great diamond known as the star of South Africa was in the hands of a native medicine-man, who used it in his incanta-tions. No sooner did the truth begin to gain credit, than a Boer, who had seen the stone, imitating the man in the Gospel, went and gave almost all he possessed, including five hundred sheep and oxen, and bought the gem. He sold it again for £11,000. Within two years of that time thousands of people were encamped in tents on the banks of the Vaal for a distance of twenty-five miles engaged in digging and washing, often making prodigious fortunes in a single day. The Kimberley mine, which is said to be the most productive area of ground on the globe, is a shaft about a thousand feet in diameter cut out of the barren rock and filled up to the level of the ground with different strata, in which the precious gems are richly distributed. Such it was up to 1871: now it is a crater three hundred feet deep divided into lots or claims. The black men are chiefly employed in digging out this deposit; thousands of them may now be seen, like ants in an ant-hill, at work at the bottom of this crater, whilst others are employed on the bank or reef, washing, sifting, and cutting the gems out of the hard bluish clay, while a thousand baskets are being lowered or hauled up with windlasses along wire ropes that stretch like a spider's web from the different "claims" to a corresponding platform on the reef. Around this centre of activity a town of thirty thousand inhabitants has sprung up, with shops in which everything imaginable may be purchased, but at enormously high prices. In 1871 the English annexed this territory, giving a small indemnity to the Orange Free State, which asserted a claim to it. The annual value of the export of diamonds is three millions sterling, the produce of a plot of ground not exceeding nine acres in superficies.

But enough, to quote Father Depelchin's words, has been said about the little piece of carbon called a diamond, for all the diamonds in the world cannot in our eyes compare in value with the infinite worth of a single soul, which cost the Blood of an Incarnate God to redeem.

The kindness shown to the Fathers by the Catholics of Kimberley, who numbered somewhat under one thousand, knew no bounds. From the good priests down to the humblest of their flock, there seemed to be but one feeling, that of a desire to make the missioners welcome, and assist them in all they could need for their further journey. One brought an offering of a dozen broad-brimmed hats, another a hundred Martini cartridges, a third a box of shoes, a fourth a dozen pair of socks, another £5 in gold, while provision merchants contributed all manner of stores.

One Sunday afternoon, the collection after a sermon by Father Law being made in behalf of the Mission, a sum exceeding £30 was collected, although no previous notice of it had been given; and, what was yet more unexpected, on the eve of their departure a deputation of Catholics waited on the Fathers at the priests' residence and presented them with a purse containing £100, and a short address expressing their sympathy with the great and glorious work to which they had devoted themselves, and their hopes that their efforts to propagate the faith might meet with all the success so noble a mission merited. "How glad we should have been to repay them in spiritual things," Father Law writes, "and to give them a retreat. The people wished it; indeed we heard on all sides, ' Why do you not give us a mission? The people would be so glad to get a mission!'" For this, however, there was no time; the delay at Kimberley was not long, and much had to be done before a fresh start could be made. Their guide, who had only been engaged for the first portion of the journey, had left them on their arrival at the town, and the drivers had all gone off to the diggings. The missioners were assured that the services of a conductor would not be needed any more, but they had hoped to keep the natives with them, and it was no easy matter to replace them. The lay-brothers had to take charge of the cattle during the time of their sojourn at Kimberley, and the Fathers took turns with them in keeping watch over the encampment at night. One evening a party of soldiers on their way to the seat of war were encamped in the immediate vicinity. The shouts and songs proceeding from their wagon warned the Fathers that these heroes were paying homage to Bacchus, and a strict guard must be kept. We will let Father Croonenberghs tell the experiences of the night in his own words.

"Hardly had I drawn my blankets over me, when I heard Brother de Sadeleer, who had taken my post as sentinel, parleying with two strangers. The conversation became more and more animated and the dogs began to bark. Raising my head a little, I demanded silence, and ten minutes after I repeated the same request in a louder tone. Then our Basuto, the only native who remained with us, thinking the occasion favourable for the display of his courage, jumped up from under his wagon, and drawing himself up before the white soldiers, shook his fists at them, and shouted: 'Depart this instant, or I will kill you.' A quarrel ensued, and although I ordered the man to leave the soldiers alone, he renewed his menaces, and received in answer a fisticuff which sent him some paces to the rear. Seizing a firebrand, he made show of striking his antagonists, but when they attempted to take him, he threw it down and ran away. The whole camp was now in commotion, and all the soldiers were bent on slaughtering the black man. I stopped them by threatening to appeal to their officers. 'John' was already at a safe distance: the next day he too left our service."

Ten days after the arrival of the caravan, the party

set out once more. The Surveyor General, Father Law's kind entertainer, gave the Fathers a detailed map of the road to Gubulawayo, besides letters of introduction to Lo Bengula, the chief of the Matabele country, with whom he had had personal intercourse and by whom he was regarded with great favour, and to Khame, the chief of the Bamanguatos. He predicted however that the missioners would have great difficulty in obtaining permission to settle in the territory of the last mentioned chief, as the Protestant missioners had made good their footing there and would exert every effort to oppose the Catholics. Sir Bartle Frere, with the kind interest he always shows in missions to the heathen, gave the Fathers a general passport, in which they were recommended to the good offices of all Government officials and friends of the British Government in the Transvaal or adjoining country. This he did lest they should be suspected of being agents of the Colonial Government.

Thus provided with credentials, the missioners bade adieu to the hospitable inhabitants of Kimberley, many of whom came out to the camp to take a final farewell of them, and on the morning of the 21st of May, 1879, they resumed their journey. They were now leaving civilization behind them, and the future was full of anxious hopes and fears. Their destination was Shoshong, but would they be received there? And if not, would they be more successful further on? In the present, too, they found themselves surrounded with difficulties and dangers. "At the moment of starting" (we quote Father Depelchin's words) "two of our black drivers were missing. What was to be done? Father Fuchs took the reins, whilst Brother Nigg, grasping the huge whip with its lash thirty-five feet long, constituted

himself conductor. They both filled their posts admirably; but the state of the road was such that the
wheels got buried to the axles in sand, and every
quarter of an hour one or other of the wagons stuck
fast, so that we were unable to reach our destined
halting-place. It is an amusing sight to see our camp
fire lit. Everybody helps of course; as soon as the
vans are drawn up and our tents pitched, a log is half
buried in the sand, and a pyramid of sticks piled up to
a good height. This is soon blazing, and we have a
fire hot enough to roast all our oxen. The evening
meal is soon ready; the *menu* is simple, one dish, *unum
necessarium*, is the general rule. After supper we sit
round the fire chatting, talking over the day's adventures, forecasting the future, then after singing the
litanies, all but the sentinel betake themselves to repose.
Our bivouac is guarded by four dogs; the largest one,
Prince, was given to Father Law at Kimberley, he is
almost like an African lion in size and appearance."

The difficulties inseparable from such a journey
were enhanced by the inexperience of the travellers.
It is usual for caravans coming from Grahamstown to
change their oxen at Kimberley, so as to start anew
with fresh teams. Our missionaries had not thought
this necessary, and their progress was much retarded in
consequence. Now and again one of the animals,
weary and footsore, lay down and refused to advance
further. It had to be left behind, and by the next day
a skeleton only remained on the spot, the bones being
picked clean by innumerable vultures, almost before
the animal had expired. Through the loss of some,
more work fell to the share of the remaining oxen, and
the substitution of a few fresh ones at intervals along
the road did little to remedy the evil. One night, at

the moment of inspanning, sixteen oxen were found to be missing. Through the neglect of one of the drivers they had escaped and roamed to a distance in search of better forage, and only after a wearisome pursuit were they recaptured. These and other minor incidents, such as the sinking of the wheels into the sand, so as to necessitate vigorous work with the spades to extricate the wagons; the having to unload one vehicle in order to get it out of the mud in the midst of a stream; the breaking of the traces, which had to be repaired by the skill of the old tar, Brother Hedley, had no worse effect than that of occasioning short but vexatious delays. One day the heavy and continuous rain rendered it impossible for them to prosecute their journey; another day the violence of the wind nearly carried away the tents they were attempting to pitch. Once a more serious danger threatened to put an end to the expedition. It was midnight, and the camp was hushed in silence. Suddenly the terrible cry of "Fire" was raised by one of the Kafirs. The Fathers sprung from the wagons, to find that a box slung under one of them, containing some things they had made use of during the day, was already in flames. Happily it was detached in time to prevent the conflagration spreading to the wagon above it, for therein was a barrel of gunpowder, sufficient to blow the whole of its contents into the air. Some pieces of wood imperfectly extinguished from the evening camp-fire had been thrown into the box by the Kafirs, and these logs smouldering had set fire to the receptacle that enclosed them. Had the party known of the terrible catastrophe that befell a traveller (Mr. Burgess) while hunting in the Zambesi country, when he himself, his wagon, and horses were destroyed through a spark falling from his pipe, they

P

would have been even more grateful than they were to Divine Providence for their narrow escape. " This barrel of gunpowder," Father Depelchin adds when relating the incident, "is a dangerous companion, but it is an indispensable adjunct to our baggage. Without it we should be deprived of the means of obtaining animal food, and should incur the risk of falling a prey to the wild beasts that prowl about our caravan by night. It does however expose us to great peril when a storm overtakes us on the open plain. I remember one night when a frightful storm burst over our heads. The flashes of lightning seemed to furrow the clouds and form rivers of fire. Peal followed peal, the thunder seemed to make the earth tremble, and it looked as if wagons, men, and oxen would be swept away by the fury of the tempest. All the while I could not forget that we were lying on the top of a powder magazine. If the lightning had struck my wagon all would have been blown up, like some warship whose magazine explodes in mid-ocean. Yet night after night we rest quietly beside our powder barrel, knowing very well that our friends in Europe and Africa are praying for us, and God's angels are faithfully watching over us. *In pace in idipsum dormiam et requiescam.*"

The towns and settlements the missioners passed were few and far between. Nevertheless in this second portion of the journey, as in the first, some opportunities of exercising their apostolic zeal offered themselves. One evening a man came up to the encampment. He was a German, a native of Treves, and a Catholic. He was delighted to see a priest, and entreated one of the Fathers to hear his confession, and to baptize an infant that had been born to him.

An old soldier, he led a nomad life, wandering from farm to farm in a house on wheels, finding ample employment amongst the Boers as a carpenter and wheelwright.

Another time a well-to-do farmer, professing himself a Lutheran, came to ask one of the priests to baptize his two daughters, as he wished to bring them up as Catholics. At the conclusion of the ceremony, the mother, touched by grace, begged that she too might be admitted into the Church; and a short conversation with the father led him to abjure his errors, and with his son, a boy of six, also to receive Baptism. Nor was this all; a young Kafir, a servant to the family, expressed his earnest desire to become a Christian and a Catholic. After an hour's instruction from Father Terörde, he too was washed in the regenerating waters. The next day was Trinity Sunday, and before proceeding on their way, the Fathers said Mass in the dwelling-house of the family, and administered the Bread of Life to the newly-baptized. Truly to them it might have been said as to Zaccheus: *hodie salus domui huic facta est.* By a singular coincidence, on the eve of Trinity Sunday three adults and three children were thus baptized in the name of the Father, the Son, and the Holy Ghost. Besides this incident, the instruction and baptism of a poor Zulu, who had been abandoned by his companions and left to die of typhus fever; and the meeting with an Irishman, who on the first sight of a Catholic priest, fell on his knees to ask his blessing, and with tears of joy took advantage of the presence of the Fathers in the solitude where he lived, in order to perform his religious duties, were consolations afforded to the missioners on their journey. For each one of them desired that it should be said of him as it was said of his Divine Master: *pertransiit benefaciendo.*

At Bloemhof a halt of three days was made to rest both men and animals. About this little town, which consisted at that time but of eighteen houses, there was nothing to account for its name, which signifies flower-garden. The soil was stony and unproductive. Three Catholic families were found there, to whom the coming of the Fathers was a source of great joy. Father Law said Mass in an extempore chapel arranged in one of the houses, two sermons were preached, and all the good people approached the sacraments with much fervour. The inhabitants of Bloemhof did not know how to make enough of the Fathers. They thought it a privilege to wash their linen, to provide them with bread, butter, meat, and vegetables, and they presented them with a fine carpet of skins for use when Mass was said in the tent. Even after they had got an hour's journey from the place some persons came after them with biscuits and milk.

Whilst in the proximity of the town the drivers proved rather troublesome. After a visit to the taverns on the first evening there was a quarrel which would have ended in a regular fight but for the interference of the Fathers. The next evening Brother Nigg was instructed to devise a means of keeping them in the camp. Seated aloft upon a wagon, the little Brother played stirring strains upon his concertina. The Kafirs soon began to dance. The louder he played, the wilder grew their antics, to the infinite amusement of the missioners. "For the first time in my life," said Brother Nigg, when the performance was ended, "I have played dance-music *ad majorem Dei gloriam.*"

The following letters were written by Father Law while at Bloemhof. The first is addressed to his father.

Here I am, all safe and sound, as far as this—a place in about 27½ S. latitude. We start for Zeerust, and then along the Marico River for Shoshong, which is in about 23½ S. latitude, on Tuesday or Wednesday. We hope to get to Zeerust in about a fortnight or three weeks. I like the wagon-life well enough. It is at least very healthy. I have not enjoyed such health for some years. I am glad to say there is a regular post to and from Shoshong, so that we can write and receive letters, as easily as if I was at Grahamstown.

The people have been very kind to us all along. I was mentioning this to some Protestants three or four days ago, and they answered, " And you deserve it." I believe you have received the paper giving an account of the Bishop's sermon on our departure from Grahams-town. It was a beautiful sermon, and I wish I was even a little worthy of the great things he said about the missionaries. Pray that I may at least profit by the great favour God has given me in choosing me for such a mission, and you will help me in thanking God for it.

The other is to the Superior of the Convent at Grahamstown.

I am so much obliged to you for your kind letter and the things you sent with it. We all of us feel we can never repay your kindness and that of the Sisters in all you and they did for us at Grahamstown. Father Depelchin said the other day you were " a true mother to our Mission," a feeling we all share. And then your

kindness did not end with our stay there, but followed
us, or rather went before us like a good angel, wherever
we went and you knew any people. May God reward
you and bless you and your dear Sisters. The Catholics
at Kimberley were so very kind. Father Lenoir, too,
and his *confrère* kindness itself. Perhaps some find the
wagon-life a little rough, but they thrive on it. I
scarcely know myself, I am so stout and well. I enjoy
the life ; the only thing is one has little time to study.
However, all the boys speak Zulu, and I pick up a
good deal from them. The Governor gave us a capital
passport, telling all who wished to be friends of the
British Government to befriend and aid us. Mr. Bailie
wrote a letter to Lo Bengula, and his brother-in-law
one to Khame. Besides we carry for them presents to
these two chiefs. We start this evening or to-morrow.
There are here two excellent Catholics, Mr. and Mrs.
Quin. Mrs. Quin keeps the only school here; she
teaches the little Dutch Protestants, eleven in number,
to say Catholic prayers, to make the sign of the Cross,
and instructs them in the Catechism. She is doing
great good. I gave her a lot of pictures as prizes
for her children. I am getting on very well with my
flute, but I put away the concertina for the present on
account of the great amount of dust.

I hope all the Sisters are well. We shall remember
them always in our prayers. Thanks so much for your
prayers for my brothers. Please continue them.

The next letter we have from him is dated from the
Limpopo River, which was reached in the second week
of July. The journey to Zeerust had lasted ten days;
it is a beautiful spot, situated in a fertile valley, with
the stream of the Marico running through it. The

travellers, who even in June had been compelled to wear their warmest garments on account of the severity of the cold, might now fancy themselves in southern Italy. The vegetation was luxuriant, and in the gardens were trees laden with oranges. Passing by a succession of farms, they stopped at one whose owner happened to be a Catholic. He was of Irish origin, and for thirty-four years had not seen a priest. Nevertheless he had not lost the faith; he was overjoyed at the opportunity of having his children baptized and himself performing his religious duties. Father Law was no less rejoiced to administer the sacraments to these good people; finding the mother of the family in good dispositions, he received her, too, into the Church.

The sight of the Limpopo River excited in the breast of the travellers no ordinary emotion. They had long known of it as a river of the far interior, but none of them had ever thought of looking down upon its waters, and it seemed like a dream to find themselves standing on its banks. Writing thence, Father Law says:

Three years and a half ago Mr. Wilmot made a very fine speech, at Port Elizabeth, on the return of Dr. Ricards with the priests and the staff of St. Aidan's College. He spoke of Catholic missions extending from St. Aidan's to the Limpopo. And often afterwards we joked about this speech, thinking the allusion to the Limpopo nothing more than a mere flight of eloquence and a flow of words. Yet here we are all safe and sound on the banks of the Limpopo, and have been quite well on the way. We are now within a few miles of the limits of our desired Mission.

Some days later, on July 18th, he writes to the Rev. Mother:

A wagon is just passing down to Zeerust, so I take the opportunity of writing just a line to Grahamstown to say we are all well so far. On Saturday Brother Nigg shot a crocodile. We hope to be in Shoshong in a few days. We have had a little rain, which will well supply us with water from the Limpopo to Shoshong, where sometimes there is scarcity. Fancy from Saturday week till yesterday (a period of nine days) we did not meet a single human being. We have heard panthers, and jackals and hyenas at night, but no lions. One of our oxen, which was too weak to return to the camp with the rest, being left where it was, was found in the morning with half of its body gone, devoured by jackals, although we had kindled a large fire to keep off beasts of prey.

The missioners had been warned, after leaving Zeerust, to be very careful to keep up their watch-fires at night, as there was danger to be apprehended from wild beasts. They took all precautions and met with no accident but the one mentioned above. The rivers in this region abound with crocodiles, which are very dangerous. "To bathe in the Limpopo," says the traveller Mohr, "is simply suicide." The monster lies still at the bottom of the pool, or floats motion-less, only the upper part of the head, which greatly resembles a piece of floating bark, being visible above the surface of the water, and seizes in an instant whoever unwarily approaches too near the stream. Our travellers had to be extremely careful lest their dogs should meet their death in this manner, especially

"Prince," who was most valuable as a watch-dog, besides exciting the admiration of all who saw him, on account of his size and handsome appearance. One day he nearly got his owner, Father Law, into trouble. Seeing some wagons on in front Father Law went to see whose they were. They proved to be those of a Protestant missionary, the Rev. W. Sykes, who was bound for the same destination as the Fathers. He took "Prince" with him, and as there happened to be a large and pugnacious dog at the Protestant camp, a fierce battle ensued, and the respective owners of the dogs had difficulty in separating the combatants.

On leaving the Limpopo, the travellers journeyed for six days through a dreary waste, dusty and dry, without game, and almost without water. "Whilst traversing the African plains we learnt," says Father Depelchin, "how important a place a good water supply holds among the necessaries of life. Many a time we suffered much from scarcity, having barely a glassful for washing purposes. More than once our oxen had to trot on their way for forty-eight hours without a drop to drink. We wondered how the poor animals performed their task so well. How grateful to us was the sight of a stream or a spring where we could, after a long march, quench our thirst and wash our face and hands!" The scarcity at times of animal food was also one of the troubles of the journey, as the native drivers became recalcitrant if no meat was forth-coming. This was generally to be obtained at the farms. On one occasion, when the provision of game consisted of one water-hen, two Boers, huntsmen, unexpectedly rode into the camp, with four fine gazelles across their saddle-bow. They were willing to dispose of two of these to the missioners for the sum of six

shillings; for a few percussion caps another was purchased, while the fourth was given them into the
bargain.

On the 20th of July our missioners crossed the
tropic of Capricorn, and entered within the boundaries
of the domain of their Mission. The next morning the
Holy Sacrifice was offered beneath a tree upon which
a large cross was cut to mark the spot where the first
Mass was said within the limits of their jurisdiction.
They were now approaching Shoshong, but they first
had to cross a shallow depression, formerly the bed of
a lake, which in the rainy season is covered with pools
of briny water, at other times with a crystallized saline
deposit. It is now known by the name of the Saltpan.

Before accompanying the caravan to the capital of
the Bamanguato territory, which they reached on the
23rd, we cannot refrain from inserting an extract from
a letter of Father Croonenberghs, describing a scene
which they witnessed as they drew near to the town. It
would have delighted an artist. "Two Betchuana
cavaliers approach our camp at full speed. They are
mounted on oxen with immense horns; a string
attached to the nostrils serves as a bridle; a couple
of trusses of hay make the saddle. These warriors
wear the uniform of nature; black, with a ruddy tinge.
A feather in the hair, a girdle round the loins, and
sandals on the feet, make up their costume. They
carry for weapons only the assegai, or iron-shod club.
But these warriors of Shoshong are on a peaceful
mission. They have come to exchange the milk of
their goats for our tobacco from the Transvaal. Then
a troop of little black children came into our camp to
sell us sheep and goats. As they stood and leant, this
one on a sheep, this one on a goat, these little dusky

angels reminded us of the St. John Baptist of Italian painters. Father Superior gave them some warm slices of bacon. The use they made of it made us laugh heartily. In the twinkling of an eye, they rubbed themselves all over with it, and then looked as if they were surprised to see each other so brilliant and handsome-looking. One might, indeed, have taken them for angels carved in old brown oak, like those with which our great artists adorned the churches of St. Jacques and Notre Dame at Antwerp."

CHAPTER XV

THE missioners (we quote Father Weld's words) approached Shoshong with beating hearts. Great interests were hanging in the balance, the eternal salvation of many souls, the success or failure of the expedition. The possibility of finding themselves without shelter and without resources in the inhospitable regions that lay to the north, or being perhaps over-taken amidst the marshes of the Zambesi by the floods of the rainy season, at which period fever is rife and it is doubtful whether it is more dangerous to advance or to remain stationary, presented itself to their minds. If we add to these considerations the thought of the sad discouragement it would be to those who sought to follow in their footsteps if ill-success should cause it to be said that much money and many lives had been rashly and foolishly sacrificed, we can understand that they must have had brave hearts indeed if they did not feel deeply anxious as to the issue so soon to be tried. They had not, it is true, burned their ships, but they had left them a thousand miles behind them, and had no thought of ever seeing them again.

They had been warned before leaving Kimberley that disappointment was in store for them, as it would be difficult, if not impossible, to obtain permission from the King to settle in his country. Shoshong was the first town within the limits of the territory assigned to them by the Holy See as the sphere of their labours; their hope was to establish a station there which would be a basis of operations for future missionary enterprise, where recruits from Europe could reside for a time, to become acclimatized and acquire a knowledge of the languages of the aborigines. Although the capital of the country, and the royal residence, Shoshong is described as a poor sort of place, its former population of thirty thousand having dwindled to a third of that number. It is surrounded by a rampart of rocky hills; the miserable huts of the natives are grouped round an open space, and divided from one another by mimosa hedges. Standing apart are some fourteen houses, whose English inhabitants are provided with all the comforts of their native country. Here the London Missionary Society has established its head-quarters.

The Bamanguatos are a tribe of the great Betchuana race. The first missionaries who penetrated to these regions were Germans; they made a few converts, amongst them the two eldest sons of the King Sekhome. But in 1860 they were ousted by the emissaries of the London Missionary Society, who have since ruled there supreme, instruction in the English language being preferred to German. When our missioners arrived, Khame was sole occupant of the throne, which he had wrested from his father some eight years previously. His kingdom presented the singular example of an African community under the dominion of a Christian ruler, for he had remained steadfast to the beliefs he had learnt in his early youth. He had even suffered some persecution on this account, having refused to comply when his father urged him to take a plurality of wives. He is

stern in his repression of wrong-doing, and has pro-
hibited the introduction of intoxicating liquors into his
kingdom.   On Sundays he always attends Divine
Service, joins in the psalms and hymns, and inflicts
condign punishment on any of his subjects whose
conduct is reprehensible.   Unfortunately the Wesleyan
missionaries enjoy great favour and influence over this
excellent monarch.   Such being the case, it will be
understood that it was a matter of vital importance to
them to prevent one who was their protector, and to
some extent their tool, from falling into the hands of
the Jesuits.   It was to avert so great a calamity, to
circumvent the designs of the wily intruders, that we
have seen the Rev. Mr. and Mrs. Sykes passing the
caravan of our travellers on the road to Shoshong,
hastening forward by forced marches to give the alarm
and prepare the defence.   Their efforts were only too
successful.

We cannot do better than allow Father Croonenberghs to give an account of the interview with Khame,
which was granted to Father Depelchin, Father Law,
and himself, on the day after their arrival.   "In the
middle of the enclosure," he says, "a number of the
subjects of the King were ranged in a semicircle sitting
on their heels.   Khame himself sat on the ground in the
midst of them, like the least of his subjects.   He wore
no mark of his royal dignity, except an enormous feather
fixed in his soft felt hat of English manufacture.   His
whole dress was like that of some townsman of one of
our prominent towns in Belgium; unpolished leather
boots, brown trousers, a flannel shirt, and coat of
light-coloured English cloth.   (Only a few of the principal inhabitants are dressed in European style; the
great majority are clad in the scantiest fashion.)

Khame, who is surnamed 'the Gentleman of South Africa,' appears about forty years old; he is tall, his skin is of a dark olive colour, his hair and beard thin. He has an intelligent and kindly expression; he says very little, and all around preserve a respectful silence."

Beside the King sat two missionaries, Mr. Sykes and Mr. Hepburn. The exultant expression of their countenances showed the Fathers that they had little to hope for; these gentlemen had taken care to make their own footing secure. However, Khame received the Fathers with civility, and offered a chair to each.

Father Croonenberghs continues: " The conversation was carried on through an interpreter. Father Depelchin began by taking out the letter of recommendation which had been given to him, but Khame would not read it or even touch it. Father Depelchin then presented to him a letter from one of his friends at Kimberley; the King took it, but would not open it. He then asked Khame to authorize him and his companions to teach his people the religion of Jesus Christ, as well as the letters, arts, and sciences of Europe. The request was coldly received; the King said he already had teachers. At length Father Depelchin asked him for a place where we could camp. The King replied that he did not know of one. He then offered the King a present of a Martini-Henry rifle. All the people seemed full of wonder at the sight of this weapon, but Khame looked at it with an air of indifference. He took it in his hand, examined it for a moment, then gave it back with thanks; he added that he would come to the camp to receive it on the following day.

" We felt somewhat disheartened at the result of the interview, but the Europeans in the place bade us not despair, for Khame never gave any decisive answer in his royal residence."

Meanwhile the large picture of the Crucifixion which had been painted for Father Law by a lady in Grahamstown, was exhibited on one of the wagons. Crowds came to gaze upon it, and for several hours Father Terörde, who, it may be remembered, had made the Betchuana dialect his special study, stood beside it, catechism in hand, endeavouring to explain its meaning to the people. He found many of these had been baptized, but they were, almost to a man, utterly ignorant of the doctrine of the Incarnation. The presence of the group of Africans at the foot of the Cross proved a sad puzzle to the native mind; the idea that their ancestors had been spectators of the scene upon Calvary was contrary to all their religious traditions, and the mystical signification it was intended to convey, the vocation of all nations to the Faith of Christ, was far beyond their comprehension. This painting was still 'on view' when, on the following day, the King's brother, also a Christian, and apparently better instructed than the common people, visited the camp. He is described as the very image of his brother; he seemed touched at the sight of the picture, and even more so on hearing who the missionaries were, whence they came, and with what object they had penetrated so far. "At half-past twelve," Father Croonenberghs relates, "the 'Gentleman of South Africa' approached us with quiet dignity, followed by all his councillors. He is a head above all his suite. He contemplated the picture for a moment with a sardonic smile, and then entered our tent. We renewed as before, through an interpreter, the requests made to him yesterday. He put a number of questions about religion to us, and expressed his surprise that there could be two religions in one religion. At last he said that he was resolved to take no more teachers for his people besides those he had already; adding: That if the two religions, the Catholic and the Protestant, are the same, there is clearly no need of having more than one of them; and if they are different, there would be constant conflict between them, and they would cause division among his subjects." The Fathers could say nothing more. They felt that the enemy had forestalled them, and could only resign themselves to God's will, and trust that this first failure might be followed by better success in another quarter. Khame, despite his firm refusal to admit them, continued courteous and kind, and showed great displeasure on hearing that they had been annoyed by some of the natives. The Protestant missionaries, too, having achieved their triumph, preserved an external friendliness. On Father Law calling upon Mr. Hepburn, he was most polite, and his wife, won perhaps by Father Law's pleasing manner, so far overcame her prejudices, that she insisted on sending him some pastry and other dainties of her own preparing.

Before leaving Shoshong Father Law wrote to his father: " Just one line to say we arrived here six days ago; but the chief would not let us stay here, as he said he had other missionaries already, *i.e.*, London Missionary Society. These missionaries will be the greatest obstacle we shall have. Otherwise he was extremely civil. We are just starting for the Matabele country, where I hope Lo Bengula will receive us. Otherwise we shall have to push on to the Zambesi. I have not been so well as I now am for a long time. Pray for me, and give my best love to all. Being a

Ω

kind of adjutant to Father Depelchin, I have very little leisure, but hope to write more next time."

To his friend in Grahamstown he also wrote as follows: "Excuse me for not having written more at length. But I have little time and many interruptions. Being 'Minister' as it is called, nearly all my time is taken up whenever we get to a town. Your picture was exhibited here yesterday at the back of one of the wagons, and there was a large crowd looking at it all day. What a pity they could not be instructed in the full meaning of the picture. But Khame unhappily declined having us amongst his people, influenced no doubt by the Protestant missionaries. Well! you cannot blame him, nor them either, for we must always suppose they are sincere, and if so, of course they would do their utmost to prevent what they in their ignorance suppose to be a false religion from entering the country. But it is a great pity, for what a fine Catholic town Bamanguato[1] would make; and they seem to be very nice people. As for Khame himself, he has quite the manners of a gentleman. We now go to the Matabele. Pray that we may be allowed to have a station there. I shall work harder than ever at Zulu now.

"You little know how unworthy I feel to be a member of such a mission. Do obtain for me by your prayers from our Lord a very ardent and tender love for Him, and especially for Him crucified. I see all the saints were so devout to the Passion. I always remember you in my Mass; we will pray for one another, that our dear Lord may give us great graces, and grant us one happy day to see each other again before His throne and that of His Blessed Mother."

---

[1] This is the natives' name for Shoshong.

We hope that we are not doing the Protestant missionaries injustice when we express the opinion that the motives by which they were actuated in their opposition to the Jesuits were not quite as unworldly as those with which Father Law in his charity credits them. The King appears truly to be, according to his lights, a pious and conscientious Christian; the religious guidance as well as the secular government of his people is entirely in his hands. The position held by the Rev. Mr. Hepburn was lucrative and honourable, but it was a mere sinecure. Although the Bamanguatos were called Christians, scarcely any had a definite notion of the true God, and they were all slaves to superstition. One day one of the Fathers was reciting his Breviary when a woman passed near him. Suddenly she stopped short, and stood motionless, fixing on him a horrified stare, until he had ended his prayers and closed the book. She imagined him to be occupied with the black art, and awaited with trembling apprehension the result of his incantations. Father Law, too, became an object of suspicion at Shoshong. He was engaged with his sextant, taking the latitude, when some natives, perceiving him kneeling before the mirror (the artificial horizon) were filled with terror. They took him for a sorcerer about to cast some maleficent enchantment over the town. An angry crowd collected. His nationality preserved him from violence; had he been a coloured man, he would have been very roughly handled, if not torn to pieces, by the populace.

At an earlier stage of the journey, a very different, though an equally ignorant interpretation was given to his scientific operations. He says, "I was one day taking observations in the Transvaal at an outspan, close to a Dutch Boer's farm. Whilst I was busily engaged looking down at the mirror with the sextant, two young Boers came up to me, and said: 'Well, old man, what are you doing? Looking for gold, eh?'"

It was with heavy hearts that our missioners took leave of Khame and his subjects in order to seek a resting-place elsewhere. They had hoped against hope that an opening would be made for them to labour amongst the Betchuana tribes; now this hope was at an end, and there was nothing left for them but to proceed onward at once to the land of the Matabele Zulus, and endeavour to obtain a footing there. Gubulawayo, the residence of the King of that powerful tribe, the neighbours and foes of the Bamanguato, was the goal of their journey. It lay before them at a distance of two hundred and fifty miles to the north-east.

They were entering now upon the most difficult part of their journey. The country they had to traverse was inhospitable and barren, and at the season at which they were travelling, great scarcity of water prevailed. Many a time the caravan was compelled to push on with hardly any halt, or they would have died of thirst; many a time the only means of obtaining water was by digging in the dry and sandy bed of a river. Occasionally, despite arduous labour with the spade and pickaxe, even this resource failed them. Once they went on for two days without meeting with any supply of water. On the 31st of July the pilgrims kept the feast of their holy Founder in the midst of the desert. The Holy Sacrifice was offered in a little tent affording shelter only to the celebrant and the server; the Blessed Sacrament was exposed during Mass, and the little band of sons of St. Ignatius supplied by the fervour of their prayers and praises whatever was wanting in outward solemnity and splendour, "Our festive dinner on the occasion," says Father Depelchin, "consisted of one dish, and not a very toothsome one; a fillet cut from the carcase of a patriarchal goat, with a preparation of Indian corn or millet less resembling bread than a block of granite in colour and consistency. The toast of the day was drunk in the best Makalapsi; and if it be asked whence came this choice beverage in the interior of Africa, we answer that there was a river of it flowing at our feet."

The missioners entered the Matabele territory at Tati, on the 17th of August, exactly four months since their departure from Grahamstown. There they found themselves once more among human beings, and the post, passing through with letters from Gubulawayo, gave them the opportunity of communication with the civilized world. Tati is a central point whence routes diverge to Shoshong, the Zambesi, and Gubulawayo. The only interest attaching to this little settlement arises from the gold-fields. Some years back a numerous company of Europeans, having heard that the country was rich in gold, gathered together to search for the precious metal. No alluvial gold was found, but strata of auriferous quartz abounded, which yielded from one to four ounces of gold per ton. A shaft was sunk in the idea that a centre of wealth had been discovered, but after a while the mines were abandoned, and the gold-seekers directed their steps to the diamond-fields of Kimberley. Our Fathers found there a community of about a score of Kafirs, and about as many Boers, who gained a subsistence by the chase of the giraffe, buffalo, ostrich, and antelope. As the rainy season was approaching, and it might

consequently be imprudent to advance in the direction
of the Zambesi River, the Superior thought it advisable
to leave the greater portion of the community at Tati,
and himself to proceed with one wagon, accompanied
by Father Law and Brother de Sadeleer, to Gubulawayo, to see how the land lay, and if possible, obtain
permission from the King, Lo Bengula, to establish a
mission in his territory.

On the day preceding his departure, Father
Depelchin, during the Mass of the community,
received the vows of Brother de Vylder, an old
Pontifical Zouave, who had fought at Mentana. He
was still a novice when sent out to Africa, and the
time for pronouncing his religious vows had now
arrived. The Fathers decorated the little altar,
erected under the spreading branches of a tree by
the riverside, to the best of their ability for the simple
ceremony, and Mass was followed by Benediction of
the Blessed Sacrament. There is something of peculiar
interest attaching to the vows of poverty, chastity, and
obedience, thus pronounced in the wilds of Southern
Africa by one who had already left the world far behind
him before he pledged himself to forsake it, and had
gone to the extremity of the earth at the voice of
obedience before he had taken upon himself its yoke.

The next day, after taking an affectionate leave of
their brethren in religion, the two Fathers commenced
their journey. They had previously sent forward a
letter to the King asking permission to approach his
capital, a most necessary precaution, without which
they would probably have been expelled from the
country. They had been warned to avoid this danger
by the fate which befell a French Protestant missionary
whom our Fathers had met on their journey through

the Transvaal, returning home from an unsuccessful expedition to Matabeleland.

Amid these new scenes and this changed manner of life, Father Law was far from forgetting his friends and spiritual children at Grahamstown. At different stages of the journey he wrote to the Superioress of the convent and to other good Catholics, who assisted him with their prayers. With the lady who had been his chief friend in the town he kept up a regular correspondence, as she still relied on him to a great extent for spiritual advice and guidance. It will be remembered that soon after his arrival he had received her, with her children, and later on some of her servants, into the Church. He was very anxious for her husband's conversion; he also took a deep interest in one of her sons, a boy of fourteen, who wished to be a Jesuit, and was going to be placed in one of the Colleges of the Society in England. Whilst at Tati, he wrote a long letter to this lady, from which we give some extracts :

We arrived here two days ago, and Father Depelchin and myself start for Gubulawayo to-morrow. We hope much to succeed in getting a station there. What joy I shall have to get to a place I have been thinking of for so many months! I am getting on with the language, and should do more if I had more time. But being Minister and Procurator, I have my time much taken up. I often think of you, especially at Mass and at Communion. It is more true to say I *never* forget you by name at Mass. For you are, as you know, to be perpetually in my Memento at Mass. I am sure I have the same privilege from you. I am myself trying to do what I urged you so much to do, that is, to live in a spirit of contrition, of love and devotion to the Passion. Cultivate contrition, the " abiding sorrow for sin " Father Faber speaks of, with an immense hope and confidence in our dear Lord. I thank God for letting me see your soul striving after this treasure of contrition. Keep to it, keep down in the dust, and God will exalt you, and love you, and never forsake you. And do not forget in your prayers at the feet of our Lord a poor sinner who taught others the way of gaining God's heart, and did but little practise what he taught. I really want your prayers. Offer up all you suffer for the conversion of your dear husband. What a happiness it would be for you to have him in the one true Church. I have very strong hopes that he will some day enter. God bless you, and give you grace to advance every day in contrition and hope and love of our crucified Lord. The devotion to the Passion that God has given you is a very precious grace; try to value it more and more.

On the 10th of September, writing to the same lady from a place about seven or eight miles distant from Gubulawayo, he says :

I must give you one line to say Father Depelchin and myself have arrived here. We have seen the King, Lo Bengula, and he received us very kindly and cordially. But he has not yet given us an answer as to whether he will give us a place in his kingdom to settle in. I fancy his answer will be favourable, but we may have to wait another month, or even more, before we get his final answer. If we get permission to settle in his domain, I am to remain there, although I may perhaps accompany Father Depelchin to the Zambesi.

It will require great grace to convert the Amandabele,[1] so please pray often for their conversion. I am looking out anxiously for a letter from you, and shall be so glad to hear how you are getting on. I am writing under great difficulties, sitting beside the wagon with a strong wind blowing, and clouds of dust. If our friends (here he mentions by name some residents at Grahamstown) could only travel for four months in a wagon, how strong they would become. Father Depelchin declares no one would know me now.

To his father Augustus writes from Gubulawayo thus :

Your letter of July 17th arrived here on the 19th (September), so I get letters about as quickly as I used to when at Hong Kong, which is not so bad. The Europeans in these parts organize a post of their own, by means of runners ; and it is so well arranged that ordinarily we get letters as easily as if we were living in Europe, and not amongst the Amandabele. . . . I have kept a journal since Bloemhof. I send it regularly to Father Weld ; I expect it will appear in pamphlets regarding the Mission. We left Shoshong on the 28th of July, and got to Tati on the 17th of August. Three of our drivers ran away and left us in the lurch two days after leaving Shoshong, so two of our Brothers had to turn drivers during the journey, and hard work it was for them, poor fellows. However, we got through all right, thank God. And for that matter we could all, I think, now manage to drive the bullocks, and yoke them in as well, if there was necessity. After a few

---

[1] The name of this tribe is usually written Matabele. In quoting Father Law's words, however, his manner of spelling it has been retained.

days at Tati to rest the oxen, Father Depelchin and
myself and a lay-brother came on here to see Lo
Bengula, and get leave to establish a mission in his
country. We are still waiting for an answer, but hope
in a day or two to get one. He is going to be married
(he has sixteen wives already) to a daughter of Umzila,
the chief of another great Zulu tribe, just due east of
this, about three hundred miles, and the marriage is
not yet over. When about eight miles from here we
visited the marriage expedition kraal from Umzila, and
saw the future Queen. We were received with the
greatest cordiality; we both agreed that Umzila's
people seemed a nicer people than Lo Bengula's. We
hope to send some missionaries to their country before
long. I only wish I could go thither with the marriage
expedition when it returns, for I was charmed with the
people. However, I like the Amandabele very well.
They are a fine people, and would make splendid
Christians, if once they made up their minds to become
Christian. But to become a Christian means in this
country, so far as I can see, to be ready to die at any
moment. If any person of note dies here, the general
opinion is that he must have been bewitched by some
one. So the witch-doctors " smell out " (according to
the expression of the country) some person or persons
who are obnoxious and unpopular for some reason or
other, and put them down as the cause of the death.
These persons, with their families, are then put to
death, and their huts burnt. The King's sister was
sick the other day; I was told that if she died, her
death would be the cause of at least three hundred
others. If any one should become a Christian, he would
surely be set down as the bewitcher on the occasion of
the next death that occurred, and made a victim of.

Possibly there is a little exaggeration here, but it is what we are told. I hope all this superstition may gradually be got rid of. The King does not believe in it, but he pretends to do so in public.

When the excitement of the long journey was over, and the interest and curiosity awakened by the arrival in a new and strange country had subsided, and the Fathers, awaiting the long-delayed decision of the King, found themselves alone—with the exception of a few European traders—amongst degraded and brutish aborigines, the slaves of a gross fetichism, it is evident that Father Law felt the isolation of his position keenly. The buoyant tone disappears from his letters, and somewhat of discouragement may be read between the lines. One may almost fancy he is thinking of his own needs when he addresses these words of exhortation to his friend: "Do you remember how I was always speaking to you about hope? I repeat it now to you again. Make frequent acts of hope. I think that is the greatest honour we can pay to God, to hope in Him. And when we see our own weakness and misery, the more we honour Him by still hoping in Him. How often does holy David calls the man blessed who hopes in God! In fact there are none made more of by the inspired singer than those who hope. We little think how our despondencies displease our Lord. He likes to be looked upon as a kind and merciful Father." And then, after acknowledging how much the separation from his friends at Grahamstown and elsewhere cost him, he adds: "Be glad that you and I are able to make to God such a sacrifice as this separation is to both of us. The harder the sacrifice, the better the gift and the greater the reward. I feel it as much as you. There will probably be another great sacrifice for me up here. It may be God's will that I pass the rest of my life here without any consolations of conversions, &c., although we must hope that conversions will come even in the Amandabele country. I suppose I shall stay here. I envy those who cross the Zambesi. I am beginning to learn better that in this world it is to do God's will, not brilliant or great things, that God requires of us. Yet you can fancy how hard it will be for me to labour here without any tangible results. So pray that at least I may at length take my soul seriously in hand. I am too much given to occupy myself in external work, and to neglect my spiritual duties. This has always been my sin. And perhaps God has punished me by sending me to a place where there are at present scarcely any hopes of actually converting the souls of others, that I may look more to my own soul. ' Physician, heal thyself,' I fancy our Lord says to me."

Excepting just at the outset, when his sanguine temperament rendered him apt to view men and things invested with rainbow tints, " hues of his own, fresh borrowed from the heart," Father Law seems to have had no very good opinion of the natives amongst whom his abode was temporarily fixed, and to have early come to the conclusion that the obstacles in the way of their conversion were insuperable. Some people of another tribe, present at the Court, impressed him more favourably, and he indulged most enthusiastic hopes in their regard. In fact, he set his heart on carrying the light of the Gospel into their country.

But we are anticipating the course of our narrative, for we must now lay before the reader a brief account of the reception our missioners met with at Gubulawayo. Before doing so, however, some portions may be quoted of a letter addressed to Mr. Law, which testifies that if Father Law was mindful of his friends in Grahamstown, they on their part did not forget or cease to regret him. And no wonder, for short as had been his sojourn amongst them, he had left behind him the good odour of Christ :

With regard to dear Father Law, I have just heard of him in a note received from Father Croonenberghs, that "he is well, and kindly gay, as always." I can only repeat here what I said in my former letter, his loss is one that can never be repaired, and we feel the grief of his absence acutely. His pure and saintly life, his wonderful simplicity and humility, his holy conversation, his great kindness and self-devotion, never stopping at any trouble if he could help or benefit others, his happy, cheery voice and manner, his warm good heart, his earnest and beautiful sermons, his instructions and guidance in the confessional, all these and a thousand other virtues, made him dear to us, and he has left a great void behind. But no, his spirit is still doing good here in many hearts, and his prayers are winning many blessings for us. Seldom do I go out without being met with the anxious inquiry, "Have you any news of dear Father Law?" I am sure it must be a great consolation to you to have such a son; I never knew a soul more wholly given to God, and I shall never cease to be thankful for the time during which it was my privilege to be directed by him. I was his first convert here; he took a most kind interest in me, and his advice is still the guide of my life, and will remain in my memory until death.

CHAPTER XVI

After travelling for eight days through a well-watered and picturesque country, Father Law and Father Depelchin reached a village about two days' journey from Gubulawayo, which forms a kind of outpost, beyond which no stranger is allowed to advance without permission from the King. Here they first came into contact with the natives whom they hoped to evangelize. Father Law's journal thus describes the meeting with them: "About 8 a.m., on the 26th of August, a black man, perfectly naked except his waist-cloth made of skins, took his seat on a rock near the wagon, accompanied by two others with guns. We found he was the *Induna* (chief man) of the place; soon after several other natives arrived, either to beg, sell, or look on. They all stayed till 1.30 p.m. The next day two orderlies brought us a message from the Induna, requesting us to bring the wagon somewhat nearer to the village. It was accordingly driven on for a couple of miles; the two orderlies stayed with us until we outspanned about four hundred yards from the village, under one of the koppies, or isolated granite rocks, whose fantastic forms constitute a striking feature in the landscape. They were fine, civil, quite gentlemanlike young fellows, full of cheerfulness and fun. One of them went through the assegai exercise for us, and explained well how the steel was made from ironstone found somewhere up the country." A day or two later he writes: "The natives have been swarming round us all the day, crying out, *tusa*, make a present, *tengéla*, buy. They brought milk in abundance, and other comestibles. We bought a native axe amongst other things. One of them, a fine strapping fellow, was most eloquent in begging me to purchase a milk-pail of carved wood. He exhausted every argument to induce me to buy it. 'Here are mere boys,' he said, looking round scornfully, 'whose things are bought; I am a man, and my things are not bought. Ah! you do not love me, you hate me.' At last I told him I was beaten by him, and gave him a gaudy handkerchief, which was the thing he was coveting all the while. He looked at it, turning it over and over, then with a short 'good-bye' twisted it round his head, and ran as hard as he could to the village, singing and shouting for joy as he went. If what we saw to-day is a specimen of the Amandabele, either they have changed much for the better of late, or they have been greatly calumniated. Certainly they weary one terribly with their *tusa* and *tengéla*, but there is nothing rude or rough about them, and for my part I was charmed with the poor simple creatures. God grant that we may be allowed to make them Christians!"

On the arrival of a letter from Mr. Fairbairn, an English resident at Gubulawayo, saying that the King would be glad to see them, and the road was open to them, the Fathers moved forward. By a kind disposition of Providence, this gentleman, for whom the missioners had received letters of introduction, was with the King when their request for authorization to enter the country was brought in, and by him it was interpreted to the monarch. Had it been delivered by any one who was ill-disposed to Catholic missions the permission would probably have been withheld. In the afternoon two young men arrived, appointed to serve as an escort to conduct the travellers to the royal kraal. "On the road," Father Law writes, "two more young men from the village we had just left, dressed in their best, came up with us, having evidently seized the occasion to get their meals provided for them. It was cool, but they do these things in such a simple way, and are so jolly, that you cannot be angry with them." Everywhere as they approached the town the inhabitants showed the same friendly spirit and absence of distrust. On the 1st of September the crowd about the tent during the celebration of Mass was so great, that the next morning they had to say it at 3.30 a.m. in order not to be disturbed. All day long the wagon was surrounded by an importunate crowd eagerly asking for gifts, amongst whom the sisters of the King and other important personages were mingled. These individuals were not easily satisfied; in fact it was no small trial to patience to listen to the perpetual cry for presents with which the Fathers were beset from sunrise to sunset.

Lo Bengula lost no time in receiving the newcomers. After offering their presents, a rifle, a musical-box, some rugs and blankets, which the monarch eyed with no small satisfaction, the Fathers withdrew, for he was too busily engaged in devouring his dinner—some large pieces of meat which he held in his hands and tore with his teeth—to attend to business or make a minute inspection of his treasures. The next day they were admitted to a formal audience.

How little of royal state was discernible in the King's surroundings may be gathered from Father Law's description: "We crawled through the entrance into the hut, which like all the others is of a circular form, and there was Lo Bengula lying on the ground with eight or nine of his wives sitting opposite. Fairbairn, who had accompanied us, explained our mission briefly, and read the passport the Governor had given us. Lo Bengula said there were many teachers there already and they had done nothing, but he did not give a final answer, and then went on to chat with Fairbairn, who seems on intimate terms with him. Plenty of Kafir beer was handed round, and afterwards meat was brought in; the King pressed us to eat." This interview concluded with a performance by two magicians, whose mode of procedure was not unlike that of the spiritualists of our own country. These mediums professed to answer questions put to them by means of a mysterious little calabash, dressed as a doll, which they held hidden under their cloaks, and of whose revelations they pretended to be the mouth-piece. The exhibition, rather an embarrassing one for the Fathers, was cut short by the King, at Mr. Fairbairn's suggestion, and at length the missioners withdrew, with good hopes of a favourable reply to their request.

On the King returning the visit he showed himself friendly and even familiar in his manner. Catching hold of Father Depelchin's beard more than once, he compared it to the mane of a lion. He partook of lemonade and biscuits, but gave the same answer as before about the mission, "that he did not want more teachers, that his boys did not want to learn, and it was better for them to work." Father Law describes

R

Lo Bengula as a man of gigantic stature and excep·
tionally dark colour, even among his swarthy race. He
affects none of the refinements of European dress, his
only article of costume being a waist-cloth. As he
returned to his hut, he was followed by a herald
singing the praises of His Majesty.

The period at which the Fathers arrived at the
Court was not propitious for the prompt settlement
of the business for which they came, as all was bustle
and excitement in preparation for the King's marriage
with some new wives, the most important of whom was
the daughter of a neighbouring potentate, Umzila.
The missioners were present at some of the festive
scenes. Being attached to the Court, they were
expected to follow the King's movements; it was
his custom when travelling from one residence to
another to be followed by a long procession, in which
European residents took part. Father Law writes in
his journal :

September 14th.—Just after breakfast we got a
message from the King that he was on the move, so
we inspanned and followed his three wagons and
Fairbairn's till we got to a halting-place. We passed
the new Queen and the new wives on the road. They
were decently draped in blue cloth. The next day off
again about 10 a.m. back to Amatze. We are much
amused at having to run about the Veldt after the King.
However, we understood he wishes us to follow him.
At 5 p.m. we walked to the camp where the men of
Umzila were ; we found them dancing and stood looking
on for three-quarters of an hour. It was a sight well
worth seeing. There were about a hundred and fifty
men and sixty or seventy women, forming an ellipse,

the women opposite the men. They danced while singing, and beat time with their feet to the song, all holding sticks in their hands, sometimes advancing, sometimes retreating, at times pointing their sticks on high, now to the right, now to the left. The tunes were very good and spirited, and were sung in beautiful time and good harmony. I was perfectly delighted; such dances must be a great recreation to the people. Afterwards we went to call upon the Induna at the head of the expedition. He was a fine, open-faced, manly fellow. He shook hands with us heartily; this was remarkable, as the natives never shake hands unless they have learned the practice from Europeans. We also saw the future Queen, who said, as did the Induna, that their people would gladly receive us. To intimate that we were not Protestants, we said we were *Abafundisi* (teachers), who did not marry, and we showed them the crucifix, as the book from which we taught. Another day we took some presents to the new Queen and the Indunas. We were received with the same hearty kindness as before and brought into a hut. One of the Indunas made a speech, explaining what we had come for; the Queen thanked us; then the other Induna made a speech. All was done with great order and decorum. The same night four or five boys came up and sat down by our fire. After a little while one of them snatched Brother de Sadeleer's cap from his head and ran off with it to the kraal. It was too dark to pursue him. On the King hearing of the theft, he said, "Why did you not shoot him? When any one is found prowling about the camp at night he is counted as a wolf." Death appears to be the punishment of every crime in this country.

Gubulawayo has advantages of situation not often found in an African town. It stands on an elevated plateau, four thousand feet above the level of the sea, and commands an extensive view over the country. The air is exhilarating, and it is considered healthy for Europeans. A few merchants, chiefly English, reside in the neighbourhood; the scale of their commercial operations may be judged of by the fact that when one of them gave up his holding and started for the coast, he did so with a train of wagons containing ten thousand pounds of ivory and four hundred of ostrich feathers. The long delay in obtaining an answer from the King gave the Fathers an opportunity of cultivating friendly relations with the white men established in the town and its vicinity. They were all very kind, with the exception of one, who at first took part with the Protestant missionaries in the endeavour to deter Lo Bengula from granting the Fathers permission to make a station there. Fortunately, however, this merchant (the one alluded to above) was desirous of leaving the country, and it occurred to him, that if the Fathers remained, he might profitably dispose of his premises to them. Immediately his demeanour changed; and on Father Depelchin agreeing to purchase his holding should the King's consent be obtained, he employed his influence with the monarch to that effect. But it was a trivial incident that determined Lo Bengula to grant the desired authorization. He happened one day, after the marriage ceremonies were all over, to go to the Father's camp. He had fixed his eye on their wagon, and wanted to buy it, as his own was greatly out of repair, and unfit for the gala-carriage of his new consort. His offer was declined, but he was assured that if he would allow the missioners to remain perma-

nently he should have it for nothing, or his own royal
equipage should be thoroughly renovated and decorated.
Consequently the long delayed sanction was given on
18th October, and immediately after Father Depelchin,
accompanied by the lay-brother, started for Tati, to
bring up an additional wagon, and some members of
the little company that had been left there. Father
Law remained alone at Gubulawayo to keep the King
in good humour and hold the position they had gained.

There is no doubt that in giving his sanction to the
Fathers to remain at the kraal, Lo Bengula was principally, if not exclusively, actuated by the conviction
that their presence there would be advantageous to
himself, in so much as they would render material
services both to him and to his subjects. The skill he
had observed in them for various mechanical arts
biassed him in their favour, and Mr. Fairbairn had
represented to him how well it would be for him if he
could have his gun and his wagon repaired in his own
capital and under his own eye. The missionaries, he
assured him, would do all such things for him, and
what was more, would teach these arts to his subjects.
The Fathers had, since their arrival, daily paid a visit
of courtesy to the royal hut, and day by day the savage
monarch had appeared more pleased with his visitors,
and gave signs of increasing confidence in them. For
instance, a venomous snake had hidden itself among
the rocks, and defied the attempts of the natives to
destroy it. The King applied to the missioners; on
the next appearance of the reptile it was despatched by
a well-directed shot from a pistol. On another occasion
a messenger came from a distance of about eighteen
miles to report that a boy had been bitten by a snake.
Father Law was sent for. The King lent him a horse,

and accompanied by the messenger, who ran all the way by the side of the rider, he proceeded to the place where the sufferer was. "Luckily for me and my medical reputation," he says, "there was not much the matter with him. I was afraid I should find him *in extremis*, as he had been bitten about five hours. But the bite was not much. I administered some medicine to the boy, of which a third part was taken at once; the second dose I ordered to be taken when the sun was half-way down the heavens, and the remainder at sunset. The snake was a kind of cobra; at some seasons the bites are less dangerous than at others." The boy recovered, and we can easily believe that the angels guardian of the poor natives had a share in the cure, on account of the confidence it seemed to inspire in the missioners. In all the villages Father Law passed through he was welcomed and regaled with curdled milk. Some of the people came to him with their mouths open, pointing to the teeth that gave them pain, but he was hardly prepared to practise dental surgery even of the simplest kind. However, he was always ready to make himself all things to all men, and he soon became a favourite with the savages around him. We have seen him in Scotland, in Demerara, at Grahamstown, attracting men to himself in order that he might lead them to God, and the same principle actuated him now. He saw the aborigines enslaved by degrading superstitions, apparently inaccessible to the higher ideas of religion, and he felt the deepest compassion for them. *Misereor super turbam*, he said with His Divine Master; he hoped by gaining their affection to obtain influence over them, and induce them to listen to his instructions. He would allow a crowd of Kafirs to collect around him and remain for hours while he

played on the flute for their amusement, although, as
is well known, the offensive odour of the black men is
almost insupportable for any length of time. One day
while the little party were at dinner in their tent, a man
stalked in and rudely proclaimed that he was hungry.
The others bade him go away, but Father Law rose
from his seat in the kindest manner and emptied the
contents of his plate, as yet almost untasted, into
the hands of the intruder. During the absence of the
other missioners he lived in the house of one of the
traders, and pursued his study of the language, a
dialect of Zulu, so vigorously, as soon to be able to
converse in it sufficiently well to dispense with the
services of an interpreter.

Meanwhile, Father Depelchin had journeyed with
all possible speed back to Tati, taking with him all
manner of supplies, including a flock of sheep and
goats, for the re-victualling of the camp that had been
established there. These provisions were most welcome
to the missioners who had been left there. For the
first four or five weeks of their sojourn in the region of
the gold-fields they had wanted for nothing, the Boer-
hunters having furnished them with game of all kinds
and eggs in abundance. But their best friends had
gone to a distance, and they had been reduced to sore
straits before the return of Father Depelchin. The
relations between the missioners and the members of
this little settlement in the wilderness had been most
cordial. The suspicion entertained by Boers for Catholic
priests is very great, and their ignorance of our religion
well-nigh indescribable. This feeling at first prevailed
over the pleasure the settlers experienced at seeing
European faces, and hearing news of the remote world.
But this state of things did not last long. One of the

Boers ventured to ask whether the Fathers worshipped a woman instead of God. This question opened the way to the removal of the distrust, and the commencement of friendship and confidence. The men listened with attention day after day to instructions on the truths of religion. Every Sunday they assisted at Mass, and heard sermons delivered in their own language by one of the Fathers; and if unfortunate circumstances had not obliged some of them to depart elsewhere, it was hoped they would have enrolled themselves in the ranks of the faithful.

They had, moreover, an opportunity of showing in a practical manner their kind feelings towards the missioners, for no sooner had Father Croonenberghs arrived in Tati, than he was laid up by a severe attack of rheumatic fever, which deprived him of the use of his limbs, so that for three weeks he could not leave his bed. It was most providential that this illness had not overtaken the good missioner during the long and fatiguing journey that was just ended, amid the vicissitudes of heat and cold, of weariness and thirst to which he had been exposed in traversing mountain and plain, forest and desert. The hunters were assiduous in their attentions to the sick man. Day after day one or other would come and sit by the bed that had been made up for him in the tent, in order to cheer the long hours by their conversation or listen to him while he expounded to them the dogmas of the faith. Never did they come home laden with the spoils of the chase without bringing what was most delicate to tempt the appetite of the invalid. The other members of the mission shared also in the kindness of these strangers, so as to enable one of them to write: "Giraffe and buffalo, antelope and wild ostrich are now our daily food."

Father Croonenberghs was sufficiently recovered by the time that Father Depelchin arrived to accompany him on his return to Gubulawayo. He was chosen for the Mission on account of his talent for painting; Brother Hedley and Brother Nigg were also selected because of their skill in various handicrafts. It may perhaps at first sight appear as if these considerations were of secondary importance in comparison to the great work which it is the object of the missioner to accomplish. But those who look below the surface of things will perceive that it is necessary to find something the savages can understand and appreciate, something by which they will recognize the missioner's superior knowledge and ability, and the material benefits he is able to confer on them, before introducing to their notice those supernatural truths which at first would prove empty and even unpleasant sounds to their ears. The true artist despises nothing that leads even remotely to the perfection of his work, and knows that the lower he lays the foundation, the more secure will be the edifice he hopes to raise on it.

Accordingly, Brother Hedley, an old ship's carpenter and sail-maker, at once set to work to repair the King's wagon, under the direction and with the assistance of Father Law. The work was done to perfection. The wagon, covered entirely afresh, looked like new. When it had been painted and decorated by Father Croonenberghs it excited universal and ecstatic admiration. The King himself was so delighted that he stood contemplating it for hours together. And when, as the finishing stroke, an heraldic device was added to this royal chariot, consisting of an assegai and battle-axe surmounted by a crown, as the Imperial arms of the Matabele monarch, his gratitude and joy

knew no bounds. In general, Father Croonenberghs'
talents gave the King great satisfaction. He received
permission to go into every part of the kraal, even into
the sacred burial-place of the kings, where it was death
to enter. Moreover he received a commission to make
a picture of the " great dance," representing the King
at the head of his whole army all arrayed in their war
costume of ostrich feathers. This dance is to celebrate a
great solemnity, the feast of the first-fruits, kept soon
after the New Year, before which no one is allowed to
touch the fruits of the season. It is interesting to see
here a rite of the Mosaic law represented by the customs
of this savage tribe. Father Law, who witnessed the
dance, tells us the sight was very fine. " Four thousand
men in full war costume, with shields and assegais, and
imposing head-dresses of black ostrich plumes, danced
and sang for about an hour. Afterwards they formed
into squares, and filed in good order back into the
kraal. As we stood just outside the entrance we had
a good view of the flower of the Matabele warriors, for
they passed us as it were in review. A finer set of men
I never saw. Amongst the dancers we noticed about
ten men whose head-dress struck us as being of a
peculiar and novel description. It consisted of a good-
sized book, which they wore spread open, fastened on
the head so that the pages fluttered in the wind at
every movement of the dancer. We discovered that
the volumes put to so original a use were Protestant
Bibles."

The answer given by the King before Father
Depelchin's journey to Tati was not conclusive. However, on the return of the missioners he confirmed the
permission granted them to establish themselves per-
manently in his kingdom. He furthermore sanctioned

their purchase of the premises of Mr. Greite, the trader who wished to leave the country. An agreement for the transfer of the property was consequently drawn up. Two cottages of stone for a dwelling-house, another of iron to be employed as a storehouse, besides a stable, all of which were surrounded by a fence, were handed over to Father Depelchin. The missioners proposed to start a farm on a piece of land attached to the property, situated about eighteen miles from the town, in a fertile and well-watered valley. They hoped, as soon as circumstances would permit, to build a house there and raise vegetables and maize, which, dressed in various ways, formed the staple of their diet. This first station in Central Africa was dedicated to the Sacred Heart. Pending the evacuation of the premises by the trader's family, the wagons were drawn into the enclosure, and the missioners continued to live in them, while they made use of the stable as a chapel. There it was that Christmas found them, and again a stable served for all that was most holy upon earth. Thus the Mass of the Nativity was celebrated amid surroundings that vividly recalled those of the great event it commemorated. The altar was decked as well as it could be in the most decent part of the building. Not far off on one side was a flock of sheep, on the other a horse. The little community and two or three white men and as many blacks took the place of the shepherds, and the angels certainly were present there, when at midnight the Victim Whose condescension and love know no end was offered up for the unhappy Africans.

The Society of Jesus had now obtained the immediate object of its desires, a footing in the capital of this powerful tribe, and the real work of the Mission

was about to begin. The first endeavour of the Fathers
was to become better acquainted with the language of
the people, and to gain their confidence more and more.
This did not prove a difficult task. The medical skill
of the Fathers was frequently called into requisition by
the natives. The King sought their aid in a severe
attack of rheumatism, and they earned the gratitude of
the Induna of a village three days' journey from the
town, by curing him of opthalmia, a malady very
prevalent among the people. When they refused payment for this service, saying it was done for the love of
"the King above," the man's astonishment and delight
was unbounded, and he promised them abundance of
flocks and herds if they would settle in the country
under his jurisdiction. Somewhat later he brought to
them his daughter, who had been ill for two years,
imploring them to cure her. For her, too, they prescribed with success. One of their earliest patients
was a poor Hottentot leper, who presented himself at
the house of Mr. Martin, a trader with whom Father
Croonenberghs, on account of his recent illness, took
up his abode on his arrival at Gubulawayo. The
loathsome disease was gradually eating away his flesh,
the first and second joints of several fingers being
entirely gone. His family had thrust him out from
amongst them ; naked and alone, the miserable outcast
wandered about seeking shelter among the rocks, only
venturing amongst men in order to obtain wherewithal
to support life, often only to be repulsed by them with
scorn. Mr. Martin charitably took compassion on him;
he was clothed and fed, and the Fathers erected a small
hut for him near their enclosure. There one or other
of them visited him from time to time, to instruct him
in the truths of Christianity. Each day he dragged

himself to the door of the mission, and laid down his porringer to be filled with meat and vegetables from the Father's table. This poor Hottentot was their first convert. It is to be hoped that when his soul was released from its horrible prison, it was carried by the angels to the presence of God.

These and other tangible benefits were enough to establish the reputation of the missioners with Lo Bengula and his people. But the crowning triumph was achieved by what appears to us a simple thing. In one of his visits to the mission, the King chanced to hear Brother Nigg, who, it appears, fulfilled the duties of tailor as well as cook, at work with his sewing-machine. Nothing would content him but that the Brother should go to the royal hut, for the purpose of exhibiting before the Court the manner of working this marvel of mechanical ingenuity. The King had seen a great many wonders, but a machine that could sew was too much. It was more than he could believe. Accordingly a solemn exhibition was arranged. The principal Queens and Indunas were invited to attend. The Brother carried the machine upon his shoulder into the hut and placed it in the centre; some skins were produced, and operations commenced. Lo Bengula watched every motion intently; in a few minutes three neatly finished powder bags were displayed to his wondering eyes. In his delight he ordered an ample repast to be placed before the Brother, the viands coming from his own royal table. The comments of this King were above those of a savage. "What people these English are" (he gave this name to all Europeans), he exclaimed in the Zulu tongue; "how clever and skilful they are! They can do almost everything, and yet they must die like ourselves!" One might almost imagine that he had read the words: "You are gods, and all of you the sons of the Most High. But you like men shall die, and shall fall like one of the princes."[1]

The Fathers did not need to be reminded by a heathen potentate that they too were mortal. Each one felt that more than most men he held his life by an uncertain tenure. The reckless indifference wherewith this swarthy despot condemned his subjects to death, warned them that should they have the misfortune to lose his favour or excite his wrath, a similar fate would probably be theirs. Besides their resources might fail, and no further supplies be forthcoming; or more likely still, they might fall victims to one of the maladies which abound in Africa and prove fatal to many Europeans. Bishop Ricards remarked to one of the Jesuit Fathers in Grahamstown, that he had felt convinced, on seeing the caravan depart, that each one of the band of missioners had· made the sacrifice of his life in the cause for which he was to labour. This had indeed soon to prove the case with one of the party who had been left at Tati. Father Fuchs, whose delicate constitution unfitted him to bear the fatigues of the journey, had rapidly lost the little strength he possessed. In January of the following year he succumbed to an attack of fever. He died peacefully, calm and resigned, with a smile upon his lips, after having received the last rites of the Church at the hands of Father Blanca, who at that time with one lay-brother, himself sick, was his only companion. He was followed to the grave by two white men, one a Protestant, the other a Catholic; and there in that desert spot rest the remains of this first offering of the

[1] Psalm lxxxi. 6.

Mission, an example of devotion, and now an inter-
cessor for the souls he sought to save.

There is little doubt that not one amongst our band
of missionaries expected ever to see their native land
again. Father Law plainly expresses his conviction
that they will never meet again on earth in a letter he
wrote to his father at the close of the year. In fact
the persuasion that he was going forth to return no
more appears to have taken possession of his mind
before he left Grahamstown, since one of the last
meditations he wrote before his departure is headed
by these words of holy Job, which foreshadow the
destiny that awaited him: "Behold short years pass
away, and I am walking in a path by which I shall not
return. My spirit shall be wasted, my days shall be
shortened, and only the grave remaineth for me."[1]
What more suitable words could he have chosen, had
he foreseen the disappointment and apparent failure
that would weigh down his spirits, the fatigue and
privations that would cut short his days while yet in
the prime of life, the lonely grave that awaited him
in the sands of an African desert before the year now
opening should reach its close. The letter to which
reference has been made runs as follows: "I cannot
expect to see any of my dear relations again in this
world, but the separation is for Jesus Christ, and He
will know how to manage that we shall be no losers by
it in eternity. I beg dearest May and you, dear Father,
and all my brothers and sisters to help me by their
prayers, and to think that as I am here, the Amandabele country is specially confided to their prayers. So
in their visits to the Blessed Sacrament, let them
sometimes repair the want of devotion to the Blessed

---

[1] Job xvi. 23; xvii. 1.

Sacrament which there is here through ignorance of the
faith.   In their acts of contrition let them grieve for
the sins of the Amandabele, who do not understand
sin or sorrow for it.   In their acts of adoration let
them give God some homage for the poor Amandabele,
who do nothing for God.   And when praying to the
Blessed Virgin Mary let them pray to her for them,
and she will be moved when she looks at such great
misery as is here."

And in the commencement of the year (1880) he
wrote to his friend at Grahamstown in a somewhat
similar strain : " I write one line to wish you a happy
new year, and the same to all my friends at Grahamstown.   I wish you abundant graces this new year, and
much progress in contrition, in the love of God, in the
love of prayer.   May I beg you to ask the same for me ?
We are hastening on to eternity.   May we more and
more often ask ourselves, like St. Stanislaus Kostka,
'What is this to eternity?'   Let us think of what
the Roman Catechism says of Heaven, 'that the
thought of it should make the hardest things we have
to bear easy and even pleasant.'   I recommend myself
anew to your prayers.   May God bless you and give
you plenty of hope.   May He grant us both a happy
death, that we may be together for ever in a blissful
eternity."

CHAPTER XVII.

A FRESH ENTERPRISE.

IT may perhaps be asked why the Fathers of the Society were so desirous of making a permanent settlement in the capital of the Matabele kingdom, instead of pressing forward to the river from which the Mission took its name. For this there were several reasons. (1) The distance from the Colony rendered it necessary to establish their head-quarters at an accessible spot in the interior which could serve as a basis of operations, and a means of keeping open their communication with the civilized world. (2) To have entered the valley of the Zambesi during the hot, rainy season, lasting from November to March, would have been to expose the whole party to almost certain death. During that period violent storms follow each other in rapid succession, the clouds deliver perfect salvoes of electrical discharges, accompanied by deluges of rain, which fill the ravines with rushing torrents, and render travelling impossible. (3) Since the authority of Lo Bengula was paramount throughout the whole region consigned to the Jesuit Fathers, it was indispensable for them to secure his protection and friendship, as no stranger is permitted to pass through the country without obtaining his sanction. But as far as the evangelization of the people amongst whom they had pitched their tent was concerned, a few months'

S

residence in their midst was sufficient to convince
the missioners that this was a task, if not altogether
hopeless, at any rate of immense difficulty. Although
the monarch and his subjects showed great eagerness
to avail themselves of the medical and mechanical skill
of the new-comers, they were more than indifferent to
their spiritual teaching. Bred to war, slaves to
witchcraft, with polygamy an institution among them,
the hearts of Matabele seemed to offer only a sterile
and stony soil wherein to sow the seeds of Christianity.
A recent traveller speaking of them says: " The people
are truly far from God. If there is such a state as
unpreparedness of mind for the Gospel, then are the
Matabele unprepared. No people could need it more;
none could be less prepared or inclined to receive it.
To preach the Gospel, in point of fact, was to condemn
their whole social system from its very roots."[1] Utterly
unable to comprehend any supernatural motive, they
recognized a power of evil, whom they sought to
appease by magical ceremonies, and had of a Supreme
Being only the vaguest idea, for they paid Him no
worship nor associated Him with any rites. *Induratum
est cor eorum,* the missionaries were compelled to
acknowledge; only a miracle of grace could change
these stones of Gubulawayo into sons of Abraham.
Even the Protestant missionaries, who had been
among them for twenty years, and had engaged in
commercial transactions, did not profess to have made
a single convert. In fact the adoption of Christianity
was forbidden in the kingdom, and the people were so
enslaved to their absolute monarch that no man would
dare, were he so inclined, to become a Christian
without his consent. " Lo Bengula," writes Father

[1] Mackenzie, *Ten Years North of the Orange River,* p. 332.

Law, "is very friendly, and is naturally of a good heart. Personally I like him very much, and he is well disposed towards white people. But the detestable Zulu system, which gives unlimited and irresponsible power to a chief, is enough to spoil the best nature. I am afraid it will be very hard to make Christians of men so utterly dependent on their chief. Only if the King's heart were touched by grace could the conversion of his subjects become possible, so complete is their subservience to this sovereign arbiter of life and death."

It will perhaps be remembered that the new Queen, whose espousals with Lo Bengula were the great event of the day when our missioners arrived at the royal residence, was the daughter of Umzila, chief of the Abagasi, another powerful tribe of the Zulu race. This Princess was accompanied to her future home by a large escort of her father's subjects, and with this party Father Law had some intercourse while the missioners were in attendance upon Lo Bengula, "running about the Veldt," as he expressed it, "after the King." The courtesy with which they received him, and the interest with which they listened to him while he expounded the object that led the missioners to penetrate into the interior of Africa, awakened in his breast an ardent desire to carry the tidings of salvation into their country. Both the Princess and her attendants assured him that he might count upon a kind reception from the chief and the people, who would gladly welcome the teachers of religion. Father Law regarded his meeting with this embassy, or rather its presence at the Court of the Matabele King at this juncture, as a providential dispensation to indicate to him the field of apostolic labour wherein he was called to work. He writes: " The people of Umzila seem a far nicer people than the Amandabele. They appeared delighted at the thought of some of us going there. The Protestant missionaries are not yet in their country. They say Umzila would receive us very kindly; of this I have no doubt. I should be intensely delighted if I were sent there, which is not impossible. When I showed them a picture of the Crucifixion, one of the Indunas, pointing to the figure upon the Cross, said, *That is true.* I was much struck with the remark. They appear to me a peaceful, well-disposed people, who already show signs of the beginning of faith. There is here a soil which if cultivated would yield a rich harvest."

Another incident, trivial in itself, that occurred at this time served to strengthen the good opinion which the interviews with the daughter of Umzila and the men in attendance on her had led Father Law to form of this people. One morning he had gone out, as his frequent custom was, to wash some linen in a little stream that ran through the brushwood about twenty minutes' walk from the place where the wagon was drawn up. About two hours after his return, just as he was sitting down to dinner, he discovered that his pocket-knife was missing; he must have left it by the side of the stream. This loss disconcerted him greatly, but he thought it hardly worth while to revisit the spot where he had been in the morning, as the Kafirs were encamped all about by the water-side, and they would doubtless have long since espied the knife and picked it up. So he resigned himself to bid farewell to his knife. Not long after, three or four of the chief men of the embassy were descried approaching; the Fathers wondered what errand of importance led them thither;

it was to bring back the missing article which they had found and were desirous of restoring to its owner. Father Law was very pleased at recovering his knife, which he had despaired of ever seeing again, and no less pleased and surprised at the honesty of the strangers, for honesty is a virtue foreign to the Kafir nature, and the missioners had constantly to be on their guard against the thievish propensities of the Matabele. This proof of the superiority of Umzila's people increased Father Law's desire to become their apostle, but no thought could be entertained of executing his design until the spring was well advanced, and the cessation of the rains rendered travelling practicable. Thus all further missionary explorations were of necessity deferred until April or May, when it was expected that some recruits from Europe, sent out by the Father General of the Society to strengthen the hands of the Fathers, would have arrived at Gubulawayo. Father Depelchin then proposed to lead a little band of labourers to the ultimate goal of the Mission, the country about the Zambesi River; and it was resolved that somewhat later, Father Law should start on the desired expedition to Umzila's dominions, the promised land of his radiant hopes.

Meanwhile preparations for the journey were entered upon, and information sought from all who were qualified to give it as to the character of the country to be traversed, and the best means of transport. The accounts given did not afford much encouragement to the intending travellers. The traders and hunters who were acquainted with the land agreed in affirming that it was fertile, and abounded in game; that the inhabitants were intelligent and, for the most part, fairly peaceable. But the route was said to be of the most difficult description; through high jungle and along roads almost impassable for wagons up to the Sabi River, while beyond that point all attempts to proceed otherwise than on foot would be utterly vain. One merchant, narrating his own experiences as leader of a caravan consisting of five wagons and seventeen men, said that he had been compelled to abandon his design of penetrating further, and to return to Gubulawayo. The journey back had only been accomplished with extreme difficulty, and with diminished numbers, four of the party having fallen victims to the African fever.

Reports such as these might have disheartened any man less sanguine and enthusiastic than Father Law. On him they had no such effect. He considered himself inspired by God to undertake this enterprise, and could not rest without obeying the Divine command. It was useless to attempt to dissuade him from the project. At one time it was rumoured that the new Queen would be returning to her own country on a visit to her royal father, and it was suggested that Father Law should travel in her suite, but the plan came to nothing. All that remained was to obtain the authorization of Lo Bengula, and determine upon the means of transport. In regard to the latter, the option lay between the wagon and Kafir porters; the wagon was chosen, as being less expensive and more trustworthy.

When Father Law spoke of asking Lo Bengula for permission to go and found a mission in Umzila's land, a merchant who had been acquainted with the King for many years told him that there was no likelihood of his obtaining it. Father Law only smiled, and said, "We shall see." Then he asked the merchant to go with him the next morning to the royal hut, and help him plead his cause. The man was evidently flattered;

he assented willingly. On the morrow accordingly they asked an audience of the King. On the way to the kraal, the merchant reiterated his assurances that they might just as well have remained at home, for any chance they had of gaining their object. Again Father Law said, "We shall see," adding, "I mean to ask him to let me go, to ask a hundred times over, if needs be." They were admitted at once to the presence of the King, who liked to receive the visits of white men. Father Law told him wherefore he had come. The King inquired for what purpose did he wish to take this journey? "To teach the people the way of salvation, not to pursue the chase or carry on commercial transactions," was the answer. After two or three inquiries respecting the arrangements of the expedition, the King said: "Very well, you may go, I give my consent." Then unable to restrain an outburst of genuine admiration for the humble religious standing before him, he exclaimed: "That is what I call a true man, for he has but one mouth; his heart speaks the same as his mouth, and his heart is good. Yes, the heart of the *umfundisi* (teacher) is very good." The merchant sitting by was not a little surprised at the result of the interview being so very different to what he had anticipated. Perhaps had his services as interpreter been employed, the reception might have been less favourable, and the royal consent less easily obtained. Fortunately Father Law was able to proffer his request and explain his plans in the Zulu tongue. Finding Lo Bengula so graciously inclined, he ventured to ask him to supply the guides he would require, offering, if he would do so, to leave with him the large handsome dog, Prince, which was a gift from the people at Kimberley. The monarch had often cast wistful eyes on the fine animal; he gladly agreed to these conditions, and the bargain was forthwith made.

Writing to his father on April 8th, Augustus Law announced his approximate departure.

Father Depelchin, our Superior, left yesterday *en route* for Zambesi. It was an affecting parting, for he is old, and going of course to a place very dangerous to one's health. Then I too start in May for Umzila's country, so that it may be that we never see each other again in this life. There are some wagons coming up with some more Fathers. Father Depelchin will first meet them and then go up to Zambesi, taking those he wants with him. Some will come here, and directly they arrive, I start. The King has promised to send me four or five men, as guides. That will be a good thing for this reason also, it will be a kind of introduction for me from Lo Bengula to Umzila. The two chiefs are on good terms. The people have never yet been taught anything about the Christian religion, so we hope much for their conversion. They are said to be a more tractable people than the Amandabele, though they too are Zulus. The knowledge of the language is now more indispensable to me than ever, as the same is spoken by both the tribes, with the exception of a few words. I trust you will pray for our expedition, and will you get all the prayers you can for the same object? For it belongs to God to give the precious gift of faith. As Father Depelchin reminded us yesterday, " Unless the Lord build the city, in vain they labour who build it." You can think of my joy on going on such a mission.

Then he turns from the pagans of Africa to one who had wandered from the faith at home. " Next month I hope to write a kind letter to poor dear Graves. I always hope about him. God will hear us if we persevere in prayer."

On May the 30th, he penned the last letter (except one brief note) which his father ever received from him. It dates from a village about nine miles from Gubulawayo, when he had already started upon the journey that was to cost him his life.

You see I am off for Umzila's. I arrived here on Friday, and am only waiting now for the King to give me his two guides, and then we start in earnest on our journey. I hope to send a letter again from Ingati, as there is a regular post from there. The direction in which I go is this: first N.E. by E. two hundred and twenty miles, till we get not far from Umtigesa. We cross the Sabi and then go down about S.S.E., until we get to Umzila's kraal. This last bit will be about one hundred and thirty miles. Umzila's is not so far as the crow flies, but we cannot go straight, as there would be at least sixty miles of tsetse-fly to pass through.[1] And as we have a wagon, we cannot pass through that way as we should lose all our oxen. Even by the route we take, we may not escape the fly altogether, but we hope the patches where the fly is found will not be so wide that we cannot run through them during the night, when the fly is torpid and does not bite. If we

---

[1] The tsetse-fly, *glossina morsitans*, is about half an inch in length, of a brown colour, striped with yellow. Comparatively harmless to man, its poisonous bite is fatal to horses, oxen, dogs, and asses. The bite is scarcely perceptible at the time ; after two or three days the effect begins to be apparent, and death speedily ensues.

succeed in getting our wagon to Umzila's, we shall have the honour of being the first wagon that ever made the journey. We shall have plenty of game on the road, and shall have to look out well for the lions. Some tell us that we shall be lucky if we lose no oxen by the lions. However, we say the *Itinerarium* every day, and so shall have God's protection. I hope you will pray much that the hearts of Umzila and his people may be disposed to receive the faith. Father Wehl, an Austrian Father, one who has just arrived from Europe, Brother Sadeleer, a Belgian lay-brother, and Brother Hedley, an English one, formerly a sailor, like myself, are my companions. It is most likely that letters will come and go more quickly between Europe and Umzila's country than between Europe and here, for Umzila's kraal is only one hundred and thirty-eight miles from the sea. There are two English traders who trade in Umzila's from Natal, and many Portuguese. So at last my knowledge of Portuguese will come in useful again. Messengers only take ten days from here to Umzila's. But we shall probably be over a month, for what with reconnoitring for the tsetse-fly, and what with making roads for ourselves in many places, and what with every now and then sticking in the mud, and having to unload the wagon, we may have many a delay. However I hope to be not more than six weeks. Good-bye for the present, dearest father. I hope you have gone through this winter all right, and that you may live for many years to encourage and bless us all.

The dominions of Umzila, to whose kraal the travellers were bound, occupy all the coast land between the Zambesi River in the north, and the Limpopo in the south, and in the west are bounded by the Matabele territory. If, as is generally surmised, this wide tract of land formed a part of the great native kingdom of Monomotapa, in former times, it is perhaps hardly correct to assert, as we did on a past page, that Father Law was the earliest pioneer of Christianity, the first to lay down his life for the salvation of the heathen in this remote and savage country. More than three centuries before it had been the scene of the martyrdom of another member of the Society of Jesus. It is recorded that the Venerable Gonzalez Silveira, a Portuguese Jesuit, while engaged in missionary work on the East Coast of Africa, was seized with the desire to explore and evangelize the vast Monomotapa kingdom, lying some hundreds of miles inland from the territory of Portugal. After an arduous journey of many months, made entirely on foot, carrying the altar furniture on his shoulders, wading through many rivers, transported over others on native rafts, he reached the capital on St. Stephen's day, 1560. The King received him favourably, and was much struck by his dis-interestedness in refusing the presents offered him, amongst which gold is specified. A statue of the Madonna seen in his house was taken for a real woman by the natives, who repeated to the King that the stranger had brought a wife with him. The King on seeing the statue, requested that it should be left with him, to which the Father gladly consented. For five nights in succession the monarch had a dream, in which a similar figure appeared to him, and addressed him in an unknown language; and so great was the impression made on him that he desired to become a Christian. He was baptized with three hundred of his subjects, about thirty days after Father Silveira's arrival.

But the missioner's rapid success alarmed the jealousy of the Mahommedan residents. They plotted his destruction, accusing him to the King of being a Portuguese spy, come to subvert his kingdom. Their machinations were successful; the King ordered his execution. Eight assassins, stealing into his hut at night, strangled him with a cord and threw his body into the river, on the 15th of March, 1561. His death was followed by a partial massacre of his converts, but led to reprisals on the part of the Portuguese, who invaded the kingdom and expelled the Mahommedan settlers. The early annals of the Jesuit missions in Africa record that the disruption of the kingdom took place shortly after; at any rate it is heard of no more in history. Those who are acquainted with this region think that a considerable portion of Matabeleland and the whole of Umzila's kingdom were included in it. If this be so, the Jesuits were led back, through the zeal and devotion of Father Law, to the very spot hallowed by the labours and death of one of their Order, and he may be said to have entered upon this mission as the heir of the Portuguese martyr. Is it not perhaps possible that the recognition of the sign of our redemption by the Indunas when it was shown them by Father Law, may have been owing to a remnant of Catholic tradition, left behind by the first apostle of the land?

However this may be, our brave missioner set forth, as will have been seen from the extracts of his letters, upon this dangerous journey, full of confidence and courage. He felt extremely happy when appointed by his Superior to lead this expedition to Umzila's country. He had already had experience of the trials and difficulties of African travel, and he did not fear to encounter the same or greater ones in order to accomplish the object on which his heart was set. All the time he stayed in the Matabele country he was constantly reading, writing, talking with natives and with others who might assist him to acquire a thorough practical knowledge of the Zulu tongue, which differs little amongst the various tribes. This knowledge was of the greatest service to him now. His practical acquaintance with astronomy too would enable him to steer his course in the desired direction by taking observations of the sun where landmarks failed to guide him, and he would besides be able to make charts of the wild and then almost unknown country for the guidance of those of his brethren who should follow after him. For a portion of the way his little caravan would travel in the company of the wagons of three Englishmen, two of whom, practical huntsmen, were going to shoot elephants in the Mashona valleys, while the third, a doctor, was desirous of exploring the country in the interests of natural science. The escort of these gentlemen, a thrifty Belgian Father remarked, would be an immense advantage to our missioners as far as providing for their table is concerned, but not in regard to their cellar, since we all know how thirsty is the hunter after the exertions of the chase.

The missionary band consisted only of Father Law and Father Charles Wehl, with two lay-brothers. Father Wehl was a pious and devoted missioner, and a great lover of solitude and prayer, as will be seen later on, when the perilous adventure he met with is narrated. Of the Brothers, one, Brother Hedley, who

was afterwards to be the sole companion of Father
Law's last hours, was a simple, unaffected man. A
sailor in the merchant service previously to his entrance
into religion, his way had lain rather on the stormy
than on the smooth side of life. Early inured to
hardships, it was no matter for surprise to find him
volunteering, shortly after he took his vows, for the
African Mission. He was much attached to Father
Law, with whom he had been associated when the first
band of missioners left the Cape Colony for the interior,
and so was his comrade, Brother de Sadeleer. This was
the Brother who had been chosen to accompany Father
Depelchin and Father Law when they separated from
their colleagues at Tati, and went onward to seek the
favour of Lo Bengula. Brother de Sadeleer was greatly
edified by many little secret acts of self-denial and
charity on the part of Father Law, which did not
escape his quick observation. One night, when the tem-
perature had fallen very low, and the Kafir attendants,
never over-burdened with clothing, lay shivering on the
damp ground, their teeth chattering with cold, the
Brother saw him fetch his thickest blanket and offer
it to them. Now every one who has had to do with
savages knows that anything lent to them is spoilt for
the use of a European, for it comes back peopled with
a colony of vermin. " I reminded him of this," the
Brother says, " but he only laughed and told me it did
not matter. I thought it would be a lesson to him, but
no such thing; he did the same again and again,
although I know the consequences were most unpleasant. More than once I saw him give his dinner
away to one of the blacks whose appetite was not fully
satisfied by his own ration. His liberality in giving
presents, and the indulgence he showed in condoning

offences, gained for him amongst our 'boys' the title of 'the very kind teacher.' And indeed he deserved it."

Two natives, besides a Hottentot called by the singular name *Cape Corps*, had been engaged for the expedition. Tom, the driver, was to receive about £4 per month; Zambesi, the leader, was to have a gun given him at the end of the journey. The guides promised by the King were not in the missioners' pay. They were, however, to receive a blanket and some beads in remuneration for their services. These guides, for whom Father Law was waiting, did not make their appearance until June 3rd. And when they arrived, he found to his astonishment that not only had they never been to Umzila's, but that they knew nothing of the way. However, with his happy facility for making the best of things, he said he was not sorry for their ignorance, as at least they would let the missioners take their own way, and not lead them astray by "a little knowledge."

The following letter, dated from the First Mashona kraal, about thirty miles from the Sabi River, was sent from Father Law to Father de Wit, who was then stationed at Gubulawayo, by some Matabele hunters who were returning thither. It narrates the incidents of the first part of the journey.

Here we are, and thanks to God, all safe and sound. We have crossed since leaving Umganini twenty-two rivers, not counting spruits and sluits, some of them difficult enough. No one should ever attempt this journey without a good driver, which Tom is. We arrived at the Poort between the mountains on the 20th June, and rested there for one day. There is a

kraal close to the Poort, from which we got a very
good guide as far as here. We gave him a red soldier's
coat and a shirt. You should have seen him dance
for joy when he got them.

On June 22nd, the gentlemen hunters left us. They
have been very kind and civil to us. It has been a
great advantage to us to travel in company with them.
One day the doctor's wagon stuck fast in the bed of a
river, and we lent him our span to pull it across.
When we were crossing the Sebakwe River we had
to have one of their spans to help us up the other side.
They always shared with us the proceeds of the chase.
The day after they left, Brother de Sadeleer shot a fine
bless-buck (antelope). This was a great acquisition, as
we have twelve mouths to fill. Our men have lived on
it ever since. Nothing more has been shot, but game
seems plentiful, and I hope we shall soon be well
provided. We still have two bucks which we bought,
and plenty of other provisions. Besides we are amongst
the kraals again now.

I got some fever about a week after leaving, and it
stuck to me three or four days. I took St. Ignatius'
water, but of course did not neglect natural remedies.
Every one else has been quite well. The weather has
been very cloudy lately, so I have not been able to
take a lunar observation, which I am sorry for. I shall
take one the first opportunity.

All our boys, driver, Hottentot leader, King's two
boys, give great satisfaction. We could not have
wished for better. The oxen are in fair condition. It
is well we took a spare one, as one of the hinder oxen
is lame from a stone bruising or cutting his feet. We
have only had one regular stick, and that was three
days ago, in a kind of half river, half swamp. At last

we had to unload the wagon, and then we got out. It is well that our wagon is comparatively light. Every now and then the bush is very thick, and then it is we are thankful we have a good driver. The leader's duty too is no sinecure, and I think Zambesi (one of the natives) will deserve the gun that was promised him before his ten months are out.

The whole kraal I should think must be sitting round us. The people here seem a nice, simple, civil people.

Rain prevented the travellers from proceeding on their way until the 1st July, and then they only covered six miles, for in crossing one of the many rivers which intersected the country through which their route lay, the wagon stuck fast for nearly two hours, and again later on it got imbedded in a marsh and had to be half unloaded before it could be dragged out, a work of great labour. The journal kept by Father Law at this time shows that his spirits and courage enabled him to catch a favourable view of his surroundings. The following extracts are taken from it :

July 2, 1880.—Fine day after 11 a.m., after very cold damp weather now for three or four days. After two miles we got to a small kraal of Amaholi. They too seemed to be nice, simple people. What a happiness if we may soon get among them. They did not seem to have any cattle except goats. Perhaps they may have found poverty. the best security against their neighbours. Got to the river Sebundo about 3 p.m., which we crossed without difficulty, as time was taken to choose a good place. We crossed a stream also near the kraal without difficulty. Our outspan this

T

morning was in quite a romantic spot. We are just
under a beautifully wooded koppie on the river. On
our left, about a hundred yards across the road (we
have just come up from the river) is another similar
koppie. All through this country the scenery is often
very beautiful.

July 3.—Brother Sadeleer and Cape Corps got on
the spoor of an eland and followed it, but soon found
two lions wanted the eland, and were following it.
Somehow or other nothing has been shot since Brother
Sadeleer's antelope on the 23rd of June.

July 4.—Crossed at about nine a river that runs across
a sandy and rocky bottom. Started again at 1 p.m.,
but stuck fast through the rashness of our good driver,
who though he heard there was a better place to cross
the stream running between us and the kraal, went
straight over a very bad place, and down went the
wheels axle deep. Our dissel-boom, sprung last night,
was finished in fording this stream. The people of
these kraals are very civil and respectful. During the
unloading and loading of the wagon, instead of crowding
round to see all we had as the Amandabele would have
done, looking for an occasion of stealing, they all stood
at some distance off. The Induna here made us a
present of a goat, and we gave him a good present of
beads and cakes. It is amusing to see how soon the
people turn anything into an ornament. We opened
some sardine boxes, and amongst the crowd we now
see two or three with a sardine box tied on the top
of their heads.

July 5.—The kraal here is pitched upon the rocks,
and in passing these rocky hills we could see every now
and then a hut half hidden amongst rocks, and the
Kafir corn stored here and there on the heights. I

suppose this is done for safety's sake. Soon after our arrival, the Induna, a venerable old man, came up and made us a present of a buck. We also made him a present. He was accompanied by his musician, who danced and sang in our honour until he was tired. Whenever he wished to show particular honour to any one, he danced up to the person and drummed in his ears.

The next day, in spite of the rain, a good many were about the wagon nearly all day. The Mahatela band was in attendance, and gave out more agreeable music than the musician of yesterday. The women, seeing the band was rewarded, set off singing, but we had to draw the line somewhere. The rain kept us from going on. We got new guides here.

July 7.—What with cutting down trees, and avoiding big stones, and crossing the most difficult river we have met with on the journey, we had not got far when the time for outspanning arrived. In crossing the river, the wagon ought by all rules of equilibrium to have capsized, by taking too sharp a turn. I really believe our Angel Guardian held it up. At least we all agreed we ought to sing a *Te Deum*, which we did.

July 9.—Since about June 25th, on an average we had to cross either a river or a stream or a marsh at least every mile. To-day I was astonished to hear the familiar words *tusa mnali* (give a present), the true mark of the Amandabele, and sure enough there were two of them. Apparently they are up here to act as spies or police. We got most important information from them, to wit, that we were on the wrong road, going direct for the district infested by the fly. Indeed I have been perplexed as to why we are going so much to the S. of E., but I was always assured we were on

the road to Sehumhum. These men pointed out where
that place was, behind some hills bearing about N.E.,
instead of S.E. as we were heading. This afternoon
two women, to welcome us, kept up with the wagon for
about half an hour, dressing themselves with branches
of trees, running here and there and occasionally
prostrating themselves before the wagon, crying out,
" Wee, wee, wee." Poor things! may this be an
earnest of what their people will do for the holy faith
before long. One good thing comes from our missing
the road. It is that we have, as it were, explored the
people through whom we passed, and a nicer, simpler
people you could not find. The Induna of a kraal close
by brought a present of a goat and an immense pot of
Kafir beer. I mention the kraal, because if we ask
Lo Bengula to let us have a mission here, it might be
well to live near the kraal. No better place for a
mission than here, there are plenty of kraals all round,
filled with nice people.

Father Law was too hopeful as to Lo Bengula's
permission to found stations in this district. He did
not care to have his own people taught, and it was not
likely that he would have these Mashona tribes, his
subjects and tributaries, better instructed than those
immediately about him.

Day by day we read the record of slow progress, and
of endless rivers to be crossed. Of one of these Father
Law writes : " We got to a river magnificent to look
at, but not to cross in a wagon. I have seldom seen
anything grander. When I first saw it the wild
confusion of masses of rock piled upon one another in
every kind of fantastic way, the large surface of table-
like rock washed clear of all once upon it put me in

mind of the floes described by Kane and others in the
Arctic regions. If the scene was grand now in the dry
season, what would it be in the wet season, with
torrents of water rushing along these rocks? We
looked at one place that was spoken of as a ford, but
it was thought better to wait till the next day and then
look well for a crossing-place. It was curious to see
the people perched on rocks some one hundred and
twenty feet high, by the side of their huts, that looked
like bee-hives at that distance." The shooting of a
zebra by Brother Sadeleer two successive days was
regarded as a happy event, as it provided the party
with a stock of fresh meat. It may be asked what
could be done with so large a quantity, but one must
remember that the numbers were increased by the
addition of fresh guides, those supplied by the King
having confessed their inability to find the way, and
also by several blacks whose assistance was required in
clearing the road. The voracity of these Kafirs too is
astonishing; their capacity for eating meat, which they
devour in a raw state, being apparently unlimited.
And if there was any meat to spare, the missioners
were glad to exchange it for Kafir corn, ground by the
women between two large stones.

Every day the difficulties of the journey increased,
and the progress became slower. This we learn from
the record made by Brother Sadeleer, who did not see
men and things invested with the same roseate hues
as Father Law did. Let it not be supposed that the
worthy Brother ever complained of the trials that were
encountered; no, he only took a more prosy view of
matters. Where his Superior saw beautifully wooded
country, he saw thick bush and jungle through which
a way had laboriously to be cut. The constant

unloading and reloading of the wagon, that Father Law took so calmly, was to the Brother's eyes a vexatious expenditure of time and strength, one too which care on the part of the leader might often have avoided. On the 16th July the caravan reached the first branch of the Sabi River. "We went over all right," Father Law says, "with no hitch, so, thank God, we are now on the other side of the Sabi, and we have just got there on a feast of Mary. May she bless us in the new country into which we have just entered!" A few hours later, however, he records that they got into a dreadful sluit, the hole being so deep that only the heads of the oxen were visible, and the oft-repeated process of unloading had to be gone through again.

A few days more took the caravan to the Sabi proper, and this important boundary was passed without any accident except a slight breakage that was easily repaired. The entrance into the territory of another chief marks a stage in the journey; after which new difficulties and dangers presented themselves, in comparison to which those that had gone before were but the beginnings of sorrows.

CHAPTER XVIII.

ARRIVAL AT UMZILA'S KRAAL.

UP to the 25th July, made memorable by the passage
of the Sabi River, our travellers' journey had been
tolerably prosperous. The difficulties of the way had,
it is true, been numerous and immense, their progress
slow and tedious, and their guides had proved incom-
petent, but no serious misfortune had befallen the little
party, no insurmountable obstacle had been encountered. The missioners' health had, on the whole, been
excellent ; the inhabitants of the country through which
they passed had. shown themselves quiet and friendly ;
and thanks to Brother Sadeleer's gun, the commissariat
supplies had not run short. Two or three weeks' more
patient travelling would take them to Umzila's kraal.

But alas ! when once they had set their feet within
the territory of the tribes that nominally, at least,
acknowledged Umzila's sway, the face of affairs
entirely changed. The attitude of the people was
hostile, even menacing, and apprehensions, hitherto
unfelt, filled the hearts of the missioners. Their
guides insisted on making a slight *détour* to a village
called Isilambeyo, alleging that it was necessary to
obtain the permission of the local chieftain before
proceeding further. On the 31st July, no happy feast
for them, they arrived near the kraal of the petty
potentate, which was situated on the top of a

mountain, and halted there. A message was sent, bidding them bring the wagon nearer. So they went on about a quarter of a mile, but the only approach to the kraal was by a tortuous path up the hill-side, bristling with crags and interrupted by ravines, which it was impossible for the oxen to climb. Brother Sadeleer felt convinced that treachery was intended, and intimated as much to his unsuspecting Superior. Father Law accordingly determined to press onward as soon as guides were procured. His journal gives an account of the chieftain's visit.

August 1st.—I heard that Amalanga's people had said we should come nearer still, so I told Lo Bengula's boy to let them know the wagon could not go nearer, and even if it could, we had done enough to show him respect, that we were on our way from Lo Bengula to Umzila, and were anxious to get on. About nine he sent down a sheep and some *utjwala* (Kafir beer). About twelve he came in person. (1) We thanked him for the sheep and utjwala. (2) We made him a present of a black blanket, and a quarter of the zebra shot yesterday. (3) We said we were afraid it was too much to take the sheep from him, as we could get plenty of game on the road. He said it would make his heart sore if we did not keep it. (4) We asked for guides for the road. Here he said we had not made him a large enough present, although we really had, so we gave him another black blanket and a little gunpowder which he asked for. He promised to have the guides ready for to-morrow.

But the third day came, and the travellers were still waiting for their guides. Father Law grew anxious, and resolved to start that evening, with guides or without them. Presently the chief came again, and asked if Umzila knew they were coming, and when assured that this was the case, he appointed three men to accompany them, to each of whom a blanket was paid before starting. Well it was that the caravan moved off that evening, for they learnt by means of one of the " boys " who understood the language of the Amaholi (the tribe amongst whom they then were), that the people proposed killing the travellers and taking all their goods, and were only restrained by one of the head men, who feared reprisals on the part of the sovereign chief. As it was, a quarrel nearly arose in the camp when the next halt was made, for the Hottentot leader, overhearing Amalanga's guides discussing the conspiracy, began to dispute with one of them, and was only just prevented from shooting him by Brother Sadeleer's prompt interference.

For the next two or three days the wagon was followed or surrounded by groups of natives, whose fierce aspect and threatening gestures were anything but reassuring. Some of them occupied the defiles so as to impede the march, and lead the travellers to fear that an attack would be made on the wagon. " In the course of the second day," Father Law says, "an Induna came up, purporting to be the envoy of another petty chief, Hambehusuku, saying we ought to go to him too. As I found this would take us far out of the road, I said it was impossible, as we were going to Umzila's. The Induna replied: 'That concerns us very little; we are masters here, and King Umzila lives far away from our kraal.' In fact Umzila's authority seems little regarded here. We went on our way, Hambehusuku's people always hovering about us. I had heard he was the chief who killed white people ; and as far as we could make out, he was in league with Amalanga, who had informed him of our arrival and intimated to him that our wagon would be a prize well worth capturing. I felt here was the difficulty, and I always dreaded a collision with the natives."

On August 6th an event occurred which sadly disconcerted the missioners, and rendered their position still more painful. In the morning the Brothers had gone to Communion, and offered special prayer for direction as to the wisest course to be pursued. After consultation, it was agreed they should make what haste they could to go forward. Father Law felt it would be weakness to do otherwise, nor would it avoid danger, so he gave orders to proceed *in nomine Domini.*

That day one of the most difficult passes had been reached. After clearing a way through thick jungle with the hatchet, it became necessary to cut away the rock, to smooth in some measure a way for the oxen. It was a long and arduous piece of work, in which the Fathers took part, with their Matabele guides ; meanwhile they were surrounded by a crowd of savages, whose demeanour was more insolent and aggressive than ever. " Now," writes Father Law, " oh, the dreadful thing I have to tell! At 5 p.m., just towards the end of the outspan, Father Wehl was missed. I had seen him about two o'clock, walking a little too far, but still in sight of the wagon, and Brother de Sadeleer, who was with me sitting in front, said : ' Father Wehl goes too far.' I said, ' Yes, I will tell him to keep nearer when he comes back.' Alas! he never came back. He was very fond of solitude apparently, and often laughed at anything like risk at being far from the wagon, when cautioned against walking at a dangerous distance from the rest of the party. We were too much occupied in clearing the road, cutting down trees, &c., to observe his absence until 5 p.m., when some one said: ' Where is Father Wehl?' We at once fired five shots, the rallying signal of the caravan, which would have told him where we were, had he been still alive. Whenever we outspanned, he had the habit of going to some retired place to study or pray, and we often had to shout aloud to bring him when the meals were ready, and even then sometimes he was too far to hear. When we found he did not reappear, Brother Sadeleer remarked, ' I do not believe he is alive!' Brother Hedley said the last he had seen of him was when he was walking at some distance, followed by a lot of Amaholi. I myself did not know of this. I am sorry he did not tell me. An hour passed and there was no sign of him; we were really alarmed. I sent out all the natives in search of him, promising them great rewards if they found him. They returned without having seen him. What a night we passed!"

For three days—days of cruel anxiety and constant dread — Father Law waited, whilst his Matabele servants scoured the surrounding country without finding a trace of the lost missioner. What conclusion could be come to but that he had been carried off and murdered by the savages? Meanwhile Father Law was assured that the wagon sooner or later would certainly be attacked, and that all outlets by which it could pass onward were being watched. The crowd of Mashonas went on increasing round the little camp, and their attitude became more and more hostile. It appeared as if all would soon be over with the lives of the missioners, and the hopes of future work be extinguished. Consequently on the second day Father Law wrote in his journal: "I came to the resolution to-day, in case we cannot find the dear Father, to leave the wagon and walk to Umzila's. My reason is this. If we go on, all of us, even our Hottentot, who is not at all afraid, says we are certain to be attacked. Rather than have this conflict, where first we should have to use fire-arms with the natives, and secondly, the probability is we should all be killed, and the wagon of course plundered, I prefer to save the lives of the people committed to my care, and to sacrifice the wagon. If I were not a religious I would go on, for then I should be sure of an out-and-out defence."

It was plain that since Catholic missioners could not think of saving their life by force of arms, the only means to escape death was to take flight, and that immediately. On the third day, a council having been held, it was decided to abandon the wagon, which retarded the march, and which moreover must soon be left behind on account of the tsetse-fly. The vestments and sacred vessels, together with the arms, should be taken out, as well as the most indispensable articles, and the party proceed on foot by forced marches in the direction of Umzila's kraal.

The wisdom of Father Law's conduct in thus abandoning the wagon seems by some persons to have been called in question. It must be remembered that (1) he alone knew all the circumstances, and therefore he alone could judge securely what was to be done. (2) He clearly took the best course for forming his judgment; prayer, deliberation, consultation with his fellow-travellers. (3) The question had reduced itself apparently to a balance between saving the goods or the lives of his little band. There could be no question as to which it was his duty to prefer. One must admire the virtue which led him to decide in a manner that was contrary to the leanings that he as an old naval officer must naturally have felt. Had it not been for his sacred calling, he would have defended himself to the last. " God knows," he said later, when writing to Father de Wit, " I acted to the best of my judgment. Brother de Sadeleer told me too he thought I did the right thing."

On the 10th August, therefore, at nightfall, under cover of the thick darkness, the three missioners, accompanied by their four faithful servitors, the two Matabeles and two other blacks, set out under the protection of Almighty God. On the preceding day bundles containing necessaries had been made up for each one, and the gunpowder all poured into a keg, that it might not fall into the hands of the natives. All was left in perfect order in the wagon, and the team of oxen attached to it, to become the prey of thieves or wild beasts. Then when the natives were asleep by the fire, they dropped silently into the bush, taking the road by which they had come, because knowing it better than any other, they could get on quicker. They started in single file, groping their way in the obscurity; the deep holes dug to entrap wild beasts, some of them with spikes at the bottom, requiring a careful look-out on the part of the leader. They had not gone far when the old horse on which Father Law was mounted, stumbled and fell on its side. It rose with difficulty, only to fall again a few steps further, this time into a hole, whence it could not be got out. It was therefore abandoned to its fate. " I was by no means sorry for this," Father Law says, "as I found travelling on horseback very inconvenient, for what with branches of trees coming in one's face and breast, I was nearly knocked off several times." The greatest possible haste was made, and ten miles were accomplished before sun-rise; as the day dawned, they found to their relief that they were on the right track. After an hour's rest, ten more miles were got over, so that towards the middle of the next day they were safe, far from the hostile Mashonas. The burdens carried by all were heavy, for the "boys," although given new blankets in place of their old ones, would not be induced to leave the latter behind, and thus were overburdened. One of the Kafirs, Zambesi, insisted on carrying a quantity of blankets; he could not in consequence keep up with the others, and though they waited for him at intervals, at last he dropped behind altogether. The rest of the party felt no anxiety on his account, as they thought he would doubtless find his way back to Gubulawayo.

Deploring the loss of their fellow-missioner, the little troop painfully made their way along the banks of the River Sabi. By day they hid in the jungle, and by night pursued their journey until the first few days were past. Walking in the darkness, they constantly stumbled, owing to the roughness of the road. Many a time, Brother Sadeleer relates, he heard the weary voice of Father Law, who was the weakest of the band, exclaim: "Thanks be to God! I have only got my feet wet," or again: "I have escaped with a bruise on my knee," "I have only hurt my arm by that fall." Fortunately the produce of the chase was good, or they would all have perished from hunger and fatigue. Besides smaller game, a rhinoceros was shot, which furnished a supply of meat for several days. On the eve of the Assumption, however, they were reduced to great straits, the people in the kraals through which they passed either could not or would not sell them any corn. All the provisions they had left was a small piece of Australian damper, utterly insufficient for a single meal. The next day Father Law said Mass on a rock in the bed of the river, and promised his companions that our Lady would help them, and not let them fast altogether on her great feast. Scarcely had they gone any distance when they fell in with some Kafirs, who sold them meal and beans, and a little salt, which they had extracted from the saline deposits in the river's bed. Later on in the day two red deer were shot. " How grateful we felt ! " exclaims Father Law, " we thought it was the Blessed Virgin who sent them. How heartily one says grace after meals, when living as we do."

That feast of the Assumption was marked by another favour that was granted to Father Law's prayers, besides the daily bread for which he petitioned. There is no doubt that when he offered the Holy Sacrifice in that wild and lonesome spot, he specially commended to God and our Blessed Lady his friends in Grahamstown. For on that very day an event occurred which had he known of it, would have filled his heart with joy and thanksgiving. The father of the family with whom he had been on terms of most intimate friendship, a man who, though not opposed to the truth, had resisted every argument to induce him to embrace the saving faith to which Father Law had converted his wife and children, urged by an impulse unaccountable to himself, on the morning of the 15th, drove a considerable distance into Grahams-

town, for the purpose of attending an early Mass.
During that Mass grace touched his heart; he hastened
to become a Catholic also.

After four days more of toilsome and harassing
march, the windings of the road and the frequent
ascents and descents rendering the distance covered
but short, the weary travellers arrived, to their great
joy, at an outlying kraal of Umzila's. It was music to
their ears to hear the Zulu tongue again; the head
man was very kind to them, and promised to give
them boys to carry their loads and to show them the
road. He gave them some meal too, and would not
take anything in payment. When Father Law told
him how much obliged he was to him for his great
kindness, he answered: "Oh, we are men of the chief,"
and told him that a wagon with white men and two
of Lo Bengula's people had been expected, in fact
emissaries had been sent to look out for it. The
people were all very indignant when they heard the
story of the missioners' wrongs, and said that Umzila
would surely take vengeance on the chiefs, and perhaps
make the Amaholi bring the wagon over. "Our mis-
fortunes," says Father Law, "may make Umzila our
friend, as by the same acts by what we have been
injured his authority has been insulted." The narrative
was told with great solemnity in the next village in
presence of the Induna and other magnates of the
place. "Do not be uneasy about the loss of your
wagon," was the comforting assurance they gave,
"you will be sure to get it again; but the loss of your
comrade is much to be regretted, for we fear it is
irreparable." Finally, on the last day of August, the
missioners, exhausted by fatigue and exposure, emerged
on the large plain in which Umzila's kraal is situated.

They had walked one hundred and seventy miles since they left the wagon, and well it was that their journey was at an end, for it could not be denied that it was telling sadly on them all. Brother Sadeleer was the only one in good health, and even he was very tired. The sturdy Fleming had carried a prodigious weight nearly all the way, and had in addition, been the principal huntsman of the party. Thus the goal of all their hopes was finally reached. Let us read the entry in Father Law's diary: " We changed our *Itinerarium* to-day for a *Te Deum.* God has indeed been good to us on the road. We all felt very grateful to Him for leading us into port, so to speak, after such rough weather." Alas! brave mariner, you think that you have at length cast anchor in a tranquil harbour, whereas in reality your bark is resting on a shifting sand, in whose treacherous depths it is doomed erelong to disappear.

All through this tedious and distressing journey Father Law had kept up his courage, all through he had shown the same cheerful, hopeful nature, the same generosity to all about him, the same readiness to be grateful to any one who treated him with kindness. But all his bright hopefulness could not render his situation at Umzila's camp otherwise than pitiable, or the prospect before him otherwise than dark and unpromising. He had not been a day in the place before he found out how grossly its aspect belied the representations that had been made to him. Contrary to what he had been led to expect, there was not a single Portuguese or any other European in the country. No merchandize of any description, not even the necessaries of life could be had there. At rare intervals a Portuguese trader went thither

U

from Sofala, a town on the coast, distant about two
and a half days' journey, otherwise white men were
never seen there, as was plain from the curiosity they
excited. It was evident that they would have to open
communication with that town, as it was the only place
where things could be obtained, but how was that
practicable under present circumstances? Moreover,
Father Law complains that he has to forego the
privilege of saying Mass. "We pray God," he says,
"to give us the daily bread, the supersubstantial bread
of Holy Mass. It is impossible at present, as we have
not a hut to ourselves, the Induna and others inhabit
it as well." In addition to this, the desired interview
with the King, whereon so much depended, was post-
poned on one pretext or another, from day to day.
"We have not seen the King as yet," Father Law
writes in his journal. And on the morrow: "Still we
do not see the King. I am very anxious to see him,
as I want to arrange to send off news to Father de
Wit (who was then at Gubulawayo), and to Europe.
I spend my time in listening to people talking, and
talking myself, to learn the language, and in meditating
the Roman Catechism. This, together with A'Kempis
and *Horæ Diurnæ*, constitutes my whole library at
present."

Although the missioners were not admitted to an
audience by the King, he did not ignore their presence
in his kraal. He had been apprised, as has been said,
of the coming of *abufundisi* (teachers) by Lo Bengula's
ambassadors, who, travelling without the encumbrance
of baggage, had taken a shorter route. He placed a
small Kafir hut at their disposal, and ordered that they
should be supplied with the food they required. He
himself sent them two hundred and fifty pounds of

Kafir corn and a young ox. This supply, ample as it appeared, did not last many days. The ox was slaughtered at once, and a feast prepared, to which, besides the missioners, their Kafir attendants and the Induna, a newly-married couple from Matabeleland, with a large party of friends sat down. Father Law, listening to the dictates of good nature rather than of prudence, made no objection to the presence at the table of these unbidden guests, who, it need hardly be said, did full justice to the viands before them. This he did much to the chagrin of Brother Sadeleer, who, when recording the fact, remarks that he thought this extravagance would displease the King, and dispose him less favourably towards the missioners. There is no doubt this surmise was correct. The gift was a handsome one, for Umzila was not rich, like Lo Bengula; his cattle were small and poor compared with those of the Matabele country, and he had not many near his kraal. On account of the ravages of the tsetse-fly, his herds and flocks were enclosed in pastures on the mountain, and no beasts were brought thence except such as were required for immediate use by himself and his Court. No one besides the monarch owned any oxen. Thus meat was considered a luxury in those regions, the principal food of the people being a kind of corn.

On the 5th of September the missioners were conducted to the King's presence. There seemed to be much more ceremony in approaching him than Lo Bengula, and the head men appeared to stand greatly in awe of him, though his surroundings were anything but regal. In his journal Father Law describes him as a quiet, sedate-looking man, of fifty or fifty-five years of age. He received the missioners graciously,

and showed them every mark of regard. He expressed
his pleasure at seeing them, and listened with interest
to the tale of their trials. They must indeed have
presented a deplorable appearance, with their haggard
looks, their tattered garments, and their worn-out
boots. Umzila wanted them all to go back at once
to their wagon and bring it up to his kraal. He
appointed six of his people, four of whom were Indunas,
to accompany them. The Mashona chiefs were to be
punished, and compelled to restore all the things that
had been given to them by the missioners. Father
Law and Brother Hedley, who were both suffering
from the fever of the country, were in far too weak
a state to attempt another journey, especially as the
natives would travel at the rate of some twenty miles
a day. Besides this, they had no shoes to replace
those which they had been wearing, and which were
now useless. They therefore told the King that they
were unfit to go. So it was agreed that Brother
Sadeleer, with Tom the driver and the Hottentot
"Cape Corps," should go in search of the wagon, the
others meanwhile should remain under the King's protection and await their return. The party started that
same afternoon. "They will be five days walking
there," we read in Father Law's journal, "and we
hope to see the wagon here in three weeks. We wanted
to send some letters to Gubulawayo, as a Matabele
who is here promised to take them for us, but Umzila
will not let us write until the wagon is here, and the
honour of his country vindicated. In the meantime it
makes us feel like prisoners."

Umzila's willingness to send a party in search of
the wagon, the speedy bringing up of which was of
such vital importance to the newly-arrived strangers,

standing as they did in urgent need of the medicines and stores it contained, was not altogether disinterested. The description given of it had excited his curiosity, and made him desirous to see it; still more was he desirous of obtaining a share of its contents, the calico and other valuables which had been liberally distributed among the neighbouring tribes. He appears to have been far less intelligent and open-minded than his son-in-law Lo Bengula, and his conduct towards the missioners was far from justifying the flattering hopes that Father Law had formed in regard to the reception they would meet with at his Court. Before entering upon the sorrowful story that remains to be told of the things that befell this zealous apostle and his companion during the three months they spent at Umzila's kraal, we will briefly relate the result of the expedition sent for the recovery of the wagon.

When Brother Sadeleer and his Abagasi escort had made their way, not without meeting with a good proportion of accidents and misadventures, to the territory of Amalanga, they fell in with that chief, attended by two hundred of his warriors. Far from attempting to intimidate the little band, he showed craven fear at the sight of Umzila's messengers, and consented at once to restore all the goods he had extorted from the missioners, as well as to pay the fine imposed on him. The wagon was found intact, for the Mashonas, discovering that the white men had escaped them, and knowing that they had taken refuge with Umzila, dreaded the vengeance of that King if they pillaged it. With the wagon was found the Kafir Zambesi, who had been too heavily laden to keep up with the rest of the party on the night of their flight. He had returned to the spot lately quitted, and resumed his former duties, the charge of the oxen. A high palisade had been erected round the wagon to protect it from the wolves, and the Zambesi, with an honesty that does credit to the Kafir nature, had carefully replaced all the things that had been entrusted to him to carry. Brother Sadeleer hastened to array himself in fresh clothes; then after two days' rest, he begged to start on the return journey, for the relief of his suffering colleagues. But this was far from the intention of the Indunas in command. Their errand would be but half performed if they did not visit Hambehusuku, the other chieftain whose people had threatened to attack the caravan, and inflict punishment on him in their master's name. They therefore set about building huts for the shelter of those that remained with the wagon while they proceeded to his kraal. To this vexatious delay Brother Sadeleer was compelled to submit. Meanwhile intelligence reached him of the missing Father Wehl. Three Kafirs came up, carrying a stick, in the top of which was fixed a letter addressed by him to Father Law. Unfortunately, this letter was written in Latin, so that the Brother could not understand it, but he learnt from the men that Father Wehl was in safety at a place some sixty miles distant.

That unfortunate Father had, on the memorable 6th of August, whilst walking on in advance of the wagon, wrapt in his own thoughts, forgotten that the path he was pursuing, comparatively easy for a pedestrian, presented difficulties almost insuperable to the passage of the wagon, and that in consequence the progress made by his fellow-travellers would be extremely slow. He got too far ahead, and mistaking the direction to be followed, took a wrong track which led to the left of a range of hills instead of to the right.

In this manner he put between himself and the rest of his party high crags which effectually prevented him from hearing the guns fired for his recall. After a hopeless search, he abandoned all attempt to regain the wagon, and determined to go southward, in the direction of Gubulawayo. For twenty-six days he wandered in the bush, in great distress, enduring incredible fatigues and privations, subsisting on a few handfuls of meal begged from the natives, whenever he passed a group of huts. Thrice he was without food for forty-eight hours. For the first ten nights he slept in trees, but unable to bear the cold, he afterwards slept in the grass of the plain, trusting in God to preserve him from lions and other beasts of prey. It seemed indeed nothing short of a miracle that he escaped being devoured by them. At length exhausted with hunger and weariness, with bleeding feet and clothes torn to rags, he was picked up by some Kafirs who took him to the kraal of a Mashona chief called Guda, subject to the Matabele King. There he stayed three weeks, at first being kindly treated. Presently, however, his captors, after holding a council as to the fate of their prisoner, decided to put him to death. Providentially, he was rescued by the opportune arrival of Mr. Roxby, an Englishman who, passing near the place, heard of his captivity, and came with four servants to release him. This gentleman, an inhabitant of the Transvaal, who had gone northward in search of gold, veins of the precious metal having been discovered in the rocks near the Sabi River, generously took the priest to his encampment, and provided him with food and clothing. They then went on to Schumhum, which Father Wehl, with the other missioners, had passed a couple of months before. Hearing that Brother Sadeleer was with the wagon at Amalanga's village, Mr. Roxby gave him guides who conducted him thither. He reached the spot on the 28th of October, and found the Brother down with fever. Nevertheless, he insisted on starting at once for Umzila's kraal, as he was anxious to rejoin his colleagues with the least possible delay, no tidings having been received from them. A somewhat circuitous route had however to be taken, in order to avoid the regions infested by the tsetse-fly, as well as the high mountains which barred the direct way. Owing to the state of the roads, they only travelled about ninety miles in six weeks, reaching Umgan, the first village in the territory immediately subject to Umzila, on the 2nd of December. There they were obliged to stop, on account of the rainy season having set in, and rendering further advance impossible.

Father Wehl was never the same, either in mind or body, after this terrible adventure. He only lived for about six months subsequently, and during that time was subject to feverish attacks, accompanied by mental aberration, and followed by complete physical prostration. We will now leave him and his companion at Umgan, while we retrace our steps, and in the next chapter inquire how the two sojourners at Umzila's kraal had fared in the interim.

CHAPTER XIX

WHEN Father Law and Brother Hedley saw their fellow-missioner depart, accompanied by an armed escort, for the recovery of the wagon, it was with the anticipation that he would speedily return, bringing with him the stores on which they depended for the maintenance of their health, if not for the preservation of their very existence. Supported by this hope of succour, they determined to await its arrival, in a month, as they imagined, at the latest, continuing meanwhile to live in the little hut given them by the King near his kraal. The quarters thus assigned them were certainly not luxurious. Fancy a round native house made of clay, and thatched with grass, in diameter some thirteen feet, height twelve feet, entirely destitute of furniture, with one entrance three feet high, serving at the same time as door, window, and chimney. This Kafir hut was not only small, but ill-constructed, ill-ventilated, and ill-situated, a veritable oven, exposed to the burning rays of a tropical sun, and admitting in many places the torrents of rain that fell at this season. To complete the discomfort of the missioners, the two Matabele guides whom Lo Bengula had given to attend them, remained with them, and lived in the same hut, so that altogether they were four in number, suffocating in a close and stifling atmosphere, and constantly subject to the visits of the friends of the two Matabeles.

For the first two or three weeks Father Law seems to have kept fairly well, sufficiently so at any rate to walk about, and find amusement in what he saw around him. In his journal he describes a dance at which he was present. " I went to see the dancing at the kraal. Umzila was there, he seemed to take great interest in it, as he danced himself, but apart from the rest, and supported on each side by an Induna. Once he went to the dancers himself to correct something in the dance. Their singing and dancing here beats that of the Amandabele hollow. It is a thing impossible to describe, the beautiful time which one hundred and fifty men in a semicircle keep with their feet, hands, heads, and sticks, the spirit of the melody, the good voices of the men keeping so well together that they sound like one voice, and the delight they evidently take in it all; the women standing in the centre, facing the men, and singing as well, and often keeping up a running clapping of the hands. All this is unique, and it would move any one who witnessed it."

At another time he was a spectator of the manner in which justice was administered amongst these savage tribes. " I called on Amakityana (the head man in command) to-day, and gave him a knife which he had asked for. I stayed there while he was hearing a cause brought before him for judgment. It put me in mind of a case of conscience at St. Beuno's. First one and then the other made a statement of the case, which was one of oxen-stealing. Then the head Induna spoke, and two or three leading men. Then Amakityana spoke, and asked if any one else had anything to say; finally, he gave his verdict, and there was some desultory talk. I still find it very difficult to catch what is said by others, for here the pronunciation is somewhat different from that of the Amandabele. They change the 1 into y here; thus, instead of *umlilo* (fire) they say *umyiyo*, and besides, some words are different."

The aborigines amongst whom they now found themselves were by no means unfriendly to the missioners. They appear on the whole to have been a simple, pacific people, too indolent or too ignorant to cultivate the soil except in so far as it was necessary to raise the corn which was their principal, almost their sole sustenance. The country was, however, beautifully fertile, and could have been made most productive, since almost anything might have been grown there. Father Law wondered the people did not cultivate more fruit and vegetables. Of course there were bananas, and plenty of tobacco. This latter was a great boon to him, for his pipe was now his only solace. The Induna gave it to him liberally, refusing payment, and telling him to come again when he wanted more. But the people were complete savages. Their favourite recreation consisted in drinking the fermented liquor of the country, distilled from grain. In large potations of this beer they frequently indulged, often inviting the white men to drink with them. Of this they were glad, as the want of any stimulant made itself severely felt. The only article of dress worn by the people was a square lappet of skin, hanging from the waist before and behind, unless an elaborate head-dress of feathers, worn on gala-days, be excepted. Father Law mentions seeing one of the King's sons decked out for some grand occasion in skins and feathers, so as to resemble a huge bird rather than a human being. Indeed, at a short distance he might have easily been mistaken for a rare ornithological specimen.

The missioners were regarded by the Abagasi as objects of great curiosity. They did not trouble them by importunate begging or unscrupulous thieving, as did the Matabele, but they annoyed them considerably at first by standing at the door of the hut gazing at them, thus blocking up the little light and air that came through the single aperture of the dwelling, or even coming inside. This disagreeable was increased when some strangers from a distance came to attend a wedding that was to be celebrated, and set up their huts close by. "We felt," Father Law says, "much as the lions must do at the Zoological Gardens. The whole day they were crowding round our hut to stare at the white men. More and more are arriving, we have a continual crowd at our door." The absence of all privacy was very hard to bear, the more so as the constant presence of intruders precluded the possibility of saying Mass. On Sunday, September 12, however, he records that he had this consolation, after a fortnight's privation. On the next Sunday it was impossible. He writes: "Alas! no Mass. God grant this may be the last Sunday without it. People still throng our hut more and more. They wonder especially at books, and when they observe me reading, ask what I see there. Sometimes I exhibit the burning-glass, which fills them with astonishment. I often see a crowd watching me when I am walking up and down meditating. Some one passed me to-day, and said: 'He is divining.' I always tell them that I am speaking to the Chief above, this satisfies but amazes them." It was no small relief when the inquisitive visitors, who had been encamped néar, took their departure on the conclusion of the marriage festivities, and "delightful quiet reigned."

But as the weeks went by, the prospect before the missioners grew more and more dark. What a position was theirs, alone in an unknown country, entirely cut off from communication not only with their fellow-countrymen and their brethren in religion, but with all civilization; at the mercy of a savage chief, without calico, beads, or blankets to barter with the natives, without a change of clothes, without medicines, without necessaries of any kind. The record of their life at Umzila's kraal is indeed a pitiful tale of disappointment, sickness, want, starvation; yet it is one which affords a bright example of Christian fortitude and patience, of heroic endurance, of sublime resignation to the will of God under the most trying and adverse circumstances.

The provisions sent by the King in the first instance, soon came to an end, and for three weeks they had been subsisting on meal of Kafir corn, with occasionally a little meat. Kafir corn is at the best ill-suited to the European stomach, and even with this they were scantily supplied. Brother Hedley's sturdy frame could not stand this meagre fare, and Father Law, whose constitution, never robust, was enfeebled by the privations he had endured, suffered terribly for want of proper food. Having during the journey through the bush lived chiefly on animal food, he felt the want of it all the more, and how was it possible for him to recruit his strength on a few handfuls of coarse unappetizing meal, mixed with water? On the 24th September, we are told, fever attacked them both, and even one of the Matabele guides fell sick. No regular

rations were supplied to them, and Father Law had to
appeal to the authorities continually, for the wherewithal
to support life.   Many a time he was dependent on the
compassion of the natives.   We read in his journal:
" The wife of a man living in a hut close to us kindly
brought us a sort of soup made out of Kafir corn.   She
took pity, she said, on the white people so much in
want."   And some days later : " The good woman next
door, Kuhlisa, is always bringing us something.   God
reward her kindness."   This charitable woman seems
to have been the only individual who made any
inquiries about religion.   " The daughter of Kuhlisa,"
Father Law continues, "asked me some questions
when I was saying my Breviary, and I said I was
talking to the Chief above. · I told her what I was able
to, and she immediately ran to her mother and told her.
The mother then came and asked: ' Is there really a
Lord above ? '   Then I spoke to her still more.   They
were much struck on hearing that we had no wives,
and the reason why—that we might give our whole
selves to the Lord above.   Another day Kuhlisa came
and asked more questions, and I explained as well
as I could, the Judgment, Heaven and Hell, the
immortality of the soul, the crucifix, &c."

On the 25th September he reports Brother Hedley
to have recovered, while he himself continued very
unwell.   How he must have longed for the medicine-
chest left behind in the wagon !   " We have now no
natural means," he says, " so like Josaphat, we must
turn our eyes to God."   On the morrow, feeling a
little better, he contrived to say Mass.   " I had the
happiness of saying Mass," he writes.   " It was a
struggle.   Yet what a consolation to get the Blessed
Sacrament once more."   From the confession that it

cost him a great effort to offer the Holy Sacrifice, we gather how weak he had become. The reader may perhaps recollect that the preceding day, the 25th, was the anniversary of Father Law's first Mass, and may wonder that he who even as a boy, was so observant of every anniversary, and invariably noted in his diary the recurrence of birthdays, or any days rendered memorable by an event of importance to himself or one of his family, should fail to mention this. Although he passes the anniversary by in silence, preferring to look forward to the things that are before him, than backward to those that are behind, we cannot help our thoughts reverting to the quiet chapel in the little Welsh town, where fifteen years before, with his dear father as server, and a brother-Jesuit as assistant, the newly-ordained priest held in his hands for the first time the Divine Victim, of Whom he humbly asked that the grace of martyrdom might be his. " That was a day of joy for all our hearts," his sister wrote. What a different scene now meets the eye! In a bare and miserable Kafir hut, the Holy Sacrifice is offered by a lonely missioner, worn with fatigue, emaciated with hunger, exhausted by repeated attacks of fever. He is now tasting the bitterness of the chalice of which he then desired to drink.

After this some of the entries in his diary simply describe the efforts he made to procure food when they had but a few handfuls of meal left. Yet there is no complaint of any kind, but excuses for every one, and expressions of heartfelt gratitude for every little gift, every act of kindness. One day, one of the ambassadors from Matabeleland went over and called him to go with him to his hut to drink *utjwala* (beer). Father Law found out that the man, with an amount of good feeling remarkable in a savage, had asked him and the Brother on purpose that the Queen (in whose suite he had come) might see that Lo Bengula and his people thought much of the missioners, and wished attentions to be paid them. She would probably mention this to Umzila, who might thereby be instigated to take better care of the strangers. "How thoughtful and kind of these two ambassadors," Father Law exclaims. "May God reward them!"

In respect to the quality of the food supplied to the missioners, distasteful and innutritious as it was to Europeans, one must not accuse the natives of inhumanity. It was their habitual food, and they naturally considered that in giving these strangers what was to them the staff of life, they did all that hospitality required of them. But concerning Umzila's conduct in leaving them without supplies, there is some mystery. The indifference he subsequently displayed with regard to their welfare, ill accords with the kind and gracious reception he gave to the homeless wanderers who claimed his protection. He appears to have held aloof from them as much as possible, but whether this was owing to his sense of regal dignity, or whether his underlings purposely kept the missioners from having access to the King, in order that they might have the management of affairs in their own hands, it is impossible to decide. Perchance his fondness for the beer of the country, and other more potent liquors obtained from traders, may have partly accounted for his unapproachableness. For days together he was in a state of intoxication, or else sleeping off the effect of his cups. Father Law, speaking of him, says: "I cannot make out Umzila. I was led from the reports I had heard, to think at first so favourably of him. We expected to find every kindness from him, and indeed he did send Kafir corn and a calf at first. But since then he has sent nothing but utjwala twice. He has never sent to inquire how we were getting on. However, he may have given us over to the care of Amakityana, who has neglected us. Of course the marriage and the preparations for it would have taken up their thoughts; that is a great excuse. I have not been to ask Umzila for more corn, firstly because I felt too unwell; and secondly because the Induna of the marriage party has been kind and sent us some meat, so we have been able to make a little soup. It was said that the Portuguese were here during the good season; we thoroughly expected to find them here, and get a few things from them. We have not seen one. Fairbairn told me brandy and wine could be got here for a shilling a bottle. As there are no Portuguese to sell it, I cannot answer that, but I do not believe any is ever brought in except for the King."

Another point upon which he felt he had been grossly deceived was the nature of the climate. He had been told that the country was *very healthy.* It proved to be the very reverse. The King's kraal and a large proportion of the native kraals were situated on a long stretch of low-lying, flat land, filled with marshes and swamps. About two miles off there were hills, but they were frequently covered with mist, the exhalations from the marshes below. Writing to Father de Wit, Father Law says: " Strong constitutions will be wanted for this country, I expect. I think, too, the Fathers who should ever come on this mission should learn the language well beforehand. The country seems so unhealthy that I am afraid many would die before they learnt the language. Brother Hedley is continually

v

ailing. For myself I hardly expect to get through the first unhealthy season. The greater number of the Matabele sent with the ambassadors are prostrated with fever, and one of them has died. And yet this is considered the healthy season of the year !"

The lack not only of good food, but of sufficient food, was at this time the most serious trouble and pressing necessity. The missioners were being subjected to a process of gradual starvation. Want, the last and sharpest dart of adversity (*ultimum ac maximum telum est necessitas*), made itself keenly felt. On September 28th Father Law writes : " My fever is gone, but I suffer much from want of food. God's holy will be done! Amakityana has evidently been very careless about us, or has been afraid to speak to the King about us, so I must go myself." In the afternoon accordingly, though very weak, he set out, accompanied by Brother Hedley, to try to obtain an interview with the King, and lay his needs before him in person. There seems to have been considerable difficulty in approaching the great man. On reaching the kraal, they looked about in search of some one who would help them, and show them the way to the King's hut. Presently they came upon a jovial party engaged in singing songs and drinking beer. They were invited to join them. " Was it good for us," Father Law asks, " both weakened by fever, to drink utjwala ? Well, we were too hungry and too much in need of something to think much about that. So we drank, and I was very glad I did. Then we asked our way to the King's hut. To my surprise every one readily showed us the way, till at last we got to his hut. I asked at the door if the Chief was in. I was told to wait, and in two minutes Umzila himself came out. I was able to tell him that our corn was out, and that we were much in want of meat, as we had been sick. He was extremely affable, and sent for the shoulder of a young ox that had just been killed, and sent it to our hut. He told us the happy but surprising news that Father Wehl was still alive."

The supply thus obtained was but a temporary relief. Three days later Father Law found himself obliged to set out again on a similar quest. This time he was received with scant civility. The monarch appeared irritated at his importunity, and sent out word that he might go to Amakityana. "Luckily," Father Law says, " this individual was close at hand, but I feared a good deal that he might treat my request as he had done two or three times before—make promises, but do nothing. So I put it to him that we had nothing to eat but one or two handfuls of meal, and that we should die if left without food. He answered more in earnest than usual, and told me to wait while he went to the King. He soon returned with five small bags of meal, a little more than half a sack. I went back glad and thankful to get this, but sad at heart at being received less kindly by the King. But he may have been occupied."

Increasing anxiety at the non-arrival of the wagon, and solicitude on behalf of his companion, weighed sorely on Father Law's mind. He writes: " I feel so sad when I look at Brother Hedley. He looks haggard and going down the hill. Dear Lord, look upon us!" And again: " How I entreat our dear Lord that He would send His angels to bring on the wagon quick! I am so afraid for Brother Hedley! He is so down-spirited. He says he cannot bear Kafir corn, and there is nothing else to eat." A few days later he writes: " Both Brother Hedley and myself are getting weaker and weaker, and I am afraid if the wagon does not arrive soon, we shall both die. When it comes, I intend to ask the King for leave to reside in the country, which I fancy he will grant readily. Then I must go at once to Sofala and get stores, and black and white beads (which are the ones which sell best here), and calico; nearly all we had went in paying the guides and men to fell trees to make a road for the wagon. If the King does not allow communication with Sofala, there will be no means of keeping up this mission, for I see no other way. Oh, what anxieties!"

On Sunday, October 10th, the entry in his diary is as follows:

Slept beautifully last night, a thing I have not done for a long time. Brother Hedley keeps well. I managed to say Mass. What a consolation! I begged our dear Lord, at receiving Holy Communion, that He would absolve me and give me Extreme Unction.

On the same day he wrote the subjoined letter to Father Weld on the back of one of the pieces of paper on which the chart of the route is drawn.

Dear Father Weld,—Pray for me. So many thanks or all your kindness to me. I can't expect to live, unless the wagon arrives very soon. The fever has weakened me so much, and there is only Kafir corn to bring my strength back, not even salt to put with it. But all these troubles help my hope that God would not send them unless in His mercy to prepare me for Heaven. When you hear of my death, write a good consoling letter to my father. May my poor brother return to the dear Faith! I hope you will receive my journal all right.

The entries on the three succeeding days are most pathetic. All hope was now at an end, and the writer evidently feels that he is entering into the valley of the shadow of death.

Monday, October 11th.—Bad all to-day; delirious in the evening. Brother Hedley so kind. God bless him and take care of him when I die.

Tuesday, October 12th.—Very weak. Jesus, I cannot pray much, but my heart is with Thee, and rests in Thy infinite mercy.

On the 13th, the two faithful Matabeles who had been their companions ever since they started upon this expedition, left them to return to their own country. Father Law does not comment upon their departure, but it must have been painful to take leave of these men, the last friends left to them in this unknown land.

Wednesday, October 13th.—Rain last night and to-day. Water came into the hut. Brother Hedley is keeping fairly well. Father, into Thy hands I commend my spirit. Lord Jesus, receive my soul. Love to all the Fathers and Brothers. The two King's boys leave us, and God is our only protection.

Before laying aside his pen for ever, Augustus Law wrote a few lines to bid a last farewell to his father. They were forwarded to him on July 15th, 1881, when nine months after their date had elapsed.

Umzila's, October 12th [1880].

Dearest Father,—I am not far off my end. I trust in the infinite mercy of God. God bless you—you were the

means of giving me the holy Faith.   Tell dear, dear
Graves to listen to my last words, and to return to the
dear holy Catholic Faith.

Best love to all.

I die of fever—but if I could have had proper
nourishment I think I could easily have got right.   But
God's will is sweetest.

Jesus! Mary!

Your most affectionate son,

A. H. LAW, S.J.

On the same day he also wrote a letter addressed
to Father Wehl and Brother Sadeleer, containing
directions which show wise thoughtfulness about the
future of the Mission for which he was giving up his
life.   He begins by saying that he is not far off his
end, and begging pardon of them with all humility
for the scandal he may have caused them by his bad
temper.   He then continues, supposing them to have
arrived at the kraal after his death :

I think the best to be done is to go in the wagon to
Sofala, and either to stay there till you get an answer
from Father Weld, or go round at once, after selling
wagon and oxen, to Port Elizabeth.   You cannot stay
here.   You have not enough to keep you alive, and you
will only die, so endeavour to go to Sofala.   If you
cannot persuade the King to let you go to Sofala—but
try hard, even by offering him the oxen and wagon
when you have got to Sofala.   But if he will not, then
I should try, if I were you, to go towards Gubulawayo,
beyond the fly, and then send an express messenger for
Father de Wit to send a wagon.   He could borrow

one. Perhaps you will find dear Brother Hedley dead too. The things will be left in charge of the good woman here. I have written to Father de Wit about the payments.

Yours in Christ,
A. Law, S.J.

Brother Hedley begs pardon of all, he wishes me to say.

On the reverse side of the paper in pencil, scarcely legible, these words are traced:

The good woman will not take share [probably charge?] of dead men's things, so these will go to those who like.

And in ink, written below the words in pencil, are these:

I give my blanket to the good woman when I die. And Brother Hedley, his when he dies.

A. Law.

The woman referred to here is doubtless the kind neighbour, by name Kuhlisa, who has already been mentioned as having ministered to his needs. May God reward the charity this poor savage showed to His servant!

After the 13th of October the entries in his journal altogether cease. But the end was not yet. For six weeks more this lingering martyrdom was to continue before his soul, purified by sufferings, was to leave her earthly prison, to receive the crown which was to be their reward.

"Silver and gold are tried in the fire," the Scripture says, "but acceptable men in the furnace of humiliation."[1]   Augustus Law was now forty-seven years of age; his life, up to a recent period, had been a peaceful and happy one.   His naturally cheerful temperament had brightened much that might otherwise have worn a dreary aspect.   No very grave trouble or grievous affliction had darkened his path, until his brother's sad change cast a permanent shadow across it.   He had been successful in his work, everywhere he had been loved and esteemed.   Now his hour of trial had come. His joyous spirits had at last given way.   The expedition of which he was in charge was a failure.   His cherished wish to found a mission in Umzila's land could not be accomplished.   The project on which he had set his heart, and to which he had devoted his life, must be abandoned.   For him "all bright hopes and hues of day, had faded into twilight gray," and the night, in which no man can work, was fast closing in. One can almost imagine him applying to himself the words of the Prophet: "I have laboured in vain, and spent my strength without cause, and in vain,"[2] when deceived, disappointed, dejected, he lay dying of starvation, an exile amongst the heathen who turned a deaf ear to his teaching.

But Father Law's happiness had rested throughout on a better basis than his natural cheerfulness and contented disposition.   He was the servant of God, employed exclusively in the work of his Heavenly Master.   The will of God was the law of his life, and his one aim was the perfect fulfilment of that law. An Angel has assigned to him the charge of a human life, and whether the soul entrusted to his care benefits

---

[1] Eccles. ii. 5.   [2] Isaias xlix. 4.

by his Guardian's ministrations, or refuses to do so, that Angel is equally well pleasing to God. Success God keeps in His own hands, and for that no man is responsible. If God sees in our heart that His will is our only care, and if we sacrifice ourselves for its fulfilment, then the want of success can only make that sacrifice more heroic.

On October 15th, St. Teresa's day, Father Law said Mass for the last time. During the journey and since his arrival at the kraal, he had never missed a single opportunity of offering the Holy Sacrifice, and had often done so under great difficulties. Now he gathered together his remaining strength for one supreme effort, although he was so weak that he could not have stood upright whilst celebrating, had not Brother Hedley fastened a rope across the hut to serve as a support for him. A large stone that the natives had used as a corn-grinder, formed the altar; everything necessary for the Holy Sacrifice, with the exception of candles, was at hand, having been carried from the wagon. That Mass was Father Law's Viaticum. Thenceforward he was to be deprived not only of all human consolation, but of all sacramental sustenance. In the strength of that Food, received on the feast of the great Carmelite Saint, he had to walk, like St. Elias, the holy Prophet of Carmel, forty days and forty nights, unto the mount of God.

After the middle of October, Father Law's strength rapidly declined. He could scarcely crawl upon his hands and knees to the door of the hut. Soon he fell into a sort of lethargy, succeeded by delirium. In his lucid intervals he used to ask Brother Hedley to speak to him of our Lord's Passion and Death, in order to encourage him in his suffering and prepare him for his

last hour. On the 31st he seems to have rallied a little,
sufficiently at any rate to be able to add a few words
—the last he ever wrote—to the letter he had already
written to his Superior. They were these:

No wagon arrived yet. God's will be done. I am
still between life and death. Brother Hedley quite
well. Kindest regards to Father Croonenberghs and
to the Brother. I am so anxious about the wagon.
Please God, directly it gets here, I go to Sofala to re-fit
and get provisions and limbo, beads, &c., and perhaps
I shall have to wait till after the rainy reason—but I
don't know if I shall live.

Pray for me,
Your son in Christ,
A. Law.

From that day forth, his forces entirely failed him.
Dysentery, from which he was suffering, took a most
dangerous form, and his fever, which had been inter-
mittent, never left him. Then there were clear
symptoms of yellow fever, and after that no hope
existed of his recovery. Brother Hedley rendered him
all the services within his power, but he too was soon
prostrated by fever, and reduced to a state of extreme
weakness. An immense abscess formed on his knee,
so that he was unable to leave the couch on which he
lay to fetch anything to eat. Thus these two brave
missioners lay perfectly helpless together on the same
bed—if indeed a skin laid on the top of a few planks
can be called a bed—left entirely to the mercy of one
of the natives in whose charge they had been placed,
and who sometimes allowed them to remain without a
meal for twenty-four hours.

It would be difficult to imagine a condition more forlorn than that of these poor missioners, surrounded by savages, destitute of all help, the one dying, the other dangerously ill. Some vague reports of their distress had reached the Fathers at Gubulawayo, and early in November a wagon had been provisioned for their relief. A trader undertook to convey it to the borders of Matabeleland, whence the provisions should be brought on by carriers to Umzila's kraal. But the rainy season checked his journey. He was unable to cross the swollen rivers, and consequently compelled to return.

Brother Hedley tells us that Father Law's calm confidence in the mercy of God continued unshaken throughout this terrible time. He counted his sufferings as nothing; no shade of impatience ever marred the perfection of his peace and resignation to the Divine will. During the last five weeks of his life he was frequently unconscious, but was in full possession of his senses when the end came. When he felt he had not many hours to live, he asked the Brother to beg pardon in his name of all for the scandal he had given. Death had for him no terrors. The last words he was heard to utter were these: "I do not think I could despair even if I tried." Towards evening on the 25th November, Brother Hedley, who was lying by his side, perceived that he was dying. He began to recite the prayers for the departing, to which Father Law responded by signs. Soon after sunset, he calmly expired; and the angels carried his soul from that miserable hut to receive the reward of his labours and of his heroic patience.

This dreadful blow overwhelmed the poor Brother, who was now left quite alone, himself in a pitiable

state of illness.   Unable to move his limbs on account
of extreme weakness, and the ulcers with which he was
covered, he remained throughout the night where he
lay, by the side of the dear Father's remains, thinking
of him, and praying for him.   When the morning
dawned, and he removed the handkerchief he had laid
over the face of the dead, he was shocked to find that
the rats had already begun to gnaw it.   Despite all his
efforts, he could not succeed in keeping them off.
Calling the Kafirs, he bade them inter the remains of
his companion.   But the superstitious natives shrank
from touching the corpse of a white man.   They
refused to remove it until the Brother had fastened a
rope around it; then it was dragged out of the hut and
buried, after what manner and in what place Brother
Hedley was never able to discover.   Thus the grave
wherein Father Law rests is unknown to man, but it
is known to God and His good angels. They will watch
over it until the day of his glorious resurrection.

CHAPTER XX.

THE reader who has followed our story thus far, will doubtless be desirous to know what befell the faithful Brother who, after Father Law's death, was left alone amongst the Abagasi to mourn his loss. Terrible as had been the first night he spent in the hut after he had closed the eyes of his beloved companion and Superior, the next night, after the body had been removed for burial, was yet more terrible. For the rats, having once tasted human flesh, would be content with nothing else. Instead of devouring the grain, as was their wont, they sprang upon the pallet where Brother Hedley lay, and not finding the dead, they attacked the living occupant of the couch. All night long he had a continual struggle to hold these voracious animals at bay. The hut was perfectly dark, for he had no means of procuring artificial light. Sometimes they gnawed his feet, sometimes they would leap upon his chest and try to bite his face. It was all he could possibly do to ward them off with a stick. What made matters worse, was that he was so utterly worn out with fatigue of body and anguish of mind, that he could not help dropping asleep, despite his tormentors, only to be awaked the next minute by a fresh attack. For about three weeks longer he remained in this dismal abode. Somewhat alarmed perhaps at the

death of one of the white men in consequence of the
cruel neglect of his subordinates, the King went to visit
Brother Hedley, and showed him great kindness. The
Brother begged that he might be assisted to rejoin his
fellow-missioners who were with the wagon.   His
request was granted. As the poor Brother was utterly
unable to walk more than a few steps, Umzila had him
carried in a kind of litter or basket, made of branches
and bamboo-sticks, by sixteen of his Kafirs, who relieved
each other in relays of four, and sang lustily as they
went.   Contrary to the King's orders, the Brother was
roughly treated by these men, who conveyed him from
place to place with the utmost reluctance, and more
than once rifled his pockets and the package containing
his few possessions with the hope of discovering some
money that he had taken charge of after Father Law's
death.

All this time Father Wehl had been in the greatest
anxiety concerning his colleagues at Umzila's kraal.
On finding, in the beginning of December, that all idea
of proceeding further with the wagon must be relinquished, he could not rest without making another
attempt to succour them. Taking with him a few
necessaries in a parcel, he set out on foot, accompanied
by two sturdy natives to act as guides. This effort
proved fruitless. At the end of a week he returned,
soaked to the skin by the torrents of rain, having been
compelled to desist from his enterprise.

Two days later, three natives arrived from Umzila
with a message to the effect that the King wanted the
wagon. At the bottom of a calabash they brought the
letter addressed by Father Law to Father Wehl and
Brother Sadeleer, given on page 326. On being
interrogated as to the missioners' health, they acknow-

ledged, with much hesitation, that the great teacher
was dead. These sad tidings were confirmed a short
time after, when two other Kafirs made their appearance in the camp. They came from Sebenal, a village
about forty miles distant, where they said there was a
white man who was sick. For the hospitality shown
to him their chief claimed twenty yards of calico. They
brought a letter from Brother Hedley pressing Father
Wehl for the love of God to go at once to his assistance.
" I am alone and very ill," he wrote; " Father Law is
dead. The Kafirs have carried me thus far on their
shoulders; they will take me no further." Father
Wehl started immediately with the Hottentot to his
relief; and about the 11th January, 1881, brought him
to the camp.

The poor Brother was in the most deplorable
condition, and presented a most pitiable sight. When
Brother Sadeleer first beheld him he burst into tears,
so dreadful was his appearance. " Never in my whole
life," he says, " did I see any sick person in so wretched
a state; his entire body was covered with sores and
ulcers, and the wounds were filled with vermin. He
appeared stupefied by the excess of his sufferings both
physical and mental. It is a wonder that he did not
succumb as Father Law did. He must have had an
iron constitution. For five months he had not changed
his clothes, which were all in shreds and tatters. The
moment he reached our wagon I set about doing all I
could to alleviate his condition. I laid him on our
blankets and washed him from head to foot. I dressed
his sores with oil and balsam, and put on him clean
linen and new clothes. He soon appeared to gain-
strength, and at the end of a few days, with good care
and nourishment, was in a fair way of recovery."

It may be imagined that as soon as the poor
Brother's strength enabled him to answer questions,
his companions made the minutest inquiries respecting
Father Law's last moments. They heard from his lips
the same edifying tale of heroic fortitude and faith
that never wavered which has already been related in
these pages, besides some additional particulars concerning the three months passed in Umzila's kraal
which will not be without interest for the reader.

Almost up to the very last all the spiritual duties
customary in the Society were adhered to with the
greatest exactness by these two faithful sons of
St. Ignatius. The morning's meditation, the mid-day
examination of conscience, the recital of the Rosary and
the Litanies, were all performed as regularly as though
they had been enjoying the advantages of community
life and perfect health. The only book of spiritual
reading that they possessed was a Latin edition of the
Catechism of the Council of Trent. Of this book
Father Law had always been very fond, and he had
studied it carefully. He was in the habit of reading it
daily for a short time, translating it into English as he
went on for the benefit of the lay-brother; after this
they would spend many an hour discussing the
various points of their reading. This regularity in the
observance of religious duties under circumstances
such as those in which these two Jesuits were placed
is far more meritorious than can easily be realized. It
implies very solid virtue. Those who are in religion
know perhaps better than those who are in the world
how difficult it is to be regular and constant in prayer
and in the performance of the religious duties prescribed
by the Rule when one is even in a slight degree out of
health. If then love of prayer, fidelity to the Rule,

patience, and many other virtues are specially tried
and tested in seasons of sickness and affliction, surely
Father Law's constancy to his religious exercises
during those last terrible months is a testimony to his
holiness of no slight weight.

Father Law took great delight in reciting the
Breviary. Excepting the celebration of Holy Mass,
it was his greatest pleasure during the day. He used
to look forward to the time for saying it as to a
spiritual feast. Never upon his last fatal journey did
he display as much concern as once when he had
mislaid his Breviary. He could not rest for a single
moment until he had found it. Brother Hedley said
the temporary loss of that book was the greatest of all
the troubles he met with. And when he was stretched
on his bed of suffering in the hut at Umzila's kraal,
he did not discontinue the recital of his Breviary until
the fever had exhausted him so much that he had not
the strength to say it any longer. Even then he could
not make up his mind to lay it aside altogether, until
one day he asked the Brother what he thought about
it. On receiving the answer that if saying his Breviary
caused him pain in his state of health, it was sufficient
reason for him to give it up, he appeared quite satisfied,
and accepted the decision in all simplicity as if it had
come from the lips of his Superior. From that day
forth he made no further attempt to say it, but asked
Brother Hedley to recite the Rosary instead. He was
too feeble to join in it himself, but he followed every
word attentively, and said it sounded like music in his
ears.

He was never a friend to private devotions, for he
considered that in the prayers of the Breviary and the
liturgy of the Church all could be found which was

w

needed to supply the wants of the Christian. Brother
Hedley once showed him a form of morning prayer
which he thought very beautiful, and he expected
Father Law to say the same. But he only remarked:
" This is very nice, but where are the beautiful prayers
of the Church, are not they preferable ?."

One might imagine that as Brother Hedley had
himself been a sailor, Father Law would often have
talked to him about his early life in the navy, and would
have had many little anecdotes to relate. But it was
not so. The Brother said he had never heard him talk
about his former life, in fact he only spoke of himself
when necessity required. One day after their arrival in
the hut, he gave proof of his humility by showing the
Brother a letter which he had just written giving an
account of their journey, asking him in the simplest
manner whether he did not think he had put himself
into too great prominence in that letter. Everything
that tended to honour and exalt him, or distinguish
him from his brethren in religion, was highly distasteful
to him. Whenever the choice rested with him, his
clothes were the oldest, his rosary the commonest, his
pipe—indispensable to him in that climate—the cheapest
that could be procured. The presents showered upon
him when he left Grahamstown were promptly deposited
in the common stock, nothing that could be of service
to others being reserved for his own special use. Not
a word of complaint ever escaped his lips. Even the
last and greatest trial, that of being called to meet
death without having been fortified by the last rites of
the Church, was borne without a murmur. It was
God's sweet will that he should thus suffer; and that
was enough. We may conclude from his MSS. that
he was not altogether unprepared for this privation.

Whilst still at Grahamstown, before he was appointed
to this Mission, he contemplated the possibility of being
thus denied the consolations of religion in his last
moments. As if with a spirit of foreknowledge he wrote
the following passage in one of his meditations: " My
death may be without the help of the sacraments. So
let me listen to our Lord when He says to us, *Sint lumbi
vestri præcincti*," &c.[1] Who can doubt that he received
abundant grace in his hour of need; that God, to
Whom he had given himself with such generosity,
vouchsafed to him a special blessing in his last
moments, and made him an ample return for all that
he had left for His sake.

Not merely during his last sad weeks of suffering
and desolation, but throughout the whole of the time
that he was with him on the journey into the interior,
Brother Hedley said he never observed Father Law
show any sign of impatience or irritability, whatever
the provocation. This is no small praise when we
remember that in his youth his temper was quick
and hasty. So complete was the conquest he had
obtained over himself, that no trace was left of this
passionate disposition. What is more, the very marks
of the struggle—and it must have been a hard one—
were obliterated, so that every one who knew him in
Africa believed him to be gifted by nature with a
remarkably gentle and placid temperament. The
patience he displayed in bearing the minor disagreeables which beset Europeans travelling in Africa, and
constitute a perpetual source of worry and annoyance
to them, greatly edified his companions. Amongst
these disagreeables Brother Hedley mentioned the
plague of flies. In some regions they were so numerous

[1] St. Luke xii. 35.

that he said one might have thought a black cloth had been thrown over the wagon, so entirely was it covered by them. Few men could help being somewhat ruffled by the presence of swarms of these pests, incessantly buzzing about their heads, ready to alight with their exasperating prick on any unprotected spot. But Father Law endured this torment, one to which his skin was peculiarly sensitive, with apparent indifference, treating it as a matter of no consequence.

It may perhaps, at first sight, appear as if the mission upon which Father Law entered with so much courage and devotion had been a failure. The reader may feel inclined to regret that so great an expenditure of time, strength, money, and the sacrifice of so valuable a life should have been made in pursuit of a scheme which proved abortive. It is true that from the time he left Grahamstown until his death, a period of about eighteen months, not a single conversion cheered his heart. He did not even succeed in obtaining a footing in the country he had hoped to evangelize—he only found there an untimely grave. Yet in a short space of time he laboured much for the Mission. The other missionary Fathers felt that his death was a very great loss to them. Of them all he was the one who could best understand and speak the Zulu language, who was most conversant with the habits and customs of the people. The Matabele vocabulary that he had compiled was of incalculable service to his fellow-labourers. He had also begun to write a catechism of the first rudiments of Christian doctrine in the native tongue, and whilst journeying to Umzila's land, he traced no less than seven charts of the country through which he passed. These maps were accompanied by instructions how to avoid the dangers and difficulties the route presented. But more valuable by far are the merits and graces he earned on behalf of the apostolic work which his zeal commenced. If in the sight of some the life of this just man may be esteemed madness and his end without honour, to those who view it in the light of faith it wears a very different aspect. The Master Whom we serve will not judge of our work or reward us according to our success, but according to the faithfulness and diligence we have displayed in His service. It is related of St. James that after several years spent in Spain, he returned to Jerusalem without having converted more than seven persons by his preaching; and that his body having been carried back to Spain by his disciples after his martyrdom, the place of its interment remained unknown for seven centuries. Meanwhile the whole nation was converted to the faith of Christ, and ever since it has preserved that faith in all its integrity. May it not be hoped that the remains of Father Law, resting in their unknown grave in the plains of Africa, may call down a blessing upon the country he desired to conquer for Christ, so that those who follow after him may enter into his labours and reap a rich harvest of souls for the greater glory of God?

Father Law's last recommendation was that the mission to Umzila's land should be given up as impracticable. Father Wehl did not share this opinion. He thought that a station might be made on a higher level, where the climate would be less fatal to Europeans, within easy distance of the King's kraal, and in communication with Sofala, on the coast. He did not live to carry out this scheme. In the middle of April, their stores being well-nigh exhausted, he went on foot together with Brother Sadeleer to Sofala to buy provisions and goods for barter. Brother Hedley was left in charge of the wagon. The journey was very fatiguing, and the Father became seriously ill. On reaching their destination, the missioners were most kindly received. The Captain of the small Portuguese garrison took them into the fort, and showed them truly Christian hospitality and friendship. Father Wehl's condition soon gave cause for grave alarm. There happened to be in Sofala at that time a Portuguese priest from the nearest seaport, who hastened to offer his services to the dying missioner. He found him unconscious, gave him absolution and Extreme Unction, and remained with him to the last. On May 12th, he yielded up his soul to God. Eight Portuguese soldiers carried this soldier of Christ to his grave in the little cemetery where he received solemn burial. May he rest in peace! When the Brother wished afterwards to defray the expenses, he was not allowed to do so; no one would accept payment.

When Brother Sadeleer had completed his purchases, he made his way back to the wagon; and before the end of June he and Brother Hedley started on the return journey to Gubulawayo. It was no easy undertaking to go back by the way they had made for themselves in the preceding autumn, as the luxurious growth of grass and shrubs had rendered it undiscernible. Of all their former companions, only one Kafir driver and the Hottentot leader of the oxen remained to accompany them. Their route lay through hostile tribes and a country infested with wild animals, but the watchful care of Providence, extended over them, amply compensated for the lack of human protection. With the aid of the heavenly help in which they trusted they arrived safe and unmolested at Gubulawayo on the 1st October.

Out of the little band of missioners whom we saw starting from Grahamstown in 1879, four priests had now gone to receive their eternal reward; Father Terörde having succumbed to fever on the banks of the Zambesi shortly before Father Law breathed his last at Umzila's kraal. Father Depelchin, deeply as he deplored the loss of his fellow-labourers—the loss of Father Law affecting him more keenly than that of all the others—yet felt hopeful as to the ultimate success of the Mission. But although other brave men came to replace the warriors who had fallen in the outset of the fight, no headway was made in the succeeding years. The stations north of Matabeleland had to be virtually abandoned, since even there, the despotic rule of the Chief proved an insuperable bar to the progress of Christianity. Of late a fresh impulse has been given to missionary enterprise in Central Africa. The operations of the British South African Company have smoothed the way for the ingress of the missioner in the territory assigned to the Society of Jesus, and the sons of St. Ignatius have been prompt to avail themselves of the greater facilities thus afforded them. A central station is now established among the bloodthirsty Mashonas, and the European may pitch his tent at Umzila's kraal without fearing to die of starvation.

The reader of this biography will doubtless share the regret felt by the writer that a letter of some length written by Father Law during his last illness has been lost. It was destroyed by Father Wehl, at a time when his mental state was such as to render him irresponsible for his actions. This document is said

to have contained most edifying expressions of abandon-
ment to the Divine will, of trust in God's mercy, of
willingness to offer his life for the salvation of the
heathen.   In it, too, Father Law begged the prayers of
the Bishop of Grahamstown, of his clergy, and of his
flock.   He also sent touching messages of humble
gratitude to his Superiors and each one of the priests
of the Society in Africa, and mentioned by name
several of the Catholics of Grahamstown as well as
friends and relatives at home.   He did not forget any
one, but entreated pardon and prayers from all.

The first intimation of his death reached England
in May, 1881.   The tidings were an unexpected and
a severe blow, especially to his father.   When the
pious old man learnt the harrowing details of the
closing sufferings of his eldest and favourite son, and
the soiled scrap of paper on which the last words of
affectionate farewell were traced was placed in his
hands, he needed all the consolations faith can give to
support him under the heavy trial.   But he felt, as one
of the Jesuit Fathers reminded him, that it is a great
thing to have a good son, a greater to have a son an
apostle, and greatest of all to have given to God a
martyr; and this thought comforted him in his anguish.
The late Cardinal Newman, writing to him on this
occasion, says:

"You have indeed great troubles on you, but you
know better than I can say that they are sure in God's
good time to turn to blessings, and that prayers which
seem thrown away will be found in time to have a
fulfilment in the event.   For the son whose death may
be called a martyrdom you cannot grieve long, and he
will be nearer to you in Heaven than he could ever be
on earth.   As to his brother, we know not what he may

do for him; and this, I dare say, has already been a comforting thought to you."

Father Law's holy, devoted life and heroic death will not have been in vain, if the remembrance of them encourages those who follow in his wake to fight the battle of life no less bravely than he did, and win the crown of eternal glory no less nobly. *Defunctus adhuc loquitur.*

A marble tablet was erected to his memory by his father in the Church of St. Mary Magdalen, Mortlake. The inscription upon it reads thus:

In Memoriam,
The REV. AUGUSTUS HENRY LAW, S.J.,
Received, when an Officer of the Royal Navy,
Into the One Fold of Christ, by Dr. Grant,
Bishop of Southwark, in this Church, on May 16th, 1852,
Died of Fever, a Missionary Priest,
On the Zambesi Mission,
At Umzila's Kraal, South Africa,
In the 48th year of his age, on November 25th, 1880.
R. I. P.

APPENDIX.

THE subjoined letter, in which the late Father Weld communicated the tidings of Father Augustus Law's death to his father, gives testimony to the high esteem and affection entertained for him by his Superiors in the Society.

May 3, 1881.
San Girolamo, Fiesole.

My dear Mr. Law,—I have a very sad duty to accomplish. It is that of announcing to you that God has accepted the sacrifice which your dear son made of his life, when he offered himself for the Zambesi Mission. Our dear Lord took him to Himself on November 25. Worn out with fever and fatigue, he peacefully gave his soul to God on that day, at the kraal of Umzila, where he had so ardently desired to found a mission, and where I feel that he has really laid the foundation of a future mission, as the character of the people and the kindness of the King give good hopes of future success, when the difficulties of communication can be overcome. He had only a lay-brother with him at his death, so I have as yet no details of his last hours, but I know what they must have been; so fervent a soul as his, one so simple and ingenuous, who had all through his religious life given himself with such generosity to God, and, in all that regarded this Mission, had made such a heroic sacrifice of himself, could not but receive abundant grace at the moment of need; and I cannot doubt that our Lord will have given a special blessing to him in those moments, and made him ample return for all he had left for His sake. There is something so like St. Francis Xavier in his death, that it is impossible not to dwell upon it with consolation. Alone, with a faithful Kafir probably by his side, in a little hut, at the entrance of the Mission for which he had given his life. God was satisfied and took him to his reward.

I knew him so intimately, and esteemed so much his fervent religious devotedness, that he has always been particularly dear to me; but remembering what life is, and what it is for, it is impossible not to look on the close of his as a blessed one for himself, and a triumph of God's grace; the sorrow we feel will pass, but the consolation will last for ever.

I shall not write any more now. Father Provincial will, I am sure, communicate to you the letter when it has been translated. It will show you what a missioner in Africa must be ready for, and what a sacrifice they make to God who give themselves for such work.

I need not say that I shall pray fervently for one whom I have always loved.

Believe me,

My dear Mr. Law,

With sincere condolence,

Yours sincerely,

A. WELD.

The meditations written by Father Law hardly deserve this name in the strict sense of the word. They consist of thoughts which struck him in his meditations, and which he briefly jotted down, in order to recall them to his memory. They are often suggestive, always pious and holy, and frequently pregnant with spiritual meaning. They are, moreover, the genuine expression of his own feelings; they breathe his spirit in every line, and are revelations of his inner life. It is this that gives them their chief value. For the hidden life with God is the important element in the spiritual life of every man, and we know that in comparison with it, external work is of little moment. For those therefore who, having seen the beauty of holiness in the apostolical career of Father Augustus Law, desire to look below the surface, and observe the virtues of which his actions were the fruit, a few selections from his MS. books are added to this biography.

ON THE ANNUNCIATION OF OUR LADY.

1st Point.—The Angel Gabriel, saluting our Lady, announced to her the conception of Christ our Lord. The Angel entering in unto her, said, " Hail, full of grace ; thou shalt conceive in thy womb, and shalt bring forth a Son."

Mary has much to do then in bringing forth Christ in our hearts. He came to the world through Mary; He comes to me through Mary. And it is suggested to me that saluting Mary as the Angel did, has much to do with the conception of Jesus in my heart. How good then often to get Jesus conceived in my heart through the Hail Mary! How Mary must delight in hearing it repeated, and then how she must wish to bring Jesus to our hearts! I will try to say it over and over again with the same burning desires and affections as Gabriel did, hoping to derive much profit from my salutation because God framed it and put it into the mouth of His ambassador.

No wonder the Rosary is so powerful a prayer, since Mary is so often saluted in it, and her salutation is the prelude to the Incarnation. And when I stand in need of some great grace for myself or others, why do I not use this great power, "the cannon-balls of our Blessed Lady," as that holy woman Margaret Hallahan called them. Certainly if any one were to salute Mary once, she would repay it; what then if over and over again as is done in the Rosary? The words, "Hail, full of grace," &c., are the first words of the news of our coming ransom and freedom. And to repeat them is an act of thanksgiving to God. How glad Jesus was when one at least of the lepers returned to give thanks! Let me gladden the Heart of Jesus by giving thanks for the mercy of the Incarnation. "Announced." This is the news that should interest me, that God has become Man. Other news dissipates, this news strengthens and sanctifies. Think what the Curé d'Ars said about news and gossip in connection with the sanctification of priests. "What does all the harm," he says, "is this news of the world, these conversations, this interest in politics, these newspapers. A man fills his head with these things and then proceeds to say Holy Mass, or the Breviary." Father Clarke in the Novitiate used to say that want of guard of the ears from curiosity was what hindered perfection in the present day.

2nd Point.—The Angel confirms what he had said to our Lady by announcing the conception of St. John Baptist, saying to her: " Behold Elizabeth, thy cousin, she also has conceived a son in her old age." God is liberal and magnificent in His dealings with us and does not just show us enough to make us believe, but he *confirms* our faith by many things, *e.g.*, He does not just give us faith enough and no more to believe that the Catholic Church is the true Church, but He confirms our belief in her truth in many ways, by her sanctity, her miracles, her firmness in teaching the truth, her uncompromising opposition to error, &c., *Vera incessu patuit Dea.* And so He was liberal and magnificent with our Blessed Lady too. Nor was it any reason that she should be deprived of these confirmations of the truth because her faith was strong. " To him that hath, it shall be given to him," our Lord said. And so to the strong in faith He gives sweet and strong confirmations of their faith as a reward. And to the weak in faith, if they pray: " Lord, I believe, help Thou mine unbelief," He mercifully gives confirmations to strengthen and encourage their faith.

Let me thank God for the many confirmations of the true faith He has mercifully given me, ever since I have been a Catholic, and ask Him for many more; especially for confirmations of truths of which I practically think so little, *e.g.*, That nothing happens to me without God knowing and permitting it. That God always sees me. That God loves me more than I can imagine. That sin is the only evil, &c. Above all, I must in this meditation ask for more and more light to confirm me in the faith of the power, wisdom, justice, and goodness of my God as shown in the Incarnation.

Again, God is accustomed to make known His

secrets to His friends, as He did to Abraham: "Can I hide from Abraham what I am about to do?"[1] So He reveals His secrets to Mary, and for a like reason: "Seeing he shall become a great and mighty nation and in him all the nations of the earth shall be blessed."[2]

Notice too that the confirmation of Mary's faith was not, as it has to be with those of little faith, by means of things that can be *seen*, but by means of *faith* in another miracle. This shows the greatness of her faith. O Jesus, grant that I may take the Creed and confirm my faith in one article by faith in the other articles, seeing the beauteous and glorious harmony of Thy truth, "comparing spiritual things with spiritual."[3]

3. Our Lady answered the Angel, "Behold the handmaid of the Lord, be it done to me according to thy word."

How perfect a picture is here presented of what every one should be, the handmaid or servant of the Lord. Now is that the position that I take? In the different arrangements of God's providence, is that what I think and say: "Behold the servant of the Lord"? Do I say: I am not my own master, I am a servant, and a servant of no one on this earth, but a servant of the Lord? What He wants, I want; what pleases Him, pleases me, for I want to be a faithful servant. Are these my thoughts? What perfection is contained in the words that Mary said, how far they reach. They are the very foundation of everything. And what conclusion can we come to after thinking over the "End of Man" but the very words Mary said? Oh, how fervently we must pray: *Fiat voluntas tua.* Our will is crooked and turned away. How we

---

[1] Genesis xviii. 17.   [2] Genesis xviii. 18.   [3] I Cor. ii. 13.

must pray to force it straight! "In thy mercy force even our rebellious wills to thee."

Did Mary see what was involved in being the Mother of God? But she "cast all her care upon Him, for He cared for her." She was the handmaid of the Lord, and she knew well Who that Lord was. She "knew in Whom she believed"—*Scio cui credidi.* She would have said with David: *Tuus sum ego, salvum me fac.* And again, *Deus, Deus meus.* What then shall I say to our Blessed Lady? She is now the Mother of God. Let me put myself at once under her care. I will ask her to celebrate her dignity by giving me, so wretched, some gift, some token of mercy.

For she is now the true Ark of the Covenant. For Mercy is incarnate within her. What devout *Aves* I ought to say to her now that she is not to be, but is, the Mother of God. She contains infinite Purity. She is the Mother most pure. She contains infinite Wisdom. She is the Seat of Wisdom. She contains Him Who has come to call sinners to repentance. She is the Refuge of Sinners. Oh, how many presents I may expect from her who is rich in every point where I am poor and naked and miserable. O sweetest Mother!

ON THE EPIPHANY.

(I.) St. Matt. ii. 10. *Seeing the star they rejoiced with exceeding great joy.*

1. I ought to think what caused this "rejoicing with exceeding great joy," that I may be able to excite in my heart the same great joy. The cause was the being near Jesus Christ. Now I do not know whether the Wise Men fully understood that they were near the Saviour of the world and their God. But I do know

x

that I know Him to be my Saviour and my God; and
I am so near Him when I stand before Him at the
altar, when I am saying Mass. Is there in me this
"exceeding great joy"? If they felt it, I ought to feel
it much more. Am I then asleep? What shall I do
to bring home to my life the blessed truths of faith?

2. Let me notice, they had not seen Jesus Christ
when they rejoiced so heartily; they had only seen
what could lead them to Him. So anything that can
lead me to Him should cause this exceeding great joy.
Humiliations, troubles, annoyances, should be hailed
because they lead me to Him. Prayer should be loved
and diligently practised because it leads me to Him,
and shows Him to me. And I am apt to shirk all these
things, I, who am a priest of God and a Jesuit. Should
not whatever tends to lead me away from Him be hated
with exceeding great hatred? Are such things so hated?

(II.) St. Matt. ii. 11. *They found the Child with Mary His Mother.*

1. If it was exceeding great joy to see the star, what
must it have been to find Jesus? What joy is there
worthy of the name where Jesus is not found? "Thou
hast made our hearts for Thyself, and they are restless
till they repose in Thee." Where do I seek my joy?
"Why weepest thou? Whom seekest thou?" said
Jesus to Mary Magdalen, and He says the same to me.
Let me ask myself this question, and obtain an answer.

2. "They found the Child." Seek and you shall
find. What were their thoughts, affections, desires,
when they cast their eyes now on Jesus, now on His
Mother? Jesus is to be found on the altar, in Communion, in thanksgiving; in meditation and the
Breviary; in holy pictures and images. Do I seek
Him in these things? These are so many stars to

lead me to Him, to enable me to find Him. Do I follow them?

3. "With Mary, His Mother." You will not find Jesus without Mary. Mary will show Him to you. It is the part of a mother to show her child. She will speak for Him, she will speak of Him, and tell you about Him. Ask her to do these offices for you both now, and after this our exile.

(III.) *Falling down, they adored Him.*

1. To find Him, to adore Him, was what they made their long journey for, and went through so many difficulties. They were well rewarded now. And so I have the same Lord upon the altar to adore, and the thought of being able every day to renew my youth at God's altar ought to carry me through all difficulties. I should look forward to Holy Mass as a time of reward, for it is truly Heaven upon earth. How do I prepare myself for adoring Him? With what faith, hope, love, humility, reverence, contrition, I ought to do this.

2. The Wise Men offered gold, frankincense, and myrrh. These gifts were spontaneous. God loves a cheerful giver. God is generous, and He loves generosity. Out of my treasures what shall I offer Him? I have long ago offered Him my property, my body, my will, by the three vows of poverty, chastity, and obedience. God is the Lord Who hates robbery in a holocaust.[1] Have I robbed from the holocaust I made of myself, and made myself unfit for the Kingdom of Heaven? If so, let me do penance, and do the first works.

3. What the Magi did has ever been repeated by noble souls in God's Church. Some have offered up property and riches; others position and rank; others

[1] Isaias lx. 8.

have sacrificed friends and companions; others their country, their health, even life itself. There have been men like St. Francis in their poverty. Others have imitated St. Ignatius and St. Francis Xavier in their zeal; Blessed Peter Faber in his love of prayer; St. Aloysius and St. Francis Borgia in their renunciation of rank and riches; St. Laurence, Father Campion, and thousands of others in shedding their blood. They were led to Jesus, and immediately they adored Him; then, captivated by His love, they could not help opening their treasures, and offering Him the best they had. Cannot I be kindled with the same fire of love? Why is not the sight of Jesus as inspiring to me as it was to them? The star has led me. I have come to adore. But when the star would guide me close to Jesus, would bring me into His presence, stingy, narrow feelings enter my heart. I adore coldly, I keep my treasures shut. I do not offer Him freely all that I have. And yet Jesus is as amiable to me as He was to them; He has done as much for me as for them. Cannot this coldness be cured? "In my meditation a fire shall flame out."[1] Is this the case with me? If not, do I not understand whence comes my coldness?

ON THE PRESENCE OF GOD.

Holy David says: "I have kept thy commandments and thy testimonies, because all my ways are in Thy sight."[2] I say these words every day at None. Why did he keep God's commandments, and why ought I to do so too? The answer is given: "Because all my ways are in Thy sight." It is the simple truth we learnt as children, that God knows and sees all things,

---

[1] Psalm xxxviii. 4.   [2] Psalm cxviii. 168.

even our most secret thoughts, and if I would act up to this most simple truth, there would soon be a happy change in me. " All my ways." These words suggest to me a method of meditating this truth, viz., to go through all the actions of the day, and then to remember that each one is done in the sight of God. My rising, meditation, Mass, meals, reading, studies, visits, sermons, conversations, breviary, examens—these are " my ways," and God's eye is on them all. God's eye is on them all, and the conclusion ought to be, " I have kept Thy commandments." Is it so with me? How I forget that unsleeping eye that St. Chrysostom speaks so much of.

2. If then I want to purify my ways, God must be kept always in sight. Mother Margaret Hallahan was much helped to live with God's eye upon her, from having seen, when a child, an eye painted to represent God's unsleeping eye. I ought to be helped by what my mother said to me on her death-bed: " Remember, Thou God seest me." How shall I now begin to live with that eye upon me? Let me say with the devout David: " I set the Lord always in my sight," and then I shall be able to add with him, " He is at my right hand, that I be not moved. Therefore my heart hath been glad, and my tongue hath rejoiced."[1]

3. " He endured as seeing Him that is invisible."[2] In these words St. Paul shows us why Moses did not fear Pharao, but was ready to endure and suffer. Little things of small account put me out, and I get impatient and angry. This is because I do not see the invisible God. When I speak to a person whom I do not see, I yet see him in one sense, because I know he is there. I know God is in every place, beholding the

---

[1] Psalm xv. 8, 9.　　[2] Hebrews ii. 27.

evil and the good. If I would only see Him, then I should also endure and be patient. " He endured as seeing Him that is invisible." I should therefore act, speak, think, as though not alone. God is there seeing my actions, hearing my words, reading my thoughts. What then are my actions, my words, my thoughts? They will not be forgotten by God. They will all be judged by a God Who is *fortis et zelotes*. What reverence, then, especially, I ought to show to that unsleeping eye, to that eye that sees me as I am. Why do I love vanity and seek after lying? I look for approbation to those who know me not as I am, and that is " seeking after lying." Let me then, as it were, see the invisible God, and I shall be patient, I shall be reverent, I shall love truth.

THE RAISING OF LAZARUS.

(I.) St. John ii. 3. *Ecce quem amas infirmatur.*

1. What a good thing when one is sick in the soul to have some friends who are also friends of Jesus! These friends for me will be the saints who have done many good offices to Jesus Christ. Let me therefore apply to the saints, and beg them to carry the news: " Behold he whom Thou lovest is sick," to Jesus, and this to Him Who is the lover of souls, will be the same as a prayer.

I ought to be one who, when souls are sick, would be able to go with confidence to our Lord and say: " Behold, he whom Thou lovest is sick." It is for the priest to be constantly interceding for the people and telling our Lord of those who are sick.

2. How Mary and Martha understood the Heart of Jesus ! They knew it was sufficient to mention the

necessity of one whom He loved without further petition. And He loves all and each one of us. It is said of Joseph, who was a type of Jesus Christ, that he "kissed all his brethren, and wept over every one of them."[1]

Each one of us is bound to say with St. Paul: "Who loved *me*, and delivered Himself for *me*."[2]

Each one is bound to make acts of hope, and those acts of hope are founded on the truth that God loves him individually.

Each one is bound to say, *Deus, Deus meus*, and to call God, Father.

The prayer of Thais : *Qui plasmasti me, miserere mei*, was founded on the fact that God loves His handiwork. And we are all, each one of us, His handiwork.

See how tenderly St. Paul speaks on this subject. "Destroy not him with thy meat *for whom Christ died*." "Destroy not the *work of God* for meat."[3] Each one of us is him "for whom Christ died," is the "work of God." So I, bad and wretched as I am, may make bold to say, not only *ecce infirmatur*, but also *ecce quem amas infirmatur*. Here let me renew my confidence in the Heart of Jesus, and say myself, and ask St. Aloysius, St. Mary Magdalen, St. Mary of Egypt, St. Margaret of Cortona, St. Augustine, St. Ignatius, St. Francis Xavier, St. Joseph, and our Lady to say: *Ecce quem amas infirmatur*. Let me present all my miseries to them to report to our dear Lord. May He say: This sickness is not unto death, but for the glory of God, that the Son of God may be glorified by it.

3. How glad and grateful the poor souls in Purgatory would be if I were often to say: *Ecce quem amas infirmatur* for them at Mass and in prayer. I am not

---

Genesis xlv. 15.   [2] Galat. ii. 20.   [3] Romans xiv. 15, 20.

sufficiently devout to these poor souls, or rather not at all devout; what have I not lost by lack of this truly Catholic devotion. Blessed Peter Faber looked upon himself as their priest, and no doubt they rewarded him for it. I ought to be particularly observant of these distinctively Catholic devotions. By God's grace, henceforth I will. I will give myself more to inter-cession. There is far too much natural activity in me and not enough love of prayer. Far more real good would be done for God's glory and the salvation of souls if more time was spent in prayer.

(II.) St. John xi. 4. *This sickness is not unto death, but for the glory of God, that the Son of God may be glorified by it.*

1. The way to look at all troubles is here taught us by Jesus; how God may be glorified by them. How easily I should ride over them if I looked simply to the glory and honour of God! This trouble, this annoyance, this worry, this difficulty is sent that God may get glory out of it. And I, whose desire ought to be, *sanctificetur nomen tuum*, should see that God does get glory out of it by my patience, or sweetness, or constancy, or if I have failed in these, by my contrition. Let me listen to Jesus speaking to me about my troubles, and showing me how they may not be unto death (so to speak), but for the glory of God. And for this let me beg grace of Him.

2. "When He had heard that he was sick, He still remained in the same place two days." And yet we have just been told that He loved the sick man, and the two who sent the message: "Behold, he whom Thou lovest is sick." What do I learn from this? No doubt some would have rashly judged our Lord for not

going at once to cure him whom He loved. But God's love is infinitely more far-seeing than man's love. Why then am I not more content with God's wise and loving arrangements?

3. "Jesus said to them plainly, Lazarus is dead. And I am glad for your sakes that I was not there, that you may believe." In so many troubles and anxieties and miseries I think our Lord has forgotten me, and all the time He is thinking of me, and "is glad for my sake," that I may learn to believe, to hope, to love. Let me count up my troubles, and hear our Lord saying, "I am glad for your sake." And just as He had not forgotten Lazarus, so He has not forgotten me. May I not take courage from this? Let me listen to St. Peter telling me what to learn from this passage: "Be you humbled, therefore, under the mighty hand of God, that He may exalt you in the day of visitation, casting all your care upon Him, for He careth for you."[1]

JESUS BEING WEARIED, SITS ON JACOB'S WELL.

(I.) St. John iv. 6. *Jesus therefore, being wearied with His journey, sat thus on the well.*

1. How is it that God has come to be wearied? Ask Him why He is wearied; what were His thoughts and desires and affections as He thus sat weary? Did they concern me? Notice His posture while sitting down to rest. What is mine when I am weary? How do I occupy myself when I am weary? The saints found rest in prayer, in reading the Holy Scriptures.

Do I weary Jesus Christ in making Him take long journeys in search of me? Has He not been wearied

[1] 1 St. Peter v. 6.

in trying to win me to love Him? *Quærens me sedisti lassus, Redemisti, crucem passus.* It was a long journey from His throne in Heaven to the Cross. It was for me that He took it. How ought I to love Him in return! What weariness I ought to be willing to endure for Him, what self-denial and self-conquest! How ready I ought to be to do all He asks of me; why am I so niggardly, so cowardly in responding. Let me remember the words of St. Augustine: It is for thee that Jesus is wearied with His journey. "*Tibi* fatigatus ab itinere Jesus. Invenimus fortem Jesum et invenimus infirmum Jesum. Fortitudo Christi te creavit: infirmitas Christi te recreavit. Fortitudo Christi fecit ut quod non erat, esset; infirmitas Christi fecit ut quod erat non periret." What wondrous love and mercy are described in these few lines! Should they not animate me to do something for God Who has done so much for me?

2. "There cometh a woman of Samaria to draw water. Jesus saith to her: Give Me to drink." Little did that woman think what was to happen to her that day, Whom she would meet, and what would be said to her. Let this warn me to be always on the watch by holy recollection for meeting with Jesus, hearing His words, obtaining from Him His graces. Custody of the eyes is a great help to this holy recollection of mind. "Turn away my eyes that they may not behold vanity."[1] It was whilst pursuing an ordinary occupation that she met Jesus. I might often meet Him in such occupations. Most of my occupations are in themselves holy, so that there is the less excuse for not finding Him in them. Yet alas! do I always find Him? Jesus is waiting at the well, ready to speak to me. But I do not come to draw water, or I come late,

---

[1] Psalm cxviii. 37.

or I leave too soon. Thus Jesus cannot speak to me, or
He cannot say all He would say at those special times
when He is to be found at the well, such as the times
of meditation or examen. Let me be more punctual at
the well in future.

(II.) St. John iv. 7. *Give Me to drink.*

1. See how Jesus employs His hours of weariness. He is always intent on the conversion of souls,
wherever He is, whatever He is doing, however great
His weariness or His suffering, even when expiring on
the Cross. Here, too, he seeks the conversion of this
Samaritan woman. He begins by asking her to give
Him to drink, with the intention of leading the conversation gradually to the affairs of her soul. For, as He
told His disciples when they pressed Him to eat, that
He had a food they knew not of, the food of doing His
Father's will and converting souls, so now all His thirst
was for souls, and their salvation. All this teaches me,
who call myself a follower of this Divine Master and a
member of the Society of Jesus, that I should always
be thinking of the conversion of souls, that this should
be my meat and drink, for which I hunger and thirst.
This zeal for souls, did I possess it, would ennoble my
life, destroy selfishness, and give me an ardent desire
for my own sanctification.

2. "Give Me to drink," He says also to me. He asks
something of me. What does He ask, and what does
He thirst for from me? "I have an intense thirst to
be honoured by men in the Blessed Sacrament, and I
find few who will slake my thirst." Such are His
words to Blessed Margaret Mary Alacoque. What
else does He thirst for from me? "Give Me to drink."

He only asks of us what we can give. The woman could give water, and He asked that of her. He asks of me what I can give. What is it that I can give? My time, my memory, my imagination, my liberty, &c. " Give Me to drink." He speaks as though we could give Him something, whereas the earth is the Lord's and the fulness thereof. What can I give to Him Whose all things are? Inasmuch as I give to the least of His brethren, I give to Him. There are many souls for whom He died, who are crying out to me, " Give me to drink." Let me discover what they are in need of, what I can give to them. For in giving to them, in ministering to their needs, I shall be giving to Him, doing something to slake His Divine thirst.

3. When the woman expressed astonishment that He Who was a Jew, should ask of her, a Samaritan, to drink, Jesus answered: " If thou didst know the gifts of God, and Who He is that saith to thee, Give Me to drink: thou perhaps would have asked of Him, and He would have given thee living water."[1] Ignorance of the gift of God, ignorance of Jesus Christ, this is the reason why there is no prayer, this is the reason why no living water is obtained. How true are these words of our Lord in their application to myself! O my soul, you complain of want of grace. But how have you asked of God? Does the manner in which you pray, in which you make your meditations and examens, in which you say the Divine Office and celebrate Holy Mass, show great fervour in asking of Him that living water? And the reason why your prayers do not deserve to be called prayers is because you do not estimate the gift of God aright. You do not value the grace of God, purity of heart, courage, and generosity

[1] St. John iv. 10.

in His service at their true price. You have not a real horror of sin.

Again, it is certain that you do not know who it is that says to you, " Give Me to drink," else you would not behave in the manner you do. If it were some earthly prince who said, " Give me to drink," perhaps you would willingly give him what he asks. But now it is your First beginning and Last end, your Creator, your Lord and Redeemer, that asks something of you. And you are deaf to His request, or you are mean and stingy in giving.

I will end with a fervent prayer to Jesus Christ that by His grace I may begin at last to give something to Him, and not something only, but my entire self.

(III.) St. John iv. 15. *Give me this water.*

1. The woman does not understand what water our Lord is speaking about. The mind running on earthly things does not easily grasp heavenly things. All things in creation are intended to raise my mind to Heaven. But my thoughts are engrossed with other things, so they have no voice for me. If I am delighted with the beauty of earthly things, let me know " how much the Lord of them is more beautiful than they. For the first author of beauty made all those things."[1] For this recollection is wanted, and careful custody of the eyes.

2. But let me listen to Jesus. " Whosoever drinketh of this water shall thirst again ; but he that shall drink of the water that I will give him, shall not thirst for ever. But the water that I will give him shall become in him a fountain of water springing up into life ever-lasting."[2] With what an earnest desire for her salvation

---

[1] Wisdom xiii. 3.   [2] St. John iv. 13, 14.

our Lord said these words to the woman! And He says them to me now with an equal love. He tells me that I cannot quench my thirst except in His grace and His love. I must love something, but I shall not rest till I repose in Him, for my heart was made for Him. Shall I then weary myself in the pursuit of any other pleasure than that of belonging to Him? Shall I not from henceforth give up all false pleasures and seek only the real?

3. Let me, *pauperculus*, come and pray like this woman: Give me this water. Let me ask for it with great fervour, for *I* know well Whom I am speaking with; *I* know well what this water is. And *I* know well how much I need it. This water makes me a partaker of the Divine nature.[1] " It makes bitter sweet, and sweet bitter; it makes the unknown known, and the known forgotten."[2] It changes our views, and makes them altogether heavenly. It brings tears of contrition to our eyes, and awakens humility and truth in our souls. It teaches me that I can do nothing of myself, and that the beginning of good in me will be my acknowledgment that I shall fall into every sin, if not assisted by our Lord. Hence the necessity of continually crying out to Him, *Domine, da mihi hanc aquam.* St. Teresa says that we shall do nothing till we are persuaded that we are powerless to do anything good without God's merciful grace. Let us learn to have complete diffidence in ourselves, complete confidence in God.

---

[1] 2 St. Peter i. 4.   [2] St. Augustine.

THE CANAANITE WOMAN.

St. Matt. xv. 22.

Here is a most finished picture of how I ought to act in prayer, and therefore it must be examined most thoroughly. On other occasions our Lord had always shown Himself so easy in granting petitions. One cry, "Jesus, Son of David, have mercy on me," was often enough. Sometimes a hint was sufficient, as when it was said to Him in regard to Lazarus: "Behold he whom Thou lovest is sick." Again, at the marriage-feast, the mere statement of a fact was enough, even though the hour was not come, when the Blessed Virgin said: "They have no wine." Sometimes a wish outwardly unexpressed prevailed, as was the case with the woman with the issue of blood. Examples such as these show the rule, here is the exception. From it we see more clearly than ever how Jesus Christ cannot refuse.

1. When the woman said, "Have mercy on me, O Lord, Thou Son of David; my daughter is grievously troubled by a devil," Jesus answered her not a word. He appeared as if He did not listen to her. But it was only appearance. He listened with great tenderness, as He does to me even though He may not appear to be doing so sometimes. So when everything appears dark, when the heavens seem as brass, let me call to mind the Canaanite woman, and take courage.

2. Then worse things happen. His disciples came and besought Him, saying, "Send her away." So it may be with me sometimes. Not only our Lord, but His friends may be, or seem to be against me. Our Lord seems to take part with the disciples, for when He speaks, instead of giving her encouragement, He

gives reasons why He should refuse her request. "I was not sent but to the lost sheep of the house of Israel." What will she do now? Give up? Oh no! She came and adored Him, saying, "Lord, help me." What blessed perseverance! What pleasure our Lord must have taken in it. He would take a like pleasure, were He to find the same courageous perseverance in me. But again He seems to refuse. "It is not good to take the bread of the children, and to cast it to dogs." As if He would say: "You are no child of Mine, My gifts are too precious to be thrown away on such a one as you." Now at least the woman will be repulsed, and withdraw. But no. She is humble, she acknowledges that she is a dog, that she has no right to the Divine gifts, but she skilfully makes use of our Lord's objection as a plea for gaining her petition. She says: "Yea Lord, but the whelps also eat of the crumbs that fall from the table of their masters." Our Lord wished to draw her out. This He did with Philip and the loaves, with the disciples going to Emmaus, &c. So He often does with me. He does not grant at once; He waits to see what I will do. He wishes us to urge our requests, to use ingenious persuasions in our prayers.

3. Then Jesus answering said: "O woman, great is thy faith: be it done to thee as thou wilt." And her daughter was cured from that hour. So if I courageously persevere in asking for what I need, for devotion to the Sacred Heart, for self-denial, for a dying life, He cannot refuse it me. As He acted in His life as we have it in the Gospels, so He acts now in His Church; the Gospel is His programme. What He did for those who came to Him in the Gospel, He will do for me most certainly. Most things recorded there were done for the body, now

we pray for the soul. The only thing to be feared is our will, not His. There was no obstacle in the bodily cures, for the will was there. In the case of the soul, the will is often the obstacle. How necessary to pray: *Nostras etiam rebelles propitius ad te compelle voluntates.*

HOW JESUS SPENT THE NIGHT AFTER THE FEAST OF TABERNACLES.

St. John viii. 1. *Jesus went unto Mount Olivet.*

1. The last words of the seventh chapter of St. John are: "And every man returned to his own house." The next words are: "And Jesus went unto Mount Olivet." Observe, all these people had their own houses; the Son of Man had nowhere to lay His Head. No doubt as, "for fear of the Jews," no one spoke openly of Him, so also, "for fear of the Jews," all shunned Him and looked upon Him as one to Whom no hospitality was to be extended. "Jesus went to Mount Olivet." See Him going, not received by any one, friendless, homeless, suspected, hated by some. "Jesus went to Mount Olivet," with what resignation, patience, with what tender feelings in His Heart for His enemies; praying for them as He went along, no angry feelings rankling in His breast, no resentment—only compassion and love for those who treated Him so ill. "Father, forgive them, for they know not what they do," was very likely His prayer as He crossed the valley to Mount Olivet.

People do not treat me as badly as they did Him, and yet I should really deserve it. But perhaps they get in my way, or they do not think as I do, or they oppose me and give me trouble—then I get angry. Let me look again at the Blessed Jesus, my God,

Y

walking along to Mount Olivet, after the cruel day
when He had been the object of so much hostile
discussion, and let me learn something profitable for
my soul from it. Let me be the *pauperculus* and beg
leave to accompany Him on His solitary way. What
shall I say or do to comfort Him? What will He say
to me? What counsels will He give? What will He
complain of in my conduct to Him? Have I not
turned Him out of my heart? He would fain find a
resting-place there, but often He cannot get it. Do I
shun Him too, then? O dear Lord, who can be my
friend, if not you?

I see our Lord unable to get a shelter in the city,
and I reflect how differently I am treated. I go to
visit my flock, and they are glad to see the priest.
Jesus came to visit His flock, and they would not
receive Him. " He would not walk in Judea, because
the Jews sought to kill Him." This is how God was
treated by His creatures, by His own favoured people
on His own earth. Such was the position of our
Blessed Lord amongst the people who ought to have
welcomed and loved Him. Let me think of this when
I go to visit people.

In connection with this point in our Lord's life, let
me remember that St. Teresa said that she got most
profit from the contemplation of those mysteries in
which she saw our Lord most abandoned. She thought
that when He was thus alone and in sorrow and
forsaken, He would for that very reason admit her
more readily into His presence.

2. Notice once more the contrast. Those men who
had been pouring out their malice upon our Lord, go to
their comfortable homes, He, the Creator of all things,

spent the night in the open air, friendless, homeless, supperless. The more one ponders over this night, the more one wonders, when one remembers that it is God Who is thus lodged. "He was in the world and the world was made by Him, and the world knew Him not."[1] What should I think of comforts when I see our Lord treated thus? See how He passed that night; how much of it did He give to prayer? All of it. The saints have learned from this example to toil often without reward, even with insults, for souls during the day, and to watch during the night in prayer. Let me pass the night with Jesus, let me watch His actions, listen to His words, and myself speak to Him. He will be pleased to see one disciple trying to console Him. I will ask of Him grace to despise and hate what is "comfortable," that I may bear the mortification of Jesus in my body, that the life of Jesus may be made manifest in my body. What will He say to me about this?

Were any of the Apostles with our Lord that night? If they had been, what a lesson of fervent prayer they would have learnt! How edifying a sight it would have been to see our Lord in prayer! What recollection, what profound reverence, what fervour! In that night, and in those many other nights which He spent in prayer to God, He merited for His saints the grace of imitating Him by spending whole nights in prayer. It must have been some consolation for Him to see so many heroic souls who would profit from His example, such as St. Antony, and others of active Orders as well; *e.g.*, St. Francis Xavier, Blessed Peter Claver, St. John Francis Regis, &c. He wishes me to learn this love of prayer.

[1] St. John i. 10.

JESUS' MERCY AND SWEETNESS SHOWN IN THE CASE OF
THE WOMAN TAKEN IN ADULTERY.

St. John viii. 3.

1. How hard it is to treat sweetly and kindly those
who would ensnare you! But see how our most sweet
Lord meets those most malicious Pharisees. They call
Him Master. They quote Moses: Moses said thus—
what sayest Thou? Jesus for His only answer, " bowing
Himself down, wrote with His finger upon the ground."
When pressed to give a direct answer, He said: "He
that is without sin among you, let him first cast a
stone at her." What a kind answer to such malicious
questions! He defeats their purpose without uttering
a harsh word. Let me learn to be sweet and gentle
in my answer to any one who would wish to say hard
words to me.

2. There is much of the Pharisee in me. I may
therefore well meditate those words, and think what it
was that our Lord wrote upon the ground. Some say
it was their sins that He wrote down. Oh, what a
catalogue He might write of mine! Are they blotted
out? What penance has been done for them? Have
I tried to make reparation for them? If our Lord is
writing my sins upon the ground, perhaps He is
repeating the words: "They that depart from Thee
shall be written in the earth, because they have
forsaken the Lord."[1] What shall I say to Jesus?
How shall I persuade Him to take pity on me, and
write my name, not on the earth, but in Heaven?

3. "He that is without sin amongst you, let him
first cast a stone at her." Stones are cast by unkind
criticism. When I am without sin then, not before,

[1] Jerem. xvii. 13.

let me presume to criticize others. Perhaps it is from my vile habit of criticizing and condemning, a sure mark of pride, that God, Who resists the proud, resists me. Let me then pray fervently that I may for ever rid myself of such a disastrous habit, that so God, Who gives grace to the humble, may give grace to me, a poor sinner, at last made humble. Thus I shall obtain the grace of dying to myself, and Jesus will begin to live in me. *Fiat, fiat!*

ON DEATH.

Job xvi. 23; xvii. 1.

1. At death the world ends as far as I am concerned. Persons, places, occupations, whether they give pleasure or pain, are at an end; so is the influence I had upon them or they upon me. I am then really dead to the world. Praise or blame will be nothing to me. All in the world will be like what is seen in a dream. Like the wake of a ship now lost in the waters, or the path of a bird through the air, so will be a life not spent for God. Hence I must look on the world as passing and myself passing with it. I must live as a pilgrim not yet *in patria*, but *in via*. And in all my plans the thought of death must enter. " They that use this world as if they used it not. For the fashion of this world passeth away."[1] Those who act otherwise God calls fools. And at the end they will call themselves fools.[2] " Behold short years pass away, and I am walking in a path by which I shall not return."[3]

2. Eternity opens. The trial is over; with what

---

[1] 1 Cor. vii. 31.   [2] Wisdom v. 4.   [3] Job xvi. 23.

result? I was born for eternity and now I am launched into eternity. How infinitely small this world looks, a mere nothing! Everything is now valued according to the measure of eternity. The opinion and judgment of men go for nothing; only God's judgment is cared for. And throughout eternity nothing else will be cared for! "My days are shortened," the stewardship is ended now, an account has to be given. Now it is understood that my stewardship had an eternal import. Here at death I am alone in eternity with all my thoughts, words, and actions before an all-holy, just, and mighty God. He has seen all, remembered all. He will decide my eternity, and from His sentence there will be no appeal. God will be all in all to me *then*. Let Him be so to me *now*. Let me live for Him, live for eternity. In eternity nothing will be worth anything but what was found to be done for God. As when gold ore is found, the ore is thrown away as useless and only the gold remains, so only those things that are done for God remain. What if my hands are empty!

3. The moment of this world's ending and of eternity beginning is most uncertain. What if it were to find one in mortal sin! And if ever I fall into mortal sin, is God bound to wait until I have repented before He takes me out of this life? My death may be sudden. Most deaths are comparatively sudden. Great fervour is seldom seen on a sick-bed, especially in those who showed no great fervour when well. *My death may be without the help of the sacraments.* Let me therefore listen to our Lord when He says: "Let your loins be girt and lamps burning in your hands, and you yourselves like to men who wait for their lord."[1] This

---

[1] St. Luke xii. 35.

we find in the Gospel for Confessors: *Sint lumbi vestri præcincti*, &c., as if to indicate to us that this watchfulness was a special mark of the saints.

FATHER LAW'S PRAYER TO OUR LADY.

O Immaculate Virgin Mary, my Lady and my dear Mother! I wish to belong entirely to Jesus and to you.

For this I give you my eyes, my ears, my tongue, my whole self. Do you take care of me, but above all things preserve me from every sin, especially sins against purity which is so dear to you.

Bless me, O Daughter of the Eternal Father, and do not permit me ever to offend my good God in thought.

Bless me, O Mother of the Eternal Son, and do not permit me ever to offend my good God in word.

Bless me, O Spouse of the Holy Spirit, and do not permit me ever to offend my good God in deed or omission. But make me always to love Him with my whole heart, and to cause Him to be loved by others!

So be it, O sweet, O pious, O loving Virgin Mary!

———

The following verses were written by Father Law for the feast of St. Gertrude (November 15), the name-day of the Mother Superior of the Convent of Our Lady of Good Hope, Grahamstown. In the Collect for the day, God is said to have "prepared for Himself a pleasant dwelling in the heart of St. Gertrude"—*Deus, qui in corde beatæ Gertrudis virginis jucundam tibi mansionem præparasti.* This is the key-note of the hymn, which evidently was composed to suit some particular tune.

The Sacred Heart is full of joy:
  And wherefore, Angels say!
Ah, joyously you answering sing,
  It is St. Gertrude's day.
    O Lover of the Sacred Heart!
      St. Gertrude, hear our prayer,
    And make us love what thou didst love,
      Grant us this treasure rare.

O blessed Gertrude, in thy heart
  Our Jesus found His rest,
Made there His happy dwelling-place
  How truly thou wert blest!
    O Lover of the Sacred Heart, &c.

O blessed Gertrude, tell me why
  He chose thy heart for this;
And tell me how my sinful heart
  May share in part such bliss.
    O Lover of the Sacred Heart, &c.

I loved to dwell in that dear Heart;
  He loved to dwell in mine.
If thou dost love the Sacred Heart
  He'll love to dwell in thine.
    O Lover of the Sacred Heart, &c.

As friend to friend, as spouse to bride,
  Did Jesus speak to thee;
What wonder then, that pleasant place
  He found, dear Saint, in thee!
    O Lover of the Sacred Heart, &c.

Then love for love, and gratitude,
  And reparation due,
This is what Jesus asks of us,
  And meets response from few.
    O Lover of the Sacred Heart, &c.

INDEX.

A.

ABAGASI, curiosity of the 316; Father Law's first meeting with the 275.

ACHEUL, ST., College of 97.

ADMONITION, mother's dying 11, 38, 42.

AFRICAN TRAVEL, dangers and difficulties of 205, 207, 224 seq., 244, 289, 293, 298, 302.

AIDAN, ST., College of, founded 192; life at 174.

ALOYSIUS, ST., chosen as patron 67; College of 103.

AMAHOLI, hostile attitude of 297.

AMAZON, exchange to the 53.

ANGLICAN ARCHDEACON, anecdote of an 130.

ANNUNCIATION, meditation on the 349.

ANTHONY, ST., devotion to 210.

APPAREL, indifference in regard to 160.

B.

BEAMISH, ADMIRAL, testimony of 64.

BEAUMONT, removal of Novitiate to 95.

BERBICE, life at 133; farewell to 145.

BEUNO, ST., College of 109, 127.

BITTS, punishment of the 43.

BOER HUNTERS, kindness of 261.

BOTTALLA, FATHER 112.

BOYS, Father Law's influence over 105, 176.

BREVIARY, Father Law's delight in the 337.

BURIAL at sea described 27.

C.

CANAANITE WOMAN, meditation on the 367.

CARAVAN, description of 200.

"CARYSFORT," the 19; alarm of fire on board 30.

CATECHISM of Trent 111, 336.

CATHOLIC CHURCH, first visit to a 33.

CHAPLAIN of the *Carysfort*, testimony of the 20, 34.

CHEERFULNESS of Father Law 113, 182, 214, 305.

CHINESE, interest in the 134; language, study of the 135, 147.

CHRISTMAS festivities at sea 31; at Gubulawayo 267.

CHRYSOSTOM, ST., admiration for 100; quotations from 155.

CHURCH, the, is One 163.

COLLIER, ADMIRAL SIR FRANCIS 40; death of 48.

CONTENTED SPIRIT, Father Law's, 34, 214.

CONTRITION, value of 151.